CHILD'S MOON

BLUE MOON, BOOK 2

Also by Carper Smith

In the Jeans
(Ryanne Brady, Book 1)

Blue Moon
(Blue Moon, Book 1)

And coming in 2025

Blood Moon
(Blue Moon, Book 3)

CHILD'S MOON

BLUE MOON, BOOK 2

CARPER SMITH

For Emily, Chris, & Nick

Thank you for letting me be your mom.

One

My home is in the high desert of New Mexico. Filled with mountains and forests of green trees that stretch to an ocean of blue sky, it's not what most people envision when they think of the desert. Usually people imagine places like Mojave where I'd lived and trained for the past month. Brown and desolate, its soaring summer temperatures ensured bushes hunkered low and warm-blooded creatures hid during daylight hours. My teacher had his own method.

Jay liked to train early in the morning—taking advantage of the cooler temperatures before retreating indoors for the afternoon. As a result, he, Cruz, and I had been outside since seven that morning. As the clock approached eleven, the temperature gauge on the back porch of the ranch house read ninety-two degrees. My own internal temperature measured well past boiling.

"Send it, Luna!" Jay's leathery skin glistened with sweat and his salt and pepper hair stuck to his forehead and neck.

"I sent it!"

My job was sending telekinetic messages to Cruz while Jay coached me—a job he performed using a blend of snide remarks and thinly-veiled insults he called *constructive criticism*.

"You sent it to the dog," Jay growled. "And whatever that

1

mess was, the dog can't do. Look at him." He motioned to the Rottweiler lying on the other side of the sliding glass door. "He's confused."

In point of fact, I *had* sent my message to the dog, and it *had* been garbled. Exhaustion made my head pound and had blurred the edges of reason an hour before. I didn't want to decide what Cruz or Bear should do. I only knew what *I* wanted to do, and it didn't involve being in Mojave. I wanted to be out searching for my missing ten-year-old son and the woman who'd stolen him as a baby. Instead, I stood here facing down an irate man while sweat trickled between my breasts.

Still, Jay had a point about the Rottweiler. Head on his feet, Bear stared up at us, the two orange spots between his eyes looking like raised eyebrows on a furrowed forehead. Then again, with the exception of the time Bear had saved my life, he always looked like that.

"Stop screwing around and send it to *him*." Jay jerked his finger at Cruz. "Before the heat exhaustion you've been grumbling about actually sets in."

Jay's face glowed red, a sure sign his patience had reached its tipping point.

Leaning against the wooden railing at the north end of the deck, Cruz's attention was divided between the desert and us. His long ebony hair shone in the sun and sweat dotted the T-shirt stretched tight across his broad shoulders. He cocked an eyebrow at me—Cruz-speak for *what's the hold up?*

I shrugged.

Inside, Bear jerked to his feet and trotted toward the front of the house.

Taking a deep breath, I prepared to send.

"Hold up." Cruz pushed off the railing. "Someone's coming." He reached for the gun holstered at his back.

I stared out at the mile-long dirt road that ran parallel to the house. "I don't see anything."

Cruz pointed. "Dirt cloud."

2

I followed the direction of his finger. Beyond the point where the road disappeared behind bushes and the rise of the land, a tiny advancing cloud of dust disturbed the otherwise still air.

When the rumble of a Harley's exhaust pipes reached us, Cruz released his gun.

"Mo?" I said.

Jay's forehead wrinkled at the mention of his daughter's name. He glanced toward the road. His gaze returned to me hard as granite. "Send the message."

"Fine."

I stepped back to the middle of the deck. Although Native American, Cruz wasn't from the Keyake tribe like Jay and me, and didn't possess the extrasensory gifts of our people, the Neme-i. Nonetheless, Jay had been teaching Cruz to *feel* a thought transferred to him. According to Jay, it was Cruz's only chance of recognizing when someone tried to control his mind—an important detail since Cruz had been hired to protect me.

I took a deep breath and concentrated on my new favorite image of Cruz—hair falling over one shoulder, cola-colored eyes gleaming down at me in bed. After that, I imagined him walking to the hose bib, turning it on, and aiming a strong blast of water at Jay. I saw the two images side-by-side—Cruz looking down at me on the left and what I wanted him to do on the right. Mentally, I slid the picture on the right over the top of the other and released both from my mind, sending them, like a feather on the wind, to Cruz.

A moment passed before Cruz dipped his chin and stared at me. "Really?"

"It's hot," I replied. "He might like it."

Jay looked at Cruz. "You got it?"

"Yeah." Cruz touched his hairline. "A faint tickle, here, like always."

As a man of the Neme-i, Jay could sense the energy of messages being sent but could only read those sent to him. "What was it?"

3

Cruz heaved a sigh and leaned against the house. "To hose you down."

Jay glared at me. "Is that correct?"

"Mmhmm." I smiled.

Jay returned to Cruz. "If you hadn't known she'd sent a message, would you have recognized it?"

Cruz crossed his ankles. "If I was alert. If not, and it was something I'd normally do, probably not."

Jay exhaled. "That may be the best you'll be able to do. It's better than most." He turned and scowled at me. "And I *wouldn't* have liked it."

"I would have."

Childish? Yes. But my pent-up frustration and anger needed a way out.

He pointed at me. "You want to find your son and protect him from the people who tried to kill you?"

"Of course I do!"

"Then stop fucking around!"

It was a slap in the face, and I deserved it.

If I couldn't protect my ten-year-old son from others who could do what I could, I'd only be a danger to him.

Inside the house, Bear barked.

Jay moved to the side of the deck as the Harley came into view and raised his hand to greet his daughter.

"Were you expecting her?" Cruz asked.

"Eventually." Jay walked to the sliding glass door and reached for the handle. Pausing, he looked back. "You two should probably come."

Cruz and I exchanged a glance then followed.

Mo—short for Maureen—had come to the house three other times in the month Cruz and I had been there. Always on her motorcycle and always alone. She never stayed long, didn't enter past the entryway, and always spoke with Jay in hushed tones. When they finished, he would kiss her forehead, and she'd leave. I didn't have much experience with father/daughter relationships, but with the exception of the kiss, Jay and Mo seemed more like business associates than family. And until now, they'd always spoken alone.

The roar of the motorcycle cut out, but Bear's alarm continued in the entryway. Cruz whistled as we approached, and the dog glanced back.

"Sit," Cruz said.

Bear stopped barking and sat. His body quivered from the strain, and an occasional *woof* escaped despite his best effort.

In the month since I'd adopted him, Bear had been in training too. I may have signed the papers, but Cruz was his master.

Jay checked the peephole.

"Guard," Cruz said.

Bear moved in front of me. Eyes on the door, he appeared almost as vicious as he had when he'd attacked the man about to shoot me.

Jay opened the door as Mo approached.

At the stoop, she removed her helmet revealing ears with more piercings than I could count, a dainty gold nose ring and red rimmed eyes.

"Check," Cruz said.

Bear crept forward and sniffed Mo's leg. Recognizing her scent as friendly, he backed away, tail wagging, then lay behind us on the cool tile.

"The count?" Jay asked.

Mo stepped in. "It'll pass. Four to three."

Anxiety welled inside me. "What will pass?"

Jay's shoulders sagged. "The vote to make the prophecies public."

My stomach sank. How would I keep my child's existence secret if any of the Neme-i could read his birth prophecy? And how would they react once they read it?

With him is born the death and birth of leaders.

5

"I thought the vote was scheduled for Sunday at the Gathering," Cruz said.

Mo tipped her head. "That's the public vote. This was the pre-vote. If no one presents an indisputable argument at the Gathering for why it shouldn't pass, it will."

Nauseated, I leaned against the coat closet. If the people who'd tried to kill me had done so because I challenged my sister's previously unopposed right to be named leader of the Neme-i, what would they do when they found out about my son—the only male heir in the bloodline? The Neme-i preferred male leaders. Because of our gifts, our women could unfairly sway the minds of people outside our tribe. The Neme-i prized harmony above all else and believed using our gifts to benefit ourselves created disharmony. Having a male leader removed that temptation from the equation.

"What about Cruz?" Jay asked. "Will the council make the exception?"

I'd refused to attend the tribal meeting without Cruz. I'd been shot at during the Gathering in Albuquerque where Cruz had been made to wait outside. I wouldn't be stepping into a meeting of my tribe without him again. I didn't care that it went against tribal law. Call me a prima donna. If the council insisted on considering me a leader-elect when I'd told them I didn't want to be, I might as well reap some reward.

Mo shifted her weight. "He can attend Luna's portion of the meeting."

Fine by me. That was the only portion I planned to attend.

"How long for the records?" Jay asked quietly.

"Due after the vote."

"What records?" Cruz asked.

"Mine." Jay glanced back. "All the prophecies I've ever received." He drummed his fingers on the door before addressing his daughter. "You remember what we talked about?"

Mo nodded and, for a second, her chin quivered.

"No matter what you hear, do as we discussed." Jay leaned

forward and kissed her forehead. "It'll be okay. We'll all be fine."

Mo stared into Jay's eyes as if hoping to absorb some of his certainty. Taking a deep breath, she said, "Be careful."

I watched her back as she walked toward her motorcycle. Closing the door, Jay stood with one hand on the handle, the other pressed against the frame.

The sound of the Harley jolted Bear to his feet, his barks echoing around us.

Jay turned. "Training's over."

Ten minutes earlier that proclamation would have made me cheer. Now, I wanted to vomit.

Two

J ay pushed past Cruz and me and motored down the hall.

I glanced at Cruz then hurried after Jay.

He stood in his room when I caught up to him. In the month I'd stayed at the house, I hadn't invaded the space. Now I stepped in without knocking. "What do you mean training's over? I thought I had more to learn."

"You do." Jay reached beneath his bed and pulled out a suitcase. "But you know enough to learn the rest on your own."

"What if I'm not ready?" I couldn't believe the question came from my mouth. I'd been so anxious to finish training and begin searching for Adam.

"Then you should have practiced more."

"That's it?" It was another slap in the face. "Don't you have any words of wisdom before you walk out of my life again?"

Jay laid his suitcase on the bed. "Again?"

Strictly speaking Jay had never walked out. Gloria had moved us. But after spending so much time training with Jay when I'd been ten, I'd sort of expected him to always be there. Once we'd moved, he hadn't been. I'd assumed he'd always be a memory until he'd shown up at the Gathering in Albuquerque and turned out to be my uncle.

"Okay, not again," I said.

Jay stepped back and leaned against his dresser. "Nothing will happen for a while. They'll have to find your son's prophecy amidst the thousands I hold. Then they'll have to figure out who it's for."

Since I hadn't named Adam—the hospital who'd delivered him while I lay in a coma had—a question mark existed in place of a name on his birth prophecy. "It lists me as his mom. How hard will it be?"

"It lists your initials. It doesn't say mom or anything like that."

My brain stumbled. "It said it on the copy you gave me."

Jay shrugged. "That's the copy I wrote for you. What I write in my records only needs to make sense to me. I have a method."

For a moment I felt stuck, unable to move on. Maybe he was right. Maybe it would take time. "Will you go directly to Summerhaven?"

A little town outside Tucson and nestled partway up Mount Lemmon, Summerhaven housed the Leader's Residence and other tribal facilities. My father's ashes had been spread there, and over the next two days, it was where the council would meet with the rest of the tribe.

Jay shook his head. "No. It'll take the rest of today and most of tomorrow to retrieve my records. If I drive through the night, I should arrive early Sunday morning." He met my gaze and held it. "I'll be there in time for the meeting."

The thought of the meeting and social activities made my stomach knot. No way did I want to attend without Jay. He'd spent his entire life amongst our tribe and knew their ways. I'd only known of the Neme-i for a month.

He pulled clothes from drawers and tossed them at his suitcase. Some were folded. Most weren't.

I walked to the bed, folded the unfolded clothes, and placed them neatly in Jay's bag.

He rolled his eyes but threw more clothes my way. "If they ask when you get to Summerhaven, tell them I'm on my way. That's all they need to know."

I reached for a T-shirt. "You will be there, right?"

"I just said I would."

I folded the shirt but held on to it. "Do you have to turn in *all* your prophecies?"

"Yes." Jay closed his drawers and walked to the closet.

"How would they know?"

He leveled his gaze with mine. "You know how."

I sighed. "Because I told Anna and Maria." My sister and grandmother were the only two Neme-i beyond Jay and me who knew I had a son. Unfortunately, they also knew what year he'd been born. "Will they know you were the seer who received the prophecy?" I didn't know how many seers there were—seers kept others' identities secret—but I sensed there were many.

"Only if you tell them." He pulled shirts from the closet and laid them on the bed.

At least that would buy me time. They'd have to look through all the seers' prophecies for that year, but with a little detective work, they'd narrow down the month as well. Gloria had died in the accident that put me in my coma. If they searched, they'd find her death record.

Jay tossed me a pair of jeans. "Relax. This vote's been coming for a while. My records are hard to understand for that reason. I won't help this train wreck happen."

Hard to understand and impossible weren't the same thing. "How much time do you think Cruz and I will have to find Adam?"

"Not sure. Hopefully enough."

Now I really didn't want to go to the meeting. I wanted to get on the road and start my search.

Jay and I continued in silence. When he finished selecting clothes, he moved to the bathroom to gather his toiletries. Securing the suitcase's elastic bands, I sat on the bed.

Cruz appeared in the doorway, eyebrow cocked. I shook my head.

Two minutes later, Jay stepped out of the bathroom to find

10

Cruz and me staring at him. He wagged his head. "Look, I need to make some calls. Go start a pot of coffee, and make me a couple sandwiches for the road. We'll talk when I'm done."

Cruz and I moved to the kitchen. He worked on the coffee while I assembled two sandwiches and summarized what Jay had said. When we finished, we sat at the table and waited.

"We could skip the trip to Summerhaven," Cruz said.

"No, we can't." I'd agreed to train with Jay for six months while the council footed all bills. If I wasn't with him in Summerhaven, the Neme-i would grow suspicious and start checking on me. Cruz and I wouldn't be able to sneak away and search for Adam in private like we planned. "We need to buy as much time as possible before they realize we're gone and start looking for us." Sooner or later, they would come.

Fifteen minutes passed before Jay joined us in the kitchen. He laid a piece of paper on the table in front of me and grabbed a travel mug from the cupboard. The paper contained a phone number and handwritten address.

"What's this?" I asked.

"The number is Mo's. If you run into trouble, call her."

"What kind of trouble?" I asked.

He reached for the coffee pot. "Any."

An image of Mo riding to the rescue on her hog flashed through my mind. The Harley didn't qualify as stealth material, but it would scare anyone with sensitive hearing.

Cruz glanced at the paper. "And the address?"

"It's for a bar outside Blythe called the Eight Ball. The owner is Regina Bowman. She was a good friend of Raina's. It's as good a place to start your search as any."

Hope lit a fire inside me. "Do you think she'll know where Raina is?"

No way in hell would I refer to Raina Bluefeather as Mom or Mother. She didn't deserve it. She'd abandoned me as a baby and eighteen years later stolen my child.

"I doubt it." Jay poured coffee in his mug. "She left Blythe

11

over twenty-five years ago."

Hope died, and I slumped forward. According to Jay, Raina had moved around a lot, trying to stay hidden from the Neme-i. If she functioned anything like Gloria, she would have moved at least eighteen times in those years.

"You think she'll know where Raina went?" Cruz asked.

Jay flashed a *you-got-it* smile.

"And then what?" I asked. "Do you honestly think we'll find someone who remembers her everywhere she lived?"

"It's possible." Jay scooped sugar into his mug. "Raina makes friends. She has to. Staying hidden requires help."

"Gloria didn't have help," I said.

"That's what you think." Jay's gaze turned steely. "Gloria knew about the Neme-i. She told you the story of the First Girls. She knew you were telekinetic and brought you to me. Trust me, she had help."

The possibility he'd raised a couple times before—that Gloria and Raina might have known each other—echoed like an evil whisper at the back of my mind.

In the past month, the things I'd learned had shaken my beliefs about Gloria to the core. Had she really found me as a baby in the backseat of her car or had I been given to her? Had we moved so often because she had wanderlust, like she said, or to stay hidden? Had she known Jay was the best trainer of the Neme-i and my step-uncle, or had her referral to him been a coincidence? And why had she asked him to train me in such a way as to make sure I wouldn't be able to use my gift?

When I put all the questions together, one fact stood out. Gloria had lied to me. About everything. But the idea of her knowing Raina was a black hole I wasn't willing to visit.

"So we go place to place, dropping Raina's aliases and hope something comes from it?" Cruz mused.

"Either that or stay with me and wait." Jay screwed the lid on his cup and took a careful sip.

"For what?" I asked.

"Your son is ten. He needs to be trained."

"You said boys don't train until they're eleven." I'd already missed ten years of my son's life. No way would I sit on my ass doing nothing while another year passed. Not when I had a clue to follow. I'd been through every other option—law enforcement, child search agencies, more private investigators than I could remember or afford, even psychics. No one had ever learned anything. This was my chance.

"That's true." Jay sipped his coffee. "But I'm in demand. If you want your child trained by me, you have to schedule in advance."

"You fit me in last minute," I pointed out.

"And I'll owe favors till I'm dead because of it."

Cruz tilted back in his chair. "Will Raina count on your friendship and wait till the last minute to schedule?"

"Or what if she chooses a different trainer or doesn't want Adam trained?" I moaned.

Jay pulled out a chair and sat. "First, she already is counting on our friendship. Most families schedule with me at least a year out. Your child's birthday is in nine months." He let that sink in. "Second, she won't choose another trainer. She's raising a child. She'll want the best."

I didn't share Jay's faith in Raina. Any woman who would walk out on the tribe she'd agreed to lead, in addition to her husband and daughters, didn't put others' needs first.

"And third," Jay said, "she has to have him trained. There's no way around it. If she doesn't, his life won't be his own. He'll feel the energy all around him and interpret it as voices in his head. That buzzing won't stop, and he'll either go crazy, get diagnosed as schizophrenic, or kill himself."

Horror began a free fall inside me. What if she allowed that to happen?

Cruz reached across the table and took my hand.

"Relax," Jay said, "she'll call. Especially when she learns you've been found."

13

"Right," I said, "because kidnappers love being caught."

Jay let out an exasperated growl. "I keep telling you, she was trying to protect your son, not steal him."

He'd told me this several times. It was the story Raina had told him. But how much was actually true and how much had she made up?

"After she helped the foster mother get your son out of Gallup, she got the baby situated and went back for you. It's not her fault you woke from the coma and left the hospital against doctor's orders. She couldn't find you."

I rolled my eyes. "And I'm sure she's been looking for me ever since."

"Probably," Jay said.

"Except there's one problem with that theory. The tribe's known about me for over a month! It's no secret I'm in Mojave with you. If she wants to find me so bad, why hasn't she called?"

Jay's shoulders sagged. "I don't know."

To hear Jay tell it, Raina was a loving, caring woman. In the only conversation I'd had with my father before his death, he'd pretty much said the same. But I couldn't reconcile their views with my experience. Raina hadn't wanted me as a baby, and she didn't want me now.

Cruz squeezed my hand. "We'll find Adam."

"And if we don't?" My fear of not finding my son was second only to my fear of finding him dead.

Cruz shifted his gaze to Jay. "Jay will contact us when Raina calls."

So many *ifs*. And my future hinged on every one.

"One more thing." Jay stared evenly at me. "Once you reach Tucson, you'll need to drive."

"Why?" I didn't mind driving, but it seemed like a strange direction.

"After the disaster in Albuquerque, the council can't risk outsiders getting into a meeting again. Our women will be sending around-the-clock messages to keep anyone but the

Neme-i from driving up the mountain." Jay looked at Cruz. "Those will affect you."

"More than the messages in Albuquerque?" Cruz asked.

"Yes," Jay said. "In Albuquerque, our women scaled back the messages so the two of you could get in the parking lot. Instead of keeping outsiders off the entire property, they focused on keeping them out of the meeting room. Since you didn't go in, you never broke the barrier. All you got was a dose of headache from getting a little too close to the door. The council won't make that mistake again. When you go up the mountain tomorrow, you'll be breaking through the messages. You'll get the full force."

Cruz blew out a breath. "Let me guess, that's part of my training?"

Jay grinned.

"If that's the case," I said, "shouldn't he be driving?"

"No. If he drives and gets through the messages, they'll know I've been training him. Not good." Jay faced Cruz. "You're a *friend* of the Neme-i because you saved lives in Albuquerque and because of your bond with Luna, but you're not Neme-i. Big difference."

Cruz nodded. Tewa on his father's side and Navajo on his mother's, Cruz had been raised between two tribes. He'd once told me he'd never felt like he fully belonged to either. I doubted he cared about being considered a member of a third.

Jay stood. "Trust me, experiencing this will be enough. You need to know what it feels like."

"What *what* feels like?" I asked.

"Being bombarded by multiple senders at the same time."

"It's different than receiving from one person?" I asked.

Jay's eyes opened wide. "Oh yeah."

Cruz gritted his teeth.

"Just remember what I told you." Jay walked to the kitchen counter.

Steel shone in Cruz's eyes. "It'll get easier over time."

15

Jay tossed the sandwiches I'd made in a plastic bag then added a bag of chips and an apple. "Stay here tonight and leave tomorrow like we planned. I'll see you Sunday morning." He grabbed the bag and travel mug and nodded at Cruz. "Can I talk to you outside?"

The moment the door closed behind them, I scurried to the living room and watched through the window. Front paws on the sill, Bear watched with me.

Jay motioned northwest then flipped his hand back and forth like a rudder before handing something to Cruz. Turning, Jay winked at me then climbed in his SUV and drove away.

"What was that about?" I asked when Cruz returned.

"Somewhere to go in case there's trouble."

The hair on the back of my neck rose. "Are we expecting trouble?"

"No. Just being prepared."

In the kitchen, Cruz opened the map of California and Arizona we'd been using. Plotting our course online would have been easier, but we'd agreed to stay off the internet. Though the thought of anyone monitoring our phones or Jay's internet connection seemed like the stuff of spy novels, the thought of me being abducted at gunpoint had once seemed equally implausible. Now we knew better.

Cruz pointed to Blythe on the map. "It's on the way to Summerhaven, but it'll add time to our trip."

I shrugged. "Not as much as it will after the meeting." When we left Summerhaven, we planned to drive to Idaho to begin our search, not return to California.

Cruz yawned and returned the map to the pile of things we planned to take with us. "Have you heard from Tomas?"

I gritted my teeth. Tomas was a difficult subject. Adam's father. Cruz's best friend. Calling the situation complicated was an understatement. But Tomas's psychic abilities left him uniquely qualified to tell us if our search plans were good. "Not since he sent the picture of Gizmo." I'd sent him several texts since. He hadn't replied to any.

"Have you checked today?"

"No." I'd been purposefully avoiding my cell due to Tomas's lack of response.

My phone lay on the bookshelf in the living room. I had a voice message from my boss in New Mexico, but nothing more. My text thread with Tomas remained the same as it had the past two weeks. His last message was the picture of my black lab sitting in front of a plate glass window that said Eureka Bakery. "Nothing new."

The muscle in Cruz's jaw pulsed.

"What?" I asked.

He shook his head. "I need to make some calls then I'm gonna lie down."

He walked away and left me wondering, as he often did, about the compass that steered the inner workings of his head.

I looked again at the picture of Gizmo. God, I missed him. I'd gotten him shortly after I'd moved out of Tomas's house and raised him from a puppy. He'd become my best friend. And now Tomas had taken him on a never-ending road trip. It ticked me off. And it hurt my feelings. Tomas had never ignored me like this.

I closed the text window and listened to my voicemail.

"Hi little one." The timber of Kurt's voice made me smile. In the years I'd worked as a wilderness tour guide, he had become my friend as well as my boss. "I know you're still on your leave of absence, but that family that wants you to lead them in the Northern Pecos, will change their vacation dates if you can say when you'll be back. Give me a call and let me know. Say hi to Cruz, and if he's giving you trouble, tell him to call me. I'll take care of it."

I chuckled as I deleted the message. The *leave of absence* had been Kurt's idea. I'd told him I had no idea when I'd be back. At the time I'd assumed I would be. Now, I'd begun to wonder.

I dialed his number and told his voicemail the same thing I'd told him the last two times he'd called about this family. I still had no idea when I'd return, and he didn't need to worry. Cruz treated me well. "I miss you."

Cruz kept saying money wasn't a concern, but I knew better. With him away, the profits for his security business had to be taking a hit, even with his friend, Derek, running the company. When the council stopped paying Cruz to protect me, he'd need to work. He spoke as if he had a little stash of money. But whatever stash he had would eventually run dry.

I dialed Hideo. He picked up on the third ring.

"Just checking in," I told him.

Within a week of being named Leader During a Time of Duress—a position meant to be probationary—my sister had *retired* Hideo from his position as groundskeeper for the leader's family. He'd been given no choice. Knowing he had nowhere to go, I'd asked him to move into my house in Chimayo and take care of it until I returned.

"Everything is fine," he said. "Your garden is doing well. It's producing so much that I offered some of the tomatoes and peppers to your neighbor."

"Mrs. Gonzalez?" My neighbor was a short, round, grumpy lady whose mean tabby cat liked to pee in my yard.

"She invited me to dinner," he said.

"*Mrs. Gonzalez?*" Surely, he had to be talking about some neighbor I didn't know I had because Mrs. Gonzalez wasn't nice to anyone.

"She's a good cook," he said. "Not as fine as Juanita, but close."

Juanita, the Bluefeathers' amazing cook and housekeeper, had been Anna's other casualty in the forced retirement process. Unlike Hideo, however, Juanita had been asked to stay, given a position of prominence—like a beloved aunt who'd been taken in by the family in her later years.

"You've already eaten with her?" I couldn't believe it.

"Yes. Tomorrow I'll be cooking for her. One of Juanita's

recipes."

My mouth hung open. "Okay," I finally managed. "Is there any mail I should know about?"

"You received a package two days ago."

I heard movement and imagined him walking through the house.

"From who?"

The movement stopped and I suspected he'd retrieved the box.

"There's no return address, but it's postmarked San Diego."

"Hmm." I didn't know anyone who lived that far south. In fact, Jay and Mo were the only people I knew who lived in California at all.

"It makes noise when I move it," Hideo said. "Whatever's inside may have broken."

Figured. "Open it." Now that he'd gotten me curious, I wanted to know what the package contained. "Please."

I heard paper ripping. "Ah." He chuckled lightly. "Not broken. It's a puzzle."

Of course. And return address or not, I knew Tomas had sent it. He loved jigsaw puzzles. "What's the picture show?"

In the second bedroom of his house, Tomas had a collection of assembled puzzles depicting images of the San Diego Zoo, several landscapes across the southwest, a Victorian mansion, a marina filled with boats, and a giant multi-colored Ferris wheel. The last time I'd seen him, he'd been working on a puzzle showing a petroglyph. Apparently he'd finished that one.

"It's a Japanese tea garden." The sound of sliding puzzle pieces came faintly over the line. "The box says it's in Portland, Oregon."

I smiled. Gloria had taken me there as a kid. "I don't think it's actually for me." More likely, Tomas had intended it for himself but sent it to my address because he didn't have someone picking up his mail. "Anything else I should know?"

"No," he replied. "I've paid the bills, and the rest of the mail has been junk unless you want me to enter you in the Publishers

Clearing House sweepstakes."

I passed on the sweepstakes, wished him luck with dinner, and thanked him once again for taking care of my home.

"I am the one who owes you thanks."

He said that every time we talked. I suspected we would playfully argue about it for years to come—who'd helped who more.

I spent the next couple hours trying to stay busy. I didn't want to think about the tribal meeting, or the prophecies, or the unknown people who wanted me dead. I didn't want to think about the Neme-i, or Raina, or what would happen if the Neme-i found out I had a son and learned his prophecy. I didn't want to think about Anna, or the look in her eye when she'd pointed a gun in my direction. But with Cruz asleep and Jay gone, I had little to distract me. I played tug with Bear and gathered the possessions Cruz and I had left lying around. I tried to read a book but couldn't concentrate. Finally, I went to Jay's garage where Cruz had hung a piece of plywood with a bull's-eye painted on it.

I pulled the knives from the sheath at my back and practiced throwing. The activity had become a sort of therapy. Throw, retrieve, find a new spot, repeat. I'd been good with knives before coming to Mojave. But after needing the knives to save myself during my first abduction, good no longer seemed good enough.

My shirt clung to my back and perspiration soaked my hairline when I heard the door squeak. I glanced back to find Cruz holding a can of Coke. Whipping my gaze to the target, I threw my knife. It stuck on the outside edge of the bull's-eye.

"Not bad," Cruz said.

"I had a good teacher."

The corner of his mouth twitched.

Early in my relationship with Tomas, I'd said I wanted to learn to throw knives. He'd told me to ask Cruz. It had been the first of many things Cruz had taught me.

"Did you get any sleep?" I asked.

"A little. Probably twenty minutes before my phone woke

me." He tipped his Coke my way.

I took a drink. "Who was it?"

"Keith calling back."

Keith Richards was Cruz's friend as well as the detective investigating my abductions. The last we'd heard, he'd run into a wall after searching my abductors' houses and the houses of the gunmen who'd killed my father. He'd come up with nothing but a description of Hernandez's girlfriend's heart-shaped ass.

"What did he say?" I asked.

Cruz nodded at the knife I still held, and I gave it to him. He lifted it up and down testing its weight before he threw. Bull's eye. "His captain's closing your case."

"What?" The words were a sucker punch to my gut. "Why?"

"Because the abductors are all dead."

"But what about the person who hired them?" Hernandez, the man in charge during both abductions, had referred to someone else who'd hired him. As far as we knew, that person remained at large.

Cruz shook his head. "No evidence of such a person." He took a drink. "I'm gonna pay Keith to keep working it on his own time."

So there we were cutting into Cruz's stash of money again.

"There's one more thing," he said.

Knots formed inside my stomach. "What?"

"Keith's captain knows Maria. She makes sizable donations to the Police Officer's Foundation every year."

My mouth opened but nothing came out. I stood there blinking until coherent thought returned.

"Is that why the captain sent Keith to us the morning after my first abduction? He wanted to keep his donor happy?" We'd been instructed to go to the police station to see Keith that afternoon, but he'd shown up at the Bluefeather house bright and early.

"Probably."

"Is his captain Neme-i?"

"No. White."

I swallowed. "Do you think Maria asked him to close the case?" Asking that felt like ripping off a scab. I didn't like acknowledging it, but my grandmother's motives and feelings toward me remained a sore spot.

I'd always imagined grandmothers as warm, dowdy women who baked cookies and gave their grandchildren more chances than they deserved. Maria didn't fit that bill. She was cool and businesslike and probably preferred corporal punishment over time-outs. Sometimes she seemed to care about me. Other times she felt as warm as a piece of steel at the South Pole.

"No."

A tiny sigh escaped me.

Cruz lifted an eyebrow. "But if the person we're looking for is Neme-i, I think *they* may have sent a message to close the case."

Oh hell. How had I missed such an obvious possibility? Any Neme-i woman could have sent such a message. "So our person is a woman?"

Cruz shrugged. "Or a man with a woman's support." He walked to the target and pulled out the knives. "Or we're wrong about everything, and they're not Neme-i at all."

⚎

After an early dinner, we walked Bear. I started toward the dirt road where we usually walked, but Cruz grabbed my elbow and nodded at the land behind the house. "Let's see what Jay was talking about."

I looked at Bear. His tail wagged and his tongue lolled as he stared at the road. "Are you sure?"

If it were Gizmo, I would have taken him in a second. But I'd raised Gizmo in the wilderness—camping and hiking at all hours. He knew to stay near and not chase anything. Bear had been raised in a fenced yard in the city. He didn't know anything.

"We could put him on a leash." Cruz's tone hinted at other options.

"Or?"

"You could tell him what to do."

22

He was right. I could send impulses and ideas to Bear telekinetically, but those impulses and ideas would only control behavior when I sent them. To keep him safe for an entire walk, I might have to send continuous messages. The thought alone exhausted me.

I stared out at the desert. "What kinds of animals could we run into?" I was used to the high desert, not the low.

Cruz shrugged. "Mountain lions, skunks, coyotes, rattlesnakes."

None of which I wanted to come across with a rambunctious untrained dog.

Cruz started forward.

"So what's your plan if we run into one of those?" I hurried around a creosote bush.

Cruz whistled.

I glanced over my shoulder as Bear discovered the change in routine. He barked once then ran full speed in our direction.

"You'll send them away."

Bear hurtled past us and raced forward into the desert.

Mentally I saw him walking beside us, keeping close, then sent the image to him.

Twenty feet ahead, he slowed to a trot and stopped. Turning, he walked back to us.

"You want me to send predators away at the same time I'm keeping Bear under control?"

"Yeah."

Easier said than done. Jay had worked with me on the ability to send different messages to different people at the same time. He called it sending simultaneous messages, and said the ability was rare. But the First Girls had been able to do it—the two Navajo maidens who'd been cast out of their tribe and formed the group that eventually became the Neme-i.

"And you are of their blood line," Jay had explained.

I'd pointed out Anna was also of the same blood line and asked if she could do it. He'd said no—that Anna hadn't trained with

23

him because Maria wouldn't allow it. And to the best of Jay's knowledge, no other trainer knew how to teach the skill.

So far, my success at sending simultaneous messages had been limited.

Cruz continued walking.

"What makes you think I'll be able to send simultaneously?" I asked.

"Messages sent to animals have to be simple, right?"

I nodded. They had to be within the animal's experience and ability level.

"Simple messages were how you succeeded with me and Jay."

Translation: if I could send simple simultaneous messages to people, animals should be no problem. Sometimes talking with Cruz was like working an algebra equation.

"That's a lot of trust you have."

Cruz stopped walking and turned. His smile made my breath catch. "I know."

We wound back and forth around cacti and shrubs for fifteen minutes. When I looked back, I no longer saw Jay's house.

"Why are we doing this again?" I asked.

"Because if something happens tonight, I'd rather know my way than search for it in the dark."

I scanned the land around us—hard packed dirt, ground-hugging and waist-high cacti, pockets of creosote and desert holly in every direction. Cruz was right. This was tough enough in the daylight. Fumbling around, trying to find an unfamiliar place in the dark would be hell.

The unrelenting sun beat down and sweat ran in a rivulet down my back as we pressed on. Dirt kicked up with every step we took, coating my shoes and legs. Bear's desire to run ahead waned, and he stayed with us without my messages. The sun dipped in the west and I estimated we had two more hours of daylight.

"Twenty minutes," Cruz said, wiping sweat from his face. "If we don't get there by then, we turn back."

We veered north at a group of Joshua trees and continued until we reached a set of five-foot tall craggy boulders. Bear found a patch of shade by a giant cropping of prickly pear and lay down.

Unscrewing the lid on the water bottle he carried, Cruz offered me a drink. I took a swig and returned the bottle. Cruz enjoyed a quick swallow then crouched and poured water in his hand for Bear. When the dog finished lapping, Cruz stood and checked the horizon.

"Can you give me some clue what we're looking for?" I asked.

Cruz turned in a slow arc, studying the land. "Not sure. Jay said you'd know."

"Me?" I spun in a circle recognizing nothing but the same scenery we'd been staring at for an hour. "How am I supposed to recognize something I didn't know existed?"

Cruz shrugged and continued to study the land to the east. Finding what he wanted, he pointed. "There."

I followed his finger to a giant boulder at the base of a cliff. "*That's* what I'm supposed to recognize? A rock?"

"Not the rock," Cruz said. "Something behind it."

To my right, pebbles slid and knocked together. I turned and spotted the red and black body of a large Gila monster. Immediately, I sent a message to Bear to stay still. Better not to mistake the venomous lizard for a toy.

I sent a message to the lizard about eggs buried several yards away. It flicked its tongue then turned and walked off to find its meal.

"Was that simultaneous?" Cruz asked.

"No."

"Too bad." He started forward. Bear lumbered to his feet and followed beside me.

As we drew closer to the boulder, I realized it wasn't a boulder so much as a wall of rock connected to the cliff that stood behind it. A fifty-foot canyon dipped between the two.

We rounded the wall, and I stopped short. In front of me stood an old, dilapidated camp trailer, its wheels half-buried in the dirt.

"Holy shit." I did recognize it.

Three

Most people have photos, videos, or other memorabilia to turn to. Tangible proof that their childhood memories are real. I have one thing. A photo of Gloria and me that used to belong to Jay. Everything else burned in the fire following the accident that left me in a coma.

Standing motionless in front of the trailer, I stared at a memory I'd thought lost in my past.

"You know it?" Cruz asked.

Dumbstruck, I nodded. The trailer's once-white walls were brown with dirt, and the blue stripe on its sides had all but peeled away. I approached the vehicle slowly, as if a shift in air might cause a sinkhole to open. Bear had no such qualms. He walked right up, gave the wheel a sniff, and lifted his leg.

I rubbed grime off the window. Inside stood the little Formica dining table and plaid upholstered bench seats. The whole thing converted into a tiny bed where I had once slept. Had I really been that small?

"What is it?" Cruz stood at the back of the trailer, balancing on the bumper, trying to see through the window into what I knew was the bathroom with the ugly olive-green vanity and toilet.

"The trailer I stayed in with Jay when I was ten," I said.

"When he trained you?"

More like, untrained. According to Jay, I'd naturally begun to use my gift before Gloria found him and asked him to train me *not* to be able to use it. Out of curiosity, he'd agreed, and over the course of a year had convinced me I was tele*pathic*. By the end of that year, I'd been so convinced I had to send words instead of images that for the next eighteen years I'd been unsuccessful any time I tried using my gift.

Looking back, I could see how my gift worked sometimes, but never when I intended it to. Unlike the other tour guides at Enchanted Wilderness, I had never come across a bear on a camping trip. All that time, I'd imagined bears staying away from my groups and had assumed I was enjoying the power of positive thinking. Who knew I'd been sending messages to bears for years?

Cruz walked around the side of the trailer and wiped a spot next to mine on the window. "Was it parked out here?"

"No." At the front of the trailer, sat the gold couch that unfolded into the bed where Jay had slept. Above it hung what appeared to be a cupboard but actually folded down into a sleeping area three feet from the ceiling. On the weekends when Jay and I had been alone, I'd slept there. When Gloria had stayed with us, that bed had been hers. "Somewhere else."

Cruz stepped back and eyed the wheels. "Looks like it's been here for years."

I walked to the door and tried the knob. Locked. "You have the key?"

Cruz pulled a key from his pocket and inserted it in the lock. He glanced back at me. "Let me go first."

I shrugged. No point in arguing. He'd do it anyway.

Hot, stale air rushed out as he opened the door. Waiting a few seconds, he stuck his head in to glance around before climbing into the body of the trailer. He peeked beneath the dining table, checked inside the bathroom, and opened the closet door next to it. Probably not big enough for an adult to hide inside, but I supposed there were child-sized murderers too.

"All clear?" I asked, knowing he'd run out of places to check. "Yeah."

I hoisted myself inside, noting the dust and cobwebs. I doubted anyone had been there for months.

Cruz turned and kicked the hollow bottom of one of the dining benches. "Storage?"

I nodded and scrunched my eyes, trying to remember what Jay had kept inside. "I think it held sleeping bags."

Cruz bent and stuck his head beneath the table to better see the cabinet door. "He locks sleeping bags?"

I crouched as well and spied a small locking unit that had been added to the door. "It didn't have a lock when I was a kid." Who knew what sat in there now.

Outside, Bear barked, and I stood. He barked again, paused, and then barked several more times. *Shit.* "Bear!" I hurried out of the trailer. No telling what he'd come across.

Around the other side, Bear stood wedged between the vehicle and the canyon wall. Front legs extended, he had his head down while he barked at something underneath. I bent down to look for myself. Two glowing eyes ringed by black stared back.

"What is it?" Cruz asked.

"Raccoon." I took a deep breath and let it out before sending Bear a message to stop barking and back out of the space he'd shoved himself into.

The barking ceased immediately. The backing out took a bit longer.

By the time Bear stood free, light in the canyon had dimmed. The land outside would soon follow suit.

"We should go," Cruz said. "We'll have to hurry to make it before dark."

I agreed.

We drank some water, locked the door, and headed out.

I couldn't believe the trailer still existed. It had seemed ancient when I'd been a kid. Now, it looked like it belonged at an auction for distressed antiques. "Did Jay say why it's parked out here?"

Cruz stopped by the craggy boulders where we'd come across the Gila monster earlier. "No. Just to go there if we ran into trouble."

Fat lot of good that would do. We'd be as stuck as the trailer. I turned around, expecting Cruz to have started forward. He hadn't. He stood as still as the boulders, his gaze down.

I took a step. He tensed and gave his head the tiniest shake. I froze. A rattle told me all I needed to know.

Bear growled, weight forward, ready to pounce. Immediately I sent a message, imagining him standing still. Mouth dry, I glanced behind and around myself before easing back. Moving in a wide arc, I saw the snake coiled at the base of the rock, about a foot from Cruz's feet. Its tail and head were up. Its rattle continued.

I pictured Cruz easing away, leaving the snake alone while Bear backed away and followed in the arc I'd walked. I imagined the harmony that had existed before we'd disturbed the snake's space—the same harmony that would return if we were allowed to keep our distance. I concentrated on Bear and the snake then noticed Cruz backing away, taking one careful step and then another. Bear backed up as well. The snake lowered its head, and a moment later, the rattling stopped.

The moment Cruz and Bear were with me, I let out a breath and Bear licked my hand. My legs quaked.

"Adrenaline," Cruz said when I held up my trembling hand.

"Why aren't you shaking?" He'd been the snake's target, after all.

He pulled me to him. "Because of you. Thank you."

"Huh?"

"You don't know what you did?"

Of course I knew what I'd done. "I sent a simultaneous message to Bear and the snake."

"I got it too."

"You did?"

"That's why I backed away."

He'd moved in the exact arc I'd imagined. Maybe he really had received the message. I hadn't intended to send it to him, but I had concentrated on him as much as Bear and the snake. I'd have to ask Jay about that. "You weren't scared?"

"Not once I got your message."

"What about before?"

He tipped his head. "Some."

I knew Cruz had run into rattlesnakes before. I'd come across a few as well. But I'd never been as close as he had, and I'd always been frightened.

"You okay?" Cruz asked.

"No." A tear leaked out of my eye. What if the snake had actually bitten him? What if I hadn't been able to send the message in time?

"But you will be?"

"Yes."

"Then let's go home."

We didn't mention the snake again, but thoughts of what could have happened stayed with me all night. I would have known what to do if Cruz had been bitten. My job as a wilderness tour guide demanded I know emergency first aid. But all that training had been in case something happened to me or a client I barely knew. Cruz was different. And the difference rattled me.

We made love that night, and as I stared into his cola-colored eyes and remembered the snake, I found myself squeezing him tighter. Every kiss grew deeper, every caress lasted longer. I didn't just want this man; I needed him. Needed the way he touched me and said my name. Needed the confidence he gave me and the comfort he provided. It wasn't the same as the comfort I'd felt with Tomas. That, I now recognized as friendship. This was different—deeper. At some point in the past month, I'd fallen in love.

╬

My watch said eleven-forty when we rolled into the little town of Blythe the next day. We stopped at a taco shop for food and directions then drove a couple blocks to a park at the corner of Barnard and Broadway. Seated beneath some trees, Cruz and I ate while Bear sniffed.

The town felt quiet and sleepy. Few cars passed and no one else occupied the park.

Tossing our wrappers in the trash can, we returned to the truck and made our way down Lovekin Boulevard until we came across a ramshackle building with a cracked and peeling eight ball painted on its side.

Cruz turned onto the hardscrabble lot and wound his way past several old trucks and a handful of cars that had seen better days. Several gleaming Harleys sat parked where a walkway should have been, and a neon sign by the door declared the establishment open.

We parked between a pickup sporting an NRA bumper sticker and a burgundy Honda Civic lowered until its muffler sat an inch from the ground.

Cruz blew out a sigh. "You got your knives?"

"You really have to ask?"

He fetched his Glock from the glove box and holstered it at his back before donning a large denim shirt that he left untucked.

We climbed from the truck as the door of the bar opened and two men came flying out. The first man fell to his knees while the second stumbled forward shouting slurred obscenities and giving the blond bouncer the finger. The bouncer crossed his arms.

"I think he's done this before," I said.

"Probably once or twice."

Opening the tailgate, Cruz whistled. Bear jumped in. "Guard," Cruz said.

Bear licked his nose.

Taking my arm, Cruz steered me in a wide berth around the two drunks.

Inside, a combination of music, pool balls, and men yelling assaulted my ears. I looked past the bar and tables to a back room where several pool tables stood in rows, all but one in use. At the closest, two men stood chest-to-chest. One by one, other games stopped and players headed toward the confrontation.

Cruz put an arm out and stopped me as the blond bouncer hurried past. "If a fight breaks out, we leave."

I didn't like the sound of that. I wanted to find Regina and learn what I could. But I didn't relish the thought of ending up in a bar fight. Concentrating, I envisioned the men at the center of the argument each taking a deep breath before stepping back and shaking hands. I imagined the other players returning to their tables to continue their games. I saw the images clearly then sent them to the people involved.

Seconds later, the yelling stopped. The men who'd been chest-to-chest eased back from one another. Those behind them looked around and stepped back as well. Tense laughter rose then turned to real laughter as people shook hands and returned to their games.

Cruz eyed me. "You?"

I shrugged. I hoped preventing the fight fell more into the category of creating harmony than personal gain. I didn't want to sew disharmony.

We found an empty table, and I glanced around for a waitress. From a nearby booth, a gray-haired man watched us, his gaze unwavering. A half-finished drink sat on the table in front of him along with a cell phone and papers. His tattooed forearms were the size of my thighs. I nodded, and he nodded back. Turning away, he raised a hand, signaling someone.

"What can I get ya'?" a raspy voice asked.

A buxom redhead stared down at us. Her voice said smoker, her jeans said she'd seen slimmer days, and the no-nonsense look on her face said she'd been around the block several times.

"Two Cokes," Cruz said.

Her upper lip curled back. "Cokes?"

"We're driving."

She blew out a breath and mumbled "Whatever" as she walked away.

When she returned, she placed the drinks in front of us. "Ten bucks."

Cruz held out a twenty. "We're looking for Regina."

The waitress eased the twenty from Cruz's grasp and put it in her apron. "I don't know any Regina."

My stomach sank.

Cruz didn't bat an eye. "My understanding is she owns this place."

"If she did, it was before my time. I been here five years." The waitress lifted her chin and motioned toward the man I'd nodded at earlier. "That's Ruben. He's the owner."

Cruz's jaw worked as he studied the man. "Would you ask him if we could have a word?"

"It'll cost you."

Cruz pulled out another twenty and handed it to her.

She nodded and took the money. "Give me ten minutes. I got other tables to work."

I drank my soda while the waitress made her rounds. A dark-haired bouncer shaped like a tree trunk spoke briefly with Ruben then disappeared through a door in the back wall. Ruben glanced at me before focusing his attention on the pool tables as he sipped his drink.

"Do you think he'll help us?" I asked.

"He's been watching you since we came in," Cruz said. "He'll talk."

The bouncer returned and handed Ruben a stiff piece of paper before retreating. Ruben gazed at the paper and frowned. When the waitress stopped at his table, he lay the paper face down.

The waitress said a few words and motioned our way. Ruben nodded, said a few things, then scooted out of the booth and walked through the same door the bouncer had used.

Shit. Ruben leaving wouldn't do. I closed my eyes and imagined him returning and coming to our table.

"Hang on," Cruz said before I could send the message.

I looked up as the waitress smiled. She held up her hand,

fingers splayed.

"Five minutes," Cruz said.

Hope kindled inside me.

My foot jiggled as I sucked up Coke. Would Ruben be able to point us to Regina?

The next five minutes were the longest since my kidnapping. I shredded my napkin, chewed on my straw, and emptied my glass. Then I started on Cruz's napkin.

Finally, the blond bouncer joined us.

"The owner wants to see you in his office."

Cruz's jaw tightened. Probably not thrilled about venturing into an unfamiliar back room.

I touched his arm. "It'll be okay." I'd send messages if needed.

The bouncer led us into the back and down a hallway with several doors to the left. Bulletin boards on the walls displayed the month's schedule and various OSHA bulletins. The bouncer stopped at the third door and knocked before cracking it open. "They're here."

Inside, a man said, "Send them in."

The room was simple—white paint, oak desk, metal file cabinet shoved against one wall. A red couch sat opposite us.

Ruben extended his hand and introduced himself. Once we were on a first name basis, he motioned to the couch and invited us to sit.

Seated at his desk, Ruben swiveled to face us. "Cynthia said you wanted to speak with me?"

I nodded. "We're looking for a woman named Regina Bowman. We were told she owned this place."

Ruben rested his forearms on the armrests. "She did until she sold it to me about seven years ago."

Cruz nodded. "Do you have an address or phone number where we can reach her?"

Ruben tapped his index finger on the chair and frowned. "Regina died six years back. Cancer.

Four

Nausea filled my stomach and my body turned cold. So much for the hope I'd felt in the bar.

Ruben's chair squeaked. "When she sold me this place, Regina had one stipulation."

Taking a deep breath, I pushed away the fear and forced myself to pay attention.

He reached for something on his desk. "I'd like you to look at this." He handed me a picture.

I held it so Cruz and I could both see.

Two women stared up at us. They stood side-by-side, smiling, with their arms around each others' waists. The bar behind them looked a lot like the bar in the next room, but painted black instead of brown. The woman on the left had bleached blonde hair teased up in a bouffant hairdo. The other had long, black hair worn in a low ponytail. My mouth fell open as I stared at the second woman. If I hadn't known better, I would have thought she was me.

"The blonde is Regina," Ruben said. "The other woman waited tables here. Do you know her?"

I could hardly make my mind process the question. My sister and I looked enough alike that I had easily posed as her when Maria first hired me. So if the photo resembled me, it did Anna too. Only it didn't. The woman in the photo seemed far too casual and at ease to be Anna. Which left only one possibility.

My heart swooped inside my chest. Part of me wanted to cry. For the first time I stared at something I had longed to see most of my life. Another part wanted to rip the picture to shreds and stomp on the pieces.

Cruz touched my hand.

I wrenched my gaze from the photo. "I believe this is my mother."

"You don't know?" Ruben said.

I shook my head. "I never knew her. I've been told I look exactly like her." My eyes fell back to the image. "This is the first picture I've seen of her."

Ruben blinked as if surprised. "Do you know her name?"

I let out a snort. "Her real name is Raina Bluefeather, but we've been told she has many aliases."

With a nod, Ruben stood and walked past the file cabinet to crouch in front of a floor safe. He punched in the combination, lifted the door, and pulled out a white envelope. Returning to his chair, he handed me the envelope. "Regina's stipulation was that I watch for a young woman who resembled the woman in the photo. When I saw her, I was to ask for a name. If she gave me the right answer, I was to give her this envelope, no questions asked."

From the feel of it, the envelope contained something hard inside some sort of padding. "Do you know what's inside?"

"No," Ruben replied, "and I don't want to. I've spent seven years waiting for you and wondering if you'd come. Now you're here. My obligation is met. That's all I need."

Ruben stood, and Cruz and I took our cue.

I held up the photo. "May I keep this?"

Ruben nodded. "It's yours."

We made our way out of the bar as another fight broke out at the pool tables. I ignored it. They were on their own to stop it this time.

Seated inside his truck, Cruz motioned to the envelope. "Let's see what's inside."

I slid my finger beneath the flap but hesitated, afraid of what I might find.

Cruz squeezed my shoulder.

I let out a breath and opened the envelope. Inside, I found a three-page letter written in beautifully slanted cursive and a tiny gold key with the number 42 engraved on one side. I handed the key to Cruz.

"Maybe a security box?" he said.

Dear Luna,

I always hoped to have the privilege of meeting you myself. But the doctors tell me my chances are getting slimmer by the day.

If you are reading this, that means someone pointed you here. Maybe an old friend of your mother's or someone I don't know. Either way, it means you're searching. Your mother hoped you would.

When I met your mom, she was in her twenties and looking for a job. She had no experience and later told me she'd never worked at all. I shouldn't have hired her. My clients are the type who eat women like her alive. But I did. To this day, I don't know why.

On her first day as a waitress, a young man grabbed her. I was tending bar and reached beneath the counter for the bat I always kept there. But I didn't need it. Your mother stared that man in the eye until he let go and sat down. He never grabbed another waitress in all the years he came here. He wasn't the only one affected by your mom. When she worked, fights stopped, people were happy, and tips flowed. Everyone wanted to work with her.

She was good with people and kind. She also had a good head for business. The pool tables and name for

the bar were her idea. She even painted the sign. Until
then, the place was called Regina's. People opened up
to her. But one thing about your mom, she didn't open
up to nobody. She had secrets. I knew that but always
figured if she wanted to share she would. I didn't ask.

She'd been working for me about a year when she
told me there might come a day when she didn't show
up. If that happened she said I shouldn't worry or
send the police looking for her. I should just know how
thankful she was that I gave her a chance when no
one else would. And she told me by doing that I'd
helped keep her and others safe. She wouldn't say what
she meant by that. About a week later, she was gone.

I did what she asked. I didn't call the police. I
pretended I'd known she was going. I wondered about
her sometimes and said prayers, but I thought I'd
never know. I didn't expect to see her again. Then one
day about eighteen years after she left, I was tending
bar and the place turned calm. The riffraff quieted
and everything seemed just right. It felt like it felt
when your mom worked for me. That's when I looked
up and saw her, standing across the bar, smiling.

I'm not what you call an emotional person. I keep
my feelings to myself. Never seemed right to burden
other people with them. But standing there looking at
your mom, I cried. I hadn't realized how much I
missed her until that moment.

That night, your mom told me a story the likes of
which I never would have believed if anyone else told
it. The likes of which I'll never repeat because no one
will believe me. At the end of the night, she told me she
had a daughter. A young woman who might come
looking for her one day. And she asked a favor. She
wanted me to give you this key if you ever did come.
When I asked how I'd know you, she told me your

name and said you'd look like her. She also said you might know her real name. A name I hadn't heard until that night. She said you might be able to calm the bar the way she had. I always hoped I'd get to see that. Oh well.

I waited and watched, but you didn't come. And now my time is running out. So I'm doing something I promised I wouldn't. I'm sharing a part of this story with someone else. Just a small part. Just in case you come.

This key will open a box at the post office in Palo Verde where your mom lived. I don't know what's inside. I just know it's for you. If you do find your mom, and I hope you will, please tell her I loved her and I kept my promise to the best of my ability.

Regina Bowman

I stared at the letter feeling numb, trying to make some part of it mean something.

Cruz reached for the map on the dashboard. "If she worked here while living in Palo Verde, it can't be far."

"It's Saturday. Do you think the post office will be open?" I reached for my phone and typed in my passcode.

"Maybe." Cruz put his hand over my phone before I could press the internet app. "You don't want anyone to know we're here, do you?"

With a growl, I released the phone and took the map.

Five

Highway 78 cut southward through acres of farmland. Cruz took the road at a speed that turned the crops into blurred splotches of brown and green.

The four-block town of Palo Verde sprang up on either side of the highway with the post office being one of the first little buildings we passed. We flipped a U-turn and sped back. The truck was still rolling when I jumped out and ran for the door.

Lights were on inside but the shades were drawn when I grabbed the handle and pulled. The door didn't budge. I tried again with the same result.

Cruz joined me and pointed at the hours posted on the door. Mondays – Fridays 7:30-4:30; Saturdays 8:00-2:00. We were twenty minutes late.

"Fuck!" I yelled.

"We'll have to come back."

I didn't want to come back. And I didn't want to wait until Monday. We were supposed to leave Summerhaven and drive to Idaho, *not* return to California.

Cruz pried my fingers from the handle. "No choice." He wrapped an arm around my shoulders and steered me to the truck.

I'd already gone ten years without my son. The thought of one more day hurt as much as every year before it. But what choice did I have? Send a message to the postmaster to open up? Without knowing what he looked like I couldn't fix an image of him in my head to send a message. Cruz was right. We had no choice.

I spent the next four hours thinking about Regina's letter and everything she'd said. By all accounts, Raina Bluefeather had been raised in the lap of luxury. Her father had been leader of the Neme-i, and she had money and privilege. Much like Anna. Neither had ever worked. Both had been groomed to assume the role of leader. The difference between them seemed to be that everyone had loved my mother. People were divided on my sister.

I couldn't understand why Raina would give all that up. Surely it hadn't been her life-long dream to slop beer to a bunch of ill-mannered people. But that's what she'd done. Shortly after being named leader, she'd abandoned the husband who adored her till the day he died. She left my two-year-old sister with him and took me only to abandon me later. Why? What could she possibly have gained? And what had she meant about Regina keeping people safe by hiring her? What people? Safe from what?

At the same time I considered those questions, I kept asking myself why the hell I cared? She'd stolen my son. Robbed me of the first ten years of his life.

Cruz's dashboard clock read 6:52 when we drove into Tucson. Tired and hungry, Cruz steered us to a park where we walked Bear long enough for him to take care of business before driving to a Waffle House where I ordered waffles and Cruz ordered a cheesesteak with a side of hash browns.

While we waited for our food, Cruz asked to see the letter again. Emotions played across his face as he read. His eyebrows bunched and his eyes narrowed. "How would she know what you look like?"

I shrugged. "Probably saw me in the coma." We knew she'd volunteered at the hospital while I'd been a patient and had known the foster mother who took Adam. Logic would dictate she'd seen me.

Cruz set the letter down and cleared his throat. "We need to consider something Jay said."

I sighed, steeling myself against the possibility that had

whispered through my mind for weeks. "That Raina and Gloria may have known each other?"

Cruz nodded.

I didn't want to think about it, but how could I not? Trying to believe that Raina had somehow come across a baby boy belonging to Jane Doe in a hospital and magically put together who we were strained the limits of logic. As did the thought that we'd all ended up in Gallup, New Mexico at the same time.

"You okay with that?" Cruz asked.

"No." The thought angered me more than all the other lies Gloria had told. "But I accept it's a possibility." What choice did I have?

Our food came and we ate, me gorging myself on sugar while Cruz filled up on sodium. After we paid, we returned to the truck.

Cruz held out his keys. "Ready?"

I only had to drive. Cruz looked like a child going to the doctor for shots. "Are you?"

He gritted his teeth.

I took Grant Road east to Tanque Verde then hopped on East Catalina Highway where signs warned of upcoming roadwork. A traffic camera stood where the road turned into Mt. Lemmon Highway.

Cruz sat up straight. "I feel it."

I glanced at him as he closed and opened his eyes wide.

"Is it different than when I send messages?" I asked.

"Yeah." Cruz blinked a few more times. "This is really strong."

"My messages aren't?"

His eyes warmed and the corners of his lips tugged upward. "Your messages feel nice." The smile gave way to a grimace. "This is like a headache. A bad one."

Fifteen minutes later, he clutched his head in both hands, his skin pale. A few turns after that he cranked the air conditioner to full blast and pointed all the vents at himself. I reached across the seat and felt his cheek. Clammy.

Half a mile later, Cruz pointed at a turnout. "Pull over!"

I did.

Throwing his door open, he hung his head out and vomited three times.

I felt helpless. There had to be something I could do to make him feel better. I wanted to send a message, but what could I send? The messages I sent were of urges to *do* something. What would I suggest he do? Get out and walk around?

I thought of Gloria. When I'd been sick as a child, she had come in the bathroom and held my hair back while I puked. Unbuckling my seat belt, I climbed on my knees and gently took hold of Cruz's shoulder-length hair.

He spit and said "Thanks" then wretched again.

I clamped my mouth shut and turned away to keep from vomiting myself. Cruz heaved again and I tasted bile.

He spit, took several deep breaths, and spit again. "I think I'm done now."

Thank God.

"Can you hand me my water bottle?"

He rinsed his mouth and face then closed his door and leaned back in his seat, skin glistening. "Shouldn't have had that cheesesteak."

I seized on the idea, somehow more comfortable with the idea of him eating tainted meat than of the Neme-i causing him such pain. "Is that why you're sick? Is it food poisoning?"

"No," Cruz said. "It's the messages."

My stomach sank. How could anyone be okay with doing this to another person?

"Do you want to turn back?" I asked.

He gritted his teeth. "No. It should get better once we're in Summerhaven."

I sure as hell hoped so. "Is there anything I can do to help?" Summerhaven remained twenty minutes away.

Cruz's eyes were closed. "Drive fast."

I steered us back onto the road and racked my brain as we

climbed the mountain. If women of my tribe could make Cruz feel this bad, I should be able to do something to make him feel better. The pain came from their messages. What if I sent messages of pleasure?

I glanced at Cruz. He looked ready to puke again. Anything had to be better than that.

I imagined the two of us naked. I thought of us on a bed with me on top. I imagined us kissing and touching and turning over. I imagined all the things he liked best and sent him the images then started all over again.

Next to me, Cruz moaned. Whether in pleasure or pain, I didn't know. But since I couldn't think of anything else to do, I kept at it. I imagined every position we'd tried in the past month and added one of us making love in the truck and outside as well.

When we passed a sign that said *Summerhaven 5 Miles*, I glanced at Cruz. His eyes remained closed but he appeared to be breathing easier. When we reached the Cookie Cabin, I looked again. This time his eyes were open. An amused grin tugged the corners of his mouth.

"Really?" he said. "I just threw up and you want to have sex?"

"I was trying to make you feel better."

"It worked." The grin grew into a wicked smile. "Where's our cabin?"

"I don't know. We're supposed to go to the Leader's Residence. Some sort of get-together. Maria said she'd give us the directions when we got there."

"She's gonna have to wait." Cruz grabbed my hand and placed it in his lap.

Heat leapt through me.

"Where's that fire road we discovered last month?" he asked.

I found it in record time.

⁜

Stars lit the sky when we pulled up to the guard shack in front of the Leader's Residence. A male guard stepped out while his female partner remained inside. Guards always worked in co-ed pairs to make the best use of the gifts.

Tall and lean, the man wore jeans and a red button-down shirt. His long, chocolate hair swung free against his back as he bent to see in the window. I smiled and he straightened up.

"Miss Bluefeather. Please go ahead. They are expecting you."

Except for Raina, the entire tribe seemed to know the youngest Bluefeather daughter had been found. Not everyone knew I'd elected to keep the name I'd grown up with.

I thanked him and continued up the lengthy driveway.

More like a lodge than a home, the Leader's Residence was lit like a convention center. When I'd first seen the Bluefeathers' place in Albuquerque, I'd thought it looked like a mansion. The Leader's Residence made that one look like a starter home.

For my father's ceremony, Cruz and I had stayed in one of the home's eight bedrooms. This visit, Jay would be staying with us, so we'd been given a reprieve. My grandmother and Jay detested each other. They struggled to be in the same room for a public meeting. Under no circumstance would they sleep under the same roof.

I skipped the parking area beyond the garage, and rolled to a stop in front of the house. Cruz rang the doorbell, and I braced myself as we listened to the extended chime. In the past, Hideo or Juanita would have answered the door. But I expected one of their replacements this time.

The door opened and a young man who stood half a head taller than Cruz greeted us. His dark hair, high cheekbones, and large lapis ring told me he was likely part of the tribe, but he looked more like eye candy than an employee.

"Hi," I said, "I'm—"

"Luna." Eye Candy extended his hand. "Of course."

His fingers were long and his skin smooth—nothing like Cruz's calloused, muscular hands. Bending, he touched his forehead to my hand in the customary greeting of the Neme-i for a leader or leader-elect. I hated it. It made me feel like a queen surrounded by peons. But respecting the Neme-i meant respecting their traditions.

"I'm Leonard," he said when he straightened up. "You must be Cruz."

The two men shook hands.

"Everyone's on the deck." Leonard led us through the open-floor plan past the sitting areas and dining table to the massive deck at the back of the house. Beyond the outdoor dining area with its giant stone fireplace, sat a fire pit surrounded by people in Adirondack chairs. A guard stood to the side of the stairs, hands folded in front of him. I presumed his female partner stood on the deck below.

Laughter exploded from the people gathered around the fire. I recognized Anna, Maria, Juanita, a cousin whose name I couldn't remember and her husband. Next to Juanita sat a young woman I didn't recognize, and between Maria and Anna sat three older women I didn't know. Several bottles of wine stood open on a table and empty plates told me we'd missed dessert.

"Ah, finally!" Anna stood as we approached. Dressed all in white, she looked like she belonged in a Manhattan high-rise. She turned toward us, wine glass in hand. I flinched, remembering the sight of her pointing a gun at me. "We expected you an hour ago."

I tried to cover the flinch with a smile. "We got held up."

"My fault," Cruz said. "I got sick on the way."

Anna and I managed a stiff, one-armed hug.

"The messages." Maria frowned as she shook hands with Cruz. "John should have told you to take sleeping pills before attempting the drive."

John was Jay's given name. Only a few people called him Jay. Interestingly, Gloria had used that name when she'd approached him and later when she'd introduced us. Until he'd shown up at the tribal meeting where I'd been introduced, I had no idea my grandmother's moody stepson, John, was the same man who'd trained me as a child.

Cruz nodded. "He warned us."

Maria hugged me then glanced toward the sliding glass door

with distaste. "Where is my delightful stepson?"

"He'll be here tomorrow." I greeted the cousin and stepped around the fire to Juanita.

In the times I had stayed with the Bluefeathers, Juanita had always eaten dinner with the family, but until now I had never seen her sitting with them after dessert. I placed the girl next to her in her mid-twenties. Her jaw-length brown hair and long face were unremarkable, but her large, honey-brown eyes drew me in.

"This is Noelle," Juanita told me. Her gaze fell. "My replacement."

I held out my hand. "I'm Luna."

"Can we pour you a drink?" Leonard offered as he topped off Anna's glass.

"No, thank you," I said. "We can't stay. Cruz needs to lie down. Jay said it would take time for the nausea to pass."

I glanced back and saw Cruz standing with a hand on his stomach. If I hadn't known how happy I'd left him on the fire road, I might have believed he felt miserable. "We just wanted to let you know we made it and get the directions to the cabin."

Maria stiffened. "Perhaps Cruz could lie down here? Anna and I have something to discuss with you."

Heat prickled the skin on my arms. What could they possibly need to talk about so badly they would leave their guests?

I looked at Cruz. He frowned but nodded.

"Shall we go to my office?" Anna suggested. "There's a couch in the sitting room upstairs where you can lie down."

"Thank you," Cruz said.

The four of us excused ourselves and filed upstairs. To the right, at the top of the steps, sat the office, the sitting room beyond it to the left.

Cruz's lip twitched, forming something between a grimace and a smile, before he left my side and continued to the sitting room. I watched his back for a moment then turned and followed Anna and Maria into the office.

Maria closed the door. My muscles tightened.

Standing in front of the windows, Anna faced me. "How was your drive? Tedious?"

"Not bad," I said. "We have Bear with us, so we stopped and got out to walk a few times. It broke the monotony."

"Bear?" Anna looked out the window as if expecting to see a man in her driveway.

I sighed. "You remember, the dog who attacked Hernandez when he abducted us? I adopted him?"

"Oh, right." Anna turned back around. "So...."

One thing I liked about my sister, she was almost as bad at small talk as me.

Our grandmother, however, was a master. She could guide a conversation like Fred Astaire leading a dance. "How is your training going, dear?" Maria circled to my right.

"Okay."

She raised an eyebrow. "Just okay?"

I shrugged. "Jay—John, I mean—isn't exactly big on feedback."

"No. I don't imagine he would be." Maria frowned. "Has he told you anything else about the Neme-i? About our history, for instance?"

What the hell did these two want? "A little."

"Did he tell you about the birth prophecies?" Anna interjected.

Maria shot her a stern glance.

My nerves hummed. "Actually, Hideo told us." I paused to see if either would ask about the former groundskeeper. He had been with the family for years, after all. But neither did.

"Have you learned anything new about the prophecies?" Maria said. "Anything specific John may have told you?"

I looked from my grandmother to my sister, wondering what they wanted and trying to gauge what I should and shouldn't say. "I know he's a seer."

"Good." Maria smiled and looked at Anna.

It was the first time I'd seen Maria smile when talking about Jay.

Anna eased forward. "Has he told you about the vote to make the prophecies public?"

I nodded.

"It won't be finalized until we meet tomorrow, but that's just a formality."

Though her position as leader wasn't cemented yet, Anna had been busy.

She walked to the desk and perched on the edge. "Once the vote takes place, seers will turn over their records and the prophecies will be available for all Neme-i to see. A small cabin farther up the mountain will serve as a library for the records."

The hairs on the back of my neck rose. "This is about my son, isn't it?"

"Yes, dear." Maria motioned to the club chairs in front of Anna's desk.

Every instinct inside me screamed, *Flee!* I moved to sit with feet made of stone.

Maria sat next to me. "Has anyone approached you and told you your child's prophecy, perhaps at your father's funeral or back in Albuquerque after the tribal meeting?"

I shook my head. True enough. No one had *told* me Adam's prophecy. Jay had handed it to me written on a piece of paper.

Maria and Anna exchanged a look. For a moment, neither seemed to know the next step in our little waltz.

Maria recovered first. "Well, at some point, perhaps even this weekend, someone will."

"Yes," Anna jumped in, "you are of the Neme-i, so your son is too, even if his father is an outsider."

Outsider. Anna said it like a simple fact of life. Like I might say my hair was black. And I supposed she had a point. Not born of the Neme-i, Tomas was an outsider, same as Cruz. But coming from a people made up of outcasts from tribes across Mexico and the American Southwest, the term struck me as hypocritical.

Determined to share nothing about Adam's father, I schooled my features. "Are you saying you're worried about my son's prophecy?"

Anna and Maria answered at the same time.

"No."

"Yes."

I looked from one to the other wondering who had stepped on the other's toes.

Maria smiled. "I suppose the answer is both yes *and* no." A graceful double step. "Do you remember we told you the council would take a tremendous interest in your son if they knew about him?"

We'd had that conversation just before the Gathering in Albuquerque. "Yes."

"When the prophecies are made public," Anna said, "the council will learn about your child." Far more direct than Maria's approach, Anna's cut deeper.

Maria scowled at Anna then turned back to me, her voice smooth and loving. "We know how much you want to keep your child a secret, dear. Once the council receives the prophecies, there will be a brief period of time before they are placed in the new library. It might be possible, during that time, to find your child's prophecy and remove it from the others—keep that one secret."

Something cold sliced through me. The hair on my arms stood up. Like everyone else's, Adam's prophecy was secret now. This law would change that. Yet here sat the new leader of the tribe and our grandmother offering to break the law they championed.

"Wouldn't that be against the rules?" I asked, backpedaling, trying to buy time. "Why would you do that?" Hadn't I asked Jay to do this very thing the day before?

"We are family, dear, and family must come first. We do what we have to."

My skin tightened. Maria had once said that for the leader and his family, the Neme-i had to come first. I felt like I was in Mojave looking at the rattlesnake all over again.

"To make the search easier," Anna said, "all we'd need is his birth date."

I thought of Cruz. Imagined his face as he'd slept the night before then imagined him knocking on Anna's office door. I imagined him coming in and pleading nausea to get us out of there. I imagined him doing it right then.

Six

I gulped as I looked from Anna to Maria. What could I say? "I, uh—"

A knock sounded on the door.

"Luna?" Cruz called.

Springing to my feet, I hurried to open the door. Shoulders bowed, Cruz stood with his head against the jam.

"I really need to go." He glanced past me at Maria and Anna. "I'm sorry."

I wanted to kiss him. "Okay." I forced what I hoped was a concerned expression before facing my sister and grandmother. "Can we please finish this tomorrow?"

Anna's eyes narrowed as Maria stood.

"Of course." Maria stepped toward us. "Is there anything we can get you?"

"No." Cruz's stomach jerked and his cheeks puffed.

"The directions," I said.

Maria joined us at the door. "There's a brochure and key on the entryway table. The directions are circled." She glanced at Cruz. "I hope this won't keep you from joining us tomorrow. We are expecting both of you for dinner."

He flashed a weak smile and let me lead him to the stairs.

A mile down the road my heart stopped pounding.

On the seat behind us, Bear paced back and forth sticking his head out the windows.

I told Cruz what Maria and Anna had suggested, and when I finished, he sat in silence shaking his head.

I had wondered why Anna would vote to make the prophecies public. She had the most to lose if Adam's existence came to light. Now I knew. She had counted on me to help keep him secret.

"We need to talk to Jay," Cruz said.

That was true about a lot of things.

⚜

Larger than my house in New Mexico, the split-level cabin had two bedrooms, a loft that could sleep four, and a second bathroom.

Cruz and I took the room on the lower level which had its own bathroom. Cruz said the choice had nothing to do with the bathroom, and everything to do with the private rear entrance at ground level as well as an entrance to the house at the top of the stairs ascending from the bedroom. He didn't want to risk being surprised if someone broke in downstairs while we slept upstairs, and if someone broke in upstairs while we were below, he liked the idea of having a way out. I liked the private bathroom.

Worn out from getting sick or the exercise he'd gotten on the fire road, Cruz fell asleep quickly. So did Bear. I lay in bed, staring at the ceiling while my mind refused to shut down.

I didn't want the Neme-i to know about Adam—at least not until I found him and knew I could keep him safe. But I didn't want to help Anna either. I didn't trust her. She wasn't truthful. Something about her never seemed right. And there was that whole unresolved gun issue plaguing my mind. Yes, our abductor, had been behind me, and yes, Anna had shot him when I'd moved out of the way, but in the seconds the gun had been pointed at me, she'd looked at me. Not past me. Not through me. And she sure as hell hadn't told me to move.

She also hadn't used her gift while Hernandez had us. She'd

told me afterward she'd been too flustered to think straight. People reacted differently under stress. I understood that. But how much thinking was required to do something she'd been doing effortlessly for twenty years?

⌗

The next morning I woke alone. When I made my way upstairs, Jay sat at the dining table drinking coffee from a green mug. His hair was mussed and a glance through the bedroom doorway at the end of the living room showed an unmade bed.

"Good morning," I said.

He looked up as if surprised to see me. "Morning." The shadows beneath his eyes spoke of a very late night.

Smelling of soap and cologne, Cruz sat on the couch, the pieces of his gun and his cleaning supplies spread across the coffee table. An orange mug and the baby monitor he sometimes used when we were in separate rooms sat beside him.

Lying beneath the table, Bear thumped his tail against the floor. I rubbed his head.

"Mugs are above the coffee maker," Cruz said.

Coffee poured, I joined Jay at the table. He offered me a strained smile.

"Did you get what you needed?" I blew on my drink.

"Yeah." He yawned and stretched. "Cruz said you made it to the Eight Ball?"

I nodded.

"And that you sent simultaneously?"

I tipped my head side to side. "I sent simultaneously to a snake and Bear, but somehow Cruz got it too. I don't understand how that happened."

Jay nodded. "It just means you're becoming comfortable sending and aren't having to concentrate as hard. Anyone else?"

"A few people in the Eight Ball."

"How many is *a few*?"

I glanced at Cruz trying to remember how many players had been at the pool tables. "Somewhere between six and twelve?"

55

"Sixteen," Cruz said.

Leave it to him to count.

"Not bad." Jay looked inside his mug. "How many messages?"

I considered. One message to the fighters and another to the surrounding players. "Two."

Jay drained his coffee. "Keep working on it." He wanted me to send four messages at a time.

"Is there a way to make the messages last longer?" I asked. "I mean it doesn't do much good for me to stop a fight if it's just going to break out again in five minutes."

"Yes and no," Jay said. "Messages have more staying power if you're touching the person you're sending to, but for what you're talking about that wouldn't be practical. In that case, all you can do is change the message."

"To what? Never fight again in your life?"

Jay stared at me like I was purposefully being dense. "I've told you, you can't send a message that will affect a person's long-term free will. Sometimes you can stretch a message maybe an hour, maybe a night. But that's it."

A series of *clicks* sounded as Cruz reassembled his Glock.

"Okay," I said, "how do I change a message to stretch it?"

Jay drained his coffee. "You're sending impulses. If your message is to back off and step away from a fight *right now*, that's what the person will do. But if your message is for the person to want to prove they can go a *whole night* without getting in a fight, that's what they'll do."

More than his attitude and his statements, the simple brilliance of ideas like that made me believe Jay probably was the best trainer of the Neme-i.

Pushing the magazine into the grip of his gun, Cruz chambered a round and joined us. "I told Jay about Regina's letter and the post office."

"Too bad about Regina," Jay said. "Can't say I'm surprised though, as much as she smoked."

Cruz fetched the coffee pot and topped off everyone's cup.

56

"I understand you talked with Maria and Anna last night?" Jay said.

I glanced at Cruz. He held my gaze. Apparently he'd left the nitty-gritty for me. "They want me to tell them Adam's birthdate so they can pull his prophecy from the public record and hide it."

For a moment Jay said nothing, just sat and blinked. Then he tipped his head back and laughed.

"You think that's funny?" I demanded.

"A little," Jay choked.

Cruz glanced at me, one eyebrow raised.

In the living room, Bear opened his eyes and peered at us.

"Come on," Jay said, trying to rein in his amusement, "you've got to admit it's priceless. The new leader votes a law into existence then immediately plots to break it. Classic."

Put that way, I did see a little humor. "But it's my son."

"I know." Jay's laughter died. "What did you say?"

"I sent Cruz a message to get me the hell out of there before I had to answer."

Jay looked at Cruz. "Did it work?"

Cruz nodded. "I pretended to feel sick and said we needed to go."

Jay nodded, all traces of humor gone. "Good. But was Anna's boy-toy there?"

"Her what?" I asked.

"Tall good-looking guy. Took Hideo's place?"

My jaw tightened.

"You mean Leonard?" Cruz asked.

Jay pointed. "That's him. Was he there?"

I nodded. "He and Anna are sleeping together?"

Jay shrugged. "Not sure. A lot of whispering about that. He doesn't know shit about gardening."

I tried to remember the way the grounds appeared the night before. The plants had seemed a bit wilder than a month ago, but it had been too dark to see much. "Are they bonded?"

"No. That's part of the whispering." Jay gulped some coffee.

"Back to your message."

The corners of Cruz's mouth turned down. "Leonard will know Luna sent me a message, won't he?"

Jay nodded. "And probably have told Anna."

I groaned. I had forgotten about Leonard. "They'll know I panicked."

"Yes," Jay said. "But no big deal. You were conflicted and wanted time to think. Understandable. You need to be prepared for the fact they know, however. You also need to think before you send messages in the future. In a room full of Neme-i, if a message is sent and moments later someone's saved from an awkward situation, it's obvious what happened."

So sending messages around the Neme-i would be like playing chess. I hated that game.

Jay tipped back in his chair. "What are you gonna do?"

Inside me, something fell. I'd hoped Jay would tell me what to do, not ask to hear my nonexistent plan. "I don't know."

"What do you *want* to do?"

"Honestly? Go back in time and skip coming here so they can't ask that question." If I was going to wish, I might as well wish for the impossible. "What do you think I want to do?"

Jay shrugged. "Don't know."

I practically felt steam pouring from my ears.

"What will happen if Luna tells them Adam's birth date?" Cruz set his cup on the table.

"Not much." Jay tipped his head. "They'll have a little head start when they try to find his prophecy, but that's all."

"And if I don't tell them?"

Jay shrugged. "Won't make much difference." He let the front legs of his chair return to the floor. "Either way, they'll look for it and try to pull it, but it'll take time."

"What makes you so sure?"

Jay stood and walked to the bedroom. He returned carrying a small, spiral bound notebook. Opening it to the middle, he folded back the cover and laid the open page in front of me. Cruz leaned over my shoulder.

Written on the paper was a prophecy. Whose I couldn't say. At the top of the page were a series of letters and numbers that made no sense. I tried everything to decipher them, birth date, initials, European date format, alphabetical ordering, Pig Latin. Nothing worked. I pointed at the gibberish. "What does this mean?"

"I told you," Jay said. "I have a system. It makes sense to me. That's all that matters."

Cruz straightened. "It's a code?"

"Yes," Jay said.

"So it can be deciphered?"

Jay shrugged. "It would take time. I change it regularly."

Having now seen the oddity of his system, a ray of hope kindled inside me. "Do all seers use a code like this?" If they did, Anna and Maria might search for years and never find the right prophecy.

"No," Jay said, "most use no code. Those who do, have their own system."

Not quite as good as everyone using a code but better than only Jay.

"Feel better?" he asked.

I took a last look and nodded. "Yes. Thank you." But I still didn't know what I would do when Anna and Maria approached me again.

Jay took the notebook back and closed it before checking his watch. "We're third on the morning's docket. We should get moving."

I showered and put on jeans and a T-shirt then added one of Cruz's flannel shirts to stave off the morning chill. We left Bear in the cabin and piled into Jay's SUV.

He drove us to the Cookie Cabin and parked next to the dumpster at the rear of the building. "Wait here."

He knocked four times on the back door then disappeared inside.

"I hope we're not having cookies for breakfast," Cruz grumbled.

I hoped not too, but I wouldn't put it past Jay. In the month we'd spent with him, I'd come to understand his idea of a decent breakfast had changed a lot since my childhood. When I'd been ten, breakfast with Jay consisted of Raisin Bran or scrambled eggs and toast. Less than a week ago, I'd found him dunking a rice crispy treat in coffee and calling it good.

Voices drew my attention to the corner of the building where a group of people stood laughing and talking. Their ages varied, anywhere from ten to ninety. Long hair, jewelry and skin tone told me they were Neme-i, and the mirth in their faces as they joked and teased with a young couple at the center of the party left a smile on my face.

The sound of Jay's voice outside the SUV made me turn.

"Ná bąą hózhǫ́!" he called as he waved.

Cruz cocked his head and most of the group waved back.

"What?"

"Means congratulations."

For the most part, the Neme-i spoke English, but the tribe did have a language, and words and phrases from it occasionally cropped up. According to Jay, the language consisted of a combination of the languages spoken by the various clans when they joined the tribe. Since Cruz understood chunks of Tewa and Navajo, he knew more of my tribe's language than I did. Yet I had to be considered for leader. How screwed up was that?

Jay opened the back door and handed me a large paper bag, warm to the touch. I placed it on my lap and inhaled the scent of something spicy.

Joining the group, Jay shook hands with several of the men and kissed an older woman on the cheek before working his way to the young man at the center of the party. A full head taller than Jay, the man's short black hair brushed his collar. Travertine earrings glistened in his ears, and his eyes sparkled as he stared down at the young woman beside him. When Jay made it to the couple, he gave the girl a hug and exchanged a few words with the young man. The man glanced at the SUV, making eye contact with me. Looking back, he shook his head and spoke. Jay nodded then smiled at the girl and kissed her cheek before returning to the SUV.

"Who's the couple?" I asked.

"George Tsossi and Noni Lonehill." Jay took the bag and opened it. "They're asking the council for permission to marry today."

I made a face as the group dispersed and piled into several cars. "They need the council's permission to get married?"

Jay pulled cardboard containers from the bag and passed them around. "The owner's an old friend. She always makes my breakfast when I'm in town. I hope you don't mind. I assumed you wouldn't want to go in."

I didn't mind at all. To the Neme-i, Jasmine Bluefeather was a celebrity—the long-lost Princess Anastasia suddenly found. Until recently, she had been a myth—daughter of the leader who had taken her and disappeared never to be found again. And most had believed she never would be. To those who'd held out hope, Jasmine seemed to represent hope—a chance that the tribe would once again experience the peace and harmony it had under my grandfather's leadership. People stared and wanted to meet me— wanted to meet the myth. But I was just Luna Ortiz—lover of nature, wilderness tour guide, and mother of a missing child. I had no desire to be a celebrity.

I opened the lid to my container and discovered an omelet.

"Smells great," Cruz said.

"Wait till you taste it." Jay eased his seat back and cut into his breakfast. "To answer your question, no, couples don't need permission to marry, not in the way you mean. Originally they did, but today it's more like a blessing. Couples don't have to have it, but most who live within our society seek it. It's thought to bring good luck to a union, and it demonstrates commitment."

"Commitment to what?" I took my first bite of omelet and

moaned as the mixture of egg, sausage, peppers, and onions hit my taste buds.

Jay caught my gaze in the rearview mirror. "She calls it a fajita omelet."

I called it bliss.

Releasing my gaze, Jay shoveled egg and sausage into his mouth. "Commitment to the Neme-i and our ways as well as each other and the future they're creating. It requires they research their lineage."

"To prevent inbreeding?" Cruz asked.

Jay nodded. "The Neme-i are mainly derived from seven tribes, Navajo, Pueblo, Yaqui, Mohave, Shoshone, Akimel O'odham, and Ute. In the beginning, the blend of tribes was enough to ensure inbreeding didn't take place. But over time, the odds of being related to others grew." He nodded to the cars exiting the parking lot. "The people in that group for instance? I'm related to half. In order to receive permission from the council, a couple must prove they have no common relations going back five generations."

"Why five?" I reached for the water I'd brought from the cabin.

Jay shrugged. "Seems to be the amount of separation necessary for the gifts to be unaffected." He checked his watch. "We need to talk about your drive up here before we go to the meeting." His gaze found mine. "Cruz said you figured out you could counter the multiple messages."

My cheeks warmed as I looked at Cruz. "You told him?"

"Not everything," Cruz said around a mouthful of food.

Jay rolled his eyes. "I don't care *how* you did it. The point is, you did it, right?"

"Yes." I gritted my teeth. "You could have told us that was possible so Cruz wouldn't have gotten sick."

"I could have," Jay agreed.

"So why didn't you?"

He loaded his fork with omelet. "He needed to experience it."

Anger filled me. "No one *needs* to experience that."

Cruz remained calm. "Why?"

"To understand what I've been saying for the past month."

"About the Gathering in Albuquerque?" Cruz shoveled omelet into his mouth.

"Yes."

Thank God one of us followed Jay's train of thought.

"The messages to keep outsiders away were sent throughout the meeting. I sensed them clearly." He glanced at Cruz. "They're likely what made you leave the lobby and step outside when you did. You were too close to the meeting room."

On the drive up the mountain the day before, Cruz's illness had started with a headache. He'd experienced the same thing outside the meeting room in Albuquerque. It had driven him outside for fresh air.

"What you experienced coming up here is what the gunmen should have experienced the minute they stepped into that meeting," Jay said. "Do you remember how sick you felt?"

Cruz closed his eyes and nodded, his face pale.

"Is there any way you could have stood there picking out targets and shooting while you felt that way?"

Cruz shook his head. "No."

A shiver slid through me.

In Albuquerque, Paul Hernandez had waited outside the conference center while his two partners entered the assembly and began shooting. One man shot randomly at anyone in the path of his gun. The other aimed for me. I still remembered the look on his face as we'd made eye contact. He'd mouthed *Anna* and fired. His first shot went wide. My father jumped in front of the second bullet.

According to Jay, it never should have happened. Just as the Neme-i had a planned escape route for the leader and council members at all meeting locations, they always had several women sending messages to keep outsiders away.

He'd been telling us that since the morning after the meeting.

63

Now I understood what he meant.

A lump formed in my throat. "Are you saying the two shooters had tribe members sending them messages like I sent Cruz yesterday?"

Jay nodded. "Yes. But not just any tribe members. Whenever the tribe needs messages to keep outsiders away, they use twenty women. That's what you helped Cruz overcome yesterday. Last month, the same twenty women sent the messages to keep outsiders out of the meeting, and they'll do it again today. To overcome that many messages, your average outsider would need an equal number of women sending counter messages—"

"But that would mean..." I calculated quickly—twenty women for the Neme-i plus twenty per shooter. "...sixty messages." My heart raced. I tried to swallow the lump in my throat, but it refused to budge.

"Exactly." Jay's eyebrows rose. "Which tells me one thing. The gunmen didn't need twenty women apiece."

His point sat staring at me. I could feel it. But I couldn't grasp it. I was too busy freaking out about the thought of forty people wanting me dead.

"They were bonded," Cruz breathed.

Jay nodded and smiled.

It was like being back in high school. Me sitting in class near the star pupil who made a giant mental leap while I struggled to find the bridge leading from one thought to the next. "Wait. What?"

Jay's smile died. "Cruz didn't need twenty of you yesterday, did he?"

And suddenly I saw the bridge. "No."

"When people are bonded, messages sent between them come through stronger. The stronger the bond, the stronger the message."

I stared at him. "But that doesn't explain why you didn't sense the messages sent to the gunmen."

Jay blew out a breath and looked at the remainder of his

omelet. "Think of the energy as buzzing—lots of it with different frequencies—but still just buzzing. Only when a message is sent directly to one of us or sent to no one in particular—a blanket message—only then can we read it. Then it's like a voice in your head."

Something shifted in my mind. Something important, but I didn't know what.

"When the message is sent to someone else," Jay continued, "it's just buzzing for me. I can tell you there was a lot of buzzing in that meeting, but none sent to me."

"But the different frequencies," I said, "aren't those all different senders? Every woman with her own unique frequency?"

"Yes," Jay replied.

"And energy leaves a trail?"

"Yes."

"So can't you decipher everyone who sent messages?"

Jay barked a laugh. "No. I'm not that talented. There are men amongst us who are—they are gifted that way—they become our trackers. But even they can't tell you what the messages said, just who sent them. And throughout that meeting, many messages were sent—some probably as simple as reminding a child to empty the trash." Closing his container, he shoved it in the bag. "There is no way to know who sent what. But I do know there were never more than forty messages sent at the same time until *after* the shooting began, and then they weren't effective."

Could that be what had happened to Anna? Had she sent messages to Hernandez but been too flustered to make them clear?

"That's why you think they were bonded," Cruz said.

"Yes. No matter how many messages a person receives at one time, the loudest, clearest one will always be from the person they are most bonded to. In Cruz's case"—Jay nodded at me—"that's you."

As part of their ability to read energy, men of the Neme-i could

65

also sense the bonds between people—parent/child, friends, lovers, etcetera. The morning after Cruz and I first slept together, every man who'd looked at us seemed to know.

"So who were those men bonded to?" I asked.

"It's not that simple." Jay swirled the contents of his travel mug. "If I hadn't been distracted by the fact that they were shooting at people, I might have noticed they were bonded, but to know who they were bonded to, I would have needed to see them with that person."

"Okay." I forked up a piece of omelet. "What about the women bonded to those men? Have you been able to sense that?"

Jay shook his head. "No. Bonds die when one of the individuals sharing them dies."

The muscle in Cruz's jaw pulsed. He had killed the shooters to save lives—his own and mine included. But taking those lives weighed on him.

"What about Hernandez?" I asked. He'd lingered for a few seconds after Anna had shot him. People had begun to spill out of the conference center during that time. "Did you see him before he died? Was he bonded to anyone?"

A bitter tension formed around Jay's mouth. "I saw him, and there was something there, but nothing healthy. He was bonded to someone, but I didn't sense anyone bonded to him."

The Neme-i placed harmony above all else. For relationships, that meant two partners giving themselves fully to each other. What Jay described would create disharmony and ugliness.

"Could that be why he waited outside the conference center?" Cruz asked. "The bond wasn't strong enough to get in?"

"Could be." Jay checked his watch and started the ignition. "Or, being at the door may have been the plan in case Luna and Anna made it out."

"You'd think your council would ask questions about that," Cruz shoved his food container into the paper bag.

Jay shrugged. "Some have."

"But not all?"

Jay put the SUV in gear. "Others still contend the gunmen were after Anna."

"Even though they shot at Luna?"

Jay pointed the SUV toward the exit. "They say regardless of who Hernandez and his partners *thought* Anna was, they were after Anna. They believe she's the one in danger."

Cruz clenched his teeth. "They're wrong."

Jay nodded. "I agree."

In both of my run-ins with Hernandez, he'd called me Anna. In the second, he'd called Anna Jasmine. He'd had our names confused, but *I'd* been his target both times. I knew it in my bones.

Jay steered us toward the exit, and my breakfast turned to lead inside my stomach. The last tribal meeting had ended in disaster. The idea of attending another had me on edge. "Where's the meeting being held?"

Jay signaled and turned onto the main road. "Tribal meetings in Summerhaven are usually held at the ski basin, but this one's at a restaurant that's closed for the weekend."

"Why the change?" I asked.

Jay glanced in the rearview mirror. "Officially? The restaurant's location is smaller and easier to police. But I also think they're trying to cut back on the crowd. The restaurant has a limited capacity, so people are encouraged to attend only the part of the meeting related to them."

"Don't people usually do that?" I asked.

Jay signaled and braked to a stop in the left turn lane. "For the most part. But the birth prophecies are a hot topic. Had the meeting been at the ski basin, attendance for that portion would have been several hundred. Those who want this law passed don't want that many people hearing arguments against it."

Set back from the road, a large wooden building crouched in a meadow surrounded by a wire fence. Several cars sat parked in front of the building, and two guards stood at the gated entrance to the property.

Jay lifted his hand and waved at a passing car. "Were they worried about security? Yeah. But they could have taken other measures." He turned in his seat and looked at me. "Take Cruz's hand."

"What?"

"He's about to be hit with a wave of messages to stay away. You'll need to counter that. Remember I told you touching him while you send messages will make yours stronger?"

I reached forward and took Cruz's hand.

Jay looked at him. "You ready?"

Cruz gritted his teeth and nodded. "Yeah."

Jay made the turn into the restaurant's driveway, and Cruz stiffened beneath my touch. I imagined the smooth flowing waters of the Rio Chama and the first rafting trip Cruz and I had taken together. He relaxed some, and I knew he was receiving.

Jay braked at the stone pillars that supported the open gate. A camera sat atop one. I recognized the young guard approaching the driver's side. His female partner watched from the other side.

Rolling his window down, Jay greeted the man.

The guard checked to see everyone in the car and grimaced when he spotted Cruz. He turned to Jay. "Your friend will be okay inside the restaurant. The messages are directed at people coming up the mountain or trying to get into the parking lot. Once he's at the walkway, they should ease up. But once you leave, the messages will go back to affecting the restaurant too. He won't be able to come back with you tonight."

"Of course," Jay said.

"One last thing," the guard said, "all speakers are asked to wait in the entrance until a council member comes for you."

Jay thanked the guard and drove forward. "Park or drop you at the walkway?"

Cruz squinted at the building ahead. "Walkway. Sit and idle until I get Luna out."

The pallor of his skin made me concentrate harder. I imagined the two of us under the stars listening to the wind and crickets.

Cruz looked at me. "Stay in the car till I signal you."

I nodded. Given what he was going through, I would have agreed to almost anything.

Jay rolled to a stop at the front of the restaurant. Cruz threw his door open and stumbled out.

"You sure that touching thing works?" I watched Cruz stagger to the walkway.

"I'm sure." Jay glanced over his shoulder. "Your energy didn't feel as strong as usual. Were you concentrating fully?"

I answered with a sigh. "No." My nerves and Cruz's pain had distracted me.

"It's all right." Lifting his chin, Jay acknowledged someone near the edge of the parking lot. "He'll be fine. Concentrate harder on our way out."

I stared. He had never let me off that easy.

Outside, Cruz paced the walkway. His chest rose and fell and his gaze remained down. I didn't know if it would help, but I sent him an image of the two of us sitting in a hot spring while snow fell around us.

"Better," Jay said.

"They knew Cruz was coming. Why are they sending the messages to him?"

Jay shrugged. "They're blanket messages. They go to anyone trying to enter the lot."

Cruz took a few more steps and looked up. Surveilling the area, he turned a pointed gaze our way. His head tipped slowly side to side.

I checked the direction he'd indicated and realized men and women stood in various positions around the lot. How had I not noticed them?

Lips pursed, Jay nodded.

"Are they guards?"

"Trackers." Jay pointed at Cruz who nodded at me through the window. "Time to go."

I climbed out and Cruz caught my elbow and hustled me to the door. Inside, he stood me in a corner without windows and scanned the room, hand rested on his gun.

Small and dark with benches on either side, the entryway reminded me of the restaurant I'd been abducted from in Albuquerque. I shivered.

Looking up, I found Cruz studying me. His gaze shifted to the walls and ceiling of the entryway, and he seemed to understand. He reached for my hand. "Come on."

He led me into the empty bar to the right of the entrance.

"You okay?" he asked.

I hoisted myself onto a barstool. "Nervous."

"Jay and I will be with you the whole time. You won't be alone."

The door opened and Cruz tensed then relaxed when Jay stepped through the entryway.

Spotting us in the bar, he walked over. "So much for waiting in the entryway."

"What'll they do?" Cruz mumbled. "Fire her?"

I smiled at that cheery little thought.

Jay turned to Cruz. "How's your head?"

"Better than it was outside. Tell me again, why the messages don't affect you the same way."

Jay grinned. "I have superior DNA." He and Cruz had batted the joke around for the past month. When Cruz didn't smile back, Jay sighed. "It's an extra-sensory thing. Luna and I—all of the Neme-i—were born with a sixth sense, something that goes beyond the five you have. Because of it, we experience the messages like outside voices which makes them suggestions we're free to follow or not. Because you don't have that sense, you can't pick the messages out for what they are. You experience them as your body speaking to you and are compelled to follow them. When you don't, your body reacts violently, like when you drink too much or eat bad meat. You get sick."

"Lucky me." Cruz's Adam's apple bobbed up and down. "Who were those people outside?"

"Trackers."

The skin between Cruz's eyebrows puckered. "Why are they here?"

Jay shook his head. "Not sure. If I had to guess, probably to get a bead on Luna."

"What?" My muscles tensed.

Jay sat next to me. "You were sending Cruz energy on our way in. You'll have to send more on our way out. The trackers will sense the energy—like dogs given a scent to follow. The more energy you send when they're around, the easier it'll be for them to recognize your energy in the future."

The hair on my arms stood up. When I'd been kidnapped and taken to a trailer in the middle of nowhere, I would have liked it if someone could have found me. But I didn't like this. "Why would they need to do that?"

Jay sighed. "Do you want the party answer or my opinion?"

"Both," Cruz said.

"The party line is that knowing Luna's energy will help them protect her. They'll be able to find her if she's ever in trouble or abducted again, provided she's sending messages."

Once again, I thought of my sister and the messages she had not sent when we were abducted.

"And your opinion?" Cruz stared straight ahead. His gaze could have cut a diamond.

"I think they're worried what Luna will do."

"About what?" I asked. No one but Jay knew Cruz and I intended to look for my child.

"Good question," Jay said. "A better one is who asked them to be here."

A dull pain formed in the back of my head. I hated this. Hated nearly every part of being around the ruling bodies of the Nemei. There were too many twists and turns, too many dark corners for things to jump out from.

"Is this normal?" Cruz asked. "Do they do this with all leader-elects?"

71

Jay nodded. "Leader-elects, leaders, leader's family, council members, etcetera. Any prominent member of the Neme-i."

Cruz scrubbed a hand through his hair. "But you don't think this is normal?"

Jay grimaced. "Nothing involving Luna has been normal."

My stomach churned.

In the back of the restaurant, sound rose, voices filled with surprise. We stood and moved toward the entryway as the surprise turned to dismay and anger. I tried to see into the back of the restaurant but Jay and Cruz stepped in front of me.

"This is bullshit!" a male voice yelled.

Chairs scraped the floor and the volume of the voices grew. Footsteps followed accompanied by the sound of tears. I stood on tiptoe to see over Cruz's and Jay's shoulders. A large group of people pressed through a doorway into the empty dining room and moved in our direction.

Many of the people I'd never seen before. Some I recognized as the group of people Jay had spoken with outside the Cookie Cabin. In the center of the group, Noni and another girl held each other and cried.

Jay caught an older man dressed in denim and cowboy boots by the arm. "What happened?"

"The council refused to give their blessing to any couple."

"What?" Jay's head jerked back. "Why?"

Noni's fiancé stopped beside the older man. A vein pulsed in the young man's temple and his fists clenched. "They want to wait until the prophecies are read."

Jay looked at the older man.

His brown eyes drooped. "They say they want to be sure the prophecies don't speak against the unions."

Jay's mouth opened.

"You told me it would be like this," George said. "I didn't believe you. I was wrong." He glanced back in the direction he'd come from and lowered his voice. "That thing you asked me? I'll do it."

Jay squeezed George's shoulder. "Go with Noni. We'll talk later."

George nodded and hurried to catch up to his fiancée.

The older man remained. He studied me. "Your grandfather would not have allowed such a thing. I hoped your sister would be like him." He looked down and shook his head. "Now I don't believe she will be."

Was he blaming me for declining the opportunity to be named leader? "I'm sorry."

"It won't last," Jay said. "It can't."

The man gave a sad smile. "Who can say anymore?" He gazed at the door as the last of his party exited. "Come by the house later. Monica is here. She wants to see you."

Jay nodded, and the old man shuffled away.

"I don't understand," I said.

Jay pointed past the dining room. "I'll explain later."

In the doorway the crowd had pressed through stood Raymond Benally, leader of the Sky clan, his right leg bent to accommodate the shorter length of his left. He nodded in our direction.

"We're up," Jay said.

My legs wobbled as I followed him through the dining room. Cruz followed me. At the doorway, Benally offered his hand.

Jay took it and the two exchanged pleasantries before Benally turned to me. With an arthritic groan, he bent to lower his forehead to our joined hands. "Miss Ortiz."

Quickly, I lifted my hand to keep him from bending so far. "Luna, please."

Benally straightened with a smile and reached for Cruz's hand. "Mr. Whitehorse, it is good to see you again."

Cruz nodded. "And you."

"We welcome you." Benally motioned for us to step into the room.

Cruz entered first, blocking the door while he checked the surroundings. Approving what he saw, he stepped aside and allowed me in. Jay stepped in behind me, and the two flanked me

73

as we made our way toward the tables placed end to end and covered in turquoise cloths at the front of the room. Behind the tables sat the council, Anna at one end with the clan leaders to her left. A male and female guard in each of the front corners completed the view.

Much like Albuquerque, chairs had been placed in two rows facing the council table. Unlike Albuquerque, they were empty. Benally ushered us to the first row then reclaimed his place at the end of the council table opposite Anna. Bypassing the chairs, Cruz opted to stand against the wall, facing the windows where he could keep watch.

"Welcome Luna, Uncle John, Cruz." Anna's brow wrinkled as she looked at Cruz standing against the wall.

In the middle of the council table, sat Ivan Yellowhair, leader of the Spirit clan—my clan. His long white hair hung in a braid that had fallen over his shoulder.

"Because we are meeting in such a closed setting today," Anna continued, pulling her gaze from Cruz, "we invite you to remain seated while you speak."

Given my rubbery legs, I appreciated that.

Ivan's face seemed to have hollowed in the month since I'd last seen him, but his eyes still sparkled with warmth as he nodded at me. "Daughter."

I smiled back.

"It is good to see you again," he said. "You look well."

"I am," I supplied.

Jay elbowed me. Tradition required that I listen to council members and elders. I was not to interrupt and only to speak when asked questions. I gave a tiny nod to tell Jay I remembered.

"As leader of your clan," words rolled from Ivan's mouth like marbles spilling out of a bag, "it is my responsibility to speak with you about your training. Do you understand?"

I nodded, and Jay elbowed me again. "Yes," I said quickly.

"Have you spent the past month training with John?"

"I have."

"How have you found the training?"

"It's hard, but I think I'm doing okay. Jay—" I winced. "I mean John, would be better suited to answer that."

Ivan nodded and shifted his gaze to Jay. "Please tell us how Luna is doing."

"Well," Jay said. "She's overcome the misdirection I gave her as a child and is successful at sending messages. Her energy is strong, and she's shown a certain aptitude for the possibility of sending simultaneous messages."

Anna gaped, and Benally leaned forward. Joseph Peshlakai, the refrigerator-sized member of the council, narrowed his eyes.

"Simultaneous messages?" Ivan's eyebrows arched as he studied at me. "That is unusual, daughter."

I blew out a breath. I'd been raised to fly beneath the radar, to believe standing out in any way brought unwanted attention. I'd begged Jay not to mention this ability. He'd said hiding it would look suspicious and that if someone found out, I'd have more unwanted attention than I could imagine.

"So far," Jay continued, "her success with simultaneous messages has been limited to animals. Whether she will be as successful with people is yet to be seen."

This was Jay's one concession to my request. He'd agreed to bend the truth and downplay what I'd done, but he'd refused to lie about it.

Seated next to Benally, Jacy Crow tucked his long, black hair behind his ears. Fire glittered in his opal earrings. In the few conversations I'd had with him, he'd struck me as fair and unbiased—a person who listened to all sides before forming an opinion.

"It is, of course, unlikely she will be successful with people," Peshlakai said.

Crow's jaw tightened.

Jay shrugged. "It is true the ability is rare, but it is not unheard of. Several of our elders tell stories of a woman who had this ability when they were children. And I have personally experienced messages sent this way."

"Nonsense," Peshlakai growled. "No one's been capable of this in years." He looked up and down the table. "Right?"

The clan leaders exchanged glances, but no one spoke. Eventually, all eyes returned to Ivan.

His gaze remained on Jay. "Have you ever trained anyone with this ability?"

"Not officially," Jay replied.

Ivan cocked his head. "What do you mean?"

Jay looked toward his clan leader, Willy Trujillo, who sat to Anna's left. A barrel-chested man in his sixties, his short, dark hair was threaded with gray.

"Your clan leader has to answer for you?" Peshlakai grumbled.

Too bad Jay couldn't smack Peshlakai upside the head for rude behavior.

Trujillo's silver bracelets clanked against the table as he leaned forward. "Our former clan leader forbade John from speaking of this."

"Are you able to speak of it?" Crow asked.

Trujillo worked his tongue behind his lips while he seemed to consider. "Parts." He turned to Anna. "With your permission?"

She blinked as if surprised then motioned for him to continue.

"When John was a teenager, he heard of this ability." Trujillo looked at Jay. "He knew a girl with impressive strength and convinced her to try to send simultaneous messages. At first, she did not succeed, but he continued to encourage her to try different ways until one day, she did succeed. This is how it came to our attention that John had the ability to teach. The other person the young lady sent to was John's teacher, former leader of our clan."

Youngest of the council members, Martin Alvarez tipped his head. His wire-rimmed glasses flashed in the light. "Is that enough experience for you to train someone to use this gift?"

Jay shrugged. "Training is not so much a process of teaching someone to do something as it is unlocking their potential and helping them direct it. Either they have the ability or they don't."

"And what makes you believe this ability exists in Luna?" Ivan asked.

"Her strength," Jay replied. "When she sends, the strength of her energy is similar to the strength of that girl's."

Strands of Crow's hair brushed the table. "Are you able to tell us the girl's name?"

Jay looked at Trujillo.

"No," the clan leader replied. "That, we are forbidden to say."

I glanced at my sister at the center of the table. Eyes narrowed, she stared at me.

Ivan cleared his throat. "Do you understand how rare this ability is, daughter?"

I'd thought I had, but the council's reactions had me thinking again. "Maybe."

Ivan smiled. "That John considers this possible for you is an honor."

Some of the council members nodded.

Ivan folded his hands on the table. "Our culture and our beliefs require that we learn to live in harmony with our world. This world is a blessing from the great spirit, as are our gifts. As such, we believe they should be used to further that harmony. As you continue your training, it is our culture and beliefs that will guide you. Before we decide whether the extra training will be blessed, we need to know these lessons will be taught."

"I've been thinking about this," Jay said. "Usually, these lessons are handed down through family and interaction in our society as a child grows. I believe being Luna's only teacher in these matters would be a mistake. As you know, I have my own viewpoints. Others have theirs. To get a complete picture, it would be best for her to learn from many people."

"What do you propose?" Crow asked.

"I would like to take her to different clans—to have her learn from our elders as she would if she'd been raised with us. I could give you a list of who I'm thinking."

Ivan tapped a finger on the table. "Most children would learn these things within their clan, but as daughter of a leader, Luna would have been exposed to all clans." He turned his gaze to the other council members. "I believe this plan is wise." He waited several moments, giving the others a chance to speak. When no one said anything, he turned back to Jay. "Please continue Luna's training as you have described."

Jay nodded.

Ivan smiled at me then turned the reins back to Anna.

She addressed the council. "Are there any other questions for our guests?"

"Yes." Peshlakai's belly jumped as he spoke. "I have one."

I braced myself. He'd never wronged or been rude to me, but something about Joseph Peshlakai set me on edge. He had the coloring of the Neme-i. He wore the jewelry of the Neme-i. But he reminded me of a greedy politician.

"Mr. Whitehorse," Peshlakai said.

My muscles tightened.

Back against the wall, Cruz regarded the large man.

"According to your written reports, you've experienced no suspicious activity since the meeting in Albuquerque. Is that true?"

"Yes," Cruz said.

Peshlakai turned to the other council members. "One month with no suspicious activity leads me to wonder if we might need to revisit our arrangement with Mr. Whitehorse. We are paying this young man a good sum of money. If the danger to Luna is gone, is that money well-spent?"

The council members eyed each other, and I dug my fingernails into the arms of my chair.

"Luna is a leader-elect," Trujillo said. "Our laws require she be protected until capable of protecting herself."

"Of course," Peshlakai said. "But we already have a payroll full of guards, each of whom has the benefit of possessing our gifts. My question is, do we truly need another guard?"

Cruz pushed away from the wall. "I'd like to answer that."

Seven

The council members turned to better see Cruz.

"Your question is valid," he said. "My services aren't cheap, and I don't have your abilities. But I believe that's an asset."

Trujillo's eyebrows rose. "How so?"

"Your way of doing things relies on your gifts. For meetings, your guards are present and your women send messages to keep outsiders away. In the past, that worked." Cruz looked from one council member to the next. "At the last meeting, it failed."

Ivan tilted his head. "Continue."

Cruz's gaze swept the room before settling on the council table. "I've been told you believe the danger died with the gunmen."

I watched Anna for some sign of reaction but saw none.

"I disagree," Cruz said. "I believe the problem lies within your tribe."

"Wait a minute!" Peshlakai grasped the table.

Ivan lifted a hand. "Mr. Whitehorse is our guest. We will hear what he has to say."

Peshlakai scowled but released the table and leaned back.

I tried not to smile.

Cruz nodded at Ivan. "I mean no disrespect. But the facts are clear. The gunmen addressed Luna as Anna and Anna as Jasmine. They knew your missing leader-elect had been found. Who but the Neme-i knew that? They made it past your messages, flushed Anna and Luna in the direction of the planned exit, and had someone waiting at the door. They knew your system. They had to have help from within."

Peshlakai's chair squeaked. Clothing rustled.

"These are points we've been discussing," Alvarez volunteered.

Trujillo and Ivan exchanged a glance.

Peshlakai's belly jerked as he cleared his throat. "Regardless of what our problem is or is not, Mr. Whitehorse, my point remains. Why should we continue to employ you?"

Cruz's gaze circled the room. "Because my way of doing things isn't known by the Neme-i. And, as unfamiliar with your ways as I am, I won't overlook things that seem ordinary to you."

Silence filled the room as the council members eyed one another.

"Martin?" Crow turned to the youngest council member. "Has employing Mr. Whitehorse put a strain on the council's funds?"

Alvarez adjusted his glasses. "No. The surge our businesses have experienced since Luna's return has more than offset the cost of her stipend and Mr. Whitehorse's employment."

Crow nodded. "Then perhaps we should hear from the person this decision most affects." He motioned at me. "Luna?"

I swallowed. My answer was simple. Either the Neme-i kept Cruz or they lost me. I glanced at Cruz. His gaze met mine for the briefest moment. He knew my answer.

"The only person I trust is Cruz."

"Only?" The lines in Trujillo's brow multiplied. "You don't trust your uncle?"

I looked at Jay. "I trust him. But it's not the same. If a gun were pointed at me again, I would run to Cruz every time." Uncrossing my legs, I sat back.

"It is good that you trust your friend," Benally said, "but do you understand messages could be sent to sway his actions?"

I met the arthritic man's gaze. "I do. But I can send messages now too." I stared at each council member in turn.

"May I remind the council that Luna remains in training?" Jay said. "As I explained when I agreed to train her, having others around with our abilities could complicate the process."

Anna leaned forward. "And yet you wish to expose her to many others with our gifts."

Jay smiled. "Not every day. On the days she is with others, she will be learning of our people. On the days she is with me, we will continue her training."

Quiet ensued as the council members eyed each other. Ivan called for a vote.

⊥⊤

"What a prick!" I said as the restaurant doors swung closed behind me.

"Peshlakai was doing his job," Cruz said.

"By voting against you?"

The vote had been five-to-one in favor of keeping Cruz on the payroll. Only Peshlakai had voted against Cruz. Anna's vote had not been needed as there had been no tie.

"By looking out for the tribe." Cruz took my elbow and hurried me toward the walkway where Jay had the SUV waiting.

"If that's looking out for the tribe, what were the other council members doing?"

Jaw clenched, Cruz opened the back door and waited while I climbed inside.

"Start sending," Jay said.

Cruz closed my door and opened the front. I took a deep breath to calm myself, but calm didn't come. I wanted to march back inside and tell Peshlakai what I thought of him.

Forcing myself to concentrate, I slid to the center of the seat and reached for Cruz's hand. I sent him an image of a field of flowers. The SUV remained stationary. Breaking my gaze with Cruz, I glanced at Jay. He stared straight ahead at a short-haired man who stood by the edge of the restaurant. A tattoo peeked beneath the man's left sleeve as he stared back.

"Who is he?" I asked.

"Ethan," Jay replied. "Keep sending."

The corners of Ethan's mouth turned upward as if he knew his name had been spoken. He lifted his hand and waved.

Jay's eyes narrowed, and he shook his head. Gunning the engine, he turned the SUV toward the exit. Gravel pinged off the undercarriage, and a cloud of dust rose behind us.

I concentrated on an image of Cruz and me lying in the field of flowers. Once we turned onto the highway, Cruz let out a breath and I stopped sending. He squeezed my hand and treated me to a small, grateful smile before letting go.

Hooking his thumb in the direction of the restaurant, he asked. "What was that about?"

"Ethan?" Jay pressed his lips together. "Issuing a challenge."

"What kind of challenge?" Cruz said.

"The kind meant to help you learn."

Jay said nothing more and Cruz didn't press. When it came to questions, Jay only answered when ready.

Pine trees and aspens dotted the roadside, their scent intoxicating. After a month in Mojave, being back amongst trees felt exhilarating.

Jay waved at a passing pickup. "I need to stop by Chester's house before we train. He's the man who spoke with us outside the meeting."

A mile past the general store, Chester's gray A-frame house sat back from the road.

Chairs and tables decorated with bright cloths and flowers lined the backyard. No doubt the gathering had been planned as a celebration. The mood felt like a wake.

Jay introduced Cruz and me to a few people then deposited us at a table with Noni and her friends before going into the house to say hi to Chester.

Cruz smiled and nodded at everyone before retreating a discreet distance to better watch the crowd and yard. Lucky bastard. I got stuck amongst a group of girls determined to bad-mouth everyone in an attempt to make Noni feel better.

The girls seemed nice enough, but the only person I wanted to bad-mouth was Peshlakai which I doubted would be appropriate for a leader-elect. I could practically feel my grandmother's disapproving gaze just thinking of it. So I bit my tongue and turned my attention to the group of children playing king-of-the-mountain on a mound of dirt behind the tables.

Most appeared between eight and twelve except one who looked closer to three or four. Wanting to play, he climbed onto the mound but kept getting bumped and tripped over and yelled at to get out of the way before he got hurt.

"Who's the little boy?" I asked the girls at the table.

Castigated, the child plopped down on the ground ten feet away, put his fingers in his mouth, and began to cry.

"You mean the one sitting down?" one of the girls asked.

"Yeah."

A sad smile tugged at Noni's lips. "Johnson Vigil."

Dirt smudged the boy's cheeks and chestnut-colored hair fell in his eyes.

"Whose son is he?" I searched the crowd for the parent keeping an eye on the boy. When no answer came, I looked back at Noni.

She stared at the table. "No one's."

"And everyone's," added the girl named Rose whose ponytail appeared to have been assembled during a windstorm. "His mother's dead, and his father's an alcoholic. Ivan found Johnson locked in a closet a couple weeks ago while his father drank himself stupid."

"Ivan Yellowhair?" I asked.

Rose nodded. "Leader of the Spirit clan."

"My clan," I said.

"Yours, George's, and Johnson's," Noni whispered.

I turned to regard the little boy again and found him pushing dirt into a pile.

"Ivan and his wife have been caring for Johnson since then,

but they won't be able to much longer," Rose said.

I looked at her.

Her eyes opened wide. "You don't know?"

I shook my head.

"Ivan has cancer," Rose supplied. "Stage four."

Sadness crashed into me. I liked Ivan. I'd spent very little time around him, but I felt more warmth toward him than I did my grandmother or sister. "What about chemo?"

Noni shook her head. "They've tried."

Johnson's fingers trailed saliva as he pulled his hand from his mouth and pushed himself off the ground.

"What will happen to Johnson?"

Noni's eyes filled with water. Pushing her chair back, she stood. "I'll see if he wants some food."

I felt like I'd shot myself with a rubber band. "Did I say something wrong?"

"No," Rose replied. "It's just—George and Noni were talking about adopting Johnson after they married."

Warmth flooded through me. It would be a good match.

"Too bad the council denied them."

I looked up. "Denied? I thought they put the decision on hold till they know about the prophecies."

"That's how they said it, but it amounts to the same thing."

I swallowed as my mind raced over the conversation we'd had with Jay that morning. "Even if it does, George and Noni don't have to have the blessing. They can still get married. Right?"

Rose gazed at the buffet table and sighed. "Technically, yes."

Technically? "Don't they love each other?"

"More than any couple I know." She played with her ponytail. "George is special. His gifts are really strong. They say he might take Ivan's place on the council when the time comes."

"So?"

Rose smiled as if talking to a child. "Noni's ordinary. No Sáanii Suntehai."

I felt my nose wrinkle at the unfamiliar expression.

"There's nothing special about her abilities."

In my mind, I repeated the phrase, resolving to ask Jay about it when I could.

"People at this party don't care that George and Noni's gifts don't match. We know they belong together. But others care. They think George should be with someone whose ability level is closer to his own."

Whispers of something Jay had once said flitted across my mind. When I'd asked if he'd been talking about arranged marriages, he'd said arranged baby-making. "You're talking about the Revisionists?"

Rose clenched her jaw and glanced around. "Yes."

"How would the council's blessing change that?"

"Once the blessing's given, it's done. The council's spoken. No one can question that. But without the blessing, people can say anything they want. And if George goes against the council, how could he represent them in the future?"

He probably couldn't. I looked toward the buffet table where Noni handed Johnson a carrot stick.

"If George and Noni don't marry, what will happen to Johnson?"

Rose shook her head. "I don't know."

The answer sat frozen and heavy inside me. For a moment I couldn't breathe. Wasn't the ability of a loving couple to marry and adopt a wonderful, already-existing child more important than the possibility of making super-babies? Who the hell couldn't see that?

My attention left the buffet table and strayed to the rest of the crowd. People whispered and drank. Men toed the ground. Women flicked worried glances toward children. Finding Adam was the focal point of my life, but these people had needs too.

Something flashed to my left. I looked over and spied Jay waving for me to come. He and George stood near the side of the house.

"Excuse me," I said to Rose.

85

Weaving through the crowd, I made my way to the two men. They watched as I approached, neither speaking.

"Luna"—Jay placed a hand on my shoulder—"I present George Tsossi. George, Luna Ortiz."

I looked up at the man who stood several inches over six feet and offered my hand. "I understand we're of the same clan."

George hesitated a second, glancing at Jay before taking my hand. Behind us, someone gasped. Before I could glance back, George's second hand closed over the top of mine and his gaze locked on me like a missile. For a second, I thought he planned to do the formal greeting of the Neme-i, but his back remained rigid. When I realized he had no intention of touching his forehead to my hand, relief whispered through me. His two-handed death grip was more than enough.

"It's nice to meet you, Luna. You are right. We are of the same clan." Another moment passed before he released my hand and nodded at Jay.

Jay grimaced. "Thank you."

For a moment, neither man said anything. Jay turned to me. "Grab Cruz. We need to go."

Out front, Jay bypassed his SUV and walked to an old blue Chevy pickup. Opening the driver's side door, he motioned for us to climb in the other side.

"What's wrong with your car?" I asked as I slid across the bench seat.

"Nothing." Jay turned the key and the engine rumbled to life. "Just making it harder for Ethan to find us."

Cruz fastened his seatbelt. "The guy from outside the restaurant?"

"That's the one."

"You think he'll look for us?"

"Yes."

Cruz's eyes narrowed. "Do I need to worry about him?"

"Not today." Jay put the truck in gear. "Today you need to see what he can do."

We pulled away from the house and made our way toward the main road. Cruz rested his elbow on the back of the seat and trailed his fingers over my shoulder. "You okay? You looked upset at the table."

I recounted what I'd learned about Johnson. "Rose said George and Noni were talking about adopting him after they got married, but now she doesn't know if they will."

Cruz frowned.

"She said something about George being special and Noni being ordinary. No—" I tried to recall the phrase Rose had used. "—sunny soonhee, soonhi, something like that."

"Sáanii Suntehai," Jay corrected.

I repeated the phrase. "What does it mean?"

He steered the truck around a curve. "Blessed women. Historically, it's a group of our most gifted women. In the early days, the tribe turned to them for messages when they needed to steer others away or sway the minds of neighboring tribes."

"Is it different now?" Cruz asked.

Jay's jaw tightened. "Now they're more like a political think tank with an overabundance of power. Maria's one of them."

"My grandmother?" Maria was a strong woman, but I'd never considered how smart or gifted she might be. "Are her gifts strong?"

"Yes. But in that group, she's average."

I couldn't picture her taking a backseat to anyone.

"What do you mean by overabundance?" Cruz asked.

Jay's face scrunched. "We're taught that the purpose of our gifts is to help create harmony in the world. The Sáanii Suntehai stopped caring about harmony years ago. Now, they're interested in power—political power—and more and more of our people seem to be following their example."

"You mean they want to be on the council?" I asked. "I thought council members had to be men."

Jay shook his head and braked for a squirrel scampering across the road. "They don't have to be, but usually they are. And no,

87

that's not what I mean. Those women have enough relationships with powerful men that they've got council members in their pockets. I'm talking about state politics for now, but I wouldn't be surprised if they had their eyes on federal seats as well."

"To what end?" Cruz pulled his seatbelt to loosen it.

"Power," Jay said simply. "There are some who believe our gifts make us stronger and smarter than outsiders, and because of that, we should be the ones making laws and ruling the world."

The hairs on the back of my neck stood up. There were power-hungry people in every society, but I hated anyone thinking they were better than others.

"You said Maria's gifts are strong." Cruz stared out the windshield. "How do you know how strong a person's gifts are?"

Jay looked both ways then turned onto the main road. "You get a sense of it from their energy. But there are also people like George who have a particular gift for knowing a person's strength just from touching them."

"Does that mean he knows how strong my gifts are?" He'd shaken my hand after all.

"Yes."

"People gasped when he shook her hand," Cruz said. "Why?"

Jay frowned. "Without an invitation it's considered rude for a person with his gift to touch one of the Neme-i—an invasion of privacy."

I'd held my hand out to George when Jay had introduced us. Had I put him in an awkward situation? "Should I not have offered him my hand?"

Jay shook his head. "No. He could have declined."

"But he didn't," Cruz said.

Jay shifted in his seat. "I asked him not to."

Eight

I blinked in surprise as the words penetrated my consciousness. "You *asked* George to shake my hand?" I didn't care if George knew the strength of my gift. Hell, I wouldn't mind knowing. But if it was considered an invasion of privacy.... "Why?"

Jay frowned. "It's hard to explain."

Cruz's feather-like touch became a vice grip on my shoulder. "Try."

I patted his hand. "It's okay."

His clenched jaw told me it wasn't okay with him.

Jay sighed. "The Sáanii Suntehai have the kind of abilities that would make what happened in Albuquerque very possible. They're organized, skilled, and powerful."

Cruz pulled his arm back. The air around him vibrated with intensity. "Why didn't you tell us about them before?"

"Would it have made a difference?"

"Yes." Cruz glared. "Individuals and groups behave differently. I would have looked at this differently."

"That's why I didn't tell you," Jay said. "You need to keep an open mind. This could be about the group or have nothing to do with them. It could even be about one person who happens to be a member of the group. There's just no way to know."

Both had a point, but neither seemed ready to concede. Silence thundered around them.

Cruz's eyes darkened. "So why did you ask George to touch Luna?"

"To apply pressure." Jay stopped at a sign and waited for a car to turn. "Anna's greatest desire is to be leader, right?"

"Right," Cruz and I replied.

"Did you notice her reaction when I said Luna *might* be able to send simultaneous messages?"

"She tensed," I said.

"Because it worried her." Jay accelerated forward. "If your gifts are stronger than hers, she'll have more to worry about."

Pieces clicked in my mind like one of Tomas's puzzles coming together. Had Anna actually been thinking about getting rid of me in Albuquerque? "You think that's why she pointed the gun at me?"

Jay tipped his head. "The possibility's crossed my mind." He turned left onto the road to our cabin. "You want to find your son and raise him. I respect that. I want to be sure our tribe's in good hands. If you're chosen for leader and you don't want it, you turn it down. But before the council fully names Anna leader, I want to know if she's innocent, evil, or a puppet in someone else's game."

"Will the council ask George whose gifts are stronger— Anna's or Luna's?" Cruz asked.

"Probably."

Tomas had once cautioned me that Anna's abilities were stronger than mine. But I hadn't known what my abilities were then. I did now. And I'd spent the last month training. "Whose are?"

"Hers." Jay shifted gears. "But your energy is brighter."

I made a face. "What does that mean?" On average, I understood about half of what Jay said regarding our energy.

He shook his head. "I don't know. George experiences energy on a whole different level. He says the brightness is important." Rolling to a stop in front of the cabin, he turned off the engine. "I don't want to risk people seeing this truck here, so we're only staying long enough to grab some food and climbing gear. Got it?"

Excitement lit inside me. "We're climbing?"

Jay nodded. "Climbing and training. Get moving."

My legs shook and my fingers ached as I clung to the jagged rocks. Seventy feet below, the earth glistened golden with pine needles. Fifty feet of sheer brown rock towered above me. I took a breath and searched for another hold.

"Nothing there." Cruz lay on his belly peering over the top of the cliff. Wisps of hair blew across his face. "Your only option's three feet to your right."

I scanned the rock until I saw what he meant. Reaching with my right hand, I came up a foot short.

"You'll have to jump," Cruz called. "There's a natural toehold and a crevice you'll catch with your right hand."

Easy for him to say. He was a natural climber. He'd made this face look easy.

I gazed at the rocks above me and once again saw nowhere to go. Too stubborn to follow the path Cruz had blazed, I'd chosen my own route and climbed myself into a pickle. Now I was stuck. Other than climbing down and starting again, Cruz's hold appeared to be my only option.

"Tell Jay what you need and trust yourself," Cruz said.

Jay remained on the ground. Working belay, he sat back in his harness, perfectly balanced against my weight and the rope that connected us. He'd made the rules clear before we'd donned the harnesses. All my communicating had to be telekinetic.

I fixed an image of his face in my mind then visualized him sitting back farther in the harness, adding tension to the rope to support me as I made the jump and sent it.

Seconds later, the rope between us tightened, and I made the jump. I caught the handhold and found a ledge with the ball of my left foot. My right side swung free until I wrapped my arm and leg around an edge of rock I hadn't seen before. My fingers wedged into a crack and my foot found a crevice. I let out a breath and reveled in the ability to put weight on my whole foot instead of just my toes.

"Look around that edge," Cruz called.

I craned my neck to see what my right side curled around and gasped. A plethora of holds peppered the cliff.

Within minutes, I finished the climb. At the top, I gave Cruz a kiss then rappelled down and wriggled out of the harness.

Jay joined me at the base of the rocks. "Not bad." High praise coming from him.

"I agree," a male voice said behind us. "Not bad at all."

I whirled around, fumbling at my back for the knives I always carried but had left with my hiking boots when I'd donned the climbing harness. Jay stepped forward and pushed me behind him. Above us, I heard a click and knew Cruz held his Glock pointed at the man approaching through the trees. And to think, I'd called Cruz paranoid for carrying the firearm during his climb.

Jay tipped his head. "Ethan. How'd you find us?"

I peeked around Jay and saw the tracker from the restaurant nodding in my direction.

"How do you think?" he asked.

Jay glanced back, one eyebrow raised, the look on his face saying, *You see?*

Trackers could trace my energy and find me. I got it.

Jay scanned the trees. "Where's your partner?"

"Around," Ethan replied.

Jay flashed me a pointed glare and mouthed, *gun*. Quickly, I sent Cruz a message to put his Glock away. Most likely, Ethan's female partner would be sending the same message. Although Cruz knew not to show his ability to recognize or resist our women's messages, when it came to my safety, he would resist first and explain later. Better to avoid the whole mess by sending the message myself.

"What can we do for you?" Jay asked.

Ethan's gaze remained locked on the top of the cliff, his jaw

92

tight. A second passed before his face relaxed, and his gaze returned to Jay and me. Cruz had clearly gotten my message.

"The council sent me," Ethan said. "They haven't been able to reach you on your cell."

Jay patted his pockets. "Shit. I must have left it in the truck."

Ethan shook his head. He reached into his shirt pocket and produced Jay's phone. "At your cabin."

"Really?" Jay sounded surprised but his steady gaze communicated the opposite.

"The council—" Ethan's gaze jumped to the cliff. "What the hell?"

I turned to see Cruz on his belly, inching his legs over the edge of the cliff as he felt for a hold with his toes. Finding one, he began his descent managing a pace only slightly slower than my rappel.

"Is he wearing a harness?" Ethan asked.

"No," I said. Though a harness would have been a nice precaution, Cruz could climb and descend a face like this as easily as I could a chain-link fence.

We stood in silence watching Cruz's progress.

Jay shivered. "Scares the shit out of me." He turned back to Ethan. "You were saying?"

Ethan tore his gaze from Cruz and fixed it on Jay. His mouth opened, but nothing came out. He shook his head as if rattling his thoughts into place.

"The council...?" Jay prodded.

"Yes. They've been texting you. Your meeting time has changed." Ethan handed Jay his phone.

Keying in his passcode, Jay scrolled through his messages. "Five o'clock." He checked his watch as Cruz joined us. "We should get going so I can shower."

"Appreciate you texting back that you received the message," Ethan said. He nodded a greeting at Cruz.

"Of course." Jay keyed in a brief message and frowned. "Looks like they sent the message around two. Have you been looking for us long?"

Ethan grinned as if the thought were laughable. "Less than an hour."

"Of course." Jay clapped Ethan on the shoulder and addressed me. "Ethan's the tribe's best tracker. I'm surprised the council wasted his time on someone like me."

Ethan smirked. "I volunteered." Nodding at me, he turned and strolled away. Twenty yards out, a woman emerged from a clump of pine trees and fell into step beside him.

Jay waited until they were out of sight before turning to us.

"Is that what you wanted us to learn?" Cruz asked. "That he can find us?"

Jay shook his head and stepped out of his harness. "No. I wanted you to learn how *easily* he'd find you."

Cruz wound the rope. "Why did he have your phone?"

"Because he dropped by the cabin searching for us." Jay unclipped the hardware from his harness.

I grabbed the duffel bag and held it open. "But if he tracks us based on my energy, why'd he go to the cabin when we're out here?"

"To track your energy, you have to be sending messages," Jay said. "When did you start sending?"

I looked at the rock face. I hadn't started until I'd begun climbing. "About thirty minutes ago."

Jay tipped his head and grinned.

In thirty minutes, Ethan had managed to get from the cabin to the dirt road we had taken off the main highway then park and hike down into the valley where we were. The travel time alone would have taken twenty minutes. "Shit."

Jay dumped his harness in the duffel bag. "When you two are out searching, you need to remember it's only easy for trackers to find you if you're sending messages."

The point hit me like a rock to the head. "If I can't use my gift, why the hell did I spend the last month training?"

"Because sometimes you'll need to use it. And then, if you

94

don't want to be found, you'll need to move. Fast."

"How far?" Cruz asked. "How far can they track from? How far will we have to move?"

Jay shrugged. "Depends on the tracker. Ethan's exceptional. He can sense energy sent or received within a five-mile radius. Most trackers have a significantly shorter range than that. A one-mile radius is required, but most have at least two."

Finding a boulder, I sat and exchanged my climbing shoes for hiking boots. "Wouldn't it just be easier to go to the police and tell them I'm being stalked?"

"By who?" Jay asked. "Ten different stalkers? Twenty? Thirty? And what's your proof? You've got a creepy feeling? If you tell them about your abductions, they'll check with the Albuquerque police, find out the abductors are dead, and your case is closed. They'll assume you're paranoid."

He'd trivialized it, but that didn't make him wrong.

"Even if they did believe you and agreed to help," Jay said, his voice softer, "how long do you think it would be before one of the Neme-i became uncomfortable and sent a message disrupting the investigation? Or, worse, a message for one of the officers to turn his gun on you?"

Silence fell between us as I contemplated the far-reaching effect of what he'd just said. "Is that why Gloria never went to the police?"

A weight seemed to descend on Jay. "I think so."

Cruz finished winding the rope and tied it off, pulling the end more forcefully than usual.

"So the parking lot this morning?" Cruz said through clenched teeth. "You were daring Ethan to find us?"

"Yes." Jay glanced in the direction Ethan had gone. "Something you need to remember: the strength of your gift is important, but the strength of your mind will always be more important. Ethan is a hell of a tracker, but I just played him to our benefit."

I blew out a breath finding the words less heartening than he probably intended. Maneuvering around the Neme-i would be a constant game of strategy.

Back at the truck, we buckled in, and Jay steered us toward the cabin.

"Does the time-change for your portion of the meeting mean anything?" Cruz asked.

Jay shook his head. "Happens all the time."

"Will it affect Maria's dinner plans?" I tried to keep a neutral tone, but there was no mistaking the hope in my voice.

"No. The dinner break is always six-thirty. If needed, the meeting will reconvene at eight."

"Will it be needed?"

"Yes." Jay glanced at me. "Have you decided what you'll tell Anna and Maria?"

"No." And I still didn't want to think about it.

⚏

"Why not take their offer?" Cruz asked.

We were at the cabin getting ready for dinner. Jay had left an hour before and Bear lay content on the floor after a walk in the forest.

"If hiding the prophecy would keep the council from learning about Adam, why not do it?"

"Because I don't know if I can trust them. Every time I remember Anna with that gun in her hand, I feel sick. If she learns Adam's prophecy and thinks he poses a threat—" I shivered. "She's willing to screw with people's lives to make super-babies. What do you think she'd do if she felt threatened by her nephew?"

Cruz tipped his head, conceding my point. "If you don't tell them Adam's birth date, what do you think will happen?"

I considered my fears. "They'll be upset and suspicious. Probably think they can't trust me."

"You think they trust you now?"

The question knocked me back an inch. "No." Why hadn't I considered that before?

"So you lose nothing."

"True. But eventually everyone would know about Adam."

Cruz nodded. "But would everyone else care about his prophecy?"

I sighed. "Probably not."

"There's no clear win." He walked to the corner to retrieve his boots. "So focus on what you think is right."

I studied his broad shoulders and shoulder-length hair, watched the way his hips seemed to roll rather than plod with each step. "Come here," I said.

He returned to the bed, and I wrapped my arms around his neck and kissed him.

His boots hit the floor with a thud and his hands slid around my waist. Our tongues met and the kiss deepened. My hands found their way beneath his shirt. He cupped my ass and curled the fingers of his other hand into my hair.

The kiss continued, and I pressed against him.

With a groan, he pulled away. "That won't get us to dinner."

Who cared? I reached for him but stopped. If I didn't make it to dinner, they'd probably send a tracker after me. Any breathing young woman would understand why I'd let falling into bed with Cruz supersede going to dinner. My grandmother would not.

<hr>

"Ah, there you are!" Anna said as Leonard ushered Cruz and me into the living area of the Leader's Residence.

Furniture had been moved to create space for folding tables and chairs, and council members, spouses, and other guests crowded the room.

"I was beginning to wonder if we should send Ethan after you."

I spotted Ethan and his partner leaning against the wall by the French doors. He smiled and lifted his glass.

I nodded curtly. Cruz squeezed my hand, reminding me to maintain a neutral facade.

"Sorry if we worried you," I muttered as Maria drifted over. "We lost track of time."

Maria bussed my cheeks and shook Cruz's hand. "We're glad you're here."

Offering us drinks, Leonard stepped away.

I turned to my sister. Her eyes shone and her cheeks glowed. "You look happy."

She beamed. "It's been a good day."

I nearly choked. She'd put a halt to the happiness of several couples. God knew what else had happened at the meeting.

I forced a smile. "I'm glad you enjoyed it."

Unable to meet her gaze any longer, I turned to the room and spotted Jacy Crow by the fireplace. "Will you excuse us? I'd like to say hi to Jacy."

Anna motioned for us to go—probably as happy to be rid of me as I was her.

Halfway across the floor, Cruz gave my hand a tug then motioned to the open stairwell. I glanced at the spot that offered the best view of the room. Nodding, I released his hand. Cruz planned to work, not socialize.

I approached Crow alone.

"I'm pleased to see you." His hair hung limp, and the droop of his shoulders told me his day had been long.

"Is the meeting over?"

He shook his head. "I believe we're in for a long night."

"That's too bad. You look tired."

"It hasn't been an easy day."

I glanced around. "Is Ivan here?"

"No. Resting. Inez insisted."

Given what I'd learned about my clan leader's health, I was glad.

Crow sipped his drink. "I understand you met Noni and George today."

I nodded, wondering how he'd heard.

"How was Noni?" His eyes reminded me of Bear's whenever Cruz and I walked out the door and left him alone.

"Hanging in there, I guess."

Crow nodded. "She's of my clan. I hoped to check on her tonight but it doesn't look like there will be time."

"You could call her," I said.

"I did. Went straight to voicemail."

Leonard delivered my beer and carried a glass of water to Cruz.

I took a sip. "How did you know I'd met them?"

Crow nodded at Ethan who now stood with his back to the party while he talked to his partner. "Ethan reported to the council. I understand you were rock climbing."

I glared at Ethan's back. I hated being the subject of gossip. "What'd he do? Give you a blow-by-blow of my day?"

"He likes us to know how good he is."

"How good is he?"

Crow grimaced. "Possibly better than his teacher."

"Who was that?" I sipped my beer.

"Joey Two Paws. Generally considered the best tracker in the history of our people. In forty years, your mother was the only person he never found."

Dread settled like a burning ember in my belly. Not only would I be searching for a woman the best trackers of the Nemei had never found, I'd likely be doing it with their newest best tracker on my tail. Great.

I made it through dinner and dessert before Maria asked the dreaded question. "Will you join me upstairs?"

I glanced around for Anna but didn't see her. Probably waiting in her office, ready to ask for my decision.

With crème brûlée churning in my tummy, I followed Maria to Anna's office. Cruz shot me a tight-lipped smile as we passed him by the stairs. I still had no idea what my answer would be. I'd considered the question throughout dinner, and every time the scale tipped one way, a different thought swung it back the other. Two main questions stuck in my mind: would I prefer Adam's prophecy be discovered sooner or later, and did I want Adam's existence known only by Anna and Maria or by everyone?

99

Inside her office, Anna stood staring out the window. Lights from outside cast a ghostly pallor on her reflection. She turned as Maria closed the door. "Have you thought about our discussion from last night?"

"Yes." I would have been hard-pressed not to.

"Based on today's meeting, I'm certain the vote to publicize the prophecies will pass. Grandmother and I can protect...." she paused as if searching for a name.

"Adam," I supplied, knowing she'd never find it on his prophecy.

"Adam." The corners of Anna's mouth twitched. "We can protect Adam if we know his birth date."

My heart pounded. "But you're the leader. Why would you vote a new law into existence then turn around and break it?"

Anna's eyes narrowed.

"Dear"—Maria stepped closer—"if the council finds out you have a child, they will search for him more fiercely than you can imagine. He will be in line to be leader, and they will be compelled to find him. We can't guarantee what will happen during the search."

I stared at her. "What do you mean, *what will happen*?"

Maria's gaze remained even. "I mean the search will be serious and of such a fevered pace, people might be hurt or worse."

My heart sped. "You mean my son?"

"No," Maria replied. "Him, they would protect. I mean anyone in the way of the search."

My heart continued to race and my voice shot up an octave. "I thought we were supposed to pursue harmony."

"We are," Maria said. "But we must start with our own. Having a leader brings harmony to our tribe."

"But we have a leader." I motioned at Anna.

"Having a leader-elect is just as important as having a leader," Anna said as if quoting something she'd been told her whole life. "In order for the tribe to feel safe when thinking about the future, there must be a leader-elect waiting to assume control should something happen to the current leader."

The reasoning made me nauseous, but I couldn't deny its logic. The night our father had been killed, the council named Anna Leader During a Time of Duress. After a lifetime of preparation, she'd been ready.

"Were people hurt when the trackers searched for me?" I asked.

Maria's face looked pinched. "No. But that was different."

"How?"

"First, we had another leader-elect. While it is always preferable to have more than one, having only one does not create the same sort of vacuum as having none."

"But they wouldn't have none without my son," I said. "They'd still have me."

"You've already professed you don't want the job."

"And yet they insist on considering me for it."

Anna's eyes narrowed.

Maria smiled and waved her hand as if shooing a fly. "A technicality created by our laws. You will not be named leader if you do not wish to be."

I sensed a loophole in her reasoning, but I couldn't see it.

"The other reason the search for you was not the same is because you're a girl. Your son, quite obviously, is not."

"And the Neme-i prefer a male leader," I said repeating the phrase I'd heard Jay use.

"Antiquated old fools," Anna mumbled.

Maria shot her a steely-eyed glare. "It may seem old-fashioned, but it's true." Her gaze returned to me. "There are many who do not trust the integrity of our women. Our gifts give us access to great power; only our sense of responsibility ensures we use it wisely."

Unfortunately, responsibility couldn't be policed.

I ran my hand through my hair. "So because Adam would be the only leader-elect and he's a boy, you're saying the trackers

101

might kill to bring him here?"

Maria leaned back in her chair. "I'm saying it's a possibility."

I bit my lips. Though ugly, I couldn't say with absolute certainty I wouldn't do the same. And in some ways, it made me *want* to employ the trackers. But I couldn't. Not until I knew whoever had tried to hurt me wouldn't do the same to Adam.

"So, if I wasn't as important as Adam would be," I said, stalling while I tried to let my brain process the rest, "why did they search for me my entire childhood?"

"Because you're our family, dear. Of course we wanted you found."

My father had wanted me found—that I had felt and seen firsthand. But Maria and Anna? To them I felt more like a duty than a treasured family member. And in all fairness, I felt the same in return.

I tipped my head as a new thought occurred. "They thought they'd find Raina with me, didn't they?"

Maria shifted in her chair. "Well that played a part, of course, but—"

I lifted my hand. "It's okay." When Raina had disappeared, she'd left the tribe stuck. My father had filled in as temporary leader, but he hadn't been able to vote in that position. With the council evenly divided on most issues, the tribe hadn't been able to progress or change. Of course they'd wanted her back even if only to punish her and force her to vote and relinquish her position.

"So, about your son's prophecy?" Anna's fingers drummed lightly on her chair.

"I told you last night, I don't know it."

Maria licked her lips. "We'd heard you were at Chester Tsossi's house today. We thought someone might have approached you there?"

"No," I replied as I studied my sister. "We weren't there long."

In the time I'd known Anna, I'd only seen her truly care about herself. She could couch her request as care or worry for Adam and me, but I knew better. This had to be about her and something she stood to lose or gain.

Maybe I'd made this harder than necessary. Maybe it was quite simple. Did I want Adam's prophecy discovered sooner or later? Did I want only Anna and Maria to know about him or everyone? Easy.

I preferred Adam's prophecy be learned later, thereby allowing me time to search for him. And as for Anna and Maria or everyone? God help me, I trusted people like Hideo, Crow, George, and Noni more than I trusted my own sister or grandmother.

I drew a shaky breath. Anna and Maria hadn't been completely forthright with me. I saw no reason to be so with them. "I can't ask either of you to break the law. It wouldn't be right. We are of the Neme-i, not above them. And if our prophecies"—I motioned between us—"and everyone else's are going to be public, then Adam's should be too...assuming he even has one."

Anna's fingers fisted on top of her chair.

I pretended not to notice as I turned to Maria. "You once told me being part of the leader's family meant understanding that tribe comes first. I think I'm starting to get that." I smiled. "Maybe I really am becoming one of the Neme-i."

Maria glanced at Anna then forced a smile and patted my hand. "You've always been one of us, dear."

⚌

I woke with a start. Darkness surrounded me. Outside the cabin, crickets called. Moonlight streamed through the gap in the curtains.

Beside me, Cruz lay asleep, his body warm.

Something had woken me. A noise?

By the corner of the bed, Bear stood staring at the staircase. I looked to the bedroom door at the top of the steps. No light shone through the crack beneath.

Floorboards squeaked overhead. I froze.

Was it Jay? But why wouldn't he turn on a light?

I touched Cruz's shoulder. He jerked upright, one arm jutting out to shield me, while the other reached between the mattress and headboard for his gun. He blinked and peered into the darkness.

"Someone's upstairs without lights," I whispered.

The floorboards squeaked again.

Nine

Cruz sprang out of bed, Glock in hand. Clad in boxers, he crept toward the stairs connecting our room to the rest of the house.

Bear moved to follow.

"Stay," Cruz whispered. "Guard."

Bear positioned himself between me and the stairs. Cruz ascended in silence. Two steps from the top, he stopped and put his ear to the door. I strained to listen, but heard nothing.

Jerking back, Cruz took aim.

A second later, a muffled whisper came through the door. "Luna? Cruz? You awake?"

Jay.

The tension in my body eased.

Cruz hit the wall switch and the bedroom filled with light as he opened the door.

Jay opened his mouth then stiffened at the sight of Cruz's gun.

Shaking his head, Cruz trooped down the steps, lips pressed into a tight line.

"I take it you heard me walking around," Jay said before following.

Cruz set his gun on the nightstand and glared at Jay.

Tail thumping against the floor, Bear whimpered.

Cruz let out a breath. "Check."

Bear crept forward and gave the requisite sniff. Recognizing

Jay's scent as friendly, the Rottweiler wagged his tail and pressed his nose into Jay's palm.

Jay patted the dog's side. "Sorry I scared you."

Bear returned to the foot of the bed and lay down as Cruz plucked his jeans off the chair in the corner.

"Why didn't you turn on a light?" I asked.

"Didn't want to risk being seen packing."

"You're leaving?" Cruz buttoned his jeans and tossed me a pair of sweatpants.

Jay took the chair in the corner. "As soon as we talk."

"The vote?" I asked, wiggling into the sweatpants beneath the covers. I knew what the answer would be, but I hoped I was wrong.

"Passed," Jay said. "Four to three. The prophecies will be part of tribal record starting tomorrow."

My heart sank.

"What time did you get in?" Cruz asked.

The clock on the nightstand said 3:20. When Cruz and I had gone to bed at eleven, Jay had still been gone.

"Thirty minutes ago."

I pulled my knees to my chest. "It took that long to vote?"

"No. The voting took five minutes. My explanation of why the prophecies should stay private took several hours."

I blinked. "You had that much to say?"

Jay shrugged. "I had that many examples."

"And you shared them all?"

Jay rolled his eyes. "Seers had to turn over their records following the vote. If I drug the meeting out late enough, I knew the council would want to sleep before they looked at the prophecies."

"What's the difference?" Cruz asked.

"Head start. I'll be a couple hours down the road before they wake up." Jay pulled a piece of paper from his pocket and passed it to Cruz and me. Names were written with locations and phone numbers beside them.

"What's this?" I asked.

Jay slouched in the chair, legs splayed. "Those are the people you need to see to complete your training. They're expecting you. They'll teach you what the council requires."

"When are we supposed to do this?"

As soon as Cruz and I left Summerhaven, we had plans of our own.

"If you don't want the council sending trackers after you, soon."

I growled in frustration.

"We'll make it work," Cruz said, jaw set.

How we'd do that, I didn't know. We already had two plans: the one Cruz and I had plotted over the past month and the one Jay had suggested where we let people who'd known Raina point us from place to place. Now this? "Will you be with us?"

"No." Jay rested his head on the back of the chair and rubbed his eyes. "When the council checks my records tomorrow, they'll send for me. I plan to be long gone. I'll stay that way as long as possible, but it won't last. They'll send trackers to find all of us once they realize we're not together."

My stomach knotted.

Leaning against the wood-paneled wall, Cruz pushed some hair behind his ear. "How do we avoid them?"

Jay sighed and rubbed his jaw. "Luck. Care."

"What do you mean?" Fear sat in my belly like a barbed weight. Surely he had better advice than *best of luck.*

"I mean, exercise care." Deep lines creased the skin between Jay's brows. "The next part of your training involves you traveling while you work on controlling your ability. The council will expect you to move around. If you're somewhere you don't mind them knowing, use your gift. But if you're somewhere you don't want known, don't. Or, if you have to, use it and move on. Move far and move fast and do it immediately."

My breathing quickened. "Why didn't you tell us this before today?"

"I hoped we'd have more time."

"But now we don't." The muscle in Cruz's jaw pulsed. "Where will you be?"

"Around. I hope."

My gaze shot back to Jay. "You *hope*?"

He shrugged. "Like I said, I'll hold the trackers off as long as I can, but eventually they'll find me. When they do, I'll be held until I break the code. After that, they'll let me go. They'll have to."

A chill slid down my spine. "How long will they hold you?"

Jay shrugged. "Depends how long I hold out."

"What will they do?" Cruz's voice was quiet, but the words frightened me.

Jay grimaced and slid a glance my way. Looking back at Cruz, he shook his head.

Whatever the answer, he didn't want to say it in front of me. Guilt laced my gut. "All this to keep my son a secret?"

"No," Jay said. "That's only part of it. We've talked about what the Revisionists want to do. You saw the beginning of it today with the marriage blessings."

Two days ago the idea of Revisionists wanting to match couples in order to breed children with stronger abilities seemed like a paranoid fantasy. But why else had they denied the marriage blessings? According to Rose, George was special; Noni was ordinary. Any children they had would likely be above average but not extraordinary.

"How will we reach you?" Cruz asked. Worry about George, Noni, and the Neme-i were not part of the equation for him. Keeping me safe and finding Adam were his priorities.

Jay pulled his legs in. "Mostly, you won't. If you have to, go through Mo. She'll know how." He checked his watch and stood. "I need to go. If anyone asks where I am, tell them I left to deliver prophecies. Good luck at the post office."

He moved to the stairs and started up.

"Wait!" I jumped off the bed and hurried to the foot of the

108

stairwell.

Jay turned.

I swallowed while I tried to find what I wanted to say. "When will we see you again?"

"I don't know." He gave a sad smiled and climbed the remaining steps before exiting the room.

The words I wanted came then: *Be careful.*

⊥⊤

Following Jay's example, Cruz and I also packed and left. We stopped for breakfast in Phoenix then continued on to Palo Verde. A little past one o'clock we pulled up outside the post office. The lights inside were on and the window shades open.

I reached for my door handle.

Cruz caught my arm. "Let's talk before we go in."

I didn't want to wait, but understood Cruz had a concern.

With a sigh, I clipped Bear to his leash, and we climbed outside. Heat surrounded me like a wet, wool sweater.

"Ugh." A day and a half on Mt. Lemmon had spoiled me.

Towering false cypress trees stood in a group to the left of the building. We retreated to their shade, and Bear sniffed until he found an acceptable spot and lifted his leg.

Cruz's gaze raked the area.

"What?" I demanded.

"What's your plan?"

Bear took a couple steps and lifted again.

"What do you mean? I'm going in there and getting what's inside the box."

"And then what? Open it?"

I opened my hands as if to say, *duh.*

"Right there in front of the postal workers, the security cameras, and anyone else who happens to come in?"

I dropped my arms and Cruz made his *tcht* noise as Bear moved toward the edge of the bushes.

"What are you saying?" I asked.

Cruz touched my elbow. "I'm saying let's do what Jay said

109

and exercise care. Wait till we're back in the truck to open it. There's no reason to think trackers will come through here, but if they do, and there's something in that box—like a picture of Raina with Adam for instance, you don't want the trackers to find out what it was, do you?"

His point took my breath away, and I closed my eyes as I realized how foolish I'd been. This was what Jay had meant about exercising care. I needed to always be thinking, not blindly rushing in.

We left Bear in the bed of the truck and went inside.

A small room stood to the left where a bored-looking postal worker leaned on a counter while typing on her phone. She looked up when we entered, nodded, and returned to her phone.

Box number 42 sat on the wall opposite the door, its gold hue matching that of the key. Cruz stood next to me, casually leaning against the wall of boxes, blocking the worker's view. My hand shook as I fumbled to insert the key.

"Breathe." Cruz trailed his fingers down my back.

I did as suggested and relaxed enough to slide the key into the lock. Inside, a small white box rested on its side. I noted the address as I shoved it in my purse. *L. Ortiz; P.O. Box 42; Palo Verde, CA.* Closing the little door, I removed the key.

As we turned to leave, I glanced at the postal worker. Cruz had been right. She was watching us.

Back inside the truck, I pulled the box from my purse, and ripped off the tape. Inside sat a plain white envelope, a leather pouch with fringe on bottom, and two keys—a gold one that might have been a house key and a smaller, silver one. To a padlock perhaps?

I dropped the keys and envelope in my purse. The fringe on the leather pouch tickled my wrist as I loosened the leather strap and dumped its contents into my hand. A ring landed face down in my palm. The hair on my arms prickled.

Swallowing, I turned the ring over and stared down at two diamond-shaped turquoise stones surrounded by six round stones of various colors. Air rushed from my lungs.

"It can't be." For the first time in ten years, I gazed upon the Leader's Ring.

In the wreck that killed Gloria, our engine had caught fire, and everything we owned had burned. I'd seen the twisted, charred hunk of metal that had been our car in the junkyard. Nothing had survived that fire. Not Gloria. Not anything else. I'd only lived because I'd been thrown through the windshield and ended up several feet away.

I stared at the round stones which represented the different clans of the Neme-i. *Opal, Mohave Stone, Chrysoprase, Malachite, Jasper, and Travertine.*

"Your purse," Cruz hissed.

I looked up.

"We're being watched." He nodded toward the post office as he started the engine.

Staring at us through the glass door as she held her phone to her ear, the female postal worker smiled.

I shoved the ring in the pouch.

"Breathe," Cruz said.

I tried.

"And buckle up."

He steered us north onto the highway. "Is that ring what I think it is?"

"I don't know." My head pounded. It certainly looked like the Leader's Ring, but how could it be? I'd been told only one existed, but maybe that was wrong. Maybe a copy had been made. I knew one way to be sure. "Can I pull it back out now?"

Cruz glanced in the rearview mirror. "Yes."

I removed the ring from the pouch and checked the back of the setting. Engraved in the bottom right corner angled up and to the right was a tiny arrow with a G and an F on either side, the mark of the artist who'd died shortly after making the ring.

My stomach churned and bile made its way into my mouth. I gagged the bitterness down.

"It's my ring," I said.

"The Leader's Ring?"

Sweat trickled down my neck. "Yes."

I turned the air conditioner full blast.

Cruz glanced at me then pulled onto a dirt road that ran between a crop of melons and the river.

Eyes closed, I leaned my head against the neck rest.

If everything had burned in the fire but me, how could the ring be in my hand? It had to have been packed with Gloria's jewelry box when we'd left Berkeley. She always kept it there. Too big for my fingers, she'd feared I'd lose the ring if I tried to wear it. She'd always said I could have it sized to fit when I became an adult. Until then, she insisted we keep it safe, nestled in her box between her parents' wedding bands and a diamond pinky ring I never saw her wear.

Cruz turned the truck to face the river and braked to a stop beneath a tree. Rolling the windows down, he shut the engine off. "May I see it?"

I held the ring out.

He tipped it back and forth, taking in the stones and the notch cut in the top. "It's gorgeous. What about the envelope and keys?"

In my surprise over the ring, I'd forgotten about the box's other contents. Pawing through my purse, I removed the envelope, but couldn't find the keys. I finally dumped everything out and found them near the bottom.

The left side of Cruz's lip snagged upward. Dumping a purse was never efficient.

I sighed. "Do you have a key ring?" I didn't want to put the keys with my day-to-day keys, but I did want to be able to find them with ease.

Cruz opened his hand and I passed him the keys. From a little cubby in the dashboard, he pulled out a ring with one key on it.

"What's that to?" I swept the items on the seat into my purse.

"Jay's trailer."

Returning the purse to the floorboard, I reached for the

envelope and froze. What if it contained a note saying *I took your son and sold him,* or *I killed him,* or *You'll never find us?* Squeezing my eyes shut, I whispered, "Let Adam be okay."

A tingle in my brain sent a warm shiver through my body, and peace enveloped me.

Working my finger beneath the flap, I eased the envelope open and pulled out two pieces of paper. A shiny brown strip fluttered to my lap. I picked it up and showed it to Cruz.

"Photo negatives?" A crease furrowed his brow. He took the strip from my hand and held it to the light.

"Can you tell what's on them?"

He shook his head. "Not really. But only two have pictures."

I leaned forward, noting the blank squares as well as the two with what appeared to be dark shapes and a blob.

"What about the letter?" Cruz asked.

My hand trembled. Neat blue lines of print marched across the pages.

My Dearest Darling Daughter,

I scoffed. Who dumped their "dearest darling" in someone else's car?

I have searched so long, I no longer know where to look. My only hope is that you are searching too.

I will be leaving the key that brings you this letter with an old friend. If you have found this, you have found her. I hope and pray, through her, you have seen a little of who I truly am.

I cannot begin to imagine what you must think of me, nor can I tell you what you should. I can only pray that by the time we are united, you will understand the choices I made. I don't dare hope you will agree with them, but I pray you will understand everything I've done has been from love.

I snorted. The woman who'd abandoned me and robbed me of my child had acted out of love? That was rich.

I would like very much to tell you where to find me, but I can't. Moving has become a way of life. Almost as regular as the change of seasons.

I have no idea when you'll find this letter or where I'll be. But there is a place you know which may provide answers. A place where answers were hidden from you long ago.

There is so much I wish to say, but no words match what I feel. And words written have become as dangerous as messages sent. If I am one of my people anymore, I do not know. But they are of me as I am of you. At my hands, you will never know harm, only the love of a mother's arms. In you lies my greatest hope and desire just as with me, lies yours.

Be careful in your travels and your trust. What you know or think you know may prove false. What you are told and what you see can lead you astray. What you smell, taste, and touch can be manufactured. But what touches you will likely prove true. Trust only the things you know in your heart and your soul. Be brave. Be the woman you were raised to be.

With all my love and prayers for a time when we may be together, I remain,
-Your Mother

I read the letter twice, gritting my teeth at the parts that were lies and shaking my head at the rest. Both times I ended thinking, *what the hell*?

Ten

My emotions ping-ponged like a ball in a fishbowl toss. I hadn't necessarily expected the letter to say, *I love you.* But what about, *sorry I left you*? Or, *sorry I stole your kid*? And what the hell did it mean? Was she crazy?

Unable to stop the bouncing of my thoughts, I offered the letter to Cruz. Maybe he'd make something of it.

Handing me the key ring, he took the letter.

As he read, I fingered the keys, watching his eyes narrow as his forehead crinkled. After reading the pages, he flipped back to the beginning and read again.

Finished, he looked up and opened his mouth. Nothing came out. Raina's letter had robbed him of speech too.

All those years feeling like trash because she'd left me. Maybe I should have been thanking my lucky stars. "She's crazy. Right?"

Cruz winced. "I don't think so. I think she's being careful."

Had we read the same letter?

On the river, an outboard motor sputtered to life.

"Look at the way it's written," Cruz said. "Everything's stated so carefully it's almost unintelligible."

"Almost?"

"Yes. Almost." His gaze moved to the rearview mirror as a pickup rolled along the dirt road behind us. "If you think about it, some of it will probably make sense."

"I am thinking about it. None of it makes sense."

Dust floated past the window and filled the cab with the scent of earth.

"That's because you're involved emotionally. You need to let it sink in." Cruz returned the letter. "When you can read it objectively, it might make sense."

"You're objective. Does it make sense to you?"

"No. But it's not to me. It's written for you to understand."

Fat chance of that.

"Let's talk about the ring." He nodded at my hand where the ring now circled my thumb. "You told me it burned in the fire."

I lifted my finger and the ring twisted face down. Even my thumb didn't fit it. "I thought it did." I remembered the charred carcass of the car. "Everything burned."

"Not you."

Exasperation made me growl. How many times had I told him this? "I wasn't in the car. I went through the windshield."

The skin around his eyes tightened.

"What?" I asked.

"That part of the story has never made sense. Unless the windshield miraculously blew out—which is unlikely—you would have been cut all to hell. I've now seen every perfect inch of you. You're not scarred."

I looked down at my body checking for scars I might not have noticed in the past ten years. "So what do you think happened?"

"I'm not sure. You obviously ended up outside the car, but I don't know how. Where was the ring during the drive? In the car or trailer?"

"I don't know." I hadn't been the one to pack our stuff. Gloria had done that. "Usually when we moved, Gloria packed her jewelry in a box along with some clothes that she carried into the motels at night. If she did that, it would have been in the car."

"So either you climbed out on your own and grabbed the box, or you had help."

The accident report said I'd been found lying alone. "From

116

who?"

Cruz leveled his gaze with mine. "Who had the ring?"

My body turned cold, and my blood stopped flowing. Then it rushed. Pounding in my temples, burning in my chest. I didn't want to believe what Cruz suggested, but the proof sat on my thumb. "How the hell would Raina have been there?"

"I don't know. We know she volunteered at the hospital when you were in the coma, so she had to be in the area. Her finding you would explain the police reports and lack of photos. She could have sent messages to the officers to report anything she wanted."

I toed the floorboard and stared at the keys I still held. All my life I had wanted answers to questions about my past. Over the past two months I'd gotten several. But it seemed every time I got one answer, new questions formed, most stranger than the ones I'd had before. And every time that happened, some fact I thought I'd known about my life proved false.

I took a deep breath and stacked the keys one on top of the other. "So what do we do?" I ran my finger along the cut of the keys, letting my nail slide in and out of the grooves.

"Stick with our plan." Cruz picked up the negatives he'd placed on the dashboard and waved them at me. "But first get these developed."

Strange. The cut of Jay's and Raina's larger key felt the same. I held them in front of my face searching for differences. "Cruz?"

"Yeah?" He seemed lost in thought.

"Look at this." I held the keys up for him.

He frowned.

"Are they the same key? I mean, they can't be? Can they?"

Laying the negatives on his lap, he took the keys, and studied them like a jeweler with a gemstone. His lips parted and his brow furrowed. He held them side by side then stacked together as I had.

On the river, the outdoor motor revved to a whining pitch.

I swallowed. "They're the same, aren't they?"

117

Cruz nodded.

What had Raina said? Answers might be found where they'd been hidden from me long ago. Jay had sure as hell hidden answers about my gift when I'd trained with him at the trailer as a child.

"The small one might go to that cupboard we saw under the table," Cruz said.

Looked like we were headed back to Mojave. I bit my lip. "If we leave now, we could be at the trailer before nightfall."

"True, but it would be dark before we finished. Better to do it in the morning." He returned the key ring to the cubby in the dashboard and lifted the negatives. "Let's get these developed."

Three hours later, we pulled into the Walmart parking lot in San Bernardino. Huge and busy, Cruz reasoned we'd be less likely to be remembered there than at a drug store.

We dropped our negatives off for one-hour developing under a made-up name and picked up two flip-style cell phones and pre-paid phone cards with a low number of minutes. Driving around, we found a park and claimed a picnic table with green peeling paint. Patches of brown grass littered the ground. Cruz straddled the bench and set up the phones while I threw a tennis ball for Bear and imagined all the things we might find at the trailer. An address book for Raina? A map showing where to find my child? The apology the post office letter had been missing?

"You understand how these work?" Cruz held up a cell phone.

"Flip it open, dial, and talk." Bear dropped his ball at my feet. I pinched the saliva and dirt encrusted toy with my fingertips and tossed it.

"Not the phones themselves," Cruz said. "How we use them."

I wiped my fingers on my jeans and joined him at the picnic table.

"They're burners," he said. "If you use one, keep the call short, then ditch the phone and get away before it's tracked."

That explained why he'd bought the phone cards with the fewest minutes.

118

Bear dropped his ball at my feet and pawed it when I didn't pick it up.

I rubbed his head. "What about our regular phones? How do we keep from being tracked through those?"

"Take the batteries out."

"Should we do that now?"

"No. Tomorrow. Before we leave the training house. Right now, if they track us, we'll look like we're headed back to Mojave, which is fine. It's what they'd expect. It's when we don't want them knowing where we are that we need to worry."

I thought of Anna and Maria. "If someone does try to track us through our phones after tomorrow, won't it look suspicious when they can't?"

"Probably." Cruz reached for Bear's ball and wiped it on the grass. "But someone searching for us that way looks suspicious to me." He threw the ball. "What are you worried about?"

"Needing an excuse for the council."

"We'll tell them I saw someone suspicious snooping around the training house and didn't want them following us."

Worked for me.

"Have you thought any more about Raina's letter?"

The change in topic caught me off guard, and it took me a couple seconds to shift gears. "A little. Other than the trailer part, it still doesn't make sense."

Cruz said nothing.

I squirmed. "How am I supposed to be objective about a woman who abandoned me and stole my son?"

A breeze stirred the leaves in the trees. Bear carried his ball to a shady patch of grass and lay down to lick the fuzz.

Cruz shrugged. "Maybe try to cut her some slack? Imagine yourself in her shoes."

I glared. "Imagine myself abandoning my child?"

He winced. "No, not Adam. Just someone. Try to imagine a scenario where you might abandon someone."

"I can't." I clenched my fists.

119

Cruz licked his lips and seemed to choose his next words with care. "Can't or won't?"

For a second I wasn't sure I'd heard him. But then anger roared inside me. Did he honestly think I would *ever* do to anyone what Raina had done to me? For a crazy second I thought of throwing one of the burner phones at his head.

"Can't," I said, my voice like steel. "Can you?"

"I did abandon someone once."

His words slammed into me, and my balloon of self-righteous anger deflated. "Your father."

He nodded. "What do you know about him?"

Everything I knew, I'd learned from Tomas and Kurt, and at least half of that had been conjecture. Cruz hardly ever spoke of his father.

"That he was an abusive alcoholic," I said.

Cruz snorted as if the words were understatements. From what Tomas and Kurt had told me, I supposed they probably were.

"What else?" Cruz asked.

"I know he disappeared when you were sixteen."

"Do you know how?"

I bit my lip and considered the tales I'd heard. "Tomas said you drove your father to Vegas the night you turned sixteen and left him there with a thousand dollars."

"And?"

I blew out a breath. The next part had always sounded harsh, but when I'd said as much, Tomas had shaken his head and said it wasn't harsh enough. "He said you hoped your dad would gamble away the money then end up in trouble with a loan shark and get himself killed."

The corner of Cruz's mouth twitched. "I never told him that, but it's true."

Hard to keep secrets from a psychic best friend.

"Did he tell you what happened to my dad?"

I shook my head. That was the thing about Tomas. He'd known the things in Cruz's heart because they were friends and spent time together. He didn't know about Cruz's dad because once the man disappeared, he had no bearing on Cruz. "Do you know?"

Emotions rolled across Cruz's face like shadows of clouds. "He died of a heart attack a year-and-a-half ago. A friend of his named Camille found me and told me."

"I'm sorry." It sounded so lame, but what else could I say?

"All she knew about his life before they met was that he'd had a family he said he didn't deserve and a son who'd been smart enough to dump his ass." The muscle in Cruz's jaw pulsed.

No wonder he tensed every time I said something about my mother *dumping* me. "How did they meet?"

"Rehab." Cruz looked toward the street. "When they got out, they moved to Lake Havasu and went into business. They owned a resort when he died. He left his half to my mom, sister, and me."

I sat blinking for a couple moments before I realized my mouth hung open. "Your dad left you a resort?" No wonder Cruz didn't worry about money.

"He left me *one-sixth* of a resort."

"More than my mom left me." I'd gotten a ring, a couple keys, and a shitty letter that made no sense.

"That's not the point," Cruz said.

"What is?"

A cloud slid in front of the sun, casting the ground in shade.

"Did I do the right thing when I abandoned him?"

"Of course you did! He was beating you."

"No he wasn't." Cruz swung his leg over the bench and rested his back against the table. "I'd moved out."

Cruz's dad had beaten the entire family, but according to Tomas, the man had been particularly savage toward Cruz. To protect her son, Cruz's mom had insisted he move out when he turned fifteen. He'd slept on couches, in storerooms, and in unlocked cars until Kurt found him after Cruz had broken into Enchanted Wilderness during a snowstorm. Rather than having Cruz arrested, Kurt gave him a job and a home.

"But he was beating your mom and sister."

"Yeah." Cruz nodded. "And if he'd continued doing that, I would have killed him or died trying."

My stomach turned at the thought of Cruz locked in the back of a police car. "So what you did was a kindness."

Cruz looked down and shook his head. "No. A desperate alternative."

His shoulders bowed, and I felt the heaviness of his words—the same weight I felt when we talked about him killing the gunmen at the tribal meeting. He'd done that to protect people, but he wasn't proud he'd taken two lives.

"You did the right thing."

Cruz took a deep breath and looked up. "What if your mom was desperate when she left you?"

The question jarred me. I hadn't expected this to be about Raina. And for a second—a moment—I almost pitied her. How desperate would a woman have to be to leave her baby? Even if she had left me with Gloria—even if she'd *known* Gloria and *chosen* to leave me with her—how desperate would she have to have been?

Reality slammed into me like a train at full speed.

Raina had stolen my child.

I had missed his first steps and words. First day of school. I had never held him as a baby or seen him stare up at me like I was everything.

"She took my son."

"Yeah," Cruz said softly. "She did."

Didn't he get it? Didn't he understand the pain she'd caused? My hands shook as I sat there, tears threatening the edges of my vision. Was he actually asking me to pity or empathize with her?

"She made her choice."

Blinking against the tears, I tried to return the pain to the darkest corner of my mind and hold on to the tiny bit of control I had.

I glanced at my watch. "The pictures should be ready."

Cruz didn't speak until we'd driven several blocks from the park. "I'm sorry I upset you."

Sure he was. He'd wormed his way beneath my defenses to the place where discomfort forced me to look at something new. Pressed against the passenger door, I stared out the window.

"I don't know why Raina left you. For all we know she was a crack addict."

I snorted at the degrading reference, but we both knew that wasn't true. With the exception of Anna and Maria, everyone who'd known Raina described her as nice and caring, levelheaded even. Which made it even harder to live with the fact she'd chosen to leave me.

"She took my child." My voice broke, and one of the tears I'd been fighting slid down my cheek.

"I know," Cruz said gently. "But if we're going to find him, we need to understand that letter. So whatever you have to do— whatever story you have to tell yourself to let your anger go— you need to do it. I was trying to help you get there."

I breathed deeply and wiped the remaining tears away. I didn't like a second of what he'd said. But that didn't make him wrong.

Back at Walmart, a middle-aged man with thinning hair fetched our pictures in the photo center. I stuffed them in my purse. In the parking lot, I reached for them, but Cruz hissed and nodded at the video cameras on the light posts. "Wait till we're on the highway."

The minute we reached the freeway, I pulled the snapshots from my purse and studied them side-by-side. In both, a three-legged Boxer sat on a bench outside a bakery. A child whose dangling legs and feet didn't touch the ground sat with the dog. In the first photo, the child's face and torso were hidden by the dog attempting to be a lap dog. In the second photo, the dog licked the child's face allowing me to view part of a smile and one eye squeezed shut. The child's messy, dark hair could have easily belonged to a boy or girl.

123

My heart skipped and stuttered. Could the child be Adam?

"What do they show?" Cruz asked.

"A dog and a kid on a bench."

"Do you think it's Adam?"

My heart sagged. "I don't know." Even if I could see the child in the photo clearly, would I know? In his visions, Tomas said Adam looked like me. But I suspected his visions were tainted by the guilt of knowing I couldn't see what he had.

Cruz steered us onto an off-ramp. "Can I see?"

I handed him the pictures.

My heart hadn't raced and no voice in my head said the child was mine, but Raina had included the negatives with her letter for some reason.

Cruz looked from one photo to the other. "Huh."

"Do you think it's Adam?" I doubted Cruz would be able to tell any better than I could, but I had to ask.

"Can't see enough of his face to tell. I was trying to judge from his hands, but he's too young."

I leaned over and peered at the child's pudgy fingers bunched in the dog's fur. "You think it's a boy?"

"Probably."

"Why?"

"The shirt." Cruz handed the second picture back to me. "That's a Spider-Man web."

The blue shirt had a red and blue graphic with black lines. I squinted at the lines and realized Cruz was likely right.

He studied the other photo. "Do you still have the picture Tomas sent of Gizmo?"

I blinked at the change in topic. "Yeah."

"Pull it up."

I didn't understand the reasoning, but I opened the shot of my dog on my phone.

Cruz glanced from the snapshot to my phone and back again. A smile blossomed. "Do you see it?"

"What?" I scrutinized the shot on my phone of Gizmo sitting

on a wooden bench in front of a window then the snapshot of the three-legged dog and boy...on a wooden bench...in front of a window. Realization dawned. The lettering on the window had changed from white to gold, but the words were the same. *Eureka Bakery.*

Eleven

"**H**oly shit!" Astonishment felt like sunshine streaming through my pores. Two shots of different dogs outside the same bakery. "What do you think it means?"

Cruz grimaced. "That Tomas should have picked up his phone when you called last week."

Cruz didn't swear often. Usually only when angry. I got that. I felt angry too. But the connection between the photos didn't prove anything. It might just mean Tomas had a vision of me looking at Raina's photos and wanted to prepare me. Which led me back to Cruz's point. If Tomas had picked up his damned phone and explained when I'd called, we'd know what it meant.

"I can try him again." I flipped back to my phone's home screen.

"No," Cruz said. "Don't." He handed the photo back to me.

Surprised, I lowered the phone. "Why not?"

"Too risky to talk about this over a cell phone." Cruz's shoulders drooped. "Probably wouldn't do any good. He's not returning my calls either."

I stared. "You've been trying to reach him?" With the exception of a couple terse exchanges when I'd worked for the Bluefeathers, he and Tomas hadn't talked since their falling out over two years before.

Cruz glanced at me before putting the truck in gear. "Yeah."

Usually Mr. Manners when it came to returning calls and texts, Tomas ignoring both Cruz and me wasn't a good sign. But if he were injured or missing, I would have heard. I remained the emergency contact on his phone. And if he went without calling his mom or sisters for three days, they called me. That left one other possibility. I winced before I said it. "Do you think he knows about us and that's why he's not calling? Because he's mad?"

"He knows," Cruz signaled and pulled back onto the road. "I told him."

Dumbstruck, I opened and closed my mouth several times before sound came out. "You did?" I'd assumed I'd have to do the telling since the two weren't talking.

Cruz grabbed the bag of chips from the dashboard and unrolled the top. "He's my best friend. I owed him that much."

How they could be best friends without talking was beyond me. Once again, I found myself wondering what they'd argued about two years before. I knew it had something to do with me, but nothing more.

"And no, I don't think he's mad." Cruz's jaw clenched as he pulled out a handful of chips. "He's too big an idiot."

I'd heard that comment enough to know it harkened back to the argument neither would talk about, so I let it go and tried not to focus on the bit of disappointment that came from knowing Cruz was likely right. Tomas wouldn't be mad. "So why do you think he's not calling?"

"Don't know." Cruz offered me the chip bag. "I'm sure he has a reason."

I shook my head and Cruz set the bag between us.

Tomas always had reasons; the reasons just didn't always make sense.

Cruz nodded at the photo I still held. "Looks like we're adding Eureka to our itinerary."

I fished in my purse for the zipper pocket and pulled out the photo of Raina and Regina at the bar in Blythe. I held it next to the photo of the dog where I could see part of the boy and also Tomas's picture of Gizmo. What were Raina and Tomas trying to tell me?

I stared at the images until darkness fell then I slipped them into my purse.

⊥⊤

Bear's tail thumped the backseat as Cruz turned onto the dirt road that led to the training house. Tires crunched in the dirt. When the house came into view, my muscles relaxed. It wasn't home, but it felt safe, and a familiar bed waited inside.

Steering with one hand, Cruz let out a contented sigh.

"Tired?" I asked.

"Yeah." He glanced at me. "It's been a long day."

I thought of all the driving and felt guilty I hadn't done more. "Has it been a good one at least?"

He shot me a funny look before making the turn into the driveway and braking to a stop. Engine off, he turned in his seat and studied me. "Did I spend the day with you?"

"Yes."

"Are you safe?"

"Yes."

"Have you forgiven me for making you mad?"

The memory of the park still stung, but I understood he'd been trying to help. I would heal. "Yes."

The air around us seemed to soften as a smile warmed his lips "And I'm about to share a bed with you, right?"

"Yes."

He ran a hand through my hair. "Then it's been one of my best."

Waves of warmth washed through me. Tingles filled my chest. Had Cruz just said he loved me?

"Has it been a good day for you?" he asked.

I stared at him, wondering how to reply. My heart pounded and my body screamed to move closer—to crawl into his lap or even inside him. But my desire had nothing to do with physical

128

proximity and everything to do with emotional. "Yes. Until a second ago."

He tensed and pulled back.

I caught his hand and held tight. "A second ago it became one of my best too."

His body relaxed and his eyes glistened. He smiled, and my heart filled.

I took a breath and told myself to say it. "I I—"

Bear whined and pawed the door.

Cruz and I turned to look at the dog.

"Dude." Cruz shook his head.

Bear whined again.

I heard the desperation. "We better let him out."

Bounding from the truck, Bear sniffed his way to the nearest bush and lifted his leg. He sniffed some more and marked enough spots to tell his competitors he'd resumed his residency.

By the time we trooped inside the house and dumped our bags in our room, I assumed the moment had vanished, but I was wrong. The minute we crawled into bed, Cruz pulled me close and whispered in my ear. "Say it."

"Say what?"

He rubbed his leg against mine. "What you were going to tell me in the truck."

Panic seized me and shyness set in. What if I told him and he didn't say it back? In the truck, I'd felt sure, confident. Now....

He held me tight. "Tell me."

I couldn't meet his eyes.

I'd felt it from him, hadn't I? Wasn't it what I felt now? Surely, he'd say it back.

I took a deep breath, closed my eyes, and let it out. "I love you."

He sighed and squeezed me tighter. "Luna." His fingers traced their way down my side. "I've waited four long years to hear that."

"Four?"

"You remember our first snowshoeing trip?"

"When I threw the snowshoe at you?" I'd thrown it because Cruz had laughed at me when I'd fallen and plowed a path down a hill with my face. It had been humiliating.

"Yeah." He grinned. "That's when I fell in love with you."

"When I threw something at you?"

He laughed. "No. When I went to get it. You were covered in snow and your face was scraped up, but you laughed. I turned to look at you, my heart leapt. I knew then. I could spend the rest of my life hearing you laugh and never grow tired of it."

Breath caught in my throat. "Why didn't you tell me?"

"You were with Tomas."

"Not for the last two years."

He sighed. "But you wanted to be. At least most of that time."

It was true. I had wanted that. "Not anymore."

His gaze bore into me. "Are you sure?"

I took a moment to ask myself the same question. I didn't want to lie or mislead Cruz. I didn't want to lie to myself. But I didn't need the moment. "Yes."

⁜

I was in the desert, a child again, glaring up at Jay. He held a present wrapped in gold paper with a red bow. Stomping my foot, I yelled. I wanted that present! He turned his back and climbed into the trailer.

I followed.

He began to laugh then faced me. The present was gone. In its place, he held a key. Still laughing, he put the key in his mouth and swallowed. I ran to him and beat on his chest.

"Open up! Open up!" I yelled.

When he opened his mouth, the key was gone, and a bark came out.

I forced my eyes open and sat up in bed. Bear let out a muffled bark.

I opened my mouth, and a hand clamped over it.

My gaze jerked left and there stood Cruz, eyes wide, as he

covered my mouth with one hand and held a finger to his lips with the other. His eyebrows arched and I nodded. I would be quiet. He removed his hand and buttoned a pair of jeans riding low on his hips.

"Someone's outside," he whispered.

I sucked in a breath and clenched my fists. "Who?"

"Don't know." He tossed me the clothes I'd left on top of my bag. "Get ready to go." He turned toward the door. "Bear, guard!"

The Rottweiler moved to the door and stood in front.

Carrying his hiking boots and gun, Cruz hurried out of the room and across the hall to Jay's room.

Hopping out of bed, I donned the shorts and slid my arms into the flannel shirt I'd worn in Summerhaven.

"Relax!" Cruz called. "It's Mo."

"Mo?" I glanced at the bedside clock. "It's three *a.m.*!" No wonder my head felt so foggy. Buttoning the flannel shirt, I hurried down the hallway. Bear kept stride beside me.

In the entryway, Cruz yanked the front door open. Mo stood on the other side, one fist poised to knock while her other hand aimed a key at the door.

She blinked in surprise then pushed her way inside, closing the door behind herself. "Get your stuff. Trackers are coming. We need to go."

"What?" I asked.

"Trackers. Coming here." Mo looked into the living room then moved into the dining area to check the kitchen.

"How do you know?" Cruz asked.

"My source." Mo returned from the kitchen and pulled up short. "What the hell are you standing there for? We've got ten minutes, max. Grab your shit. Let's go."

"Follow us and explain," Cruz said.

Mo rolled her eyes. "Fine."

With the exception of a couple things, most of our stuff remained packed in the two bags we'd brought into the house. Everything else remained in the truck. I shoved my sleep shirt and bra into my bag and went to the bathroom to gather the toiletries I'd left out while Mo explained she'd gotten a call from Summerhaven forty minutes before. Her source said that after the council had discovered Jay, Cruz, and me missing and searched the mountain for us, they'd sent trackers to Mojave.

"Are Cruz and I in some sort of trouble?" I asked as I jammed toiletries inside my bag.

"All I know is they're coming here and you're trying to avoid them." Mo pulled the comforter tight over the top of the bed.

We hurried down the hall and out the door with Cruz removing the batteries from our phones on the way.

"We'll have to drive blind a little while since the road can be seen from the house," Mo said as she opened the door to an old, dented Jeep Cherokee. "Turn your lights off when I do, and try not to use your brakes. If you notice someone behind you, don't worry. I've got a friend covering our tracks."

"Where are we going?" Cruz asked as he tossed our bags in the bed of the truck.

"Another friend's house," Mo said.

I settled Bear in the backseat and Cruz and I climbed in his truck.

"Do you trust her?" I asked as Mo started forward down the dirt road.

"No." A moment passed before Cruz put the truck in gear and followed. "But Jay does."

When we got to the intersection where we usually turned right to get to the main road, Mo continued forward. Cruz and I exchanged a glance. We'd walked past the intersection before, and I'd wondered where the road went. In the mile or so we'd walked, we'd only seen more desert.

Two miles later, Mo turned off her lights and Cruz followed suit.

The dirt road made a long slow curve to the left and began to climb. I looked out Cruz's window and noticed headlights in the distance—a line of five cars moving in a southerly direction. The line broke apart as I watched, and the cars pulled alongside and behind each other.

Cruz glanced out the window. "Is that the training house?"

A black patch sat in the midst of the headlights beneath the silvery glow of a nearly full moon. "I think so."

"Looks like she earned some trust," Cruz said.

Five cars to find Jay, Cruz, and me? That seemed like overkill. Surely they weren't all trackers. "Could be an elaborate hoax."

Cruz looked again. "Pretty damned elaborate."

A deep pothole bounced the truck in a jarring manner, and Cruz glued his gaze forward. The higher we climbed, the narrower and rougher the road became. We hit a couple switchbacks, and I continued to watch the training house, but after five minutes, it disappeared from view.

The lights of the Jeep lit back up and Cruz turned ours on as well. Behind us, another set of lights clicked on.

I turned to look out the window and thought I saw a pickup, but the lights made it hard to be sure. "How long's that been there?"

"Couple minutes."

I didn't like the feeling of being sandwiched between two vehicles, but neither seemed intent on running us off the road, so I took that as a good sign.

The road leveled out and made a sharp right turn before jogging left and ending at a paved road. Mo turned right onto the road, and we followed her another quarter mile before turning into a driveway belonging to a light-colored ranch house.

Pulling off the cement driveway beside the garage, Mo motioned for us to follow. The car behind us stopped. Around the back of the house, a Doughboy swimming pool sat next to an old wooden building that looked like it belonged in a horror movie.

Mo parked next to the building and jogged over to us. "I'll open the door. Park inside."

As far as I could see, there were no windows on the building. "We're hiding the truck?"

Mo nodded.

"Expecting visitors?" Cruz asked.

"You never know." Mo scurried to the building and opened the large door.

"You and Bear get out," Cruz said.

"Huh?"

He glanced in the rearview mirror. "In case you're right, and this is a hoax, I'd rather one of us was out here if the plan is to lock us in there."

Good point. I opened the door and Bear and I jumped out.

Cruz rolled forward into the building while I stood next to Mo. She had a hand on the large door, but didn't seem inclined to close it.

Cruz killed the engine and climbed out, retrieving the two bags we'd had at the training house.

A light inside the ranch house revealed someone moving around.

"Who's your friend?" Cruz asked as we followed Mo toward the back porch.

"Name's Fish," she replied. "The less you know about each other the better."

"Is this his house?" I asked.

"No."

Cruz caught my elbow and pulled me to a stop. "Whose house is it?"

Mo turned and noticed we'd lagged behind. "Walter Chino's. He was my father's mentor."

"He's not here?" I asked.

Mo retraced her steps with a sigh. "He was a seer. He's in Summerhaven with the other seers. Can we go inside now?"

Cruz didn't budge. "Why are the trackers at the training house? What are they looking for?"

"My father. You two."

"Why?" Cruz asked.

She blew out a breath and her gaze strayed to the house.

"Come inside. I'll explain what I know there."

As Mo started forward, Cruz released his grip on my elbow. I could still feel the tension rolling off him, but he motioned for me to follow her.

Inside, Fish stood at the kitchen sink refilling a water bottle. Colorful tattoos covered his arms and I could see a few peeking out beneath the neck of his shirt. He turned the water off and screwed the cap on the bottle. Turning our way, he glanced at Cruz and me before focusing on Mo. "We good?"

"Soon," she said. "How many?"

"Six cars."

"Six?" I said. "I counted five."

"You missed one." He turned back to Mo and nodded toward the front of the house. "I'll wait outside."

He left the kitchen and seconds later I heard a door open and close.

"Have a seat." Mo motioned to the wooden table and four chairs in the center of the room.

Cruz and I sat as she filled three glasses with water. Placing them on the table, she took the chair opposite me. Cruz gave a quiet whistle and pointed. Bear took up position in the kitchen doorway.

"Why are the trackers looking for us?" Cruz asked.

Mo shook her head. "Not sure. The obvious assumption is they're upset my father's prophecies are coded and want them translated. But they sent too many trackers to just be that."

"Exactly how many did they send?" I asked.

"Six cars means six sets."

A shiver ran up my spine and the hair on my arms stood up.

"The prophecies explains why they're looking for your dad, not Luna and me."

Mo rolled her eyes. "You're supposed to be with him, aren't you? All my source told me was they were coming. We're lucky I got that information in time."

"Who's your source?" I asked.

135

Mo's expression hardened and turned blank.

Jay had given me the same look whenever my questions crossed a line. I suspected it meant the same with Mo.

"I'll make some calls in the morning," she said. "Someone will know something. For now, you should get some sleep."

A simple clock with a picture of a rooster hung above the doorway between the kitchen and living room. The hands read close to four.

Cruz glanced at the clock. "Luna and I need to go to your dad's trailer at dawn. Will it be safe?"

Mo's forehead wrinkled. "The one in the canyon?"

I nodded.

Her eyebrows lifted, and she blew out a breath. "There's an ATV in the garage. You know how to drive one?"

Cruz nodded.

"Keys will be in the ignition. If you take that and don't linger, you should be fine. The trackers will head into the desert, but it'll take them time to find the trailer. I'll draw you a map to get there from here."

"Thank you," I said.

Cruz's eyes narrowed. "You're not going to ask why we're going there?"

Mo shrugged. "I assume you'll tell me if you want me to know."

"How did you know we were at the training house?" I asked.

"There's a camera outside the house with a motion sensor. It captures anyone who approaches the front of the house." She picked up her glass. "My computer's linked to its video feed. I saw you drive up."

Cruz and I sat silently.

She sighed and set her glass back down. "My father called yesterday during the dinner break. He said you might be back today and asked me to watch for you."

Cruz leaned forward on the table. "Why?"

Mo sat back and crossed her arms. "I'm supposed to help you

136

any way you need."

I blinked. "Why?"

"I don't know." She spoke through clenched teeth. "My father doesn't exactly share his motivations."

"How much do you know about our plans?" Cruz tapped his glass.

"Only that you'll be traveling and need to steer clear of trackers."

He nodded. "Can you help with that?"

"Yes."

"How?" I blurted.

She uncrossed her arms and seemed to relax. "By helping you get things."

"What kinds of things?"

"Whatever you need. Vehicles, food"—she lifted her hand and motioned around us— "shelter."

"Information?" Cruz asked.

"Sometimes."

I took a drink of water. "How do you get those things?"

Mo turned her frank gaze on me. "Does it matter?"

"Yes." I didn't want to drive around in a stolen car after all.

"I don't steal, if that's your concern. I borrow and barter."

There was a catch. I could hear it in her tone. "Will the person you borrow things from *know* you borrowed them?"

Her eyebrows arched. "Sometimes."

I looked at Cruz. He tipped his head. It was something.

⌁

The sun had just peeked above the horizon when Cruz and I mounted the ATV and left the garage. We'd seen no sign of Fish or his car, and Mo had been passed out on the couch when we crept by. Good to her word, she'd left a map on the table and keys in the ignition. Cruz drove while I sat behind him, holding his waist and hoping I didn't fall asleep and tumble off the back. The hour of rest he and I had gotten after our talk with Mo hadn't been enough.

137

Mo's map took us onto the road we'd driven up the night before then onto paths too small for cars but perfect for horses and ATVs. I tried to watch for trackers, but my eyes kept closing in spite of my effort.

We reached the trailer in twenty minutes and found it gloriously untended. Cruz used Raina's key to open the door. Inside, the trailer looked exactly as it had days before.

Handing me the key ring, he nodded toward the cupboard.

I knelt down and crawled beneath the table, saying a silent prayer, before inserting the smaller key. It worked. The cupboard door swung open and darkness stared back at me.

I looked at Cruz. "Did you bring a flashlight?"

Cruz had never been a Boy Scout, but he lived by their motto. Reaching into his left pocket, he pulled out a miniature Maglite and handed it to me.

I shined it into the cupboard. Happily, no glowing eyes stared back, just the edge of a shoebox and a small book. Knocking away cobwebs, I pulled out the items and handed them to Cruz.

"We should go," he said.

Neither of us moved as we stood staring at the box and book lying on the table.

"Quick peek, then we go," I said.

"Fine."

I reached for the book while Cruz pulled the lid off the shoebox.

Handwriting and black marker filled the pages of the book. The one line I allowed myself to read said something about the temperature dropping. "Journal," I said.

"Letters," Cruz replied.

Inside the box, an army of envelopes marched in a line. I pulled one up and froze. It was addressed to Gloria in Kansas City.

"What the hell?" I pulled up another envelope and another. They were all addressed to Gloria. "Why would Raina have letters addressed to Gloria?"

Cruz tipped his head. "Same reason she had the Leader's Ring?"

It seemed odd, but I couldn't think of another viable explanation. I'd never known Gloria to receive or keep letters. I glanced at the upper left corners. Each bore a name but no return address. Rainelle Trujillo, R. Zepeda, Ann Onestar. That name seemed vaguely familiar.

Cruz touched my hand. "You need to look later. We've gotta go."

As much as my fingers itched to pull out a letter and start reading, he was right. I jammed the envelopes in the front of the box, and Cruz lifted the lid to replace it on top. Something colorful flashed underneath.

"Wait." Taking the lid from him, I turned it over and stared down at a photo of a child with a sheet over her head holding an empty pillowcase that hours later would be filled with Halloween candy.

"What?"

I nodded at the photo. "That's me."

His mouth opened as he looked from the picture to me and back. Then he took the lid, stuffed it on the box, and scooped it up along with the journal. Grabbing my arm, he led me out of the trailer. I locked the door while he secured our booty to the rack on back of the ATV.

As we bounced along, climbing the hill back to Walter's house, I felt behind myself to make sure both items remained on board. At the same time, my mind wandered back to that Halloween when I'd been seven and allowed to go trick-or-treating for the first and only time. Beneath that sheet, only my eyes and oversized red tennis shoes could be seen. But I'd worn the biggest smile I'd ever worn when Gloria snapped that photo.

At Walter's house, Cruz pulled the ATV into the garage.

"Tell me about the picture," he said when we climbed off.

I told him everything. The smile, the trick-or-treating, the promise I'd made to Gloria that I'd stay covered all night or we'd come home.

Everything had gone well until I'd tripped over my second-hand shoes, stepped on the sheet, and it had come off my head. Gloria had grabbed my hand and marched me home immediately. She'd always been a woman of her word.

"Why did she want you hidden?" Cruz asked.

I shrugged. "It was Gloria." For most of my life, those three words had answered so many questions, but now my mind delved deeper. "Maybe she worried someone was watching me?"

Cruz grimaced.

I glanced at the box and book. "Do you think I'll find answers in these?"

"Some."

I stared at the items knowing what he didn't say. In addition to answers, I'd probably find more questions.

Picking up the box and journal, I hugged them to my chest. "I'd like to go to the bedroom and start reading."

Cruz nodded. "I'll run interference."

Dressed in the same clothes she'd worn the night before, Mo sat at the kitchen table, a cup of coffee steaming in front of her. The muffled sound of talking came from the phone pressed to her ear. She nodded at us and motioned toward the coffee pot on the counter.

Cruz touched my shoulder. "I'll bring you a cup."

I smiled a thank you and hurried down the hall to the bedroom Cruz and I had used.

Kicking off my shoes, I closed the door and got comfortable on the bed. Setting the journal aside, I pulled out the letters I'd held earlier.

Cruz entered carrying two cups of coffee. He placed one on the nightstand beside me. "You okay?"

I smiled up at him. "Yeah."

He'd been present when I'd opened the letters from Raina and Regina, and I'd been okay with that. But those letters had been written to me. These were written to Gloria.

"I'm gonna need some time," I said.

"Okay." He kissed the top of my head and left.

My first sip of coffee made my tongue pucker and my mouth turn down. Mo liked her coffee strong. Returning the cup to the nightstand, I picked up the three letters.

The envelope from Rainelle Trujillo was postmarked Silver City, New Mexico. R. Zepeda's letter was addressed to Gloria in Kansas City and postmarked Weston, Missouri. Odd. I remembered Weston and Kansas City being less than an hour apart. Why write a letter? The third envelope, from Ann Onestar, whose writing strongly resembled Rainelle Trujillo's and R. Zepeda's, came from Boise, Idaho.

Really just an index card, the letter from Rainelle Trujillo said:

G,

Made it. I miss you.

-Rainelle

I set the card aside and pulled out the letter from R. Zepeda.

G,

Thank you for the pictures. I can't believe how fast she is growing. I know you said like a weed, but she looks more like a wildflower.

The dreams are a concern. I will leave right away and draw attention from you. As long as they don't get worse, stay for the two weeks. Leave when L's play is over.

A memory flashed through my mind. Something distant. A Christmas play for school. How old had I been? Seven? Eight maybe? I checked the date on the postmark. Seven. My part hadn't been big. I'd been one of several elves in Santa's workshop, but my teacher had given me a speaking line. "Look everyone, it's Santa!"

At the end of the performance, after all the bows, I'd met Gloria in the audience. She'd hugged me and told me she was proud then walked me out. At the edge of the lot, past all the other cars, I spied our station wagon, packed and hitched to our trailer. I'd cried for thirty minutes on that drive out of town.

Shaking the memory from my mind, I looked again at the letter.

When you land, send the address to GD at 5.
-Rina

What was GD at 5?

I sipped coffee, wincing at the bitter taste, and turned to the letter from Ann Onestar. It had been sent from Boise to Reno in December when I'd been twelve.

G,

It is snowing here. Has been for days. It reminds me of home.

I saw the neighbor's children making snow angels yesterday and thought of you. Have you and L made snow angels yet? Does she like the snow? Is she excited about Christmas?

I skimmed through the melancholy letter then returned it to the box and pulled out the second to last envelope. It had been sent to Berkeley and postmarked Ipswich, Massachusetts. The envelope said R. Gonzalez, and the letter was signed Rhea.

Rhea. I knew that name. I'd seen it written on a piece of paper along with several other names Jay had given me. Some of Raina's aliases, he'd said. Desperately, I tried to remember some of the others. R-Ray-Rainette! Raylene. Perez. With shaking fingers, I yanked out envelopes, flipped through pages, combing through names. I found them all along with at least a dozen others.

An avalanche rumbled inside my chest. Yesterday I'd struggled to accept that Gloria might have known Raina and never told me. But this was worse. They hadn't just known each other, they'd been in contact my entire childhood. The betrayal was absolute.

Why? Why hadn't Gloria told me? Why all the lies and secrecy? Why had she allowed me to think my mother knew nothing about me and didn't give a damn? What purpose had it served?

I ran a finger over the tops of the envelopes. There had to be close to a hundred. If the two women who'd been my mothers— one by birth and the other by practice—had been this close, why hadn't they raised me together? Why had they left me to believe I'd been abandoned? Left like a piece of trash?

But even as the question pounded my mind, the answer floated in too. I hadn't been left to think that. In fact, I'd been discouraged. Gloria had never used the words abandoned or left when discussing the matter. She'd always said placed. I'd been placed in her car, wrapped in a blanket with obvious care. And she'd insisted the note and ring left with me were signs I'd been loved—that whoever had placed me there must not have had a choice.

I wanted to scream. Nothing about it made sense. Why had Raina left the Neme-i? Why had she split her family in half and gone into hiding? Why take me then leave me? What purpose had it all served?

There were too many questions. Too much left unanswered. Frustration and anger tangled inside me. I jammed the letters back in the box. I didn't care about dates or placement. But when I got to the bottom of the pile and picked up the last letter, the one that had been second from the back, one word caught my eye and made me stop. Pregnant.

Twelve

I looked at the postmark on the letter's envelope and my anger evaporated. The letter had been mailed around the time I'd told Gloria I was pregnant.

G,

Please forgive me for taking so long to answer your letter. I was stunned when I received it, and I won't lie, I was angry. But not at you. Never at you. You have done more for L and me than I ever had a right to ask.

Pregnant at 17. My God. Is she sure she wants to keep the child? She is so young.

I agree with you. The decision should be hers. No matter what she chooses I will support her. But if she keeps the child, everything will change. We will have to tell her.

This is very important. Even if she doesn't want to tell you who the father is, or (God forbid) can't, you must nail her down on how far along she is. Halfway through her second trimester, about the time the baby begins to kick, he or she will begin putting out energy. No matter how buried L's gift is, when the child's energy combines with hers, it will be a beacon for anyone searching. They will begin moving in. You will have to move. Do NOT wait for the nightmares. If you do, it will be too late.

If she chooses to keep the baby, send me the date, and we will meet as we planned so many years ago.

Until then, I am with you and her, supporting you every step of the way.
-Rhea

I read the letter again, paying special attention to the paragraph about moving. I remembered sitting with Gloria in Berkeley, both of us with our hands on my stomach feeling the baby kick and laughing as he did.

And I remembered her dreams. Gloria had had terrible nightmares. They seemed to come and go. Returning off and on over the years. And every time they returned, we moved. They had returned in Berkeley.

I looked at the box. One letter remained. I felt confident I knew what it would say, but I had to be sure.

G,
Leave now. They are on to you.
I will do what I can to draw the attention, but you must leave. There is no time to waste.
Shiprock. Saturday.
My love to you and L,
Rhea

The letter had been mailed ten days before our accident.

Numbness engulfed me as I placed the envelope back in the box.

We'd stayed in Berkeley as long as we had because I'd hoped Tomas would return and I could tell him I carried our child. Gloria had talked about leaving a month before we did. But I'd begged and cried to stay until she'd relented. Was I the reason she was dead?

In the end, I'd agreed to the move because Gloria said we'd go to Taos and look for Tomas. Maybe she'd meant that. I would never know. Apparently she'd intended to go to Shiprock first.

Could that be why we'd gotten such a late start leaving the motel in Arizona that day? Had she planned the trip so we'd drive through Gallup in the middle of the night when I would likely be asleep? She could turn north before we got to Albuquerque that way, and I'd never know or be able to throw a fit.

Something warm and wet hit my hand, and I realized I was crying. I wiped a couple tears but they kept coming so I wrapped my arms around myself and let them fall.

All my life I had wanted answers. But these answers hurt worse than the questions. I eyed the box of letters and the stack I'd pulled out then hastily shoved back in the middle. With a sigh, I pulled the letters back out and started the painstaking process of refiling them in chronological order. There were answers in this box, and if I had to go through the heartache of getting them, I wanted to do it in order.

As I replaced the envelopes I began to notice a correlation between the places I'd lived with Gloria and the postmarks on the envelopes. When Raina's letter came from Blythe, we'd lived in Los Angeles. When we'd been in Sacramento, she'd been in Folsom. Tahoe; Carson City. Las Cruces; Silver City. She'd never been far away. Had she come around to visit sometimes, and I just hadn't known?

But all that changed the year I turned ten and we moved to Hemet. The year I'd begun training with Jay. From then on, Raina kept her distance. We'd lived in California; her letter came from Washington. We'd lived in Nevada; she'd been in Idaho. At the very end, when we'd been in Berkeley, she'd been in Massachusetts. Why had things changed? What had been different? My energy, obviously. But hadn't Jay buried that when he'd buried my gift?

My head hurt as I tried to reason it through. I just didn't know enough. I needed to talk with Jay. But he wasn't here. Who else could I speak with about the energy? Who else would know the answers and could be trusted to keep my questions secret? Mo wasn't a teacher. I doubted she knew as much about the energy as Jay. I doubted anyone understood it like Jay. But there had to be someone I could talk with. Jay had given us a list of places to go, clan members to see. Perhaps one of them could help.

I put the lid back on the box and shoved the journal into my purse. Reading could be done on the road. My question for Mo had to be answered now.

Jay's list sat folded inside Cruz's bag. I pulled it out and grabbed my coffee mug.

In the kitchen, Mo stood at the counter pouring a fresh cup of coffee. I wondered if she had any stomach lining left.

"Where's Cruz?" I asked.

"Transferring your things from the truck to the Jeep." Leaning against the counter, she blew across the surface of the rotgut.

"We're taking your Jeep?"

"You're taking Fish's Jeep."

"I thought he left."

"He did." She sipped the coffee. "He'll be back."

I started to ask whose car Fish had driven the night before but stopped, unsure I wanted to know. Instead I asked, "Do you always drink your coffee this strong?"

"Yep."

Clearly her stomach lining was superior to mine.

Carrying my mug to the sink, I washed and dried it and returned it to the cupboard she indicated. "I have a question."

Mo lowered her cup to the counter.

"I need to talk to someone about our energy and how it works. But I need the conversation to stay confidential. Your dad gave us this list of places to visit. I'm wondering if you could recommend someone in one of these areas?"

She took the list and read.

The sliding glass door opened and Cruz stepped in. Seeing me, he raised an eyebrow.

I waffled my hand back and forth.

He nodded. "Did Mo tell you about the truck?"

"Yeah."

Still studying the list, she moved to the table.

Cruz's brow furrowed when he caught sight of the paper.

"I have a question about our energy," I said. "I'm hoping she can recommend someone to answer it."

"Someone who'll keep it quiet." Mo pointed at the paper. "Here."

Cruz and I walked over and stood on either side of her.

"There's a woman who lives in this area. She should be able to help you."

Mo moved to the counter and pulled a pen and pad of paper from the drawer. They made a *smack* as she tossed them on the table in front of me. "The lady's name is Catherine Rivers."

Reaching for the pen, I wrote the name and number Mo dictated.

She took a sip of coffee. "Unless you need anything else, you should get going. The trackers will be here at some point. Best you're gone before then."

Cruz and I retreated to the bedroom where I gave him a brief description of the letters I'd read. He listened and nodded without interrupting.

"I think I need to read them in order." I shouldered my bag and reached for the shoebox.

"Makes sense." Cruz remained still, his bag at his feet. "You okay?"

I bit my lip. "Maybe?"

He pulled me in and wrapped his arms around me.

I tried to lean into him, but the bag on my shoulder made it awkward.

He held me anyhow. "I know this isn't easy."

I took a deep breath and tried to keep from shaking.

"You're the strongest, bravest person I know."

I stepped back and stared at him. "Are you kidding? I'm not strong or brave. I'm a great big cream puff, and I'm terrified every time I think I won't find Adam."

148

"But you keep trying."

"I don't have a choice."

"Sure you do," he said. "You always have a choice. Yours are the reason I love you."

My heart caught and a warm tingle worked its way through my body.

Cruz kissed my lips then released me and reached for his bag. "Let's go. We've got a long drive."

⚔

The map put the drive to Eureka at close to twelve hours. The map didn't know squat about Southern California traffic. We lost an hour just getting out of the county.

As Cruz inched along, I sucked on coffee and wolfed down a breakfast burrito. The shock from what I'd read earlier still stung, and I found myself unable to open the box and read more of the letters. I would get to them, but I needed time. So I tried the journal.

The cover appeared to have once been decorated with brown and yellow flowers but now looked like water, coffee, and God knew what else had been spilled on it. Inside, the writing matched that of the letters. At the top of each entry sat a day of the week and what I guessed had once been a date, but had since been scribbled out or covered over with permanent marker. Several things had been treated to that sort of redaction.

Weds. ▅▅▅▅▅

Oh God. What have I done? What am I supposed to do? I'm so sorry. Daddy, forgive me. Please! Show me what to do. God help me!

I wasn't sure what to make of the first entry. But a part of me ached as I read it. Memories of leaving the hospital following my coma flooded my mind. I had been desperate—not knowing what to do or where to go. I'd never prayed much before that, but I'd prayed like hell afterward, asking for anyone or anything to help

149

me find my way.

Sat. ███

We're staying in a hotel. Jasmine cried all night. I think she senses my fear.

Oh Anna. My beautiful girl. What must you be thinking? Are you crying too?

You weren't supposed to be with your grandmother! You were supposed to be home! What was your father thinking? Damn it. How can I protect you?

Raina had intended to take Anna too? Not just me? Wouldn't that be nice for my sister to know.

Sun. ███

We moved again yesterday. So many hotels these past couple weeks, I don't even know where we are. They are looking for us. I can feel them. I have to find a place where Jasmine and I can stay. ███ gave me money, but it will run out. I'll have to get a job. Doing what??? I've never had a job.

I must keep Jasmine safe and get to Anna. I can't protect her if she's not with me.

For now at least, the prophecies are safe. No harm will come to the girls while that holds true. At least I've been able to give them that. Please God, let that last.

Prophecies? Which prophecies? All of them? Or just some? And how had Raina kept them from hurting Anna and me?

"Cruz?"

He glanced at me.

"Do you remember talking with Hideo at some point and him telling us Raina's leaving affected the tribe's ability to make changes?"

Cruz seemed to consider. "Something about the council not

being able to vote for changes in tribal policies."

"Because they didn't have a leader, right?" Was that what Raina meant about keeping the prophecies safe?

"Yeah. Why?"

I flipped to the beginning of the journal and reread everything to Cruz then continued on.

"Thurs., ▮▮▮▮

They're getting closer. ▮▮▮▮ called last night and told me I had less than an hour to clear out of the hotel before we were found. I grabbed Jasmine and everything I could hold and ran. I left so much behind.

We rode a city bus for five hours and slept on it in the bus yard. Thank God the driver and watchman weren't Neme-i. I had to use my gift to keep us safe. I know it was risky. But I had no choice. We had nowhere to go.

Mon., ▮▮▮▮

Today a man I've never met brought us food, money, and clothes. I cried when he handed me the suitcase and told me what it contained.

He drove us to the train station and told me he didn't want to know where I chose to go. He said it wouldn't be safe for him. I hugged him before he left and asked why he would do this for someone he'd never met. He said ▮▮▮▮▮▮▮▮▮▮▮▮▮▮▮▮▮▮▮.

I don't even know if he was Neme-i. No matter what he is, Jasmine and I will forever be in his debt.

Fri., ▮▮▮▮

The council called ▮▮▮▮ for inquiry. No one knows where the meeting will be held. ▮▮▮▮ has been gone for several days. It is no longer safe to contact either of them. It's no longer safe to contact anyone. We are on our own.

I am going back and crossing out all names, dates, and places. If this diary falls into the wrong hands, I don't want it used to hurt those who have helped us. If something happens to me and this should end up in the hands of my children, please know everything I've done has been to protect you.

I turned the page, but the next one was blank as was the one after that and all the rest. What had made her stop writing?

I flipped through the pages once again.

"What?" Cruz asked.

"The rest of the pages are blank."

"All of them?"

"Yeah."

He quirked an eyebrow. "So Raina's leaving had something to do with the prophecies?"

"Looks like."

"And she didn't leave with the intention of leaving you or Anna?"

"Maybe not." After twenty-eight years of believing I'd been dumped on purpose, accepting something different felt like putting on someone else's skin.

"Wonder what changed." He glanced at the shoebox nestled between us on the seat. I could read the question in his expression.

"You think the letters might explain it?"

He shrugged. "Maybe."

I couldn't argue his point, but I had my doubts. The letters had been written after the fact. And from what I'd read already, they were more about day-to-day life than past decisions. But I did need to read them. And maybe it would be easier with Cruz listening. At least that way, I wouldn't be alone.

In the backseat, Bear let out a loud yawn. Standing, he turned a tight circle before lying down again.

I pulled out the first letter and read it then returned it to the box and read the next and the next. With each new letter, I pointed out the dates on the postmark as well as the proximity between the letter's destination and origin. Cruz listened without asking questions.

The letters often thanked Gloria for pictures and drawings. Sometimes they talked about the weather or included a brief mention of work. Occasionally there were answers to unknown questions and once in a while, advice: yes, the story of the First Girls would be okay, but not to explain it too much or give it a title. No, standing in line to visit Santa at a mall would expose us to too many people with nothing better to do than stare at others. At the end of some letters would come the odd scribble I'd seen before, GD at 7 or GD at 1. There didn't seem to be an order to the numbers, but they'd clearly meant something to Gloria and Raina.

By the time we stopped for lunch, I'd made it halfway through the box and reached the year I'd turned nine. We picked up hamburgers and drove to a rest stop where Bear could stretch his legs and sniff around.

"They're not telling us much, are they?" Seated on a bench, I worked to suck strawberry milkshake through a narrow straw while Bear explored the weed-choked patch of dirt around us.

"I don't know." Cruz dipped three French fries in a pool of ketchup. "I'm curious about what they don't say."

"What do you mean?"

The French fries disappeared into his mouth and he took a moment to chew. To the right, Bear took a step beyond the twelve-foot radius Cruz had deemed okay, and Cruz made a tcht sound. Immediately Bear returned to the safe zone. I really needed to learn to make that sound.

Cruz tipped his head. "People usually talk about their lives when they write letters." He took a bite of hamburger and chewed. "These are all about you. It's like one side of a conversation between two parents discussing their kid."

He was right. It was exactly like that. Had I actually had two mothers growing up? One had just been invisible?

We said little else until we were back in the Jeep, cruising north on I-5 through the farmlands of California's central valley.

153

"G,

Thank you for your letter. It couldn't have come at a better time. I've been feeling blue, and your words cheered me immensely.

No, I don't think she's stealing. I imagine she was given the things you found. It is a natural step in her coming of age. It means her ability is coming through. It also means it's time to find J. I know that means another move, but you can't delay. Her ability will continue to grow stronger. It will be best for him to work with her before she realizes what she is doing.

Do as we discussed. When you get hold of J, tell him the story we planned and make the request. He'll have his work cut out for him to reverse what she is already doing, but if anyone can do it, it's him. I told you how the teacher reacted when J helped me. He is as close to a miracle worker as you'll find."

I stopped reading and checked the date on the postmark. The letter had been written around the time Gloria had found the gifts from my classmates under my mattress and moved us to the desert.

The letter J had to refer to Jay. I wondered if that's all his name had ever been. Just an initial used to hide his identity. Had I simply heard it and assumed the J-a-y? I'd never seen it written anywhere.

I continued reading letters all the way to San Francisco when I finally reached the last one. By that time, my throat was dry and my voice sore. I offered to drive, but Cruz told me to rest. When it came to driving, Cruz found a zone and stayed there. About thirty miles south of Eureka, we reached Humboldt Redwoods State Park. Cruz pulled off the highway and turned down smaller and smaller roads.

"We're not going all the way to Eureka?" I asked.

"Don't know where we'd stay if we did." Cruz turned right onto a road too narrow for two cars. "We'll camp here tonight and finish the drive in the morning."

I tried to remember the last time I'd slept in a tent. It seemed a lifetime ago. To some degree it had been. Back before I'd heard the names Jasmine or Raina Bluefeather or known my heritage. Back when I'd thought my son as lost as the foster mother who'd taken him.

Sandwiched between Cruz and Bear, I fell asleep listening to the profound quiet of the forest. In one way, it was bliss. And yet, even in that bliss I missed Gizmo and knew a part of me would never be whole until I found my son.

⽕

Fog filled the morning, hugging the Victorian buildings of downtown Eureka. "Cute," I said as we cruised down a street.

Cruz grunted.

I took that to mean he agreed, or might have if it hadn't been for the quarter-mile visibility he'd struggled to find his bearings in while driving us out of the forest.

We found a café and ordered coffee and breakfast sandwiches then asked for directions to Eureka Bakery where, Cruz said, we'd been told we could get the best donuts in town. The girl seemed to think another bakery offered better donuts but gave us the directions anyhow.

Taking our coffee and breakfast to go, we headed down the road, and Cruz found a parking spot across from the bakery.

Butterflies jetted inside my tummy as the little bit of breakfast I'd eaten turned to lead. What would we find? Surely the pictures from Raina and Tomas couldn't be a coincidence. There had to be a reason for our coming here.

Cruz killed the ignition and I reached for my door handle.

He caught my hand and squeezed. "Wait."

"For what?" The answer to my son's location might lie across the street.

"To be sure this isn't a trap."

Incredulity filled me. "Tomas wouldn't send us into a trap."

"No, he wouldn't," Cruz agreed. "Can you say the same for

Raina?"

I couldn't. Though my hand fell away from the door, the desire to cross the street remained a red-hot ember inside me. "How long do we wait?"

"Until it feels safe."

How the hell long would *that* take?

I jiggled my foot and gnawed my nails while staring at the glass front of the light-yellow building. Intermittently, I tore off pieces of my ham and egg breakfast sandwich and ate them before jamming the whole thing back in the bag and throwing it on the dashboard. By the time I resorted to cracking my knuckles, twenty-eight minutes had passed, and Cruz deemed it safe.

We entered the shop to the tinkle of a little bell above the door. The scent of sugar and pastry filled the air and despite what I'd already eaten, my stomach growled as I gazed at the cases of donuts and éclairs. My eyes zeroed in on the filled pastries, and my tongue parked itself on my lips.

Cruz chuckled. "We'll order some."

A red-haired woman wearing a long white apron stepped out from a back room and greeted us with a friendly smile. "How can I help you?"

I took a step toward the counter, and my mouth went dry. What should I say? *Do you know where my son is* didn't seem appropriate.

Taking a breath, I told myself to calm down. I'd been raised by Gloria. I knew how to spin a lie. I opened my mouth, and an order for a dozen donuts came out.

The woman reached for a pink pastry box.

I sighed. "Let's start with four lemon filled." I had to do better than that. I swallowed as a lie finally sprang to mind. "Um, I recently came across a photo taken outside this shop amongst my mother's things. She's not with us anymore so she can't tell me who the child in the photo is. I'm hoping you can?"

The woman smiled and wiped a hand on her apron. "I'll try."

I slid the photo across the counter. Cruz sauntered to the wall to peruse a bulletin board.

Picking up the photo, the woman smiled with recognition. "That's Jacob."

"Jacob?" Could Jacob be Adam?

The woman returned the photo. "The owner's grandson."

"Owner?" Did she mean Raina? Were my son and mother living in this town?

"Barbara Stinton. She and her husband opened the bakery back in"—the woman screwed up her face and stared at the ceiling—"nineteen—eighty-six, I think." Satisfied with her statement, she smiled waiting for the next part of my order.

"Four jelly filled, two éclairs, and two frosted with sprinkles," I said. "Is she possibly in? The owner?"

The smile fell. "You just missed her. She stepped out to get her hair done. She should be back in a couple hours."

I nodded as the ember inside me sputtered. A couple more hours before I'd know if the child in the photo was Adam.

"If you come back, you should be able to talk to her. I'm guessing she knew your mom?"

"That's my guess too," I said. "Thank you." I tucked the photo inside my purse and started to turn, but looked back as another idea seized me. "I have no idea how long ago the picture was taken. The boy—Jacob?" I checked to be sure I had the name right "—looks like he's about four or five. How old is he now?"

The woman grinned. "Just celebrated his seventh birthday. Got a new bat and ball and already broke a window."

She laughed and I forced myself to laugh with her as the ember inside me died.

Gloria's *guesstimate* of my birthday had allowed me to go through life passing as someone three months younger than I actually was. No one had ever questioned it. Least of all me. But no way would a ten-year-old boy pass as seven. The child in the picture couldn't be Adam.

I stepped back on wooden legs.

"Luna?" Cruz motioned for me to join him.

157

I stumbled over. He nodded at the bulletin board. A rainbow of flyers advertised sales and local events. A band called Burgundy Sky would be playing at Morton's on Saturday, and Mary's Beadwork had all crystals marked down twenty percent. My gaze swept the board before returning to Cruz. I didn't know what he wanted me to see, and I didn't care. He tipped his head again, angling his gaze toward the bottom left side. I narrowed my search to that section of the board. A local college student offered responsible, in-home dog sitting services, and The Carpet Guys were running a two-for-one special. I glanced again at Cruz. His gaze hadn't wavered, but this time he added a finger jab in the direction of a photo with curling edges dangling from the bottom corner of the board.

With a sigh, I smoothed back the corners of the photo and froze.

The boy named Jacob was once again featured sitting on the bench outside the bakery, but this time another boy sat with him—an older dark-haired boy with a dimple in his left cheek like Tomas and eyes that looked like mine.

Shivers ran up my spine and tickled my scalp. Warm tendrils circled my heart. Something inside me whispered words I didn't understand but emotions I did. That child was mine.

My eyes jerked toward Cruz as I shifted closer to the bulletin board. I wanted the picture. I *needed* that picture. It would be leaving with me.

Cruz nodded. "I'll distract her."

He turned on his full-wattage smile and stepped away. "What did she order?" He jerked his thumb at me. "Did she leave out my crullers?"

The redhead glanced up, and her mouth fell open.

"She always pretends to forget them. She thinks it's funny." Cruz leaned against the counter, blocking my view of the woman and her view of me.

Quick as lightning, I snatched the photo off the bulletin board and slid it into my purse.

The woman mumbled unintelligibly.

I walked over to Cruz.

He shot me a playful glare. "Trying to deny me my crullers again."

I shrugged. I didn't even know what a cruller was.

The woman licked her lips, helpless against the onslaught of Cruz's testosterone. "Should I put two of the other donuts back?"

"No." Cruz winked at her. "We'll take them all."

Thirteen

I couldn't stop staring at the photo as Cruz drove around Eureka, searching for a place to make copies.

"You think it's him?" Cruz asked.

"Yes." I didn't think; I knew. Somewhere deep inside, I *knew.* He had Tomas's dimple and jaw. He had my eyes and nose. No one could look that much like the two of us and not be related—could they?

"Are you sure we have to put it back?" I asked. I didn't want to let the photo go for anything.

"Unless you want them to realize this picture was more important to you than the one you showed them."

I didn't want that. On the off-chance trackers came through here, I didn't want to risk anyone telling them about a snapshot that meant so much I'd stolen it.

At an office supply store, Cruz pried the picture from my fingers and made two copies of it. The minute the copies came out, I snatched them up and stared at them—stared at my beautiful child. I cradled the images against my chest as we walked to the Jeep.

Cruz didn't put the keys in the ignition as he sat in the driver's seat.

"What?"

He grimaced. "I don't recommend getting attached to the picture."

"Why not?"

He spoke in a soft voice. "It might not be him."

"Of course it's him! Who else could it be?"

He took the copies I jabbed in his direction and nodded. "I'll admit, the child looks like you and Tomas, but that doesn't guarantee it's Adam."

A part of me knew Cruz was right. An hour before, I'd thought the boy in the other picture might be Adam. But I hadn't felt this certain.

"If you get too attached to this photo, and we look for *this* child, we could overlook the real Adam."

The logical part of me understood the validity of Cruz's point. But logic played no part in this. This was visceral. It existed in my core. Still, I forced myself to take a breath, turn the photo over, and lower it to my lap. My heart ached as I did it. Cruz laid the copies face-down between us.

"Now what?" I said.

He caressed my shoulder. "Let's go somewhere Bear can run."

We ended up at the beach, eating donuts and drinking coffee while Bear ran in and out of the surf, chasing the ball Cruz threw for him. That whole time, the photo stayed in the Jeep, and that whole time my entire being ached to hold it.

After I looked back at the vehicle for about the hundredth time, Cruz came and sat beside me. Bear settled behind us.

"It's still there," Cruz said.

True. The vehicle remained parked where we'd left it, and I supposed the photo did too.

"What are you planning to say at the bakery?" he asked.

I shrugged. "Same story."

"What will you say your mom's name was?"

Good question. Given the number of aliases Raina had used, choosing the right one would be like identifying the card someone drew from a full deck. "Probably go with the truth." Raina had left me the photo showing the bakery after all. She'd wanted me to come here. It stood to reason she might have told the truth to the owner like she had Regina.

"If this woman doesn't know anything and can't point us anywhere, where do you want to go next?"

Behind me, Bear lay down, his side a comforting warmth against my tailbone. The fog had burned off, but after living in Mojave for a month, Eureka felt downright cold and the sweatshirt and jeans I wore weren't cutting it.

"I'm thinking we stick to our plan and go to Idaho," I said. "But I'd like to stop in Nevada and talk to that woman Mo told us about."

"Is she on the way?"

"Close. About an hour east."

Cruz tipped his head. "Not bad. If we stayed the night, we could also see the person Jay wants you to visit."

I nodded as I watched the waves rolling in. How had Jay put it? Keep the council thinking I was a good little leader-elect.

⌗

The donut selection had dwindled significantly by the time we returned to the bakery. We still had a half dozen in our box and would have had more if I hadn't made the mistake of sharing one of mine with Bear. After he'd had a taste, he'd wanted more and managed to sneak a jelly-filled out of the box before we'd realized it. As we stood inside the bakery, he sat outside tethered to the bench with his tail between his legs. Cruz really liked jelly-filled donuts.

At the tinkle of the bell, the woman who'd helped us that morning stepped out of the back.

"Ah, you're back." The smile that lit her face felt genuine. "Give me a minute." She ducked into the back again, and Cruz took advantage of her absence to return the photo to the bulletin board. He stood at my side by the time the woman reappeared with an older woman in tow.

I'd expected the owner to be short and round, not thin and striking. With shoulder-length gray hair and large silver hoop earrings usually worn by younger women, the owner looked more like a retired model than someone's grandma.

At the sight of me, she started, her eyes growing wide with wonder.

I held out my hand. "I'm—"

"Rae's daughter." She took my hand. "Luna."

Maybe I should have been surprised she knew my name. But I was getting used to it.

"I'm Barbara," she said, "Barbara Stinton." Her gaze jumped to Cruz and her eyebrows arched.

I got the feeling she wondered if she should say anything more in front of him. I stepped back to give her a better view. "This is Cruz Whitehorse, my...." I froze. What the hell was Cruz to me now? Way more than a friend, but could I call him my *boyfriend*? Would he be okay with that?

I glanced at Cruz. He cocked an eyebrow at me, clearly amused by my discomfort.

"Ah." Mrs. Stinton nodded. "I understand."

Thank God someone did.

"Do you have a few moments?" I asked. "We'd like to talk with you about a picture."

She offered to take us into her office, but Cruz wanted to stay near Bear—or more likely, keep Bear near me.

We ended up sitting on the bench in front of the shop with Cruz and Bear flanking us on either side.

"Your dog seems very nice," she said after Bear had given her a thorough sniff. "It's too bad my grandson isn't here."

"Your grandson," I repeated, "Jacob?"

"Yes." She smiled. "He loves dogs."

I slid Raina's image of Jacob and the three-legged dog from my purse. "This is the picture I wanted to ask you about. Is that Jacob's dog?"

She took the photo and glanced at it. "No. That's Harley. He lives with a man up the street. Oliver used to walk him. He loved Oliver."

"Oliver?" I asked.

CARPER SMITH

She turned to face me, her gray eyes boring into mine. "Your son."

My heart leapt. Everything else ceased to exist. "You…you know my son?"

Cruz tensed. His gaze snapped to mine. I understood. I'd been trying to hide the fact I had a child for his safety, yet I'd just admitted his existence to a perfect stranger. It might have been a mistake, but I couldn't help myself. For the first time, I was speaking with someone who claimed to know my son—someone who offered a tangible link to him still being alive.

"Yes."

"How do you know he's my child?"

"He's Rae's grandson, and you're her daughter. Seems obvious to me."

I swallowed trying to take it all in. I wanted it to be true. Desperately I did. But how could I be sure? "I don't know anyone named Rae." But I did know Rae was one of Raina's aliases.

Barbara nodded. "The last time I saw her, she told me you would probably know her as Raina. But to me she was always Rae. She left something for you."

My heart raced. "What?"

"I don't know." She nodded toward the shop. "It's inside a fireproof safe in my storage room."

I glanced at Cruz, thinking of all the things we'd been given so far, a letter, keys, a photo, a diary. What next? "You haven't looked inside?"

"It's not my safe."

Cruz's brow furrowed. "She gave you a whole safe?"

Barbara nodded. "It's not that big. Just the size people use to hold documents."

Cruz and I exchanged a look. An entire safe seemed extreme. Whatever it contained had to be important. Would it be an address to where I could find Raina and Adam?

"What can you tell me about Oliver?" Though anxious to see the contents of that safe, this woman knew my son. She could tell

164

me what he liked and if he was happy.

Barbara smiled. "He's a wonderful boy."

A warm tingle filled my chest.

"He's kind and funny. Loves animals. And he's very patient." Her smile saddened as she glanced at the photo and returned it to me. "My grandson, Jacob, is what is known as selective mute. Outside our house, he doesn't talk to anyone. He'll talk to me, but only if no one else is around. His teachers have gotten a couple words from him, but that's all. Oliver is the only exception. Jacob spoke to him within a month."

Pride swelled and cocooned around me.

"It broke Jacob's heart when your mom and Oliver moved."

"How long ago was that?" I asked.

"A little over two years. Right before school started. Rae came to see me the night before they left, and that's when she told me about you and asked me to keep the safe. She showed me a picture of you when you were pregnant so I'd know what you looked like. But she didn't need to. It's obvious you're her daughter. You look just like her."

Her observation didn't surprise me. But the photo of me pregnant did. Gloria must have sent it before we'd left Berkeley. "Do you still have the picture?"

"No. She kept it. She said it was more important than I could imagine that no one know you have a child."

For once, Raina and I were in agreement.

"Has anyone else come through here asking about Raina or Luna?" Cruz asked.

A blue truck rolled past. Its driver raised his hand in greeting.

Barbara smiled and waved back. "No." She shot a glance at me and winced. "You'll forgive me for saying this, but Rae always seemed a bit paranoid. I don't know who she thought followed her or why, but she believed someone did."

I forced a smile. I'd once considered Gloria paranoid. After what I'd read yesterday, I doubted I ever would again.

"Paranoid or not," Cruz said, "after today, there's a chance

165

people will come through here asking about Luna. We'd appreciate it if you'd try not to mention any of this."

Barbara sat back and folded her hands in her lap. "Rae was one of the best friends I've ever had. She helped me a great deal after my husband passed. My promise to her doesn't end simply because I've met you."

I touched her forearm. "Thank you."

"Also"—Cruz scratched his neck—"you might want to take down that picture on the bulletin board of Jacob and...we're guessing it's Oliver?"

Barbara paled. "It's back?" Eyes closed, she shook her head. "I've taken that photo down at least a dozen times. Jacob keeps finding it and putting it back. I've told him how upset Rae would be if she knew, but he does it anyway. I don't know why. I'll tell you what. Why don't you take it? He won't be able to put it back that way."

I wanted to say yes, and I opened my mouth to thank her, but what came out surprised me. "Is that Jacob's only photo of Oliver?"

Barbara nodded.

"Then I don't want to take it." We'd made copies. They would do. From what Barbara had said, my son had been a good friend to Jacob. I didn't want him to forget that. I touched Barbara's arm again. "Maybe you could put it in a locked drawer or something for the next six months. Somewhere Jacob won't get to it. After that, I don't think it will matter if people see it."

By that time, the prophecies would likely be decoded and the council would have made its decision about who would lead the Neme-i. Whether or not I had an heir would no longer matter as much.

Tension lined her face. "Rae never told me what this was about. Can you?"

I glanced at Cruz. His frown made his opinion clear. I shook my head. "I'm not sure we know yet. I'm sorry. Will you please keep the photo hidden?"

"Of course."

"Thank you."

A couple cars drove by and a middle-aged man in dirty clothes pedaled past on a child's bicycle. Cruz tracked them all. Bear stood up and shook, sending slobber onto the leg of my jeans.

"Would you like to see that safe now?" Barbara asked.

She led us to her storage room at the back of the donut shop. A corner had been set aside for a desk, executive chair, and couch. In the opposite corner stood shelves filled with flour, sugar, confectioners' sugar, and oil. Next to those sat another set of shelves piled high with binders that Barbara said contained recipes. On a bottom shelf beneath such a stack sat a brown, metal chest about a foot tall and a foot and a half wide. "That's it." She removed the binders stacked on top of it then stepped back so Cruz could lift the safe.

He carried it to the desk and set it down where Barbara indicated.

The door had a keyhole and a numbered dial. I looked from it to Barbara.

She opened the top of a four-drawer metal filing cabinet and reached into the back. "I have a key, but not the combination. Only your mother has both. She said you'd know the combination."

She passed the key to me as I stood and stared.

Her smile faltered. "You don't know it?"

I took the key and shook my head. "I've never met Rai—my mother." I had to force the word out of my mouth, but once I did, I realized it didn't feel as false or distasteful as it had a week before. "I don't have any idea what combination she would have chosen."

"Oh." Barbara didn't seem to know what to say.

Cruz feathered his fingertips across my shoulder. "If Raina thought you'd know it, I'm sure she chose a number you'd be familiar with."

I nodded and blew out a sigh. It made sense. Inserting the key,

I tried the most obvious set of numbers, Adam's birthday—5-2-4 and pulled. No luck.

"Naturally." Why could nothing ever be easy?

I tried the next set of numbers that came to mind—my birthday. I tried the birthday I'd grown up celebrating as Luna and then the date I'd actually been born and named Jasmine Bluefeather. After that I tried Anna's birthday and my father's. I even tried Raina's. I was out of ideas.

Cruz, who'd taken to leaning against the edge of the desk as soon as Barbara had left us, raised an eyebrow.

"I don't know what else to try." Tears threatened as I rocked back on my heels, but I held them back. Desperately, I wished for a sledgehammer so I could pound away until I'd dented the safe enough to pop the door open.

"What have you tried?" Cruz asked.

As calm as he seemed I wondered if he'd sat through hours of unsuccessful safe cracking in the past.

I recited the list of dates I'd tried, and he made a few suggestions of his own. "Street addresses, phone numbers, Jay's birthday, Gloria's birthday, the day she died."

My back straightened. That was it! In my mind, Adam's birthday and Gloria's death were inextricably linked. But the dates weren't the same. Gloria had died in the accident. Adam hadn't been born until the wee hours of the following morning. I leaned forward and dialed in the numbers. A click sounded and I smiled at Cruz before pulling the door open. "You're a genius."

Cruz pushed away from the desk and stood behind me peering over my shoulder.

Inside, a small spiral bound notebook lay atop a manila envelope folded in half. I pulled out both items and flipped quickly through the book. Another journal—this one fuller than the last. The sealed and taped envelope contained something lumpy. A small black tray rested at the top of the chest. Cruz slid it out to reveal a silver chain with a heart-shaped locket attached. He opened the locket and turned it over before handing it to me.

The pictures inside were of my sister and me, both as babies. I recognized the photos from the albums Maria had shown me.

"Look at the back," Cruz said.

I closed the locket and read the inscription. *My love forever. Gilberto.*

Tears stung my eyes as I stared at the words. I'd only known my father a few hours before he'd been killed. We'd been able to sit and talk for nearly two of them. Even then, twenty-eight years after my mother had taken me and run away, his love for her had been evident. Of all the people who had a right to hate her, his had probably been the greatest, and yet he'd loved her. I didn't understand it and doubted I ever would, but the words etched on the back of the locket were so completely his that reading them was almost like having him in front of me again.

I looked at Cruz. The love in his eyes took my breath away.

"Put it on," he said.

I wanted to, but habit made me wary. "What if someone sees it and recognizes it?" I didn't know who the hell I worried about or what I thought they'd think, but worry was as familiar as my name.

Cruz took the necklace and opened the clasp. "Unless you start wearing low-cut shirts, no one will see it." He secured the chain and let go.

The locket fell between my breasts and nestled against my bra several inches beneath the neck of my shirt. I touched it through the material and smiled. Maybe it didn't make sense, but I felt more connected to my father and maybe to Raina too.

Cruz took a step back. "If we're going to Nevada tonight, we better get moving."

"What about the safe?"

He shrugged. "Leave it. Maybe Barbara can lock that picture inside."

I found a piece of paper and pen on Barbara's desk and wrote down the combination as well as my phone number. On our way out, I handed it to her.

"Thank you," I said.

"You're welcome."

I glanced at the bulletin board and realized she'd already removed the snapshot of Adam and her grandson.

"You know," she said, "Jacob would love to meet you. Would you like to come to dinner tonight? It's just leftover stew, but believe me, there's plenty."

Part of me wanted to stay, to hear more about my son, but another part knew we were racing against a clock. "Thank you, but I'm afraid we need to go. We've taken enough of your time."

"Nonsense," she said. "It's been a pleasure. And if you change your mind, we're the only house on South Hillsdale with a swing set in the front yard."

We left the bakery then drove by the harbor on Waterfront Drive Finding a parking lot next to some grass where we could walk Bear, Cruz pulled in and parked. Still tired from his morning on the beach, I doubted the dog would need much time to do his business, so I elected to stay in the Jeep while Cruz stood nearby and Bear wandered.

Reaching for the envelope, I removed the tape and opened the flap. Carefully, I unfolded the paper inside to reveal a finger painting.

A bright circle of yellow sun lay in the middle of the paper. Beneath it, a brown outline of a house sat on top of green grass. Next to the house, and larger than it, stood three people made up of circles and triangles—two tall and one small. In neat, black teacher's print above the figures were three names: Meemaw, Max, and Mommy.

My heart skipped. Tears blurred my sight.

"Luna?" Cruz sounded alarmed as he stood next to the window. "What's wrong?"

Words failed me, so I held up the painting for him to see. As I did, I noticed the words Max, Age 5 printed on back. Was Max another name for Adam? It had to be. Why else would it have been in the safe? Pulling the painting away from the window, I returned it to my lap and stared. How many names had my son used in his short life?

Cruz whistled for Bear and they rejoined me in the Jeep.

"Meemaw means Grandma, right?" Cruz said as he settled into his seat.

In the backseat, Bear's tags clanked until he lay down.

"It's a southern term," I said. "Like nana."

"So I take it you think that's you, Raina, and Adam?"

"I want it to be." My voice came out as a whisper. But what if Adam had grown up thinking of Raina as his mother? Or what if the Mommy figure in the painting was simply a fantasy of who Adam imagined his mom to be?

"You know it might not be though?"

I nodded as a tear spilled past my lashes. More tears followed. I swiped at them angrily then moved the painting to protect it from the drops. Cruz placed it on the dashboard and gathered me in his arms. I cried against his shoulder while he stroked my hair.

"I hope it's you," he said into my hair. "I just don't want you hurt if it's not."

I sniffed. I'd be hurt. No way around it. But I'd spent so many hours of my life considering the possibility that Adam wouldn't know or want to be with me that I doubted the hurt would be anything terribly new. Besides, I'd only know who the people in the painting were meant to be if I found him, and that joy would overwhelm everything else.

Tears under control, I pulled away from Cruz and wiped my nose with the back of my hand. I glanced at his shirt and winced at the combination of tears, snot, and saliva I'd left. "Sorry." Grabbing a napkin, I dabbed at the mess.

He glanced down and the left side of his mouth twitched upward. "Don't be. I want to be the one who holds you when you're upset."

I motioned at his shirt. "I'm guessing you'd prefer to go without the mess, though."

He chuckled. "Anything else in the envelope?"

171

In my excitement over the painting, I'd forgotten the envelope. Picking it up, I turned it upside down. Two pictures and a puzzle piece slid out.

I grabbed the piece, frowned at its funny edges and blue-gray hue and tossed it on the dashboard. "That had to be a mistake."

Turning my attention to the photos, I held them side by side. In one, I recognized a younger version of Gloria, seated in a rocking chair and holding a baby with a head of black hair I assumed to be me. I recognized the rocking chair. It had moved with us from place to place my entire childhood. In the other picture, holding the same baby in the same chair sat a woman who looked very much like me.

Cruz studied the pictures then me as if concerned I might cry again.

He didn't need to worry. I didn't feel like crying; I didn't feel like anything. Raina and Gloria had known each other; I'd come to accept that. Gloria had lied. Big surprise. At least both women seemed happy holding me.

Cruz started the engine and steered us out of the parking lot. Taking a left on M Street, he continued forward a block to an intersection with cobblestone crosswalks. He rolled through slowly. To his left, a divided road led up to a giant Victorian home outside his window. My scalp prickled, and the hair on my arms stood up.

"Stop!" I called as we passed the intersection. "Go back."

"What? Why?"

"That Victorian house down there. I've seen it before. Go back. Please."

He pulled to the curb and let a car pass before flipping a U-turn. At the divided road, he turned right, then stopped at the intersection in front of the house.

Painted green with darker green trim, the mansion boasted a brown roof with multiple spires and peaks and all those beautifully carved, decorative touches that had disappeared with the Victorian era.

"You've seen this place?" Cruz asked.

"Yeah." It had been a different color in the picture I'd seen, but it was the same beautiful place. "Tomas has a puzzle of it."

"You're sure it's this place?"

A sign to the left of the building read Carson Mansion. The cover of the puzzle had called it that too. "Yeah. Weird."

"Do we need to stop?" Cruz asked. "Looks like they offer tours."

If I ever returned to Eureka on vacation, I would do it, but we didn't have time this trip. "No."

As we drove away and joined the highway, a jittery, unhappy feeling settled in my tummy. I tried to ignore it. I ate the remainder of my breakfast burrito and sucked down some cold coffee. Then I devoured one of my remaining lemon-filled donuts. Unable to sit still, I retrieved the painting from the dashboard and stared at it a few minutes before returning it to the envelope. I stacked all the napkins we'd accrued in a neat pile and put them in the center console. Then I grabbed one and used it to wipe dust off the dashboard.

Cruz watched me out of the corner of his eye but didn't say anything.

Seeing the puzzle piece we'd found in the envelope, I picked it up and twirled it between my fingers.

Sitting back, I thought of Tomas's puzzle of the Carson Mansion and of Barbara and all the things we'd learned. From my purse I pulled out the copies of the picture of Adam and Jacob. I smiled at the image of my beautiful son. Something tugged inside my head.

We'd missed something.

I sat up straight. "We need to go back."

"What?"

I knew it in my gut. "We need to turn around."

His eyebrows arched. "Why?"

"I'm not sure exactly. We're missing something." Desperation built inside me. "We need to go back. Please."

"Back where?"

My mind cast about. Where were we supposed to go? "Barbara's."

"Why?"

"I don't know." My tone reached a level between desperate and crazy. "I'm sorry. I know this sounds crazy. But we *need* to go *back*."

Cruz exhaled loudly and took the next exit. He pulled over on the shoulder and put the Jeep in park. "What's going on?"

"I don't know how to explain it. I just know it. I feel it inside my body. It's the voice inside my head."

His mouth opened and he blinked a couple times, eyes clouding as he looked at me. "You hear a voice in your head?"

I rolled my eyes. "Not literally. It's just this thing I have. Intuition or whatever. It *never* steers me wrong. The only time I go wrong is when I don't listen to it. Please. We've got to go back."

"You realize this will put us back a day?"

"I don't care. We need to go back."

He let out a breath.

"*Now*," I said.

Mumbling, he turned us around and joined the opposite side of the highway. "Sends messages with her mind. Hears things in her head."

I jerked my gaze to him. "What?"

"Nothing."

I glared until I knew he wouldn't say more then I turned and stared at the acres of redwoods rolling by outside my window. "I don't actually *hear* things."

I kept my back to him until the turns and dips in the windy road made me woozy. Holding my tummy, I faced forward and watched the road.

"Car sick?" he asked.

"A little." My tone remained chilly.

He sighed and eased off the accelerator. "If you don't hear

anything, why do you call it a voice?"

I thought about it and shrugged. "I don't know. What do you call it when something inside you tells you to do something?"

"Instinct?"

"Okay fine. It's an instinct."

"However, over the last month," he continued as if he hadn't heard me, "I've begun to receive other things that we've been calling *messages*."

I frowned. "What are you saying?"

"How do you know someone's not sending you a message— trying to get you to return to Eureka? Someone like a tracker for instance?"

I froze. Could that be what had happened?

Women of the Neme-i could receive messages, the same as anyone. But they couldn't pick out energy or identify it like our men could. I hadn't experienced receiving, as far as I knew, but Maria had once told me it felt like her head got warm and that Anna experienced it as a brain itch. I hadn't felt either of those things. But still....

"When you get messages," I said, "does it feel the same as your instincts?"

Cruz tipped his head. "Not exactly. Thanks to Jay I'm aware of a little tingle in my head when I get the messages. My instincts come with a feeling in my gut. How long have you been hearing this *voice*?"

"Off and on since my coma."

Cruz nodded. "So a lot longer than the Neme-i have known who you are."

I smiled, relieved. "Not the trackers then."

"Probably not," Cruz agreed. "But we'll still be careful."

He wasn't kidding. As soon as we reached Eureka we rolled past the bakery whose sign declared it closed and then around residential streets for close to an hour before he determined no one had followed us.

South Hillsdale was a small street, and we found the swing set in front of a modest blue house with white and gray trim. Cruz rolled two houses past and parked on the street. Leaving Bear and me in the Jeep, he doubled back and checked the backyard then peeked in windows to make sure no one held anyone at gunpoint. In one way, it seemed a little drastic. In another, I appreciated the effort. I'd already been held at gunpoint twice. I had no desire to do it again.

Returning to the driveway, Cruz whistled. Bear and I joined him at the door where we rang the bell and listened to voices and footsteps inside.

The white door opened and Barbara stood on the other side. Her mouth opened and her eyes grew wide.

"Oh my God!" She pushed the screen door open. "You have no idea how happy I am to see you." She called down the hall for her grandson. "He threw a fit when I told him you came to the shop today but had already left town. He hasn't had a meltdown like this since he was three."

I didn't know what to say.

Little steps sounded in the hall and Barbara held out her hand. "It's okay," she said. "Look who's come back."

A little boy with dark-brown hair and large eyes peeked around the corner.

Barbara beamed. "This is Oliver's mother and her friend, Cruz."

The boy peered at me and Cruz then at Bear who sat clipped to his leash behind me.

"This is Bear." I stepped aside to give an ample view.

The boy's eyes sparked and a smile tugged the corners of his lips.

"Would you like to pet him?" I asked.

He took a step forward while I crouched beside Bear. "Hold your hand out so he can sniff you."

Once Bear and Jacob were introduced and on a solid petting/hugging basis, I stood and apologized to Barbara for dropping in unannounced.

"Are you kidding?" She led us into her living room. "He's been crying and yelling for the past hour. Something about a promise to Oliver and a puzzle piece. I haven't been able to make heads or tails of it."

"A puzzle piece?" I glanced at Cruz.

He met my gaze then looked past me. Turning, I found Jacob standing next to the couch, eyes wide as he stared at us.

"Did Oliver promise you a puzzle piece?" Cruz asked.

Jacob nodded.

"Did he say his mother would give it to you?"

Jacob's nod came a little faster.

Cruz turned to me. "Did you leave it in the car?"

I shook my head. Except for the box of letters, I'd put everything we'd received in my bulging purse. It felt safer. But at the rate we were going, I would soon need a duffel bag.

I shifted my bag to my lap and pulled out the envelope. Locating the puzzle piece, I held it in my open palm. "Is this it?"

Jacob took a tentative step toward me then plucked the piece from my hand. With his other hand he motioned for me to follow him. I stood, and he pointed at Cruz and motioned for him to come as well.

Barbara stood at the same time, but Jacob shook his head at her.

"Not me?" she said.

He shook his head again. She slouched back, letting her legs splay in front of her. As tired as she looked, I didn't think she'd exaggerated about the yelling.

Jacob rubbed Bear's head and made a *come* motion by patting his leg. He walked down the hall to the last bedroom and Cruz, Bear, and I followed.

A dresser and desk stood against the wall opposite Jacob's single bed. From the ceiling hung a model of the solar system and another of a spaceship. Bookshelves by the closet held a few books and a menagerie of army men and action figures. Closing the door behind us, Jacob walked to his closet and slid open one of the doors. He reached behind a box pushed up against the wall and pulled out a piece of cardboard folded in half and tied with string. Laying the cardboard on the floor, he untied the string and opened it. Inside lay a puzzle, completely assembled except for one piece. Jacob looked back at us then placed the puzzle piece I'd given him where it belonged. Wholly satisfied with the completed image, he smiled.

Cruz tipped his head and crouched behind Jacob to study the puzzle. It showed a giant metal suspension bridge above fall-colored trees.

"Pretty," I said.

Cruz frowned. "Do you still have the box this came in?"

Jacob returned to the closet and rummaged through games and toys until he found the box.

Cruz read the side. "St. John's Bridge. Portland, Oregon."

I'd lived in Portland for a year as a child. I didn't remember a bridge that led into a forest. Just bridges that crossed the river from one side of the city to the other.

I knelt next to Jacob. "Did Ad—I mean Oliver—give you this puzzle? Did you do it together?"

Jacob gave a tiny nod.

I licked my lips unsure of my next question but knowing I had to ask. "Did he want you to show it to me?"

Another timid nod.

"He thought we would meet?"

Jacob beamed.

Confusion wriggled in my belly as I turned to Cruz. "How would he…?"

Cruz's eyes darted as if searching mental files for an answer. "He's Tomas's son."

Tomas's son. A memory of something Jay had once said fought its way into my conscience. He'd said he liked the possibility of tribal members marrying outsiders with gifts of their own because those gifts were sometimes passed on to their children along with the gifts of the Neme-i. He felt it strengthened

178

the tribe. When he'd said it, he had stared straight at me.

"Oh shit." My legs trembled and I plopped down on my butt.

"Luna?" Cruz said.

I shook my head. I needed to think.

Was Adam clairvoyant like his father? Did he possess gifts beyond that of the Neme-i? And if he did, how much more would the Neme-i want him?

I don't know how long I sat there thinking it all through, but when I looked up again, the light in the room had changed. The puzzle had been disassembled and sat in its box next to Cruz. He and Jacob sat on the bed playing with action figures. Neither of them spoke, but Cruz made quiet shooting sounds while Jacob moved his arm like a giant bulldozer over legions of carefully positioned army men.

"I need a cell phone," I said.

Fourteen

We ate dinner with Barbara and Jacob, and Barbara convinced us to stay the night. I tried to enjoy my time with this loving family and ignore the questions burning in my brain, but they refused to go away. So at six the next morning, when Cruz and I said goodbye and climbed in the Jeep, taking the puzzle Jacob had insisted we keep, I was relieved.

"Do you think Tomas will respond?" Cruz asked as we climbed the same stretch of twisty mountain highway we'd driven the day before.

He'd asked the same question after I'd used Barbara's phone to dial Tomas's number the night before.

My response remained the same. "We'll know when we get to Winnemucca."

Although I wanted to attach the battery and check my cell now, I didn't dare risk alerting anyone to our presence east of Eureka. Bad enough they would know our location when we made it to Winnemucca.

My question for Tomas had been simple. "Can Adam do what you can?" I hadn't expected him to answer his phone when I'd dialed though I'd hoped he would. But I damned well expected a response. Tomas knew me well enough to hear the seriousness in my tone.

I propped my feet on the dashboard. "Tell me again what Mo said."

After I'd called Tomas, Cruz had used one of our burner phones to call Mo.

"She's meeting us in Winnemucca."

"Did she say why?" We'd only needed her to set up a meeting with Catherine Rivers, not attend it.

"Something about recent developments."

Great. Developments that required a face-to-face visit. That tied knots in my muscles.

On the other side of the mountain, the road straightened out, and I turned to the journal sitting in my purse. I'd put it off long enough. Raina's letters had left me with questions that had us pointed toward Nevada for answers. Likely, the journal would leave me with more. Better I knew them before we reached Winnemucca.

Taking a calming breath, I opened the cover. The writing matched what I'd seen in the letters and earlier journal but seemed older too. More mature. The stroke of the pen on the page surer— the letters less loopy. I sensed it had been written more recently, by someone who no longer cared how pretty her writing looked.

Many years have passed since the things I am about to write took place, but I will tell them as faithfully as my memory allows. I know you must have questions. If you've found this then you must know there are holes in your knowledge. I wish they did not exist. I wish there had never been a reason for them, but even with the passage of time, when I look back, I see no other way.

I took a deep breath, trying to steady the shaky feeling in my stomach.

My father was a wonderful man and an exceptional leader. Proud, loving, wise. People sought his advice and opinions. As a girl, I wanted to be like him. As an adult, I've learned I never could be. Our paths were too different. Wherever he is now, wherever our spirits go when they shed our bodies, I hope he is still as proud of me today as he was the day he died. I hope that's still possible.

When he died, I had a husband and two beautiful daughters I adored. Except for my father's illness, I couldn't imagine a better existence. He had cancer, and his death was painful and long. It took a toll on everyone. But I am thankful I was able to be with him to the end.

The night before he died, he told me my birth prophecy.

At that time, a proposal sat before our council to make the birth prophecies public. My father spoke adamantly against it. But I, like many others, supported it. I was young. I had a romanticized view of life and the world and therefore of the prophecies. I considered them a quaint part of our heritage, and I expected to hear a fairy tale. All the prophecies people talked about were wonderful. I had no way of knowing prophecies could be nightmares. People don't speak of those. Even all these years later, I understand why.

My prophecy said, "She will give birth to two girls. One will lead her people. The other will try to destroy them.

I stopped reading and stared at the book. Something dark raced to fill my insides.

Anna was the leader of our people. Did that mean I would try to destroy them?

"Luna?" Cruz sounded concerned. "What is it?"

I looked at him, unable to find words.

There had to be a mistake. I had no intention of destroying anyone. "Her prophecy."

"What's it say?"

I read it to him.

His eyes opened wide, and his mouth opened and closed before he finally spoke. "It can't mean what it sounds like."

"Why not?" I said. "Anna's the leader—"

"During a time of duress," he said.

"Fine. During a time of duress. Whatever. She's going to be the leader. I'm not taking that job." Unless… What if taking the job was the only way to keep from destroying a group of people? Would I take it under those circumstances?

Cruz blew out a breath. "You remember what Jay said about the prophecies—that they come true but not always how you expect?"

I remembered. "He said they're best understood at the end of a life looking back."

"Exactly. I know you, Luna. You wouldn't intentionally hurt anyone."

My stomach knotted. "I threw a couple knives into Paul Hernandez and knocked him unconscious, didn't I?"

A tiny grin played across Cruz's lips. "But you didn't kill him."

No, my sister had done that.

"Maybe we're looking at this wrong. Maybe the point isn't the prophecy. What else did Raina write?"

I read him everything from the beginning and then went on, finishing the paragraph I'd stopped on.

"If that were your prophecy, and you had two daughters you loved equally, one of whom had a prophecy that spoke of greatness, would you share your prophecy with others? Or would your fear for the other child keep you silent?"

I stared out the windshield. I didn't have to think about the question. Compared to Raina's prophecy, Adam's was vague, and yet, from the moment I'd heard it, I had worried.

"If Anna or I have a prophecy that talks about greatness, do you think the other's says she's evil?"

Cruz frowned. "I doubt it. I think Raina would have mentioned that."

"Unless it's mine and she's trying to protect my feelings."

He looked away from the road long enough to study me. "Your prophecy could say you're the spawn of Satan, and it wouldn't change things. You're not evil." He tipped his head to the side. "Anna, on the other hand…."

I remembered my sister pointing the gun at me and shivered.

Cruz took my hand. "If you're worried, we'll ask Mo. Maybe your and Anna's prophecies are already published."

Sunshine peeked through the clouds of my mood then dashed behind them again. What if the council had also found and published Raina's prophecy?

"Why don't you keep reading?" Cruz suggested. "Get past the prophecies to the part where Raina left you with Gloria."

"I did everything I could to keep the proposal from passing. Now understanding my father's concern on a primal level, I took his position and furthered his arguments. Looking back, I know I should have made my own. But fear stopped me. What if people wondered what had changed my mind? What if they guessed? How would you and your sister be treated? Would they try to cast one of you away? Ban you from our people? From me?

When it became clear my arguments would fail, I did the only thing I could think of; I played ill. No vote could take place without me. By the time playing ill could hold the vote no longer, I had enlisted the help of a friend who lived outside our society. He put me in touch with a contact to help me escape.

I planned to take both you and your sister. We were to meet the contact and leave the morning the vote was scheduled to take place. However, when I woke, I found your sister gone. Your father had left a note, saying he worried about how sick I had been, and had taken her to his mother's. If you hadn't been breast feeding, he would have taken you too.

I lost my mind that morning. I couldn't reach my friend and couldn't hold off leaving any longer. I tried to get your sister from your grandmother, but they'd gone shopping. I had to make a choice. Protect one daughter now and try to get the other at a later date or protect neither. I made the hardest choice I have ever made. It tore my soul in

184

two. I left your sister, knowing she would be safe with her father and grandmother and took you, hoping to keep you safe with me.

I don't expect anyone to understand this. Unless you've been faced with the same choice, how could you? I did the best I could. I made what I thought was the best choice. If I were in that position again, I would likely make the same choice. But it has come with a price.

I tried many times to get your sister, but I never succeeded. Our people have kept her so protected, I couldn't get close. In the end, maybe that was best. I loved your father. How could I deprive him of both his daughters?"

So that explained it—why I'd been taken and Anna had not. There'd been no choice or desire involved. It had simply been circumstances. No one had come out ahead.

"We wandered for some time, staying in hotels. Trackers searched for us. Sometimes we were ahead of them. Other times, we barely escaped. Slowly it became clear that I couldn't ask for help from our people anymore.

I cut all ties and used our remaining money to rent a home and secure a caregiver for you while I looked for work. However, without experience or references, no one would hire me. I didn't dare use my gift and risk calling the trackers to us. Before I knew it, we were out of money and homeless in Colorado. Soon you developed a cough and then it began to snow. Desperate for cover, I ducked into a parking garage outside a hospital determined to find an unlocked car we could shelter in. That's when the miracle happened.

A car pulled into the lot, and I watched a nurse get out. She had bright red hair and a no-nonsense manner. I tried to hide from her, but she heard you cry and came over. In a matter of seconds, she deduced the desperation of our situation, and she did the most unexpected thing. She gave me the keys to her car. She told me to stay inside it and run the heater as often as needed but not to fall asleep. She even promised to bring food on her break. I'd thought I would have to use my gift to get us into a car for just an hour, but here was a kind-hearted woman offering us so much more. Her name was Gloria."

My heart skipped. All those years believing Gloria's story about finding me abandoned in her car, and the past month when that belief had been destroyed. Finally the truth. The story about finding me in her car had been a lie, but like all of Gloria's lies, it held elements of truth.

Raina and Gloria became friends. One night turned into a week then a month. Slowly, they learned to trust each other and Raina told Gloria everything. Having been raised by an abused mother on the run, Gloria knew about running and hiding and taught Raina. And after three months, when the trackers showed up at Gloria's hospital flashing pictures of Raina and me, the three of us ran together. It took a few more months and few more desperate escapes before Raina realized the only way to keep me truly safe would be to leave. The trackers were looking for her and me together, but they would never think to look for a Native American baby with a white guardian. She said she'd never been as lost or felt as empty or alone as she had the day she'd left.

Eventually, Raina had found a job working at the Eight Ball. She and Gloria remained in contact by phone and letters. They made big decisions together—like the one to have me mistrained to keep me hidden from the trackers.

"Most of the time, the mistraining worked. But on occasion, without realizing it, you still used your gift. That is how they came close to finding you. They would stumble upon your energy and have a sense of where you were. It was at these times that Gloria began to have nightmares. And at these times you were moved. Sometimes, like your last move, Gloria waited too long. She did it out of love for you. She wanted you to know some semblance of a normal life—to experience joy and love and all the things that make this life worth living. In Berkeley you

wanted to wait, hoping the father of your child would return. So Gloria waited as long as she dared and longer still. The day you moved, trackers were at a neighborhood store showing sketches of a young woman who resembled you."

Raina had not been far behind us on the road to Shiprock and had happened upon Gloria's and my accident first. After pulling me from the car, she dialed 911, then set the fire that destroyed everything to hide all evidence of who we were. She'd used her gift to make sure no pictures were taken and to ensure the investigation remained brief and undetailed. According to her, it was the first time she had used her gift in years, and though she'd known it was a risk, she'd done it to protect me.

"You were right about the windshield," I told Cruz.

He nodded without comment.

"I stayed in Gallup to be sure no one happened across my energy and looked into what had happened. I convinced the hospital to take me on as a volunteer and spent my nights holding the babies in the nursery. I found a way to bring your child to you each night, to place your baby in your arms, hoping you might wake, and to strengthen your bond."

My breath caught. I had held my child? Could that be true? Desperately I wanted to believe my son had felt his mother's arms, had heard my heartbeat and known on some level who his mother was. Tears filled my eyes.

Cruz touched my leg, a question in his eyes.

"I want it to be true," I said. "I want to know I held him at least once in his life."

Cruz nodded and squeezed my thigh. He remained quiet, allowing me time before I returned to the journal and read how Raina befriended the foster-mother assigned to my child and convinced her to leave her loveless marriage and take Adam with her. Although Adam was no longer with the woman, Raina said

187

the foster-mother was alive and happily remarried, living in Canada with her new husband and three dogs.

I flipped the page and found the next one blank. So I flipped again and again. They were all blank. Except for some occasional doodles, there was nothing more.

That couldn't be it. It had to be here. Where was my child? She'd told me all the rest. She *had* to tell me that.

I tried again and again. But no matter how many times I looked, the results were the same. No writing appeared. No clue was offered. I slammed the journal shut and threw it on the dashboard.

"What?" Cruz asked.

"That's it." I felt hollow inside. Betrayed.

"There's nothing more about Adam?"

"No." Nothing about his health or location. Nothing about where to go next. I wanted to scream and hit something. I wanted to break the windows.

"It's probably better that way."

"What?" Cruz's words were a fist to my heart.

He grimaced. "She took a huge risk revealing as much as she did. What if someone else got hold of this journal?"

My mouth opened, ready to argue, but his point robbed me of words. What if someone had gotten hold of it? They'd know my true history and that I had a child, but at least they wouldn't know where to search for him or what he looked like. They wouldn't even know he was a boy. She'd only said child and baby. Anyone else who came across this journal would be at the same dead-end we were. More so, even. I didn't know whether to be thankful or not.

⚜

Mo stood on the sidewalk outside a coffee shop in Winnemucca. An army duffel bag lay at her feet. She lifted her chin in acknowledgment then opened the back of the Jeep and threw her bag in before climbing into the backseat beside Bear. The two eyed each other. Neither appeared happy to be sharing the seat.

"You need a bigger car," Mo said.

She was right.

"How are you?" I asked.

"Hot and tired. Make a U-turn," she told Cruz.

He followed her directions out of town. "You said there were developments?"

"Yeah. The council says Walter's prophecies are missing."

I'd learned so many names in the past two months that it took a couple seconds to make the connection. "Walter Chino? The man whose house you took us to?"

"That's the one," Mo said.

"He was your dad's mentor, right?" Cruz said. "I thought he was in Summerhaven."

"He was."

Cruz frowned. "Did the council ask him where his prophecies were?"

"Of course," Mo said. "But he doesn't know. Records are passed from mentor to mentee. When a seer stops receiving prophecies, he gives his records to the seer who's taking his place. They become that person's responsibility."

"So your dad had them. Do you think he hid them?" Confusion filled me. Jay had refused to hide Adam's prophecy. Surely he hadn't hidden others.

Mo glared. "No."

"What then?"

"They're lying," Mo said flatly.

"Why?"

"I'm guessing there's a prophecy they don't want shared."

Considering Anna and Maria had offered to hide Adam's, it wasn't a stretch to think they'd hide others. "Whose?"

"Hard to say. There were some doozies."

"You've read them?" asked Cruz.

"Who do you think rewrote them all in code?"

My muscles froze. That meant... "You know?"

189

"Know what?" she said. "That you have a son? Yeah. I know."

"You haven't...." I gulped, unable to get the words out.

"Told anyone?" She stared at me like I was stupid. "Not my business."

The shock of learning someone else knew I had a child tempered my relief.

Cruz looked at me and raised an eyebrow.

I didn't know what to feel. In the past several hours, my emotions had been up, down, and everywhere between. One more twist on my emotional roller coaster hardly seemed worth noting.

Cruz glanced in the rearview mirror. "Whose prophecy do you *think* they're trying to hide?"

"Given who's on the council?" Mo said. "Probably Luna's mother's."

I felt the blood drain from my face. "You know it?" What else that I wanted hidden did Mo know?

"Yeah. Do you?"

I glanced at Cruz. "We recently learned it."

"Then I'm sure you can understand why Anna might want it hidden. Until her prophecy and yours are found, she's got something to worry about."

Didn't I know it.

"So they haven't found Anna's or Luna's yet?" Cruz kept his tone neutral.

"No."

"But you think they've broken your dad's code?"

Mo sighed. "If I'm right, they've broken one. He has several."

Cruz nodded. "Will you tell us when they do find Anna's and Luna's?"

"Sure." Mo leaned forward and motioned with her hand. "Take the next right."

Catherine Rivers raised sheep on thirty acres of land. A large two-story house sat half a mile from the entrance to the ranch, but we didn't stop there. According to Mo, Catherine seldom stayed at the house, preferring the traditional Navajo hogan her late husband had built in the center of their property. Her kids lived in the main house and, for the most part, took care of the business interests of the ranch. Catherine was called when a sheep got sick or a ewe needed help lambing.

"Leave your phones in the Jeep," Mo said as we pulled up outside the hogan. "Catherine doesn't appreciate interruptions."

Built of wood and laid out in a hexagon, the hogan had a modern door in the east facing wall and two windows on side walls. Mud coated the rounded roof and a smokestack poked out its center.

We waited in the Jeep almost five minutes before the door of the hogan opened and a thin woman with long gray hair worn in a single braid stepped out. She squinted at the windshield and held up one finger.

"One person only," Mo said to me. "That's you."

I reached for the door handle.

Cruz grabbed my arm. "I don't like it. Someone could be in there."

"She'll be fine," Mo said. "No one messes with Catherine."

Cruz glared at her. "My job is to keep Luna safe. I go where she goes."

"Well, you're not going in there." Mo blew out a breath. "Look, there's only one door. We'll see anyone coming or going."

The muscle in Cruz's jaw pulsed as he studied the little old woman.

I patted his hand. "I have my knives. I'll be fine."

His jaw tightened, but he nodded. "Stop in the doorway and look around. You see anyone or feel anything off, step back out."

"Okay," I agreed.

Eyes narrowed, he glanced at Mo. "Can I at least stand outside? Walk around the perimeter?"

"I'm sure that'll be fine." Mo cast a sideways glance at Bear. "Take the dog with you. His breath stinks."

Cruz clipped Bear to his leash and the three of us climbed out.

Bear and Cruz stopped at the front of the Jeep while I continued forward.

"Mrs. Rivers?" I offered my hand. "I'm Luna."

She wore jeans, cuffed at the ankles and a denim shirt. "Catherine," she said, ignoring my hand. "Come in." Turning, she stepped back into the hogan, leaving me to follow.

I paused in the doorway like Cruz asked, but saw no one else. Just a tidy little home with a dirt floor, simple bed, and a large wooden loom supporting a half-finished blanket. I stepped over to the loom and admired the bright blues, yellows, and greens. "It's beautiful."

"Hmph." Catherine motioned to one of several blankets spread on the ground surrounding the oven at the center of the room. "Sit."

I sat where indicated.

"John's daughter said you have questions about our energy."

"Yes."

Seated next to me, she waited.

"I know that girls begin their training when they're ten and boys at eleven," I said. "I'm wondering why?"

Catherine shrugged. "It is the approximate age when the energy matures."

"What do you mean? Matures in what way?"

Catherine frowned. "When it becomes fully what it will be. When all its strength is there."

"And this is the time you begin to teach and mold it?"

"Yes."

I licked my lips. "Does anything else happen at that time?"

"Many things. The body changes, the mind changes, outlooks change."

"No, I mean with the energy. Does anything else happen with the energy?"

Catherine stared at me blankly. "Everything is energy, so everything happens with the energy."

I blew out a breath. Doing a dot-to-dot without numbers might have been easier. "Can we back up and start again?"

Catherine motioned for me to do what I wanted.

I took a moment to center my thoughts—remember why I'd wanted to come. It had been Raina's letters, the proximity between the postmarks and Gloria's addresses. After being so close for ten years, why had Raina suddenly moved so far away?

"Let's say, hypothetically, that a young girl is about to turn ten. Is there any reason why a mother who had been in the same area as the child, though they'd been separated, would suddenly need to move a much greater distance away?"

Catherine stared at the air in front of her. From somewhere outside, I heard the distant bleat of sheep.

"Your mother was my student," she finally said.

"You were a teacher?"

She nodded. "She was a good student. I liked her. But she was no leader. Nothing about her ever said leader."

My mouth opened, but I didn't know what to say.

"A leader must be strong. Have their own opinions and not care what others think. Your mother was a follower. She tried too hard to be her father."

I thought of Raina's journal entry. She'd said she'd tried to use her father's arguments instead of her own. "She wasn't much of a mother either," I muttered.

Catherine's lips formed a tight line. "What you ask involves the bonds. When a child's energy matures, the bonds that were already there strengthen. A bond that was basically controlled by one person's energy is now controlled by two. It doubles. The energy of a child who has not yet been trained will call out to the energy it is bonded to. The other energy will answer. It has to."

"Would that make the energy more detectable?" I asked.

"Yes."

"Would distance make it less detectable?"

"No." Catherine paused. "And yes." Her body swayed back and forth. "Energy is energy. It comes and goes all the time, but it can only be traced to the place it came from or goes to. If both parties involved in a bond are within a certain distance of each other, it's possible that a tracker who comes across one will also stumble upon the other. Once they've come across both, they can put the two together and recognize the bond. If the two parties involved are farther apart, the chances of inadvertently stumbling across the second bit of energy or recognizing the bond are much less."

I sat quietly for a moment, allowing the information to penetrate. That might explain why Raina had suddenly felt the need to live farther away, but if so, how had the trackers continued to find Gloria and me? "How do trackers find people?"

"By tracking their energy."

I gritted my teeth. Talking with Catherine reminded me of talking with Cruz. "I mean, how do trackers track energy?"

Catherine paused and nodded a couple times as if mulling the answer over. "Every tracker is different. Some see the energy in colors, others say it has sound. Some say it has a taste or a scent. Some feel a vibration in the air."

"So they track it using their senses?" I asked.

"Yes."

"And every tracker is different?"

"Yes."

I shifted on the blanket. "Does the energy call out to them in some way?"

"No."

"They just have to stumble across it?"

"Yes."

"And they magically recognize it?"

The creases around Catherine's eyes deepened. "There's no magic. Is it magic when someone calls from an unknown number, but you know who they are from the sound of their voice?"

"No."

"Why not?" she demanded.

"Because I know their voice."

"Exactly. The same way you can distinguish different voices,

194

trackers can distinguish different energies."

Suddenly I felt like a point might exist in all of this. "But everyone can distinguish between voices. Are you saying everyone can distinguish between energies?"

"To some degree. But trackers are more adept. The average Neme-i man can distinguish six or seven energies. A good tracker can distinguish over a hundred."

"But to know someone's voice, a person has to have heard it. How would the trackers have tracked me as a kid if they'd never known my energy?"

Catherine scoffed. "Have you never met a child who sounded like their parent?"

I thought of Tomas's sisters. The two of them sounded so much alike on the phone that I had to use caller ID to distinguish between them.

"We are all products of parents. We get everything from them—appearance, voice, IQ, gifts, energy."

I jerked my gaze back to Catherine. "Gifts?"

She huffed like I'd failed in comprehension. "The strength of a child's gift is directly related to the strength of his parents' gifts."

Which led straight back to the Revisionist argument in favor of arranged coupling.

"Is that always true?" I asked.

"Nothing is *always* true."

My mind whirled through thoughts, flipping from one recently learned fact to the next, desperate to make sure I hadn't missed anything. Adam. Was there anything I hadn't asked in relation to him? Yes.

I bit my lip as I tried to decide how to phrase it. "So let's say, hypothetically, a tracker hadn't known my mother, but came across her and me as a child. Would they have known we were related?"

"You mean despite the fact that you look alike?" Catherine's brown eyes penetrated mine.

I wanted to squirm. "Yeah. Despite that."

"Yes."

"How?" I heard the hum of a passing vehicle.

Catherine's brow furrowed as she glanced at the window. "The mother/child bond is strong. Perhaps the strongest there is. There is no mistaking it."

"Does it matter how much time a mother and child spend together in terms of strengthening that bond?"

"Nine months is a long time to share a body. It forges an unbreakable bond. After birth, once the child touches or sees her mother, the energy knows. The bond is cemented. Can it get stronger? Of course. But it can never be broken."

A radio sounded outside the hogan as a vehicle rolled to a stop.

"What if the child never sees or touches her mother?"

"Then she will forever be restless. Always searching, never quite whole, until the bond is completed."

Was that why Raina had brought Adam to me while I lay in my coma? To cement our bond?

Voices spoke outside and someone knocked on the door.

Alarm buzzed inside me and I reached behind myself for my knives.

"Ká'ü!"

I recognized the Neme-i word for mother.

"My son," Catherine said as she pulled her legs beneath her. Climbing to her feet, she moved to open the door.

A large man with long hair overflowed the frame on the other side. He flicked a glance at me then returned to his mother.

I relaxed my grip on the knife.

Head bowed, the man spoke in a hushed tone. Catherine stiffened then sagged. A moment passed before she spoke, and when she glanced back at me, I knew I no longer belonged in the hogan.

She whispered to the man and closed the door.

I stood. "Are you okay?"

"I am needed. Do you have more questions, child?"

196

If I did, I no longer knew what they were. "Can I do anything to help?"

She shook her head and turned away, but suddenly turned back. "Stop the council."

"Stop them from what?"

Catherine turned her back. "Go."

I stood staring a moment then stumbled toward the door.

Outside, Catherine's son leaned against the hood of a filthy white pickup. Cruz stood midway between the Jeep and the house. He raised an eyebrow as I stepped out and quickly walked to meet me.

"Are you okay?" he asked.

I nodded and glanced back at the house. "She has to leave."

Mo remained in the Jeep, staring at her phone. "Where's Bear?"

"Guarding the back." Cruz whistled and Bear came running.

We piled into the Jeep. Mo's fingers flew over her phone, pausing so she could glare at Bear after his tail smacked her in the face.

Cruz pointed the vehicle back the way we'd come.

"Do you know what that was about? Why her son came?" I asked.

Mo shook her head. "I'm working on it. Did she say anything?"

I thought of the look in Catherine's eyes. It had burned at the same time it had been filled with pain. "She said to stop the council."

Mo stopped typing.

Cruz cocked an eyebrow. "From what?"

"I don't know."

Fifteen

Mo directed us to a barbecue restaurant at the north end of town and told us to wait in the car while she went in. Cruz and I took the opportunity to check our cell phones. I had two voice messages—one from Maria and one from Hideo—and a text from Tomas. I checked the text first. In reply to my question about whether Adam could do what Tomas could, it simply said More.

I inhaled. I'd expected him to say yes, Adam could do what he could, or maybe some of it, but I hadn't expected "more." Did he mean Adam could do what he could plus what the men of the Neme-i could? That would make sense. But the chill in my gut told me otherwise.

I texted back. Need 2 talk. Then I waited, hoping for a reply that didn't come.

Next to me, Cruz held his phone to his ear, listening to what I guessed were a slew of voice messages.

I sighed and played my own messages while I watched a young man in a stained apron smoke a cigarette next to the dumpster. Hideo wanted me to know everything was fine at home. Maria expressed disappointment that we'd left Summerhaven without saying goodbye. I had my doubts her disappointment had anything to do with that, but so be it. Both of them wanted me to call. Both would have to wait.

The guy on the smoke break looked our way. Probably

wondering why two people would be sitting in the parking lot on their phones and not going in. After extinguishing his cigarette, he tossed the butt in the dumpster and pulled out his own cell. Holding it up, he turned slowly until he seemed to find a good signal then pressed a couple buttons and headed inside.

Cruz tossed his phone on the dashboard and looked at me. "You get a call from Maria?"

"Yeah. You?"

He nodded.

That seemed odd. Calling one person would be effort enough for Maria. "Do you think someone asked her to call us? Maybe Anna?"

Cruz nodded toward the restaurant where Mo stepped through the door carrying two bags. "Even if Anna is leader, I don't see Maria taking orders from her."

Mo passed between two cars and glanced both ways before continuing forward.

Cruz tapped his thumb on the steering wheel. "Did you hear from Tomas?"

"Yes." Sort of.

Mo walked around the side of the Jeep and reached for the handle.

"Tell me later," Cruz said.

I opened my door and took the bags from her. No way would she be able to sit next to Bear and keep his nose out of the food.

"That was fast," I said as she climbed in.

"Lallo called ahead."

I recognized the name from the list of names Jay had given us. "Who is he?" Cruz asked.

"Lallo Edmo," Mo said. "He's a shaman. We'll be staying with him tonight."

She directed us farther north and halfway up Winnemucca Mountain to a dirt road with trees on either side. Dream catchers hung from the limbs of trees as well as something that looked like a mobile made of animal bones.

The road continued for close to a mile, and at the end of it sat a pleasant log house.

I checked the one-lane dirt road behind us. "Will the trackers look for us here?" If they did, they could easily block the road.

"This property covers close to a square mile. Most of it is holy land," she said. "They won't enter uninvited."

A large medicine wheel occupied the front yard, its outer circle marked by rocks laid out in a fifty-foot diameter. The eight spokes of a smaller inner circle marked the cardinal and non-cardinal directions. Past the wheel sat a smaller building made of logs.

"Sweat lodge?" Cruz asked.

Mo checked the direction of Cruz's nod. "Yes."

We climbed out of the Jeep, and Bear found a bush and lifted his leg. I glanced at the medicine wheel thankful Bear hadn't chosen it.

An old man with heavily wrinkled skin a deep shade of reddish brown stepped around the side of the house. He sported short white hair and a basketball-sized belly. "Mo," he said. "Did you bring my ribs?"

Mo held up one of the food bags and the man's face lit with childish delight. "Don't tell my granddaughter."

Mo shook her head. "Not a chance. Last time I did, she yelled at me for fifteen minutes."

The man smiled as he stepped toward us. He gave Mo a quick hug and told her to go into the house then turned to Cruz and me. Bear stood firmly in front of me.

"I'm Lallo." He stared into my eyes. "I've been expecting you." Bending down, he held a hand out for Bear. "Who is this?"

"Bear," Cruz said. "Check."

Bear sniffed Lallo's hand and allowed a pat on his head before following Cruz's direction to sit beside me.

"I'm Luna," I said. "This is Cruz."

"Of course." Lallo took my hand and cupped it with his other, smiling as he studied my face. Then he turned to Cruz and shook his hand. "I welcome you both. Please come inside. We have

200

much to discuss. But first there are ribs."

Books covered one wall of Lallo's living room. A leather couch and recliner faced the fireplace and a beautiful handmade wool rug covered the floor. A dining table sat in the corner behind the couch where Mo laid out food and plates.

"Beer?" Lallo offered.

Mo froze. "You're not supposed to have beer."

"Not supposed to have ribs either." Lallo grinned and disappeared into the kitchen.

We ate dinner making small talk, but mostly I watched Lallo. I couldn't remember the last time I'd seen anyone enjoy his food as much. By the time he finished his ribs, I doubted even an ant would find a scrap of meat on the bones. Afterward, Mo and Lallo did the dishes while Cruz and I took Bear for a walk.

"You heard from Tomas?" Cruz said.

During dinner, I'd forgotten the anger I'd felt over Tomas's brevity, but it quickly returned. "Yeah. A one-word text message."

Cruz frowned. "What did it say?"

"More."

"That's it?"

"Yep."

Thirty feet ahead, Bear investigated a hole in the ground.

Cruz shoved his hands in his pockets. "Sort of tells you nothing and everything."

I nodded. It also gave me more to worry about. Adam being clairvoyant, in addition to being able to read energy, meant the Neme-i would want him. If he could do even more, they'd go crazy over him—some in a good way, and others as if threatened, like I feared my sister might.

Back at the house, Mo sat in the living room playing with her phone. No telling where Lallo had gone.

"We think we know what Catherine's son wanted." Mo looked up long enough to direct the comment at us.

"What?" I asked.

"Her niece tried to kill herself today."

I stumbled. "Who's her niece?"

"Noni Lonehill."

My heart contracted, and I sank onto the couch. Noni had been so radiant amidst the crowd outside the Cookie Cabin. To think of her broken left a crater-sized hole inside me. "How?"

"Sleeping pills."

"Because of the council's decision?" Cruz asked.

"Probably. Lallo's talking to Crow now."

"Will she be okay?" I asked.

"Not sure yet."

Cruz studied me. "Are you okay?"

"No." I ground my teeth. I had never asked who had voted to deny the marriage blessings but I had no doubt it was the same four who'd voted to make the prophecies public—Peshlakai, Alvarez, Benally, and Anna. "Fucking Revisionists."

"Has anyone checked on her fiancé?" Cruz asked.

Mo continued typing. "He's at the hospital with her. Refuses to let anyone see but her family and Crow."

I shook my head. "Will they want Lallo to come?"

"Maybe. He's of Noni's clan."

We sat in silence while Bear sprawled in front of the fireplace. The air felt heavy and stiff—suffocating almost. Just as I stood to make a beeline for the backdoor and fresh air, Lallo stepped from the hall into the living room.

"She's going to be all right."

I let out a breath then sucked in the oxygen that seemed to refill the room.

"They were able to pump her stomach," he said.

"Do you need to go to her?" I asked.

Lallo shook his head. "The hospital will keep her overnight and then George will bring her here to stay with her aunt. I'll see her tomorrow."

"Why her aunt?" I asked. "Is Catherine her only family?"

"No," Lallo said. "But Noni and Catherine have always had a

202

special bond. Better than Noni and her mother. Also, Catherine can shield her from the rest of the tribe. Keep her away from the politics and everything else going on."

"Will George stay with them?" I wasn't sure how three people would fit in Catherine's hogan, but families had done so for centuries.

"No. It is best they be apart for now." Lallo touched his temple. "In Noni's mind, her strength is tied to her relationship with George. She needs to find her own inner strength again. When she has that, Catherine will call for him. In the meantime, George has decisions of his own to make."

"Is there anything we can do to help?" Cruz asked.

Lallo nodded. "With Luna's help, we can send strength to both of them."

"My help?" Confusion swam through me.

Mo dropped her phone on the couch and stood. "Where?"

Lallo nodded at the space in front of him. "Here will be fine."

I hesitated before stepping over to join them. "What do I do?"

"You join hands with us," Lallo said. "We will all think thoughts of Noni and George being strong and at peace and you will send them for us."

The last thing I wanted to do was broadcast my presence at Lallo's house by sending a message. "What if there's a tracker nearby?"

Mo shook her head. "Nothing to worry about. Something about this place makes it hard to perceive individual threads of energy."

"It's the spirits," Lallo said. "Spirit energy is very strong here. That is why this is holy ground. The energy confuses the trackers and leaves most people ill at ease."

"But not you?" I asked.

He shrugged. "I have learned to walk with the spirits."

I hesitated. Something felt wrong about this. I looked at Mo. "Can you send the thoughts?"

Her expression went from almost friendly to hostile. "No. I'm pihwappyh."

I stared at her not understanding.

"Broken," she barked. "I don't have the gift."

I inhaled sharply. Apparently I'd stumbled upon a sore subject.

Lallo shook his head. "You are not broken." He looked apologetically at Cruz and me. "Mo's mother was angry at John and our people and refused to allow Mo to be trained. Mo taught herself to use the gift in her own way."

"I was trained," Mo said through clenched teeth. "When I was sixteen and moved in with my dad. It didn't work."

"Because he couldn't unteach what he hadn't taught you," Lallo said. "You are gifted, Mo. No other seer has an assistant like you. No one gets the results you get when you ask for things."

I looked at Cruz. He shrugged. He didn't appear nearly as uncomfortable as I felt. I widened my eyes, silently begging for help.

He stepped forward. "Are you confident Luna's energy won't be tracked?"

"Yes." Mo sounded relieved to be off the topic of her.

Cruz gazed at me, eyebrows raised. The decision was mine.

"Okay." I wanted to move beyond the previous topic. "How do I send your thoughts?"

"Simple," Lallo said. "We hold hands, and as you think and send your own thoughts, our physical connection will allow our strength to flow through you as well."

I remembered the way touching Cruz allowed my messages to flow more strongly to him. I had never imagined the strength could go both ways.

Mo, Lallo, and I stepped into the center of the room.

Lallo turned toward Cruz. "You too."

Cruz's eyes narrowed. "I'm not Neme-i."

"That doesn't matter. You are made up of energy, same as every living creature. We are all connected."

Warmth blossomed inside me. My grandmother, Anna—many of the Neme-i I'd dealt with—saw Cruz as an outsider. They accepted his presence but would never see him as one of us. Lallo had just included him and, by extension, every other person who had mattered in my life. Lallo had joined the short list of Neme-i I truly respected.

Cruz joined our little circle, and we all held hands.

I closed my eyes and imagined Noni and George. I saw them separate and happy. I saw them flourishing individually. I pictured them in separate places, both staring up at the stars and finding strength in their beauty. Then I imagined both of them as they'd been before the tribal meeting.

As I prepared to send the message, my hands tingled, and colors seemed to flow through me. Behind the thoughts in my mind danced a rainbow with dark red and orange-yellow hues. The colors glowed and swirled inside my body until, with the release of a breath, I sent them along with the message from my mind.

When I opened my eyes, Cruz, Lallo, and Mo all stared at me.

I smiled. "That was different."

Mo dropped Cruz's and Lallo's hands and crossed her arms. She looked like she wanted to let loose a string of expletives.

"It certainly was," Lallo agreed.

Cruz's brow furrowed as he stared at me.

"What?" I asked.

"You don't know?" he said.

I looked to Lallo who patted my arm.

"You didn't just send our energy with yours," he said. "You *drew* energy from us."

Now I stared. "Huh?"

"We call it mukutekka," Lallo said.

"Spirit thief," Mo muttered.

Fear sliced through me. "I stole parts of your spirits?" My breathing turned shallow. I looked at Cruz. Had I hurt him?

"No." Lallo smiled gently. "Not literally. It is called mukutekka because our energy comes from our spirit. When you pull, you pull from there. But our spirits are filled by the endlessness of the Great Spirit. They remain whole. We are fine."

"Speak for yourself," Mo grumbled as she stalked toward the couch.

I glanced at Cruz and mouthed, *Did I hurt you?*

Gentle understanding played across his face, and he shook his head.

"We have much to talk about." Lallo's gaze remained steady on me. "John asked me to teach you about our spiritual beliefs. But I think for now, we should stay in the context of this. We can talk more about spiritual beliefs next time."

"Next time?" I said. "I'm coming back?"

Lallo gave an enigmatic smile. "I am hoping we will visit often." Turning, he moved toward the kitchen. "Come. I'll make tea."

Seated on the couch, Mo seemed to shrink away from me as I walked past. Probably afraid I'd steal more of her spirit.

Cruz nodded at the dining table where I knew he would stay until Lallo and I finished.

In the kitchen, Lallo stood in front of the sink adding water to a pot. He nodded toward the breakfast bar. "Sit."

I did and watched his back for a moment before I glanced toward the dining room. Cruz had said I hadn't hurt him when I'd sent the message to Noni and George, but Mo's reaction left me uncertain.

"Am I—" I struggled to find a word that would work. According to Jay, it was considered rude for George to touch people without their permission. Was I like him? "— untouchable?"

Lallo turned off the water and carried the pot to the stove. "No. You have control of when you send messages. Only when you are touching people who are concentrating on the same thing as you will you draw their energy." He scooped tea leaves from a jar and added them to the water.

"But people need to know before I do that?"

"Yes." He turned on the burner and pulled two mugs from the

cupboard. "They should be given the opportunity to say no."

"Does it hurt when I pull energy from someone?"

He seemed to consider. "It can be mildly uncomfortable if one does not trust and relax, but if you do, it is like skiing down a gentle slope with your mind. When used for good, being mukutekka can be very helpful. Because of your ability, Noni and George will receive all of our messages."

"But like all things that can be good, it can also be used for ill?" I said.

"Yes. You will have to choose when to use it and when not."

Lallo's tea tasted like bark. He said it would calm and strengthen my spirit. Then he talked about harmony and the interconnectedness of things. How all things were created in harmony and existed in balance. Day and night, sun and moon, birth and death, male and female. He talked about the gifts of the Neme-i, which also existed in harmony—the ability to send with the ability to receive.

"All things in this world desire harmony, including our spirits. Yours will tell you when it is right to use your gift. But you must learn to listen and be aware."

"Aware of what?" I took a sip of the tea and tried not to make a face.

"Of your surroundings and of those who would help you. Only when you are in harmony with them will you be able to send true harmony."

I thought of Raina and the things I'd read in her journals. Had she considered the question of harmony when she'd taken me and run? Or had desperation to protect her children erased all reason from her mind? Anna and I had definitely remained safe, but at what cost? The wake of pain and destruction Raina had left was immeasurable.

I choked down another sip of tea. "How will I know if I'm creating harmony or if I just think I am?"

Lallo lifted his mug and smiled. "A good question." He took a sip and seemed to consider. "At first it will be difficult, but it will grow easier. Listen to your spirit. It will know."

I sighed. Lallo had more faith in my spirit than I did. Two days ago, my spirit had told me my mother was a terrible person who didn't care about her children. Now I wondered if she'd cared too much.

"I can see you are troubled," Lallo said. "The spirits tell me you are facing a crossroads and will have decisions to make. They tell you not to worry. Your path will be clear."

A breeze stirred the air. Lallo turned toward the screen door. Setting his cup down, he stood and stepped outside. I moved to the door and watched him walk to the edge of the patio. A gray fox walked within five feet of Lallo and stopped. There it stood, staring at the man. For several moments, neither moved.

"Liohbwana, sai," Lallo finally said. "Thank you, brother." Returning to the house, he shut and locked the glass door. "We should join the others."

"Is everything okay?" I collected both of our mugs and followed him.

"The fox is an old friend. He visits me when trouble is nearby. For now, we are okay."

I wasn't sure what to make of the answer, but my gut told me to trust him.

In the next room, Cruz and Mo sat at the dining table. Puzzle pieces lay before them in some sort of organized system while the edges of the puzzle formed an empty frame.

I stopped short and double-checked to make sure Cruz sat before me and not Tomas. As far as I knew, Cruz hadn't assembled a puzzle in…ever?

"What's going on?" I asked.

He and Mo glanced up.

Lallo nodded to Mo who yawned and stood to follow him.

"I think I'm on to something," Cruz said after the other two stepped into the kitchen.

The jigsaw box Jacob had given us in Eureka sat on the table above the puzzle pieces. From beneath his leg, Cruz produced

Raina's latest journal. He flipped it open to the pages decorated with doodles. "I was thinking about the drawings."

"Why?"

"They're a change of pattern."

I tried to speak but nothing came out. I'd looked at the doodles and thought nothing of them.

He glanced back to be sure we remained alone then flipped forward through several pages. "Most of the drawings are childlike."

The lines were shaky and the curves lopsided. No way to tell what they even represented. Monsters or aliens maybe?

"All but this one." He flipped to a dog-eared page and pointed.

The perfect lines and curves told me the figure had been traced, not doodled. "A puzzle piece?"

Cruz nodded. "I'm trying to find the piece from the safe."

I looked from the jigsaw back to the drawing. If Adam had left me the piece and traced a drawing of it in Raina's journal, was he trying to tell me something? Was my son communicating with me?

Sixteen

My heart skipped as my mind raced. How had the puzzle appeared when Jacob pulled it from his closet minus one piece? I motioned to the upper left quarter of the puzzle. "It went somewhere in this section."

Cruz nodded. "Where the suspension cable meets the top of the bridge."

Seated beside Cruz, I attacked the puzzle with a fervor I'd never felt when staring at a jigsaw. By the time Lallo returned, I'd placed three pieces.

His eyes lit. "A puzzle! May I help?"

"Please," I said. The more people who worked on it, the sooner we'd find the piece we needed.

He pulled out the chair opposite Cruz. "I always find it helps to start with the sky."

Usually I would have agreed. But Cruz had divided the pieces into four piles—dark green trees, lighter colored trees, sky, and bridge—and he and I were desperately trying to assemble the bridge.

Fifteen minutes passed before Mo stepped into the living room. "You were right," she said to Lallo. "They're there." Beer in hand, she took a seat at the table and eyed Cruz and me. "We need to talk."

Something about her voice sent butterflies jetting through my tummy.

"The trackers know you're here."

A heavy, sinking feeling made me grit my teeth. "You said they wouldn't sense the message I sent."

"They didn't," Lallo said as he placed two sky pieces. "Too much interference here."

Mo nodded. "He's right. I don't know how they tracked you here, but it wasn't that. Maybe one of Catherine's kids talked. Maybe they were already in town watching for you. Lallo's name was on my dad's list."

"Where are they now?" Cruz asked.

"At the base of the driveway and the edges of the property." Lallo compared a light-blue sky piece with others. "They won't come closer."

"No," Mo said, "they'll wait for you to leave."

Lead filled my belly and my mouth turned dry. If they stopped us, what would we say when asked about Jay's whereabouts? That he was delivering birth prophecies? And how would we escape them? No way would they let us out of their sight. Or what if the reason they wanted us had nothing to do with Jay and everything to do with my mother's prophecy?

"Is there another way out?" Cruz asked.

"There's a back road, but it'll be guarded. You're gonna have to hike." Mo took a drink.

"To where?" Cruz asked.

Liquid fizzed as Mo righted her bottle. "There's an old radar station at the top of the mountain about seven miles from here."

Cruz tapped a puzzle piece against the table. "Is it operational?"

"No." Lallo scanned the pieces in front of him. "They closed it many years ago."

"It's pretty run down," Mo said, "but it will offer some cover which is important. You'll likely have to wait out the day. The soonest I'll be able to pull you out of there safely will probably be tomorrow night."

Cruz nodded. "We'll need food and water."

"Of course." Lallo snapped another piece into position.

"Will you be the one to come for us?" I asked Mo.

"Doubtful. The trackers will keep an eye on me until they're sure I'm not with you. I'll probably have to send a friend. Do you know where you're going next?"

The word *Idaho* sat on my tongue, but I couldn't force it past my lips. Something about it felt wrong. "Not yet."

Mo's eyebrows arched and Cruz cocked his head.

"We're working on that," I said.

"You need to figure it out, so I can plan."

The corners of Cruz's eyes crinkled before he turned a smile on Mo. "Just a vehicle—something bigger than the Jeep. We'll take it from there."

Mo blew out a breath. "Fine."

I turned away and tried to concentrate on the puzzle, but thoughts of the trackers and where we should go plagued me.

"Worried?" Cruz asked after I'd held the same puzzle piece for several minutes.

I nodded.

"I'll look around later, see where the trackers are. As long as we can get past them, we should be fine."

When it came to being in nature, Cruz was the most gifted person I'd ever seen. He could sneak up on a jackrabbit and had an infallible internal compass. Clients at work who marveled at my skill in the wilderness had never hiked with Cruz. Those who had, still told stories about the Native American boy who'd helped them do things no other guide would dare try. That was part of the reason I had such a hard time imagining Cruz running his security company. Invoices, employees, an office—those things weren't part of Cruz. Cruz *was* the land.

"What about Bear?" I asked. Cruz and I could hike and be reasonably silent, but Bear would bark and growl at everything we wanted to avoid.

The corners of Cruz's mouth tightened. He turned to look at the sleeping dog. Bear's legs twitched in the midst of a dream.

"You could send him a message before we leave."

Even though Lallo and Mo said energy couldn't be tracked here, the trackers had shown up for some reason. "But the trackers—"

"They already know we're here."

I blew out a breath and wondered what kind of message I'd need to send. "I don't think I can send a message that will last the whole hike and possibly all of tomorrow."

"You could borrow our energy for extra strength," Lallo suggested.

I jerked my head up. "Whose? Yours and Cruz's?" No way would Mo consent to another tug on her soul.

"And Mo's." Lallo placed a piece of sky that brushed the top of the bridge.

"Speak for yourself," Mo said from the couch. "Not interested." Head down, she appeared engrossed in her phone.

Lallo shot me a wink. "If you don't help, they'll have to leave the dog with you."

Mo's gaze shot up. "Not gonna happen. I'm not taking the dog."

Lallo kept his gaze on the puzzle. "What's wrong with the dog?"

"He slobbers."

"All dogs slobber."

"Not as much as that one."

Lallo shrugged. "Then I guess you'll have to decide which you want less, twenty-four hours with a dog that slobbers or a few minutes of mild discomfort."

I stared at Lallo. For a holy man, he was surprisingly adept at manipulation.

"Fine," Mo said through clenched teeth. "I'll help."

Lallo held another piece poised above the puzzle. "We'll do it right before they leave for maximum effect."

"Any idea when that will be?" Mo asked.

Cruz worked it out, calculating four hours for the hike plus one more in case something went wrong. "We'll leave in three hours."

That didn't leave a lot of time to finish the puzzle. Blocking all thoughts of the trackers from my mind, I buckled down on the jigsaw.

I'd placed six pieces when Cruz tapped my foot. Looking up, I followed his gaze to the puzzle. He tapped the piece where the suspension cable met the support. A scream welled inside me. I held it in. Back straight, butt on the edge of my chair, I celebrated with a wide-eyed stare at Cruz.

Picking up the piece as if it hadn't fit, he palmed it. "Let's take a break." He led me to the kitchen and outside onto the back porch. The second he closed the sliding glass door, he pulled the journal from his waist band and compared the piece to the drawing.

"Perfect match." He pulled me to him in a hug. "He's telling you something."

Tingles filled me with warmth. My son was talking to me! For the first time ever, my child and I were communicating. But as Cruz released me and the cool night air replaced his body heat, reality set in. I had no idea what Adam was saying.

"What do you think it means?" I asked.

Cruz tipped his head. "Don't know. Everything Raina's left has pointed us in a direction. Maybe this will too."

"To where? That bridge in Portland?"

Cruz shrugged as if he understood how ridiculous it sounded.

"And then what? We just hope someone shows up and tells us what to do?"

"Worked in Eureka."

He had a point. And regardless how flimsy it seemed, it felt more concrete than going to an area in Idaho where Jay believed Raina had lived many years ago. At least in Portland we had a specific destination.

Thirty minutes before we needed to leave, Cruz woke me. After our puzzle break, Lallo had shown me to his guest room

214

where I'd promptly fallen asleep. Cruz had declined the opportunity to sleep, electing instead to do some outdoor reconnaissance. When I woke, a blanket lay on top of me, and it took a minute to remember where I was.

Cruz shoved a cup of coffee in my hand and turned on the light. "We need to talk."

I squinted against the brightness as I took my first sip. "Did you see the trackers?"

"Yeah. They're watching the roads and there are a couple around the edges of the property."

"Can we get past them?"

"As long as we're quiet."

I let out a breath.

Cruz motioned to the foot of the bed. "I grabbed some clothes. Put them on."

A pair of black leggings and a navy-blue T-shirt lay beside the black sweatshirt I'd pulled out earlier.

"Are our packs ready?"

He nodded. "In the living room."

Usually, the prospect of a hike sent tendrils of excitement through me. Knowing we'd be hiking to flee tonight had me on edge.

Standing with his fists balled, Cruz seemed to be experiencing his own sense of unease.

I peeled my shirt off. "What?"

"Something I heard." He sat on the edge of the bed. "Two of the trackers seemed confused."

I pulled the dark shirt on. "About what?"

"Why they're here."

"They don't know they're looking for us?" Shimmying out of my shorts, I reached for the leggings.

"No. They know that. They just don't know why. Apparently Jay's the only one the council asked Ethan to find."

"So why the hell are they looking for us?" I reached for my hiking boots. "They think we'll lead them to him?"

215

"They mentioned that possibility," Cruz said, his tone noncommittal.

"What else?"

"They wondered if Ethan's taking directions from someone outside the council."

As far as I understood, the council ruled the Keyake tribe. The Neme-i lived according to the laws voted on by them. Was there some person or ruling body above them? "Who?"

"I don't know." Cruz scrubbed a hand through his hair. "I'm hoping Mo or Lallo might."

Out in the living room, Mo and Lallo sat at the table, the nearly finished puzzle between them. A topographical map of the area sat next to it. I assumed Cruz had been studying it.

"I'm addicted," Lallo said with a guilty grin. "I want to finish before you leave."

Mo rolled her eyes.

"Why don't you keep it?" I said. "We can't bring it. It'll make too much noise."

Lallo nodded as if I'd bestowed a great gift. "I would be happy to."

"We need to ask you something." Cruz told them about the conversation he'd overheard and asked if the trackers would be answering to anyone besides the council.

Mo and Lallo exchanged a glance.

"There have been rumors," Lallo said.

"What rumors?" Cruz's gaze hardened.

"That there's division. Someone else calling shots," Mo said.

An owl hooted outside.

"Any idea who?"

Lallo shrugged. "Some say the Sáanii Suntehai."

"Others say the Revisionists have a ruling group."

"Would Ethan follow one of them and ignore the council?" Cruz tightened the drawstring on his pack.

"Ethan likes power," Mo said. "He'd follow anyone offering it."

216

Lallo's face scrunched. "Maybe. But Ethan's strength has always been his approach. You expect him from the front or back and he comes at you from above. He thinks on a different level. It is possible he is simply going through you to get to Jay."

I hoped that was it, but if not, who had sent him and why would they want us?

"Is there any way of finding out?" I asked.

Mo tipped her head. "Maybe. I'll see what I can learn."

"Thank you."

The owl hooted again.

Cruz glanced at the clock. "We need to get going."

"Let's send your message," Lallo said.

I'd been thinking about what message I should send. We needed Bear quiet and beside us, but it would also help if other creatures kept their distance. I would have loved to send a similar message to the trackers, but they would know. The four of us joined hands in a circle, and I sent the message to every four-legged creature on the mountain.

"That was different," Lallo said when I'd finished sending.

I'd felt the difference too. I'd seen the colors sitting behind the thoughts again—a rainbow of hues with dark red and blue most prominent. When I'd released the message, the colors shot out with it, only this time they swirled and traveled in all directions instead of just one.

I glanced at Mo. Teeth gritted, she stuffed her hands beneath her armpits.

"Thank you," I said.

She took two steps back. "Sure." Her hands didn't budge.

Lallo watched me, and I could see the question burning in his eyes.

In the short time I'd been around the Neme-i, I'd learned gossip moved amongst them at the speed of technology. Word about my simultaneous messaging ability had probably gotten out after the tribal meeting. I didn't know who had talked, but someone clearly had.

"It was a simultaneous message," I mumbled.

Lallo's eyes lit like they had when he'd seen the puzzle. "I heard you could do that."

Cruz lifted my pack.

I slid my arms through the straps. "Do you suppose we could keep it between us?"

Lallo shrugged. "I won't speak of it, but it won't matter. If I've heard the whispers, others have too."

I'd spent my entire life trying to live beneath the radar. Being amongst the Neme-i seemed to render that impossible. "Nonetheless."

Lallo nodded. "I will say nothing."

"Thank you."

We said our goodbyes, and Lallo cautioned us to keep our distance from the trackers. "No more messages," he added. "Once you leave here, they'll be able to sense your energy."

We thanked him and called for Bear then slipped out the backdoor.

In the cool night air I pulled up the hood on my sweatshirt and drew my hands into the sleeves. I would warm up once we got hiking, but for now, I appreciated the added layer.

Cruz and I crept behind the house and into the night. About a quarter mile out, we wound around a boulder and crouched behind a bunch of creosote bushes. Cruz motioned to our right. Squinting into the moonlit night, I made out the shapes of two people about thirty yards away. Cruz put his finger to his lips and started forward bent at the waist. I followed his lead, stepping carefully to keep from kicking up a spray of pebbles.

The farther we got from the house, the more my nerves settled. Other than the trackers Cruz had pointed out, we saw no one. The only dark shapes I noted belonged to bats passing overhead. Bear remained at my side like a dog who'd mastered obedience. The land began to rise, and the dirt we'd been walking along gave way to dried grass and weeds. Soon we were lifting our knees to get through it. Eventually we came upon a path and followed it.

Looking ahead at the remainder of our climb, I noticed a dark swath cutting a twisting path up the mountain. A road. I pointed it out.

Cruz nodded. "We'll cross it twice on the way up. After the first crossing, another path diverges off this one. Lallo said it's steeper and a lot less used. We'll take it."

We continued on for some time before we came to the first road crossing—a berm atop a three-foot slope. Cruz started up the slope, and I felt a tug in my head. Something was off.

"Wait." I grabbed the back of his shirt.

He stepped down. "What?"

I shook my head. I didn't have an explanation other than the voice in my head. Then I heard a familiar sound.

Cruz and I looked at each other. "Car!"

He led me into the tall grass to the left of the path and we both crouched. I pulled Bear close and pushed his butt into a sitting position.

A set of headlights crested a hill in the road and drove in our direction. The car slowed to a crawl as it moved past. Ducking my head, I hid my face in Bear's fur. The crunch of tires on the road stopped, and I sucked in a breath, worried I'd give off some trace of myself if I exhaled.

"Did you send a message?" Cruz whispered.

I shook my head.

Car doors opened and I heard footsteps on the road. Heart racing, I glanced up. Cruz eased his hand toward his gun.

Pain shot through my right knee and my calf muscles tightened. I needed to shift, but I didn't dare move and disturb the grass around us. I tried to think of something else—anything—to distract my mind, but my muscles threatened to cramp, and the pain in my knee persisted.

"Over here," a male voice said.

The footsteps drew nearer.

"Was it her?" a woman asked.

"I think so."

Oh shit. Hand trembling, I reached for my knives.

One set of footsteps stopped. The other set continued.

"Wait," the man said. "Holy shit!"

"What?" the woman asked.

"It can't be." The man sounded flustered, excited. "We've got to go. This is huge."

"What about—"

"I was wrong. It wasn't her." The footsteps retreated. "It's better."

Car doors opened.

"Better how?" the woman asked.

The doors closed. Gravel crunched beneath tires and soon the sound of the car faded.

I breathed a sigh of relief and sat.

"You okay?" Cruz whispered.

I nodded as I stretched my leg and flexed my ankles. Slowly, my muscle relaxed. "What just happened?"

Cruz shook his head. "We got lucky."

Pulling my leg in, I rubbed my calf. "Do you think they were trackers?"

"Yeah." He watched me a moment. "How'd you know to stop?"

"Funny feeling," I said.

"The voice in your head?"

"Yeah."

He nodded and helped me stand. "Let's get moving."

Fifty yards past the road, the walking path divided in two and we took the less worn path. Whereas the original had been wide enough for people to walk two and three abreast, this path demanded a single-file trek and within minutes we were climbing large boulders and steep inclines. Several times, Cruz had to reach back and offer me his hand or grab Bear's shoulders while I shoved him up from behind. Without packs and a dog, the path would have been demanding. With them, it was worse. And with me looking back for trackers every two minutes, progress was slow.

Sweat poured down my neck and back by the time we reached the second crossing. Crouched behind boulders, we listened and watched, then scurried across the road and continued another ten minutes before stopping.

"Almost there," Cruz whispered. He nodded toward the top of the mountain, and I could see we'd made it through the worst of the climb.

We took a short rest and a couple swigs of water before continuing toward the top.

Abandoned buildings came into view. Shabby looking from a distance, they were worse up close with whole chunks of roof missing. The doors and windows were boarded to keep trespassers out, but Cruz found a door with a loose piece of plywood that had obviously been removed and replaced several times.

"Vandals?" I asked. "Junkies?"

Cruz climbed inside and shined his flashlight around. "Teenagers. It's safe."

I handed him my pack and crawled beneath the upper board, motioning for Bear to follow. Cruz shone his flashlight on a blanket in the middle of the cement floor with a couple of candles around it. Apparently we'd happened upon someone's love nest.

I took in the dirt and cobwebs and wondered how many bodily fluids coated the blanket. "Romantic."

Cruz grinned. "Can't be too picky when you're a teenager."

He had a point. And I had no room to scoff. Adam had been conceived under some trees in the hills behind UC Berkeley.

We set up our tent on the cement floor then placed our sleeping mats and bags inside. It wasn't as nice as sleeping under the stars on a pine-needle cushioned bit of ground, but it beat the hell out of the blanket.

⌁

I woke once, early in the morning, and stayed awake long enough to eat a granola bar, feed Bear, and empty my bladder.

221

The next time I woke, Cruz lay beside me wearing nothing but a pair of shorts. Eyes open, hands at his sides, he stared up at the mesh crown of the blue tent.

I wiped sweat from my hairline then sat up and searched for a water bottle. The air felt like a blanket I couldn't remove. "How hot is it?" Spying my canteen in the corner, I reached for it.

"You don't want to know."

I pulled the zipper on the door flap, letting in some of the building's stale air. "Is it cooler out there?"

"Maybe a degree or two."

Good enough.

I dressed and crawled out of the tent. Breathing deeply, I enjoyed the musty and slightly foul odor of the somewhat cooler air. Bear scrambled out behind me and I spent some time scratching behind his ears and calling him a good boy. He hadn't barked or left our sides.

Cruz joined us, and we walked around inside the building, sticking to the shadows. Even five feet away from the light streaming through the hole in the roof I could feel the temperature climbing.

Bear sniffed the floor like a blood hound.

I had no idea how hot it was, but as the day wore on, I knew it would get ugly. "Do you think we have enough water?"

"If we're careful."

"What if Mo's not here by nightfall?"

"We'll wait until midnight. If she's not here then, there's some military housing still in use a little way from here. We'll hike there, find some water, and hike out."

"To where?"

He shrugged. "Don't know. Maybe back to Lallo's."

"What about the trackers?"

Cruz grimaced.

"What do you think they'll do if they find us?" I hadn't allowed myself to voice the question until that moment.

"Ask questions. Try to figure out where Jay is. Maybe insist

222

on staying with us. They're not my biggest concern though." He kicked at something on the floor then made the *tcht* sound. "Leave it," he told Bear.

"What is it?"

"Dead rat. Mostly just bones." He looked around for something to move the remains with.

I spotted an old beer box and tossed it to him. I didn't want to see the rat.

Using his foot, Cruz eased the remains into the box while whispering in Tewa.

"What is your biggest concern?"

"The possibility Ethan's reporting to someone besides the council." He placed the box on a support stud out of Bear's reach. "If he's reporting to the council, anything the trackers do will be public knowledge. That's good. Your tribe won't let you be hurt. But if he's reporting to someone outside the council, it can all be kept secret."

The granola bar I'd eaten turned sour in my stomach. "You're worried the person he's reporting to is the same one who tried to hurt me in Albuquerque, aren't you?"

"Yes." Cruz met my gaze from across the warehouse. "Just because they haven't made a move this past month doesn't mean they're gone."

I thought of Detective Richard and his plan to keep investigating my case after his captain had closed it. Nothing had been learned in the month the case had been open. I doubted that had changed in the past week, but I hoped so.

Our day passed in sweaty drudgery. The only relief came from the few times I managed to fall back to sleep. When I did, I dreamt of Raina and Gloria, and never stayed asleep long. Cruz seemed to have better luck.

By the time darkness fell, we were practically scratching at the plywood door in our desperation to get out of the building. After exiting, I stood still gulping in the relief of open space and staring up at the night sky. I couldn't imagine anything more peaceful.

The sound of something in the distance caught my ears and I listened until recognition hit me. A radio and a car engine.

My insides froze as I stared at Cruz. Fifteen feet away, he stiffened as he looked from me to the building. "Get back inside."

Seventeen

Cruz whistled for Bear then followed us into the ramshackle building, replacing the plywood against the door. "Go to the other end."

I did as instructed. Bear followed, keeping himself between me and the door.

The car engine and radio grew louder until both cut out and were replaced by the sound of doors slamming and two voices—one male, one female.

I glanced at Bear. Teeth bared, he stood ready to pounce. A low growl emanated from his throat. Had my message worn off? Taking his collar in one hand, I put my other on his head and hoped like hell he wouldn't start barking.

Cruz hurried away from the door and joined us. "Kids," he whispered as the plywood came free of the doorway.

"I'm telling you it's in there," the female said. "It has to be. My mother will kill me if I lost it."

"Yeah, yeah, yeah," the male said.

In the moonlight, I made out the silhouette of a person stooping and entering the doorway.

He moved toward the tent—a sure giveaway someone had been in the building—and scratched on its side. "Hello? Mo sent us."

I blew out a breath as Cruz stepped out of the shadow and into the moonlight streaming through the roof. "Hi."

The boy was named Jimmy, and the girl, Kate. How they knew Mo, I didn't know, but they explained they'd been hired to act like a young couple arguing while they smuggled us off the mountain. Cruz and I rode in the trunk of their rusted-out Oldsmobile while Bear lay in the backseat.

I'd never ridden in a trunk before, and by the time we were through, I never wanted to again. It was cramped, hard, and smelled like rotted gym socks.

We met Mo outside a series of storage units near the edge of town. When I managed to extricate myself from the trunk, she stood leaning against the side of a light blue panel van. Cruz followed me, stretching his limbs one at a time while I tried to stomp life back into my sleeping appendages.

"Anyone follow you?" Mo asked Jimmy.

"No," he said. "You were right about a couple being on the road though. They were stopped and had their hood up like they were having engine problems, but they were way too interested in seeing inside our car for that to be the case."

"Did you stop?"

"No," Jimmy said. "Just kept arguing like you said, and they looked away."

"But you slowed down on the way back," Kate said as she closed the trunk.

Jimmy made a face at her before turning back to Mo and scratching his head. "I don't know why I did that."

I had an idea.

"It's okay," Mo said. "Did they see anything?"

"Don't think so." Kate moved to the side of the car and opened the back door. "The dog stayed under the blanket chewing on that bone you gave us."

Bear jumped out and trotted over to Cruz and me, tail wagging. Sure enough, he carried a beef rib bone, most likely left from the night before.

I patted his side. "Good boy."

Mo stepped away from the van and handed Jimmy a hundred-dollar bill while thanking him. Jimmy told her to call him any time then he and Kate drove away.

Cruz nodded at the van. "What's this?"

"Our new ride."

"Ours?" Cruz said. "You're coming with us?"

"They'll be looking for me now too, so yeah." She opened the cargo door. "Get in."

I stepped forward expecting to see an empty cargo hold. Instead, I found a carpeted floor and a double mattress with pillows and bedding in the back.

"If we sleep and drive in shifts," Mo said, "we won't have to stop. I'll drive first to get us out of town." She walked around the front of the van, opened the driver's side door, and hoisted herself in. "Let's go."

Cruz looked at me and shrugged then motioned for me to go first. Bear followed carrying his new treat, and Cruz climbed in last, sliding the door shut behind himself.

Mo told us to figure out our sleeping and driving order, and Cruz volunteered me to sleep first. Considering how much we'd slept at the radar base, I doubted I'd sleep at all, but I was wrong. I closed my eyes, and when I opened them, we were stopped at a gas station somewhere in Oregon.

Cruz drove next while I sat in the passenger seat.

Stars shone bright in the sky as we drove through the high desert of central Oregon. The endless low-lying bushes illuminated by the headlights reminded me of home.

Cruz glanced over his shoulder. "Is she asleep?"

I looked back. Mo lay sprawled on the mattress unmoving. "I think so." My ears popped, and I wiggled my jaw to unblock them. I hadn't seen a sign yet to tell me the elevation, but we were well above sea level.

Cruz let out a heavy breath. "I think we should tell her what we're doing. She can't help if she doesn't know."

"You trust her?" I asked.

"She hasn't led us wrong yet."

No, she hadn't. She hadn't been particularly friendly about it, but she had been helpful.

"I don't think she likes me," I said.

"She doesn't know you."

But she'd sure as hell formed an opinion. I thought about that. About opinions in general and where they came from. My opinion of Raina had been formed on assumptions. In the past week, however, that opinion had changed a lot. I didn't understand the choices she had made, and I didn't condone them, but I didn't hate her either. She hadn't dumped me. She'd left me with someone who loved me. From what she'd written in her journals, the decision hadn't been easy. It had hurt a great deal. But she'd done it to protect me. Wasn't that what a good parent did? Anything necessary to protect and care for their child?

I couldn't excuse the fact that she'd taken my child, but what if Jay was right? What if she had been trying to protect Adam? To save him for me?

The thoughts rolled through my head over the next two hours, right up until Cruz yawned and asked if I was ready to drive.

He pulled into a gas station where he filled the tank and woke Mo while I visited the restroom and mini-mart to stock up on coffee and pre-packaged breakfast pastries. As I stood in line, Mo stepped inside, eyed my selections and rolled her eyes. She walked away and returned with a box of strawberry Pop-Tarts. I couldn't fault her choice.

Back at the van, Cruz lay on the mattress while Mo and I settled into the front and buckled up. I'd barely driven ten miles when I heard the deep, even breathing of Cruz's sleep.

"Must have been tired," Mo observed.

I had no idea what Cruz's normal sleep schedule was, but since he'd signed on to protect me, I doubted he'd had more than a couple of eight-hour nights. "He needs it."

As I drove, I thought about Mo and whether or not I trusted her. Jay obviously did, and I trusted him. That should mean something. Plus, she already knew my mother's prophecy and that I had a son. The fact we were looking for them seemed minor in comparison.

The highway began to bend and curve in Mount Hood National Forest. Foliage grew taller and denser, the air cool. On the road, sun and shade fought for prominence. I looked at the trees, so dense in places that walking through them would have been difficult. The sight left me homesick.

The sound of a sharp breath caused me to glance in the rearview mirror. Cruz sat upright, his gaze darting about.

"You okay?" I asked.

He caught my gaze in the mirror and seemed to calm. "Nightmare."

Mo whipped around. "How bad?"

Cruz must have made a face because she repeated the question.

"How bad? Was it a normal nightmare for you or worse?" She watched him like a hawk targeting its prey.

I glanced in the rearview mirror. Cruz seemed as confused by Mo's reaction as I felt.

"Worse, I guess."

"Assholes," Mo growled. "Come up here."

"What?" Cruz said.

"Come up here. Jesus, why do I have to keep repeating myself? You need to touch Luna. Now."

Cruz made a face, but scooted himself to the front of the van and took my hand. Shadows ringed his eyes. His face looked pale.

I squeezed and something passed between us—a feeling like a sigh or an unexpected breeze on a hot day. My body relaxed. When I glanced at Cruz, his skin tone had returned to normal and though the shadows remained beneath his eyes, they didn't seem as dark.

"You feel that?" Mo asked.

Cruz and I both nodded.

"What is it?" Cruz asked.

Mo scowled. "Pull over. I'll drive the rest of the way. He's gonna need you to juice him."

"Juice him?" I said.

"Your bond just got attacked. You need to build it back up." She pointed at a sign. "There's a turnout coming. Pull over there."

I did as instructed.

Mo threw her door open then stalked around to the driver's side. "You two need to get in back and keep touching. It'd be better if you could send a message, but it's too risky. Touching will have to do." She nodded toward the back of the van. "Go."

I turned to obey but Cruz blocked my way.

"Not till you explain," he said.

Mo gave an exasperated sigh. "Would it be okay if I explain while we drive?"

"Will you?" Cruz said.

They glared like two chunks of granite, both unwilling to give.

"Yes," she finally said.

"Fine."

Cruz and I crawled onto the mattress. I sat between his legs and leaned against his chest while he wrapped both arms around me. Mo climbed into the driver's seat, checked the mirrors, and steered us back onto the road.

"What happened to Cruz is called tenkuane'e. It's the ability to send messages through dreams. If the message is unpleasant, the dream's experienced as a nightmare. If the message is about doing something the person already wants to do, the dream's a good one."

I thought of Gloria's nightmares and Raina's letters cautioning Gloria to move us before the nightmares started.

"If the dream can be sent right before the person wakes, the message is strongest which is why the nightmares tend to be the only messages people remember receiving."

"Because they wake the person?" I asked.

"Yes."

I remembered a series of dreams I'd had while I'd posed as Anna and stayed at the Bluefeathers' house. The voice in my head had woken me from most of them. The dreams hadn't been

230

nightmares in the traditional sense, but they'd been disturbing as hell.

"It's not reliable," Mo said, "and it's considered reprehensible—forbidden. Unfortunately, there's no way to regulate it. Even Neme-i men can't recognize who sends a message when they're dreaming. When they wake, they know they received one but not who it came from. Something about the brain being too relaxed or something."

"So let me guess," I said, "everyone's just on their honor not to do it?"

Mo glanced in the rearview mirror. "Yeah."

"Great," Cruz said. His voice sounded distant and cold.

Talking about my nightmares always helped me. "Do you want to tell us about it?"

"No."

The harshness of his tone sent a chill across my skin.

He tightened his grip on me.

"Was it to hurt her?" Mo asked. The words sounded so gentle, I almost didn't believe she'd spoken them.

Cruz looked away without responding.

I twisted to better see him. Pain and anger radiated from his eyes. For a second, I thought he might cry.

"I wouldn't do it," he said, staring at me as if desperate for me to believe him.

I reached up and cupped his cheek. "I know. I trust you."

The lines around his eyes smoothed, but I could see the pain that remained. I turned back to Mo. "Why now? And how would they have known he was sleeping?"

"It's dawn," Mo said. "Not hard to guess he might be waking. When's the last time the two of you didn't sleep together?"

"Do naps count?" Cruz asked.

"Hard to predict when someone's napping."

"Then—" I glanced at Cruz. We'd slept together every night since we'd first had sex.

"Albuquerque," Cruz said.

231

Mo tipped her head. "That's why."

My mind raced as I tried to think of the next logical question. "Why does it matter if I'm with him?"

Mo met my gaze in the mirror. "When you're touching, your bond is strongest. The feelings that make up that bond act like a shield keeping anything that goes against it from getting in."

"Because Luna's messages will always be strongest for me?" Cruz asked.

Mo nodded. "As long as that bond lasts."

I still had so much to learn.

Cruz leaned against the wall of the van. "At least we have proof now."

"Proof of what?" I asked.

"That someone's still trying to hurt you."

"Except you don't," Mo said. "It's just your word. The council members who don't want to believe it will say you're lying or it was just a regular dream. After all, you're not Neme-i; you can't know when a message is received."

Cruz blew out a breath. "Fuck."

He and I ended up lying down. He seemed anxious about going back to sleep, but he needed it, so I held his hand and rested my forehead against his while I stared into his eyes. Eventually, his lids drooped then closed and his breathing evened out. I continued to hold him.

The idea that someone could send a dream message like that turned my insides cold. Cruz and I could sleep together—that wouldn't be hard—but what if the person who'd sent the message for Cruz to hurt me sent one to someone else? I didn't know who they'd target now, but what about in the future when I returned to my normal life? Would they target Kurt or my clients on a camping trip? Who would I trust?

How had Gloria and Raina done it? Gloria didn't have the nightmares all the time, and she sure as hell didn't sleep with me. The thought was almost laughable. Until I considered Adam. If the person who sent the message could make Cruz want to hurt me, could they make him want to hurt Adam? The thought sent a terror through me I'd never known.

I looked at Cruz. So peaceful as he slept. He wanted to love Adam. I believed that. He would never *want* to hurt my child. But could he be made to?

⊥⊤

Summer still held Portland in its grip when we arrived. People wore shorts and summer dresses and the sky shone bright and blue.

"Where to?" Mo asked.

Cruz pulled out a map and gave her directions. We took Highway 84 to Interstate 5 then got off on Lombard and passed businesses and houses for several miles. When we turned onto Philadelphia, the bridge loomed in front of us.

"Whoa," Mo said. "It's big."

With four lanes, St. John's Bridge didn't look any bigger than I remembered the rest of Portland's bridges being, but its swooping cables, massive green towers, and rows of old-fashioned light posts made it beautiful.

We started across the bridge and Cruz pointed out a park below. Across the river, barges carried cranes and warehouses huddled on the shore. At the end of the bridge, stood an impenetrable wall of dark green trees.

"Right or left?" Mo said.

We went right until we found a place to turn around then drove back across the bridge and wound around the streets until we made it to Cathedral Park.

Compared to Nevada, the air felt crisp and comfortable. Most people seemed happy in shorts. I appreciated my pants.

Though not particularly quiet with the bridge above it, the park was pretty. Parents and kids dotted the grass, some on blankets, some playing catch, others riding bikes and skateboards. My gaze zeroed on the nearest kids. Could one of them be Adam?

Cruz nodded at the cement pathway. "Let's walk."

"I'll be by the river," Mo said and started across the grass.

Taking my hand, Cruz led me onto the walkway which followed the parking lot before looping left.

"You need to pull out your picture and check the kids against it," Cruz said. "I don't know why we're here, but there must be a reason."

In the three days since Barbara had given me the photo of Adam, I'd memorized every inch, but I fished it out nonetheless. It had been two years since the photo had been taken. Adam would be taller. He might be heavier or thinner, and his hair could be a different color if they'd dyed it. When he'd been in Eureka, it had been black like Tomas's and mine, and I hoped it still would be, but I had no way of knowing.

Heart racing, I studied the children in the park. Desperately I wanted to run up to each and yell, "Are you mine?"

"Anything?" Cruz asked.

"No." I heard the desperation in my tone.

Cruz slowed to a stop. "Take a breath."

I did. "I don't know what to look for. There're too many."

Cruz nodded and surveyed the park. "You've got to narrow it down. Start with age. Look at the ones in the right range. Then check skin tone. He's not going to be white or black. After that, watch their movements. Listen to their laughter. Is there anyone who moves or sounds like Tomas or you?"

I did as he said and it eliminated some of the faces swimming in front of me. I pulled back further, watching the young boys run and listening to them yell at each other. I didn't see Tomas in any of them. Or me. "I don't think so."

"Let's move on."

The path continued to curve until we were opposite the parking lot near the bank of the river before straightening out beneath a small grove of trees. A gentle bend to the right took us beneath the bridge. I continued to watch the children, but none of them caught my eye.

It would have been so much easier if I could send a message, but Jay had explained it many times. Sending to a person based

234

only on a photo of them would leave me sending to the photo, not the person. People were so much more than images.

"I don't think he's here." The admission made my heart ache.

"I agree." Cruz stopped and turned around. "None of the kids paid us any attention."

"So?" Kids seldom paid attention to adults.

"We think he's looking for you, right?" Cruz said.

"Yeah."

"Judging from his finger painting, he's got some idea what you look like."

"Okay." I drew the word out.

"We don't look like we're from here. You have the same skin tone and hair color he'd be used to seeing in the mirror. If he were here, he'd notice you."

It made sense, and it allowed me to breathe more freely.

"Chances are he doesn't live here anymore," Cruz added. "He left the puzzle in Eureka. He probably lived here first."

His logic jived with the feeling in my gut, but that didn't mean I liked it. "If that's the case, why are we here?"

Holding my hand, Cruz started back the way we'd come. "Hoping for another clue."

We stopped where the path ran closest to the river. Mo sat on the bank farther ahead, leaning back on her elbows, watching the water flow.

"Have you thought any more about telling her what we're doing?" Cruz asked.

"Yeah." I was leaning toward telling her.

Mo stood as we approached.

"Relaxing?" Cruz asked.

She shrugged. "Now where?"

Cruz and I exchanged a glance.

"Somewhere private where we can tell you a story."

"Fine," she said. "Motel. We all need sleep, and the two of you need showers."

I hadn't thought about how we probably smelled after

235

spending the previous day sweating it out in an abandoned building and driving through the night, but a glance at Cruz revealed him looking—still hot, but not as devastatingly sexy as usual. I suspected I fell well below both marks.

Cruz grimaced. "We can't use a credit card."

"Not one in our names," Mo agreed. "But we can use Julie Clawson's."

"Who's that?"

Julie Clawson was an alias—a fake ID owned by Mo along with a matching credit card. Apparently, Mo possessed several.

We ended up at a no-frills, low budget, economy motel with two double beds, an exterior walkway, and a mini fridge, but no coffee pot. After stepping in the door, Mo announced she would go find food and be gone an hour. She made a not-so-subtle hint that Cruz and I might want to shower together and do what we could to *strengthen our bond* during our private time. We did our best.

By the time she returned, Cruz and I were passed out in the bed nearest the door. I opened my eyes to see who'd come in then promptly fell back to sleep. The next time I woke, sunshine slanted through the west-facing window. Dust motes floated in the air.

Sporting wet hair and a different set of clothes, Mo sat at the little desk typing on her laptop.

"Where's Cruz?" I asked.

"Walking the dog." She continued typing. "There are sandwiches in the fridge."

I'd finished half a turkey sandwich when Cruz returned carrying three sodas from the vending machine.

Mo typed a couple minutes more then closed the computer before turning in her chair. "What's this story you want to tell me?"

I told her everything. How I'd given birth while lying in a coma and how Adam had been placed in foster care and disappeared with the foster mother. I told her what Jay had said about Raina actually having Adam and why. And I told her about the Leader's Ring, letters, pictures, and journals.

When I finished, Mo's forehead crinkled and one eyebrow lifted. "So we're hoping he's here, but he's probably not, and we're here because a puzzle told you to come?"

I shrugged. Put that way, it sounded ridiculous.

"Show her the puzzle piece and journal page," Cruz said.

I fished both items from my bag.

Mo flattened the page on the desk and compared the puzzle piece to it. "Is this why you were in such a hurry to finish that puzzle at Lallo's?"

I nodded. "Trust me, it's not because I love puzzles. Adam's dad can attest to that. He's always trying to get me to help him with his."

Cruz frowned. "Tomas has been doing puzzles?"

"I didn't tell you that?" I said around a bite of sandwich.

He shook his head.

"He started having these visions of puzzles. Puzzles of places. He said the visions were unusually strong—not normal. So he found the puzzles online and started buying and putting them together. He thinks it has something to do with Adam." I sucked down the last of my Sprite.

"Your ex has visions?" Mo's Coke can dangled from her fingertips.

I winced. Apparently I hadn't done the best job with details. "Yeah. He's clairvoyant."

Her eyebrows rose.

"What if all these puzzles are images of places Adam's lived?" Cruz said.

The thought made me pause. It made sense. But it seemed too far-fetched, like trying to force a puzzle piece where it didn't belong. "You honestly think there's a puzzle of every place Adam's ever lived?" I knew one didn't exist of every place I'd lived.

"Could be."

237

I shook my head. "It feels like reaching."

"Maybe not." Mo set her can on the desk with a clink. "If your psychic ex sees things in visions, there's a chance your kid does too. Puzzles are usually of local sights, right? Things you go see if you're a tourist."

I nodded and ate the last of my sandwich.

"You said you think Adam and Raina are trying to guide you to them. What if your kid saw his dad putting together puzzles in a vision then started doing puzzles of places he lived, hoping his dad would see him too?"

The thought rendered me speechless. I looked at Cruz.

He shrugged. "Makes sense."

Yes, it did.

"You said Tomas had a puzzle of that mansion in Eureka," Cruz said. "Adam lived there. What other puzzles has Tomas done?"

I closed my eyes and tried to remember. "There's one of a giant Ferris wheel that would make Crayola proud. A couple from San Diego, a waterfall, some of canyons." I opened my eyes. "He was working on a petroglyph last I knew."

Mo stood. "What petroglyph? What waterfall? Where in San Diego?"

I closed my eyes, trying to remember the exact images. "The zoo in San Diego and a marina. The rest, I don't know."

Mo opened her computer and stepped away. "Then get over here and figure it out."

I hesitated. "Won't the trackers be able to find us if we go on the internet?" My fear of being found sat in my tummy like curdled milk. No way would I do anything to help the trackers succeed.

Mo shook her head. "I use a VPN. The IP address is hidden and the information will be encrypted."

I didn't understand much of what she'd said. I glanced at Cruz, knowing he would. He nodded in approval.

Seated in front of Mo's computer, I googled *giant ferris wheel*.

Several images came up, but none of them were correct. I narrowed the search by adding the word *jigsaw*. Several new sites appeared. I opened them one at a time.

Standing behind me, Mo pointed at an image of a Ferris wheel lit in neon pink. "What about that one?"

"No," I said.

"You sure? It's bright."

It was bright, but it didn't make me think of crayons. "I'm sure. Not enough colors."

Ten minutes later when I still hadn't found the right image, Cruz said, "Skip the Ferris wheel. Try one of the others."

I typed *canyon puzzles* in the search bar. Several images came up. I pointed at one from the Grand Canyon. "Not like this," and then at one from Bryce Canyon where the rocks were red and there were other small canyons in the background. "More like this. But this isn't it."

Cruz crouched beside me, his head near my shoulder. "Try Canyonlands puzzles."

I pulled up a screen full of images from the national park, many of which were close but not exact. I pointed at one with a red arch. "Tomas has one of an arch like this except shown at night."

"That's Arches National Monument," Cruz said.

I pointed at another with a river making a horseshoe bend through a canyon. "This might be the same river as one of his puzzles, but it's a different angle."

Cruz stepped back. "Canyonlands and Arches. Both in Utah."

Mo had moved to the unused bed and sat reclined against the headboard. "Try the petroglyph."

I found the glyph easily. A single man who appeared to be wearing earrings. It was called Moab Man. The waterfall proved easy too: Multnomah Falls in the Columbia River Gorge of Oregon.

"Is that nearby?" Mo asked.

I looked it up and mapped its distance from Portland. "Thirty miles east."

Mo grabbed her keys. "Let's go."

The falls were beautiful. A viewing area at the bottom offered a clear view of both falls—a longer one from the top and a short fall into a small pool of water at the bottom where moss clung to the rocks surrounding it. A path led up to a bridge spanning the distance between the rocks on both sides of the pool. Old pine trees on either side stood slightly taller than the top of the rocks where the waterfall began. The cool scent of water filled the air and a fine mist licked my skin as we stood on the bridge.

Back at the lower viewing area, we waited for over an hour. No one approached us, and nothing stood out to suggest Adam had ever been there. As we climbed the path to the van, I confronted the disappointment in my soul. It wasn't that I'd expected Adam to be there, but if the puzzle had sent us to the falls, there had to be a reason. Silence reigned on the drive back to Portland.

I told myself I'd been stupid to expect much. Even if Raina and Adam were searching for me, they couldn't leave a person at the falls 24/7 just in case, one day, I happened to wander by. Probably, I should have been smarter. But things had happened with such ease at the post office and the bakery that I'd thought maybe....

"What are we doing for dinner?" Mo asked.

"I need vegetables," Cruz said.

That sounded good. I imagined a nice big salad of vegetables picked fresh from my garden. A pang of sadness washed through me. Over a month had passed since I'd seen my home, smelled the familiar scents, slept in my own bed. I wished I could see my garden flourishing under Hideo's care. How long had it been since I'd called him? What had we discussed—his dinner plans with my neighbor? My mail?

Realization hit like an electric shock. "There's another puzzle."

Seated in the passenger seat, Cruz whipped his head around.

"I completely forgot about it. It came in the mail to my house. Hideo opened it. It's of the Japanese Tea Garden here in Portland."

Mo signaled and exited the freeway. "Sounds like we've got a starting point for tomorrow." She made a few turns then pulled into the parking lot of a run-down-looking diner. "They'll have vegetables."

No doubt they would. Whether they'd be fresh or not was another matter.

⌶

"I don't like it," Cruz said as we sat in the van outside the Japanese Tea Garden waiting for it to open the next day.

"Don't like what?" Mo asked.

After checking out of the motel, we'd picked up breakfast and coffee, and now sat in the van enjoying our dining experience.

"This place and the falls—they're places you go see once or twice. They're not places you go regularly or hang out."

"Like your job or a bakery?" I said catching on.

Once again, Mo had driven and Cruz had taken the passenger seat leaving me to lounge on the mattress with Bear. Probably not the safest spot in the van, but definitely the least visible.

Cruz nodded. "Exactly."

"What's your point?" Mo dumped a pack of sugar in her coffee.

"The bridge," Cruz said. "It's different. Pretty, but not exactly a sight-seeing stop."

"So why it?" The question swirled through my brain as sausage, egg whites, and flakey biscuit delighted my taste buds.

Mo replaced the lid on her coffee. "Maybe he saw it a lot?"

Cruz nodded. "Why?"

"He might have gone to that park regularly," I said.

Cruz bit into his breakfast sandwich and chewed. "That's a neighborhood park. If he went there regularly, he probably lived in the area."

"Maybe his house had a view of the bridge." Mo tipped her head back and sucked down several gulps of steaming-hot coffee.

Cruz lowered his sandwich. "If he lived in that area, he probably went to school there."

My breath caught. "You think there'll be some record of him?"

Grabbing her phone, Mo let her fingers fly over the screen.

Cruz tipped his head. "I think there'd be a memory."

"A memory?" I made a face. "How do we go about finding someone with a memory?"

"Everywhere we've gotten a clue, you've been recognized," Cruz said. "Someone wanted to talk to you."

"There's an elementary school less than two miles from Cathedral Park," Mo said.

"That's where we go."

Cruz wanted to show up at the school just before it let out. We'd be able to blend in with other parents waiting for kids that way. If no one recognized us, we'd go into the office after most of the kids were gone and tell them a story about having a child we intended to enroll. We'd ask if we could take a peek at the school.

Once we'd set the plan, we went into the Tea Garden for good measure. Nothing came from it.

⁂

A large two-story brick building housed the elementary school. Cars and busses lined the roads while parents stood on the sidewalk staring at cell phones and waiting for children.

Unable to find parking, Mo pulled into the driveway that accessed the school's dumpsters. An older janitor in denim coveralls stared at the van as Cruz and I exited.

Mo eyed the man warily. "He'll be pissed if I park here. I'll circle the block till something opens up."

Cruz and I thanked her and watched her pull away. The janitor turned his gaze on us.

Cruz smiled at him. "Which way to the office?"

The man pointed and motioned with his chin. "Around the

front of the school. Big sign directing you. Can't miss it." The sun caught the whiskers on his chin turning the grays to silver.

"Thank you." Cruz put his hand on my back and guided me to the front of the building.

We stood across from the main entrance where teachers leading classes of younger students would see us. The bell sounded, and the doors popped open. Kids and teachers streamed out. They glanced at us, but no one did a double take or stared. No one stumbled. They kept moving, glancing over us like one more set of parents in a growing sea of them. Soon, I gave up on the teachers and focused on the children, applying Cruz's method to narrowing the field. Right age range, tan skin, possibly dark hair. Any who met the criteria earned second and third looks. A couple students appeared to be Native American but didn't resemble my picture of Adam.

As the sidewalks began to clear and the busses pulled away, I realized I'd been staring so hard, I'd nearly forgotten where I was.

"Anything?" Cruz asked.

My stomach sank. "I forgot to watch the teachers."

"I watched them. No one noticed us. Did you see anything?"

"No."

We moved to the office where no one gave us a second glance or seemed any more interested in us than our story merited. They did, however, hand over visitor's badges and agree to let us walk the halls with an escort after copying our IDs and questioning us thoroughly about our fictitious child. A few kids remained in the hallways—stragglers working their way toward the doors—and others could be heard inside a few classes. The lower grades were housed on the first floor with the upper grades on the second. From the stairway that led to the basement came the sounds of music—a piano being used to tune a couple violins.

The classes were warm and inviting with colorful rugs and miniature chairs and desks. Less than two weeks into the school year and finger paintings and drawings already decorated walls. At the end of the hallway sat another set of stairs. I doubted a look at the second floor would net us anything more than the first, but our escort, who looked like she'd taught Ben Franklin, started up anyhow.

"Excuse me?" The janitor we'd seen outside stepped out from beneath the stairwell.

I pulled my foot off the step and moved back to better see him. In his baggy coveralls, he appeared doughy around the middle and he stooped as he stepped nearer. His hands shook, but his brown eyes were sharp and clear. The moment I gazed into them, my senses seemed to vibrate.

This was the person we'd come for.

Eighteen

The man glanced up at our elderly escort then lowered his voice for me. "I saw your ID in the office. I've got somethin' for ya."

My breath caught and Cruz put a hand on my shoulder.

The janitor nodded at the escort. "Say you parked where you shouldn't'a, then go check out with the office. I'll meet you by them dumpsters where you got out the van."

"Ten minutes," Cruz said.

"Fine." The man glanced down the hall then shuffled to the stairwell and headed down.

I exchanged a look with Cruz who mumbled an excuse for our escort before we returned to the office and handed over our visitor's badges.

Outside and across the street, Mo sat tipped back in the driver's seat of the van with the window down. She popped an eye open as we drew near. "Anything?"

"Maybe." Cruz stopped beside her window. "Can you pull around back and park where you let us out?"

Mo turned the key and the motor rumbled to life. As Cruz and I walked around the corner toward the back of the school, Mo drove by and stopped at the curb ahead. Cruz and I remained on the sidewalk outside the school's fence. Inside, children played on the blacktop, bouncing oversized playground balls and jumping ropes or chasing each other. A young African American man and a dark-haired girl dressed in matching purple shirts supervised the kids. We smiled at them and they nodded back.

"I thought school was out," I said.

Cruz glanced at the playground. "After-school program."

I smiled at the children, loving their squeals of delight. Everything seemed to be an adventure for them.

The girl in the purple shirt faced us and held up her phone as if taking a picture.

"What the—?"

"Shh." Cruz cut me off. His gaze traveled from me to the playground to the van with Mo inside. Grabbing my elbow, he steered me several steps beyond the playground. "Probably not good for two adults with a panel van waiting to stare at a bunch of kids who aren't theirs."

Put that way, I could see how our presence might be construed as creepy and worth snapping a picture.

We moved to the driveway where the dumpsters sat to one side. Putrid scents emanated from them, and I tried to stand as far away as possible.

The janitor appeared pushing a cart with a trash can and various cleaning supplies on it. He pulled a wad of keys from his pocket and unlocked the gate then pushed the cart through and locked up behind himself. Leaving his cart by the dumpster, he joined us and held his hand out to me. "Name's Henry. Henry Price."

Henry's brown skin was wrinkled and calloused, but his grip was strong.

"I'm Luna."

"I know who you are." He nodded at Cruz. "You trust him?"

Some men would have bristled at the implication. Cruz merely smiled.

"Yes," I said. "This is Cruz."

The two men shook hands before Henry glanced around. "How 'bout her?" He nodded at the van. "You know her?"

I nodded.

"Okay." He pulled an old handkerchief from his pocket and dabbed the perspiration on his brow. "Three years back, a little boy went to school here. Named Gilbert. Funny kid. Nice though. Liked helping me clean the cafeteria after lunch. His grandma came and volunteered in his classroom a couple days a week."

"Do you remember her name?" I asked.

"Ms. Onestar," he said. "She told me to call her Reza, but I called her Ms. Onestar."

I sucked in air. Reza and Onestar were two of the names Raina used in her letters to Gloria.

Henry leaned against the brick wall. "Some of these parents look at me like I'm trash. Not Ms. Onestar. She treated me fine. Sometimes brought me cookies. She made real good oatmeal raisin cookies."

I remembered the cookies Juanita made at the Bluefeather house and wondered if it was the same recipe.

Henry took a deep breath and I glanced at Mo. She sat in the same reclined position she'd been in before moving the van. Birds sang and a distant lawnmower roared to life. The laughter and calls of the children disappeared and a quick glance told me they'd gone inside.

Henry stared out at the street, but his gaze appeared to be elsewhere—focused on a time long since past.

"One afternoon," he said, "when the kids were in the auditorium listenin' to a speaker, Ms. Onestar and Gilbert came to my office. Ms. Onestar said Gilbert had somethin' to tell me. Now I don't know what you believe about God and the afterlife, but I's always taught there's a heaven and a hell and we go to one or t'other. I never thought much beyond that. But Ms. Onestar told me Gilbert had a gift—that he could talk to others who had...*crossed over*, she called it. If anyone else told me that, I would've pushed past them and told 'em to save it for someone else. But Ms. Onestar had always been nice to me, so I thought I owed it to her to listen."

Was this what Tomas had meant when he'd said Adam could

do more than him?

A strained sort of pain washed over Henry's face. "'Fore I go any further, I should tell you, I had me a daughter. Real pretty girl named Missy, like her mama. She was grown up and married and expectin' a little girl of her own. She and her husband planned to name her Minna. They lived in a little house with a hot tub out back."

Pinpricks of fear crawled over my skin.

"In the summer," Henry continued, "Missy and her husband used the hot tub like a pool, just to get in and cool down. No one knows what happened exactly. We think she must have slipped tryin' to get out and hit her head on the side. Her husband found her floating face up. He got her breathing a little and called the ambulance, but the doctors said she lost too much air. They did a C-section to try and save the baby, but Minna was stillborn. Missy never woke up again. The doctors said she was brain-dead." A tear squeezed out his eye and fell down his cheek.

I reached for his hand.

He flashed me the saddest smile I had ever seen.

"Missy's husband and the doctors thought we should take Missy off the life support, but her mama and me, we couldn't do that. Just couldn't bring ourselves to let go of our girl. After three months, Missy's husband moved away. Said he couldn't take it no more and had to get on with life. Six months later, Ms. Onestar brought Gilbert to see me. He said he had a message. Said there was an older woman wantin' to tell me something. Said her name was Louise." Henry looked from me to Cruz. "That was my mama's name—Louise. Gilbert said my mama'd talked to Missy and that Missy wanted me and my wife to let her go. Said it was time. Missy was ready to cross over. She wanted to be with her little girl, but she couldn't do it till we let go."

Henry swallowed hard and his voice grew hoarse. "That boy, he squeezed my shoulder just like my mama used to when I was young. Then he looked at me like he was the man and I was the boy. *Let her go Mr. Price,* he said. *She loves you and she knows you love her, but it's time now. You have to let her go.* That night, I went home and told my wife what happened. Next day, we sat with Missy while the doctors disconnected the life support. It was the hardest and most loving thing I've ever done."

Tears streamed down my face and water glistened in Cruz's eyes. Beyond him, the female after-school supervisor walked past the gate. She glanced at us, but kept moving. Maybe seeing us with Henry would help calm her suspicions.

Henry wiped his face then offered his handkerchief to me. I took it and dabbed at my cheeks before handing it back. Folding the cloth, he returned it to his coveralls and pulled out a lunch-size paper bag.

"Couple weeks later, Ms. Onestar came and told me her own story about a daughter she hadn't held since she was a baby and a little boy who wanted his mama." Henry smiled at me like a father might. "She told me about you. Said there was a chance you might come through here one day, and if you did, I should give you this." From the bag, he produced an old stationery box tied in string with a beautiful gray and white feather knotted in the bow. "She said the feather was from Gilbert."

I took the box and gently traced the edge of the feather. Had my son once done the same thing? Was I now touching some trace he had left behind?

Henry reached into the bag once more. "Two days after Ms. Onestar's visit, Gilbert came to see me. Said he knew his meemaw—that's what he called Ms. Onestar—had brought me something to give you. He wanted to give you something too." This time Henry pulled out a long macaroni necklace with a circular laminated photo at the bottom. "He made it in his class. Was real proud of it."

My jaw trembled as I took the necklace and studied the picture. A dark-haired boy with a beautiful dimple and smile minus two bottom teeth stared back. He held a sign decorated with lopsided hearts and flowers that said Happy Mother's Day. My chest burst with sunshine as my vision clouded with tears.

Cruz checked the picture then lifted the necklace over my head. He smiled at me before turning to Henry. "It's her first Mother's Day gift."

Unable to speak, I turned to the janitor hoping he could see all the joy and thanks in my heart.

He nodded at me as if remembering his own macaroni necklaces. "I should get back now." He walked toward the dumpster to retrieve his cart. "It's snack time for them kids. They'll be lookin' for me. I wish you well." He stopped and held out his hand. "I'm real pleased I got to meet you."

I bypassed his hand and threw my arms around him.

For a second, he stiffened then he patted me on the back and finally wrapped his arms around me, his whiskers tickling my forehead.

"Thank you," I whispered before stepping back.

The older man walked through the gate and secured the lock on the inside. Giving us one last nod, he returned to the building.

A pinwheel of happiness twirled inside me as I stared at my new necklace and the box in my hands.

"You ready?" Cruz asked. A gentle spark shone in his eyes.

I practically skipped toward the van.

"Jasmine?" someone said behind us. "Or Luna?"

The hair on my arms stood up. Turning, I found the girl in the purple shirt standing at the gate, fingers laced through the chain link.

"Oh my god!" she squealed. "It *is* you!"

Something cold slithered inside me. Cruz's face turned to granite.

I stepped forward. "How do you know me?"

Cruz edged in front of me.

"The website." The girl bounced up and down, her face aglow.

"Website?"

"The game." She said it like everyone knew about the game and the website. "I'm of the Neme-i. On my father's side."

I knew there were Neme-i everywhere. But I didn't know

about a website or game. I forced a smile as the girl continued to bounce.

She whipped out her cell phone. "I'm the second person to enter your location!"

Location? Alarm bells rang inside me. My instincts screamed, *flee!*

"We need to go." Cruz grabbed my arm.

"Glad to meet you," I lied as I hightailed it away from the girl.

"Mo!" Cruz called. "Start the engine."

Her head snapped upright as we scurried around the front of the vehicle.

Cruz slammed the cargo door behind me and scrambled into the passenger's seat. "Go."

"Where?" Mo asked as she pulled away from the curb.

I knelt behind the seats and glanced through the window.

The purple-shirted girl remained at the fence with her phone pointed in our direction.

In the driver's side mirror, I noted a blue car rolling toward us from behind.

"Anywhere," Cruz growled. "Go!"

Mo accelerated forward.

"Faster!" Cruz stared at the passenger side mirror.

"Are they following us?" I asked, terrified of the answer.

"Maybe."

Bear moved toward the window. I caught his collar and settled him beside me.

"Take the next right," Cruz told Mo.

She did, and for a moment, no one seemed to breathe.

Eyes still locked on the mirror, Cruz said, "Shit."

I sat down hard. Panic curdled inside me. I swallowed it down.

Bear whined and licked my face.

"Ideas?" Mo asked.

Cruz grabbed Mo's phone off the dashboard and opened the maps application. "Can you get back to that bridge we went to yesterday?"

"Yeah," she said slowly.

"Good." Cruz glanced back at me. "We're going across it."

"The forest?" I asked.

He nodded.

"Are you sure?" Disappearing with a vehicle inside a national forest was one thing. Doing it on a couple acres of forest in the middle of a city was another.

"If we have to, we'll ditch the van."

Other than engaging in a car chase sure to draw attention, I had no ideas. The forest was out best option. I sucked in a breath. "Okay."

As Mo wound through side streets trying to lose our pursuer, I shoved the items Henry had given me in my purse and jammed it inside my backpack. The tent got strapped to the bottom of Cruz's pack and the leash to Bear's collar. I placed all three bags by the cargo door in case we had to leave the van in a hurry.

"There," Cruz said.

Up ahead, Saint John's Bridge loomed.

"Once you get across," Cruz said, "go right, then take the second left. You'll have to punch it after that." He looked back at me. "This could get bumpy."

I nodded and moved to the mattress with Bear.

Mo turned right at the end of the bridge and glanced back at me in the rearview mirror. "Get ready."

Wedged into the corner, I patted the mattress and told Bear to lie down.

The van jerked left then right. My head hit the wall and pain exploded through me. For a second I thought of Micky—the violent hulk of a man who'd knocked me out during my first abduction. I couldn't risk being knocked out again. Grabbing the pillow, I stuffed it behind my head.

"Floor it," Cruz growled.

The trees I could see through the windshield turned into a dizzying blur.

We skidded around one bend then another. Cruz grabbed the

wheel and helped Mo steer through the next turn.

"Brake, brake!" he yelled.

Then he yanked the wheel right and we bounced off the road into the forest. He directed Mo this way and that between and around trees until we were hidden so far beneath the canopy, darkness surrounded us.

"Keep the engine running," Cruz said when Mo reached for the key.

I held my breath, not daring to speak or move for what felt like ten minutes. Birds sang outside, and I heard cars from a distance, but nothing that sounded like one drawing closer.

Finally, Cruz turned and said, "I think we're okay."

Pent-up air whooshed out of me. My heart raced as if I'd been running. I rested my head in my hand. That had been way too close.

"Is someone going to tell me what the fuck's going on?" Mo demanded.

Cruz pointed forward. "Get back on the road. Same way we came."

Mo put the van in gear and we bounced along the forest floor while I explained about the girl and the website.

"Probably the Keyake site," Mo said as we pulled onto pavement.

"We've got a website?"

Cruz and Mo ignored my question.

"Did you get a look at the people in the car?" Cruz asked as he studied the map on Mo's phone.

"No. You?"

"The woman."

"Did you recognize her?" Mo asked.

"No."

"So we aren't sure they were trackers?" Hope raised my voice half an octave.

"You know someone else who wants to follow you?" Mo asked.

I didn't, but I also didn't know how they would have found us so easily.

Mo braked to a stop at the main road, and Cruz told her to turn left away from the bridge in case any other trackers were on the way.

"Do you think they followed us from Winnemucca?" I asked.

"Doubt it," Mo said. "More likely they were already here."

"For what?"

"Don't know. Probably something unrelated. You two and my dad can't be the only people they're looking for."

╬

Cruz directed us across the river into Vancouver, Washington. He wanted us out of Portland and off the road, so Mo checked us into a motel with two queen beds and an in-room coffee maker—an improvement from the night before. Using her cell, she made a call and said, "I need a car and a drop spot." After listening, she hung up.

Opening her laptop, she typed something in. "This is the website."

Cruz and I stood behind her and peered over her shoulder. A *Members* tab took her to a sign-in screen where she quickly tapped in a username and password.

"Won't they know you signed in?" My heart rate ratcheted up.

Mo shook her head. "It's a friend's account. They'll think she logged in." She clicked on something. "Shit."

I bent down to better see the page with a picture of Cruz and me on the left and one of Jay on the right. The title read *Where Are We?* A paragraph lay below followed by two columns of boxes and, at the very bottom, a map of the United States.

Cruz knelt beside Mo. "They've turned this into a game?"

My eyes got stuck on the left-hand column.

Name: Branson Dovesong
Sighting: Smokey's BBQ, Winnemucca, Nevada.
C

I remembered the employee on a smoke break playing with his phone in Winnemucca. Probably Branson Dovesong.

Name: Thania Morris
Sighting: James Elementary, Portland, Oregon.
C

"What are the C's for?" I asked.

Mo studied the screen and groaned. "Confirmed."

"By who?" Nausea flitted like butterflies inside my tummy.

"Trackers, I assume." Mo sat back in her chair.

Dread flooded me. "They'll go to the school, won't they?"

Mo sighed. "There's a good chance they're already there."

"And they'll talk to"—Cruz checked the computer screen—"Thania?"

Mo turned to face us. "Probably the janitor too."

I stumbled back a few steps and sat on the bed. Every set of trackers included a woman. A woman who would send Henry messages to tell them everything he'd told us. The nausea twisted my stomach and the air became heavy. "They'll know about Adam." Had I just endangered my child's life?

Mo pushed her chair back and stood. "I need to move the van. You two stay here. I'll bring back food. If I'm not here by nightfall, leave."

Perspiration broke out along my hairline.

Mo left and Cruz looked at me then walked to the bathroom. Water ran in the sink and moments later he placed a wet cloth on the back of my neck.

The mattress dipped as he sat beside me. "Breathe."

I took several deep gulps and felt my heart rate slow. Bear rested his head in my lap, his big brown eyes like liquid chocolate staring up at me.

"Do you think Henry will tell them Adam can talk to spirits?" I asked.

"If they send him messages, yes."

I'd known the answer, but I'd hoped Cruz might lie.

"Oh God." I put my head in my hands.

Cruz took a breath. "They would have learned about Adam from the prophecies."

"I know. But they wouldn't know about his extra gifts. Now they will. The Revisionists will want him, and Anna will probably hate him."

"Maybe." Cruz rubbed my back. "They don't know where he is though."

I snorted. "Neither do we."

"But we may have a clue." He pointed to the stationery box I'd dropped in the corner.

Tingles slid across my shoulders as I stared at it. I'd nearly forgotten about the box.

"Should I stop looking for him before I make this worse?" They were the hardest words I'd ever uttered—like I'd stabbed myself in the heart.

Cruz stared straight ahead and seemed to consider. "No," he finally said. "The trackers know about him now. They'll search for him. If we're going to keep him safe, we need to find him before they do."

He was right. I felt it in my gut. What I didn't know was what we'd do after we found Adam. How would we keep him safe?

"Check the box," Cruz said.

I retrieved it while Cruz returned to Mo's computer.

"They've spotted Jay a few places," he said.

"Where?"

"Kansas, South Dakota, Atlanta."

I couldn't picture Jay in Atlanta. I had a hard time imagining him in any big city.

Cruz pointed at the screen. "They're tracking it on the map."

Blue dots appeared in the places Jay had been and a blue line connected them all.

I checked Nevada and Oregon. Red dots connected by a red

line showed our progress. "They're tracking us like animals." Would they do the same with Adam?

In that moment, I hated the Neme-i. Or at least the group within them determined to invade our privacy. "How do we avoid them?"

Cruz frowned. "We may need to travel at night."

"Fine."

"Beyond that, we need to talk to Mo." He clicked a few keys. "Check this out."

Four columns of pictures ran down the screen with names beneath them.

"Who are they?" I asked.

"Trackers."

I looked more closely. Sure enough, Ethan's picture came first with his partner's name and picture beside it. I recognized a couple other faces, people I'd seen at some of the gatherings but whose names I'd never learned. Halfway down the page, Cruz stopped scrolling and pointed. "She was the passenger in the car that followed us."

The picture showed a woman with medium brown hair parted on the right and a bleached-blonde stripe fronting the left. Though unremarkable in features, her blonde stripe stood out. No wonder Cruz recognized her.

"Rebecca Two Paws," he read.

I jerked my gaze to her name. "Crow said a man named Two Paws was the tribe's best tracker before Ethan. Raina was the only person he never found."

"Probably a relative."

If so, would he be helping this woman? My hands shook, and I realized my breathing had turned shallow again. I turned away from the computer. I didn't want to see any more.

Seated on the bed, I removed the string from Raina's box and carefully separated the feather from it.

I lifted the lid and found bits of my childhood staring up at me. Pictures, folded pieces of paper, even the orange rabbit's foot that had precipitated Gloria taking me to Jay.

"What is it?" Cruz closed Mo's computer and turned in the chair.

I pulled out the stack and quickly thumbed through the contents. "Stuff from my childhood."

"Can I see?"

I nodded and scooted sideways making room for him on the bed.

Sitting next to me, he reached into the box and pulled out the rabbit's foot. "What's this?"

"A girl in my class gave it to me when I was nine. It and a few other things were how Gloria realized I'd started to use my gift. It's why we moved to Hemet."

"So Jay could train you?"

"More like mistrain me," I mumbled as I separated papers from pictures.

"Or maybe contain you?" The tenderness in Cruz's tone told me he was treading lightly.

He didn't need to. "Maybe." Gloria and Raina had been trying to protect me. They'd wanted my gift hidden so I couldn't be found, just as I wanted Adam hidden.

The pictures showed me at different stages of my life—the first as a chubby infant sitting on an ugly flowered couch. Another of me in a swimsuit running through a sprinkler.

"How old are you in this?" Cruz asked.

I shrugged. "Five, six maybe." I took a closer look at the house in the background. San Antonio. "Six."

My second grade school picture came next.

Cruz took it from me. "You're wearing a bow?" A grin spread across his face.

I scowled and snatched the photo, glaring at the ugly, white hair bow. "Gloria made me." She'd also forced me to wear the purple dress with the stupid lace collar I'd hated.

The parade of memories continued, and although the photos were nice to see, fear of the trackers searching for Adam overshadowed any excitement I might have felt. I wanted a clue, not a trip down memory lane.

But then I came to a photo of Gloria and my heart caught. "I took this."

I'd snapped the shot right after I'd cried my heart out and told her I was pregnant. I'd been terrified she'd be angry with me or disappointed. She'd told me she was disappointed for me, not in me. *Never in you*, she'd said. I'd been so relieved and touched by her love that I'd insisted on taking the photo. I'd wanted to remember the moment forever. Turned out, I hadn't needed the snapshot for that. But I liked seeing it just the same.

"Maybe that's a photo that should go in your locket," Cruz said after I relayed the story to him.

I fingered the locket beneath my shirt. "No. In a frame. On my dresser." I didn't want to cut a single part of this picture away.

He kissed the top of my head as I put the photo on the bottom of the stack.

"This isn't giving us a clue," I said.

He motioned to the papers. "Maybe those."

Returning the photos to the box, I picked up the stack of papers.

A note I'd once written to a friend I no longer recalled, a page from a magazine with a photo of a hot air balloon that didn't ring any bells, a list of cities written in Gloria's hand, a birthday party invitation for the only party I'd ever had, and finally a list of names written in my own penmanship that stole the air from my lungs.

"What is it?" Cruz asked.

"My list of possible baby names." I'd started it in my second month of pregnancy and continued it into my seventh.

"Daisy?" Cruz said.

I rolled my eyes. "That was before I knew he was a boy."

"Why are some crossed off?"

"Narrowing down the list."

He leaned in tighter and pointed at the paper. "How come you crossed off Cruz? Not good enough for you?"

I looked at where he'd pointed. Sure enough, there sat Cruz's name, third in line right below Alex and Tomas. I'd forgotten I'd put it on the list. I'd liked the name but I'd crossed it off almost as soon as I'd written it. The fact that I'd met Cruz before Tomas and been more attracted to him—at first—had made it seem disrespectful to Tomas.

"Sorry," I said. "I didn't know how Tomas would take that."

He chuckled. "I'm honored you considered it." Pointing again, he asked, "What are the check marks for?"

I looked more closely. "I—Those aren't mine." Nor was the writing where Gill had been crossed off and Gilbert written next to it. "Wait a second." I examined the list. Gilbert, Oliver, and Max all had checkmarks. I pointed at the names. "Here, Eureka, the finger painting."

The left side of Cruz's mouth tipped upward. "This could be how they choose his names."

I scanned the names with check marks. Alex, Oliver, Maxwell, Ian, Hector, and Gilbert. "Do you think he goes by one of these now?"

Cruz blew out a breath. "Maybe?"

I understood the question in his tone. All of this—all our assumptions—were just conjecture. We didn't know anything for sure.

I glanced at the papers lying beside me on the bed. The names were a boon, but... "There still aren't any clues about his location."

Cruz frowned.

"Unless you saw something?"

He shook his head. "No. It's just—" His words trailed off and I waited for him to finish the thought. "Everything else she left had one."

⚔

By eight o'clock, when Mo returned with pizza and a baseball hat to disguise me, Cruz had gone through the contents of the box

260

twice more with me and once alone. We still hadn't found anything.

While he looked, my mind had returned to the trackers. Were they close enough to sense my energy? Would they break into our room tonight? And if they did, what then? Also, what would they do if they knew about Adam? Like a song set to repeat, the questions played through my mind in a never-ending loop.

I assaulted Mo with questions as she slid the pizza box onto the desk.

Shoulders bowed, she held up a hand. "Slow down." Seated on the bed nearest the bathroom, she untied her Doc Martens and loosened the laces. "I need to eat. I'll answer questions after."

I didn't like it, but I understood the need for food. My stomach had been growling for the past hour.

Mo returned to the pizza box. "I didn't know what you guys like, so I got everything." She flipped the lid back. "Well, everything but pineapple. I hate that shit."

I loved it.

We all took a slice and ate while standing around the box.

"Any problems with the car?" Cruz asked.

Mo shook her head as she chewed. "We've got an old, blue Suburban. It's parked behind the liquor store next door."

"Why there?" I asked.

"We can get to it without going through the lobby."

"Where's the van?" Cruz shoved pizza crust in his mouth and reached for a second slice.

"In a parking garage in Portland."

"Anybody find it?" he asked.

Mo spoke around a bite of crust. "Not by the time I left. But they will."

After she and Cruz had each taken a third slice, Mo settled herself against the headboard on the empty bed and asked me to tell her my questions again. I repeated them as I reached for the last slice.

Mo nodded. "About feeling your energy when you're not

sending messages? Any of the male trackers could from the walkway outside." She motioned to the window. "A few would feel it from the parking lot, and one or two from the road."

Was that why the trackers had stopped beside the road on Mount Winnemucca? Had they sensed my energy? But if so, why had they left? "What about Ethan?" The way he'd tracked us in the forest outside Summerhaven haunted me.

Mo pressed her lips together. "Probably within a block."

I closed my eyes and told myself that wasn't such a big space. Finding the right block in any given city wouldn't be easy. Of course, if he limited his search to blocks with hotels, the search got easier.

"If they track us to this motel," Mo said, "they won't break in. They'll knock on the door."

I swallowed my fears regarding Ethan's prowess. "Then what?"

She shrugged and ate her last bite. "Most likely? Ask us to accompany them to Summerhaven."

"Following that?" Cruz's voice had that deadly calm that sent shivers down my spine.

"Not sure." Mo leveled her gaze with his. "I don't intend to find out."

Cruz nodded once.

They were saying we would fight like hell before we let them take us, and I agreed with the plan. Thoughts of it coming to that scared the shit out of me, however. I touched the throwing knives holstered at my back.

"As to what they'll do if they've figured out you have a kid?" Mo adjusted the pillows behind her. "They're supposed to report to the council. Based on what Cruz overheard in Winnemucca, I don't know if they will."

My stomach churned. No longer hungry, I offered the remainder of my pizza to Cruz.

He pushed my hand away. "You need it. Eat."

I took a bite. It tasted like cardboard and glue. I forced myself to chew and swallow. "That dream thing—the nightmare Cruz received—is that something one of the Sáani Suntehai could do?"

Mo tipped her head and seemed to consider. "Probably. It takes a certain amount of strength."

"How much?" Would Maria be able to do it? Or Anna?

"Hard to say." Mo leaned forward. "If you think of the gifts as an ice cream sundae, the basic gift is the ice cream. Some people get a bigger scoop. Some get smaller. Same with the extras—mukuttekka, simultaneous messages, tenkuane'e. They're kind of like hot fudge, caramel, whipped cream."

"Are there other toppings?" Cruz asked.

"Sure. Gifts like George Tsossi's, the trackers', even my dad's. Those are all extras. Above and beyond the basic messaging gift. They're what make people special to the Revisionists."

Tomas's text said Adam could do more than he could. We knew he could speak with spirits, but could he do more than that? If so, what would the Revisionists make of him?

Cruz touched my shoulder. "Adam?"

I nodded and rested my hand on top of his.

Mo shrugged. "If he can see and speak to the dead, like you said, or if he takes after his dad, he'll be considered special. Nothing you can do about that."

"I'm scared the trackers will go after him," I said. "If Anna's involved, I'm scared they'll hurt him."

Mo tipped her head. "You could...." She winced.

"What?" I asked.

"You're gonna hate it, but it might work."

"Just say it," Cruz said.

"You could share the fact you have a son with the council members and others from the tribe. Send them all a message. If people know he exists, no one would be able to hide him away or hurt him without hurting themselves even more."

The pizza I had eaten turned to lead in my tummy. I sank onto the bed.

Cruz eyed me, one eyebrow raised. "It could work."

I nodded and bit my lip. Logically, I understood the idea. It made sense. But it went against everything I wanted to do. "Only if we're desperate." Which we weren't. Yet.

"On that cheery note"—Mo clapped her hands together—"when's the last time you checked in at home to see if you had new packages?"

Cruz took Bear outside while I borrowed Mo's cell and called Hideo. He picked up on the second ring.

"I'm glad you called," he said. "I was beginning to worry."

I apologized and explained that making calls had become difficult.

"I imagine so," he said. "I saw the website."

A frustrated sigh escaped me. "Me too."

"I'm guessing you would rather not stay on the phone long?"

It wasn't a brush-off. I could hear the concern in his tone. How the hell had I thought of this man as *Old Creepy* when I'd first met him?

"Probably best I don't."

"What can I do for you?"

"Have I received any more mail?"

"Mail?" He sounded taken aback, but then his voice brightened. "As a matter of fact, you've received two more packages."

I heard movement on the other end of the line. "Do they sound like the first one?"

"Yes." He chuckled. "Just like it. Shall I open these as well?"

"Please."

"Just a minute." There came a small clunk as he put the phone down followed by the sound of ripping paper. A few moments later came the fumbling sound of him picking the phone back up. "They are what you expected."

"What do the pictures show?"

"The first looks like a church but it is," the sliding sound of pieces came over the line, "the California Dome at Balboa Park."

264

I wrote the name on a piece of paper from the motel notepad. Mo looked over my shoulder and nodded.

"San Diego," she whispered.

"And the other?" I asked Hideo.

"This one is different," he said. "It doesn't show a place. It's more like a chart showing different kinds of dinosaurs."

"Dinosaurs?"

"Yes."

"Does it give a location?"

"No."

Mo motioned at the pad clearly expecting me to write something. I put a question mark to appease her.

"Both packages were postmarked San Diego, if that helps." He paused. "There is one more item. You received a postcard from Arizona yesterday."

I couldn't remember ever receiving a postcard.

"It shows a painting of the Madonna and Baby Jesus."

I didn't know what to say. Tomas was the only person I knew who was traveling, but I couldn't imagine him sending a religious postcard. "What's written on back?"

"It says…" Hideo paused. "…he sees us. It's signed, T."

He sees us? What the hell? I wrote the words on the paper and tossed the pen down.

"Does that make sense to you?" Hideo asked.

"Not really. But that's okay." When I finally talked to Tomas again, I could ask. "Is there anything else I should know?"

"Only that you are missed."

A lump formed in my throat. "I miss you too." And then to keep myself from crying, I said, "You're not killing my plants are you?"

Hideo chuckled. "No. They're doing well."

Most likely they were flourishing, but Hideo wouldn't brag. I thought about my little garden and backyard. About my house and bedroom. About Gizmo. I missed it all. I imagined Adam, looking as he had in the picture with Jacob, running around inside my house—our house—and my heart leapt.

By the time I hung up with Hideo, Cruz and Bear had returned. For Bear to do his business that fast meant we'd kept him inside too long. I felt bad about that. The dog needed to walk or run. So did I. Probably Cruz too. Mo? She'd probably prefer a motorcycle ride.

I told Mo and Cruz about the things Tomas had sent. When I got to the postcard, Cruz made a face. I imagined I'd made the same face when Hideo had described the card to me.

Mo glanced from Cruz to me. "What?"

"Tomas isn't religious," I said.

Cruz perched on the edge of the desk. "It's out of character."

"So were the puzzles according to you," Mo said.

She had a point.

"Maybe he saw a painting of it in a museum and it reminded him of you and Adam," she said. "You know, Madonna and child?"

I made a face. "Maybe." It felt off though. I'd attended art exhibits with Tomas. Religious works were something he usually hurried through.

"I'm more interested in the puzzles," Mo said. "The first one's from somewhere in San Diego. Didn't you say he had other puzzles with pictures from there?"

I shook off thoughts of the postcard and tried to remember the puzzles hanging on Tomas's wall. "One of the zoo and another of a marina."

"What about the second puzzle?" Cruz tossed a glance at us then returned to staring out the window like a sentinel.

"It shows a bunch of different dinosaurs," I said, "like a chart. Not an actual place."

"But it came from San Diego?" Cruz said.

"Yes."

"Sounds like that's our next destination." Mo pulled off her boots and dropped them on the floor.

The lines around Cruz's eyes deepened.

266

"You disagree?" I asked.

He shrugged. "It seems too easy."

"I thought we were looking at the puzzles as clues to your kid's location," Mo said.

"We are."

"Well, we've got three puzzles from San Diego. Doesn't get more straightforward than that." She fluffed the pillows behind her and lay down.

I refrained from pointing out that was exactly what Cruz had a problem with.

Resting a hand on his knee, I watched him, waiting for his opinion. Darkness clouded his features. A moment passed before he nodded.

"Okay. San Diego it is." We had no other ideas.

⚜

"Luna. Wake up."

I opened my eyes and shot upright. Cruz stood next to the bed. A sliver of light shone beneath the bathroom door. Otherwise the room remained dark.

"What's going on?"

The clock on the nightstand said 4:03.

"We need to go. *Now*." Cruz pulled the covers off me and handed me a pair of jeans. "Trackers are on the way."

My heart rate spiked. I jammed my legs in the pants and jumped up to pull them on. "Where's Mo?"

Bear stood at the foot of the bed.

"Loading the car."

I buttoned the jeans and crammed my feet in my hiking boots.

Cruz handed me the baseball cap Mo had purchased. "Put this on."

I threw it on my head as Cruz peeked through the curtain.

"Fuck. We gotta go." He grabbed my arm and Bear's leash and led us to the door.

My heart raced. "Are they out there?"

"Maybe."

He handed me the leash and reached for his gun. After a glance through the peep hole, he opened the door, looked both ways and stepped into the hall reaching back for me. He pushed me in front of him to the right, away from the lobby. We jogged to the end of the hall where Cruz cracked the door, checked in all directions, and motioned for Bear and me to follow.

Outside, a small walkway ran alongside the wrought-iron fence surrounding the pool. A floodlight on the side of the building lit the area. From the parking lot to our right, came the sound of voices.

Cruz pushed me the opposite direction. "Behind the pool, through the bushes."

I stumbled forward, my legs shaky.

Trackers. *Shit.*

I tried to keep my mind blank. Tried not to let lose any sort of mental energy. I didn't know if that was possible, but I tried. At the end of the walkway, I turned right and scurried along between the fence and a flower bed. The bushes sat twenty feet ahead. Bear jerked to a stop. I yanked his leash, but he wouldn't budge. A figure appeared around the corner of the building. Smallish. Most likely female. I ducked behind Bear.

Standing just past the splash of the floodlight, I couldn't make out the woman's features, but I could clearly see the blonde streak at the front of her dark hair.

She stared in our direction, and I could swear straight at me. My breath caught and my heart threatened to burst through my chest. Blood pounded in my ears. I didn't dare breathe. Cars passed on the street. Tightening my grip on Bear's collar, I prepared to run. A voice called, and the figure turned away. She glanced back once more, yelled "Nothing" and jogged to the front of the building.

I sucked in a gulp of air and nearly screamed when Cruz touched my back.

"Go," he whispered.

I went. Faster than I knew possible.

Beyond the shrubbery, a large Suburban sat next to the liquor store, its back end open.

Mo waved from the driver's seat. "Get in and lay down."

Bear and I jumped in the back. Lying on my side, I held his collar to keep him low. Cruz closed the rear door and hurried into the backseat. My entire body trembled and I had to clench my teeth to stop them from chattering.

The vehicle started forward.

"Do you see them?" My heart raced as I thought of the woman with the blonde streak. She had to be the same woman who'd chased us earlier, the one Cruz had pointed out on the Keyake website.

"Two cars," Mo said. "There'll be more." She turned left out of the lot.

Bear pulled against his collar. I put my hand on his back and told him to stay. Curled against him, I tried to leach his warmth to make myself stop shaking.

"How did you know they were coming?" I asked.

"Paid a guy to hack into the security systems of a couple nearby motels. Once the trackers showed up at one of them, I knew they'd head here too."

My mouth opened as my mind went blank. I didn't even know what to say to that.

"Are we clear?" Cruz asked.

"No."

Wind filled the vehicle and I realized Mo had rolled down a window. I heard a flick and saw the glow of a lighter before cigarette smoke filtered back to me. "What the hell?"

"It's my disguise," Mo said.

Another puff of smoke flew over my head.

Mo swerved slightly then eased off the accelerator before hitting the gas and causing the Suburban to jump forward. Apparently she'd chosen a drunk smoker disguise.

"Good," Cruz said.

She turned right, and I heard the turn signal come on a second

269

later. More smoke swirled through the vehicle.

I covered my mouth with my T-shirt and concentrated on breathing. Deep breath in. Out. Repeat. My heart rate slowed.

"They gone yet?" Cruz asked.

"No."

An image of the tracker with the blonde streak crossed my mind and my pulse ratcheted up again.

Mo turned left.

Bear shifted and I moved with him.

Two right turns later, Mo sighed. "Okay. We're clear."

I sat up and looked behind us. We were on a residential street with cars parked on either side of the road. "Why didn't they sense me?"

"They probably did." Mo extinguished the cigarette and rolled down all the windows. "But they sensed you in the general area, not this car specifically."

"Why not?"

"Did you send a message?" she asked.

"No."

She tipped her hands palms up as if I'd answered my own question. Maybe I had, but I didn't understand.

"It's not an exact science." She powered the windows up. "They know you were in the area. And by now, the desk clerk's given the two at the motel our room number. The group will check there before worrying about some random drunk driver."

⸸

I took over driving while Cruz conked out in the backseat. Predawn light shown in the sky east of North Salem.

The freeway cut through forests of trees, and clouds filled the sky. Rain began to fall. Probably just a sprinkle outside the SUV, but enough to require wipers while speeding down the interstate.

The idea of going to San Diego sat like a giant piece of uncertainty inside me. Nothing in my gut screamed *no* about it, but nothing screamed *yes* either. The only thing my gut seemed to scream was get the hell away from the trackers. But if they could track me even when I didn't send messages, how would I hold them at bay? How would I keep from inadvertently leading them to Adam? Yet if they were even now beginning to track him, what choice did I have? I had to find him first. I had to keep him safe.

Cruz woke when I pulled into a gas station with a mini-mart in Ashland. We used the facilities and Mo bought food and drinks while Cruz consulted a map and I clipped Bear to his leash.

I walked the Rottweiler to a little patch of dirt and weeds. He looked at me like my bathroom choice fell well below his standard.

"This is as good as it gets," I told him.

We stood still, glaring at each other, both waiting for the other to cave.

Out of the corner of my eye, I saw Mo return to the SUV and noted Cruz had moved to the driver's seat.

He started the engine and rolled down the window. "What's wrong?"

I motioned at Bear. "He won't go."

Cruz made his *tcht* noise and Bear lifted his leg.

Back in the SUV, Cruz steered us onto the interstate and exited a little bit later to follow the signs for Old Highway 99 South. He wanted to wait out the daylight and resume driving that night. The road led us deeper into the forest. Cruz took smaller and smaller roads until he seemed satisfied we were reasonably hidden and parked amongst some bushes alongside the road. From there, we grabbed our packs and hiked about half a mile to a little clearing with a creek nearby. Bear took care to scent as many trees as possible on the way. Apparently the forest qualified as bathroom heaven.

Cruz pitched the tent while Mo and I anchored our little ice box in the creek to keep everything cold. After that, she crawled into the tent to sleep while Cruz and I walked Bear.

I inhaled the scent of pine and listened to the songs of birds punctuated by the occasional thunderous crack of falling branches. Cruz held my hand while Bear ran ahead, reveling in his freedom. If I'd been able to shake my fear of the trackers, it might have been perfect. But no matter how much I enjoyed my surroundings, the worry remained.

Despite the care we'd taken over the past week, the trackers had found us. Twice. Would they continue to do so? Our plan to travel at night was good, but we couldn't live like vampires forever. At some point, we had to return to normal society. We had to work. We had to live.

Was this why Raina had left me with Gloria? Had she known the only life we could have together would be filled with constant running and fear? Had leaving me with Gloria been an attempt to spare me that pain? As it was, Gloria and I had run enough, moving to a new city every year for most of my childhood. But if it had been me and Raina, would it have been worse? Would it be like that for Adam and me?

"What are you thinking?" Cruz asked.

"I'm scared."

He stopped walking and faced me. "Of what?"

"The trackers. What they'll do if they find us. What they'll do with Adam. Who's directing them. What the hell is going on?"

Cruz's cheeks puffed as he regarded the ground. "That's a lot."

"It's like we're running blind. Trying to find our way in the dark."

He nodded.

"We need answers."

"To what? Specifically."

I stiffened. Based on the fears I'd just voiced, I'd thought it obvious. The expression on Cruz's face told me it wasn't. Did I even know? Releasing his hand, I walked to the nearest tree to consider.

Gears turned, my mind like train wheels fighting for purchase. What specific answer would help me answer all the other questions?

"I want to know who Ethan's answering to."

Cruz nodded. "Maybe Mo's heard something."

I nodded and let my eyes blur while I tried to think of anything I'd missed. Bear nudged my hand with his snout.

Cruz gave the dog a pat. "I'd like to know why that person wants you."

"Wants *us*," I corrected.

Cruz shook his head. "Not us. You. I'm just conveniently with you which gives them the advantage of looking for two people instead of one."

If looking for two people provided an advantage, how much more benefit would there be when we had Adam with us and were three? Or what if Tomas joined us and we were four? Or five if we had Raina?

"How sold are you on going to San Diego?" Cruz asked as we headed back.

I shook my head. "I'm not. But I don't know where else to go."

He plucked a stick off the ground and threw it for Bear. "I keep thinking, Tomas was in San Diego. If he'd found something there, he wouldn't have left."

"Makes sense."

Bear skidded to a stop and sniffed sticks until he found the right one and returned with it.

"Do you have another idea of where to go?"

Cruz took the stick and threw it again. "No." He frowned. "I wish I understood the dinosaur puzzle."

⚓

Back at the campsite, I pulled out Raina's box and flipped through the contents while I sat on a boulder between the creek and the tent. Cruz had been right. Everything else we'd found from Raina—the journals, the letter, the photos—had pointed us in some direction. It made sense the box should too.

As I leafed through the items, memories returned, but less intense this time, allowing me to look with more detachment. I inspected every inch of the photos and studied the words and dates written on the backs. Nothing stood out. I turned to the papers and studied them front and back as well, reading them top to bottom and bottom to top just in case that offered anything. It didn't.

Mo continued to sleep while Cruz played fetch with Bear.

"Find anything?" he asked.

"No." I slid the list of names to the bottom of my pile. There had to be something.

"You're looking at everything?"

"Yes!"

"Does anything seem unusual?"

I groaned. "No. Everything is exactly what it looks like. The most unusual thing here is the magazine article."

Cruz threw the stick and joined me. "What's unusual about it?"

"The fact that it means absolutely nothing to me. Everything else, I recognize."

He stood beside me. "Can I see?"

I fished the article about the hot air balloon tours from the stack and held it out to Cruz. A breeze rippled the page as he reached for it and something on the back snagged my attention. "Wait a second." I pulled the glossy page back and turned it over. The article continued on the back with a couple more pictures.

"What?" Cruz asked.

I shook my head. "I don't know." The page appeared the same as the other times I'd studied it.

Cruz reached for the article, nudging my hand out of the way, and there it was. Hidden beneath my thumb. A tiny picture of a tent. A tent that looked exactly like the last one I'd owned. I sucked in air as the hairs on the back of my neck rose.

Nineteen

"What?" Cruz asked.

I tapped the picture of the tent. "I got a new tent a few months back, but my last tent looked like this one."

Cruz glanced at the picture. "You mean the shape or the brand?"

"I mean everything. The brand, size, shape, colors. *Everything.*"

Cruz looked more closely. "That's weird."

Something caught inside my brain, a tiny spark.

Cruz opened his mouth, but I held up my hand to silence him.

The spark sputtered into the tiniest flame. Something about the puzzles, maybe? Dinosaurs and a building in San Diego? The flame dimmed. No. Not that. What else had Tomas sent? The postcard showing a Madonna and child. What had he written on the back? Something about God watching us. No, seeing us. God sees— No! *He!* "He sees us."

"What?" Cruz made a face.

"Tomas wrote that on the postcard. He sees us."

"Yeah?"

"What if he didn't mean God? What if he meant Adam?"

Cruz tipped his head, eyes opened wide.

The implied religious message hadn't felt like Tomas. But using the obvious implication as a decoy?—that felt very much like him.

"Tomas said Adam can do what he can, right?" Cruz said.

"Yes."

"That makes sense. Tomas sees parts of our lives. Adam must too."

I nodded. "But Tomas usually has to have something of ours in hand or be touching us. What if Adam doesn't need that?"

Cruz sucked in a breath. "That...."

"Would make him clairvoyant as well as a medium." Mo said as she unzipped the tent and peered out at us. "Not entirely unusual."

I wondered if we'd woken her or if she'd already been awake. "What's the difference?"

"A medium is someone who sees and communicates with spirits. A clairvoyant sees things happening to someone else without any sensory input." Mo crawled out of the tent and zipped the flap behind her.

"What did you mean about it not being unusual for a person to be both?" Cruz asked.

Mo shook her head. "People with extrasensory abilities often have a few different kinds. They don't always fit into tidy categories."

"So a clairvoyant and a medium," I said. "Is that something the Revisionists would be interested in?"

"Of course," she said as if it were obvious. "Not just the Revisionists though. Most of the Neme-i. People like the idea of tribe members with extra abilities—it gives the group more strength."

Great.

Cruz studied the magazine page. "So maybe Adam's seen you in your tent. Maybe he knows what you do for work."

Something tugged at the back of my brain. A thought or a memory. Something small.

"If the tent is the clue," Cruz said, "which of the places shown in Tomas's puzzles would require the use of a tent?"

"Definitely not San Diego," Mo mused. "No camping by the marina or zoo."

I thought of the puzzles hanging on Tomas's wall. "Bryce, Canyonlands, and Arches National Monuments…Utah."

Mo nodded. "Lots of camping there."

"Does Utah have anything to do with dinosaurs?" Cruz asked.

The three of us stared at each other until Cruz pointed out Mo had the internet connection.

She hauled her phone from her pocket and keyed in a search. Scrolling with her thumb, she read the titles. "Jurassic Journey, Canyonlands, Moab, Dinosaur Mecca."

"Moab?" I stood.

"Yeah."

I glanced at Cruz. "Tomas had the Moab Man puzzle."

"Pull up the article," Cruz said.

Mo read us the highlights then touched a link for something called Moab Giants. Her eyes slid back and forth as she read, and a smile bloomed across her face. "It's a museum near Moab with full-sized dinosaur reconstructions along an outdoor track. You actually get to walk along and see these things in nature."

Warmth caressed my body and something vibrated inside me. Certainty. Clarity. This was it.

⚓

We watched the sun set, then waited another thirty minutes before driving out of the forest and joining southbound Interstate 5. Agreeing it would be best to avoid Winnemucca, and any trackers who might still be there, we had plotted a course going through Reno. I drove while Cruz sat in the passenger seat and Mo sat in back. For once she didn't have her phone out and sat quietly staring out the windows. She hadn't heard anything about Ethan reporting to anyone besides the council, but she'd sent out some more questions.

I concentrated on the road and the lights of the cars around me. Though well-traveled, the freeway wasn't busy, and traffic remained spread out. I wanted to press the accelerator to the floor and get us to Moab as quickly as possible, but the prospect of being pulled over or catching unwanted attention kept my cruise control set at seventy-five.

Nearly thirty minutes into our drive Mo's phone rang. She jumped and fumbled with the device as she tried to check the screen. I caught sight of a smile that softened the hard edges I'd come to associate with her.

"Hi," she said, her voice a warm whisper.

I glanced at Cruz. The corners of his mouth tipped upward. You didn't have to be a genius to know Mo loved the person on the other end.

Seconds passed before she spoke again, and when she did, her tone sounded curt, professional. "Go."

For several minutes, the only words out of her mouth were one or two-word sentences. "When?.... Got it.... Understood.... Where?" She scribbled something on the back of a receipt she'd found on the floorboard and passed it to Cruz.

He frowned. "Sáanii Suntehai?"

I made a face. What the hell did that group of women have to do with anything?

Unable to see a connection without questioning Mo, I gritted my teeth and tried to concentrate on the road. Nonetheless, snippets of her conversation filtered forward.

"Don't worry.... I'm coming.... Be ready."

When Mo hung up, silence enveloped the car. A glance in the rearview mirror showed her still clutching her phone while staring straight ahead. I didn't know what the conversation had been about, but I knew it had been more important than the message she'd handed Cruz.

"Are you okay?" I finally asked.

I waited, wondering if she'd heard me. Cruz shrugged when I looked at him. Clearing my throat, I opened my mouth to ask again.

"They've got my dad." Mo's voice sounded small and quiet...vulnerable.

278

"Where?" Cruz asked.

"Don't know." She nodded at her phone. "She only knew they had him."

"She...who?" I asked gently.

Mo sighed. "I suppose it doesn't matter anymore. Noelle."

"Noelle?" A memory of the doe-eyed girl I'd met at the Leader's Residence slid across my mind. "You mean Anna's cook?"

"Yeah." Mo barked out a dismal little laugh. "Anna's cook."

"She's your source?" Cruz said.

Mo nodded. "My father's idea."

I didn't know what to say. Even if it had been Jay's idea, Mo appeared to be kicking herself for it. "Is she okay?"

"She's scared. She saw some paperwork. They want to mate her with George Tsossi."

I blinked, and my mouth dropped open. "*Noni's fiancé?*"

"Yep."

"But he—" Cruz said.

Mo cut him off. "Doesn't matter. Isn't gonna happen." She sat up straighter and her voice turned to cement. "When we get to Reno, you'll drop me at the airport. I'm going to get her."

I didn't know what to say.

"Then what?" Cruz asked.

"Then I'll find my dad."

"Where will you look?"

Bear poked his head over the back seat. Even he seemed interested in the answer.

Mo shrugged. "She said Ethan found him—"

Which explained why we hadn't come across Ethan in Winnemucca or Vancouver. He'd been chasing Jay.

"—so I'll search for him."

And while she did, Ethan would likely search for us. Great.

"What about this?" Cruz held up the paper Mo had handed him.

She nodded. "That's who Noelle thinks Ethan's answering to."

"The Sáanii Suntehai?" The hair on my arms rose. "Why does she think that?"

"She's seen him at her aunt's house a few times recently." Mo looked between us. "Her aunt is the leader of the group."

Cruz turned in his seat. "I thought the Sáanii Suntehai were a political think tank."

"That's what they're supposed to be." Mo unbuckled her seatbelt and climbed onto her knees to pull her duffel bag from the cargo area.

"Do you think Ethan's the only person they're directing?" I had my doubts, but it didn't hurt to hope.

"Have you met any of those women, besides your grandmother, I mean?"

Her tone dashed my hope, and when she reeled off several names, I realized I had met a few. They'd been on the deck with Anna and Maria when we'd arrived in Summerhaven.

"They're ambitious," Mo said. "*Fiercely* ambitious. I doubt they'd limit themselves to simply finding my dad. If they had Ethan searching for him, they had reasons."

"Like what?" Cruz asked.

Mo shrugged. "Who knows. Publicizing birth prophecies? Denying marriage blessings? Matching couples to make stronger babies?"

"The council denied the blessings," I said.

"True," Mo agreed. "But who do you think steers them?"

My stomach churned. Peshlakai I could believe. He was constantly kissing up to my grandmother. He'd probably do anything she asked. And maybe Raymond Benally and Martin Alvarez too. They often sided with Peshlakai. But the others? Ivan, Crow, Willy Trujillo? I couldn't see that.

I continued driving until we reached Burney Falls and Cruz took over. Mo remained in the back using her phone to book a flight and make arrangements. As I sat in the passenger's seat, I stared out the window at the stars, searching for my favorite constellations.

Jay had once told me that part of the reason the Neme-i preferred a male ruler was to keep things on the up-and-up. To make sure the tribe conducted their business on even footing with outsiders. Though the First Girls were revered as the founders of the tribe, the Neme-i considered what they had done to ensnare the Navajo warriors wrong—slavery really. Harmony would never exist in taking away another person's will and binding it to one's own. That was a temptation our women constantly had to fight.

Had the women of the Sáanii Suntehai lost that battle?

⊥⊤

We dropped Mo outside the Diamond Casino in Reno shortly after two in the morning. She wouldn't let us take her to the airport, citing the fact that she wouldn't be available to get us a new car for several hours if we fucked up and let a camera catch sight of us in our current vehicle.

She patted Bear on the head, shook Cruz's hand, and pressed her phone into my palm.

"You might need it," she said. "I have another waiting in Tucson. Its number is programmed into this one under the name Shirley." Climbing out of the Suburban, she shouldered her bag, and slammed the door.

I watched her cross the parking lot and disappear around the corner of the building.

We left Reno and headed east, driving hard. As the pinks and purples of dawn began to streak the sky, we reached the edge of the Humboldt-Toiyabe National Forest in Nevada. Cruz did his thing, turning down road after road until we reached what he considered a reasonably secluded area. Then he pulled the truck off the dirt road and parked behind some bushes. We hiked a short distance and pitched the tent beneath a group of pine trees and slept the day away.

That afternoon, we found a stream and washed off the best we could. My mind wandered over the past two days and snagged on the memory of leaving Vancouver. The flood light by the pool had been painfully bright. The tracker with the blonde streak should have seen us. The only way I could imagine she hadn't was that she'd been blinded by the light. We'd been stupid to wait as long as we had to leave. We couldn't be that stupid again.

Twenty

Millions of stars danced in the sky as asphalt sped beneath us. We anticipated the drive to Moab would take eight hours. Where we'd go once we got there I had no idea. I could only hope something would point us in the right direction.

That something came around midnight in the form of a text message from a number I didn't recognize.

Luna. It's T. R u there?

I read the message to Cruz and felt, more than saw, the furrow of his brow in the darkness.

Tomas usually signed his name T, but I hadn't called or texted him from Mo's phone. How would he have the number?

T who? I replied.

A moment passed before the response came. T who begged u never 2 make pot roast again.

I laughed. I had forgotten about the pot roast I'd burnt the first time I'd tried to cook for him. "It's him."

Cruz nodded. "What's he want and how'd he get this number?"

I typed the second question into the phone.

Will explain when I c u, came the reply. Know where ur going. Paid room 4 u at Virginian in my name. Expecting u & C. Dog 2.

The hair on my arms stood up. "How does he know where we're going?"

"Good question," Cruz said.

I typed back, How do u know where we r?

I gripped the phone tight, staring at the screen, willing a sensible answer to appear. When it finally did come, the vibration of the phone made me jump.

He told me.

I stared at the message, trying to make sense of the response. He who? Besides Cruz and me, only Mo knew our plan.

"I don't trust it," Cruz said. "Anyone can send a text."

I typed, Call me, and pressed send.

Two minutes passed before the phone rang.

"Same number as the text messages," I said.

"Put it on speaker."

I did and said hello.

"Luna. It's good to hear your voice."

Tomas's voice was as comfortable and familiar as my own bed. It warmed a part of me I hadn't realized had been cold.

"I've got you on speaker phone," I told him. "Cruz is here."

"Cruz," Tomas said, "how are you?"

A moment passed before Cruz said, "You tell me."

"You're fine," Tomas said. "We all are. But you're probably tired and you'll be exhausted by the time you get here. Go to the inn and get some rest. I'll bring food around noon and tell you everything."

"Everything?" I asked.

"Everything."

I could hear him holding something back. Something that shouldn't be discussed over the phone.

"Drive safe," he said and hung up.

I sat staring at the phone for a minute before I laid it on the dashboard and turned to Cruz. "What do you think?"

"He found something."

I agreed.

"You'll have a lot to talk about."

In the light from the dashboard, I saw the muscle in Cruz's jaw pulse.

"We'll *all* have a lot to talk about," I said.

⸭

The town of Moab sprang up on both sides of Highway 191. A giant mountain of rock formed a wall on its west side. We googled directions to the Virginian and found it one turn off the highway. Cruz pulled up in front of the lobby and turned off the engine. Slouched in his seat, his entire body seemed to droop with exhaustion.

We sat in silence, staring at the lights in the lobby. Cruz took a deep breath and let it out, probably digging deep for energy. He glanced at me and behind us at Bear who danced around the backseat excited to be stopping.

"Put your hat on," Cruz said.

I grabbed the cap from the dashboard and we climbed out and plodded into the lobby.

A heavy-set woman with curly brown hair sat behind the desk reading a romance novel with a bare-chested man on the cover. She held up a finger at our approach, turned her page and read a few more lines.

A satisfied sigh escaped her lips before she dog-eared the page and looked up. I don't know what she expected to see, but it wasn't Cruz. Her mouth fell open as her eyes drank in every inch. Probably mentally replacing the man on the cover with an image of Cruz.

If he noticed the reaction, Cruz didn't show it. He probably thought all middle-aged women reacted that way to younger men.

Catching sight of me, the woman cleared her throat before glancing back at Cruz. "Can I help you?"

He shot her a grin she'd likely dream about for months. "A friend said he reserved a room for us in his name. Tomas Vigil. He said you were expecting us."

She shuffled through some papers. "Your names?"

Cruz slid a glance my way.

As easily as the trackers seemed to find us, I had no desire to share our actual names, but Tomas had told her something.

The woman quirked a heavily penciled eyebrow. "A color perhaps?"

Cruz and I spoke at the same time.

"White."

"Blue."

The woman's second eyebrow lifted to join her first. "Right." She shook her head and made a note on her paper, "Mr. and Mrs. White."

Mr. and Mrs.? I guessed we had Tomas's approval.

⚓

The gurgle of the coffee maker woke me. I inhaled the deep scent of caffeine and looked at Cruz standing across the room with wet hair and a different set of clothes.

He smiled. "Coffee will be ready soon."

Sunlight spilled through a break in the curtains. "What time is it?"

He checked his watch. "11:10."

I sat up and rubbed the crust from my eyes. "How long have you been awake?"

"Long enough to shower." He nodded at the phone charging on the dresser. "Tomas texted. He'll be here in half an hour."

I tossed the covers off and padded to my pack where I pulled out my last clean pair of underwear and the T-shirt I'd worn two days ago. I gave it a sniff and decided it and the shorts I'd worn the day before would have to do. "We need to do laundry."

"Yeah." Cruz snorted.

I scrutinized his shirt. I'd seen it a couple times in the past week as well.

"Smelled better than the others," he said.

I brushed my teeth and thoroughly scrubbed my body while luxuriating in the hotel's hot water.

Dressed, I sat on the bed next to Cruz and sipped coffee while he flipped aimlessly through TV channels. His shoulders hunched and the glaze in his eyes told me his mind whirred faster than the changing channels.

"You okay?" I asked.

Tension flooded his face. "You…and Tomas…."

I took his hand. "You're worried?"

He nodded.

"About Tomas?"

Creases formed around his eyes. "About your feelings for him."

I wanted to tell him not to worry, but I couldn't promise anything. The last time I'd seen Tomas, we'd shared a kiss that could have easily led to more. I didn't know what I'd feel when Tomas showed up. But I knew what I felt right now.

I set my coffee aside and reached for Cruz with both hands. "I love you."

"I love you too," he said.

I kissed him, but I could feel the worry still sitting there in the bunch of his muscles and the tension beneath his skin. I climbed on my knees and straddled him, deepening the kiss until his hands found my hips and one slid beneath my hair, pushing my mouth tighter against his.

A knock on the door made us both jerk. Cruz groaned and the heat that had pooled between my legs echoed the sentiment.

I looked him in the eye. "Okay?"

He bit his lip and nodded.

Slowly, we both stood and adjusted our clothes. I started toward the door, but Cruz caught my hand and shook his head.

"Bear, guard."

Even if Tomas stood on the other side of the door, Cruz would do his protective thing.

The dog jerked upright from his sleeping position and walked over to stand in front of me.

Satisfied, Cruz moved to the door and checked the peep hole. Blowing out a breath, he unfastened the locks and opened the door. Tomas stood on the walkway holding a large paper bag.

For a second, neither man moved, then Tomas reached out and pulled Cruz into a one-armed hug. "It's good to see you."

A second passed before Cruz returned the hug. "You too."

A healthy back slap ended the moment and Cruz stepped back to invite Tomas in. Seeing me, Tomas smiled. He handed the bag to Cruz and stepped toward me.

Bear growled.

Tomas stopped.

"Bear," Cruz said, "check."

Teeth bared, Bear edged forward and begrudgingly sniffed Tomas's outstretched hand.

"Friend," Cruz instructed.

Bear relaxed and sniffed with more enthusiasm. Tomas rubbed his head.

"Friend," I repeated, patting Bear's side then nudging him aside.

"Good dog," Tomas said.

Standing on my tiptoes, I kissed his cheek and hugged him. The strength of his arms around my waist felt familiar but different too. Things had changed between us.

"It's good to see you," he said.

"You too," I replied. "How's Gizmo? Where is he?" I eyed the walkway as if expecting my dog to materialize.

"He's safe. He'll be happy to see you, but I thought it would be better if we talked first."

I exchanged a look with Cruz. He glanced at Tomas and motioned to the burgundy armchair in the corner. "Have a seat."

Tomas didn't budge. His gaze locked with mine. "I found him, Luna. I found Adam."

Twenty-one

Everything stopped. My heart, the air, Cruz, Bear. Nothing stirred.

And then everything did.

My pulse raced as I gulped and stumbled backward. Cruz caught my arm.

"Oh my God." *Our son.* Tomas had found him. "Where is he?" Suddenly I had my purse in hand and was headed toward the door.

Tomas stepped in front of me. "Wait."

"No!" I reached around him for the door handle. "I want to see my son. Where is he?" I had to get to him. Had to see him. For ten years I'd been trying. Now I had a path. I had to take it.

Tomas leaned back against the door. "He's in school right now. He's fine. You'll meet him this afternoon."

Meet. The word hit me like a stone wall. I had to *meet* my own son. Like a stranger. I stared at Tomas. How could he stand in front of me this way? How could he stop me?

"Right now you need to listen," he said.

I looked at Cruz. If I asked, he would remove Tomas from my way. But then what? What school would I go to and what would I do once I got there? What name would I give for my child— Max, Adam, Gilbert, Oliver? The office staff would think me a lunatic. They'd never let me near my child. A vice-like pressure clamped my heart.

"Please," Tomas pleaded, "I need you to listen."

I hesitated. Cruz raised an eyebrow, waiting for my call.

"Please," Tomas repeated.

I turned and eased back, standing beside Cruz. Bear stepped in front of us.

Tomas took in the sight. A wan smile crossed his face. "Why don't we all sit down? There are things you need to know." He no longer leaned against the door, but he remained in front of it.

The man I'd once thought my greatest ally in finding our son now stood between me and Adam. My fists curled. He wanted to talk? Fine.

"What time does school get out?" I demanded.

"Two-forty. I'll pick him up when the bell rings and bring him directly to you. I swear."

I glanced at the clock. Two and a half hours. Pressure filled my chest. I didn't want to wait ten minutes. I swallowed and forced myself to breathe. "When did you find him?"

Tomas winced and motioned to the bed. "Sit. Please."

Cruz gazed at me.

I glanced back at Tomas. His short black hair was about two weeks past the point he'd usually cut it. Dark smudges shadowed his eyes, and he appeared to have lost weight. He'd once been the kindest man I'd ever known. I'd believed he'd never intentionally hurt me. Letting out a huff, I walked to the bed and perched on the edge.

Eyes closed, Tomas sighed and stepped away from the door. "Are you hungry?" He motioned at the bag Cruz held. "I stopped at a deli not far from here. They make a great pastrami—"

"I don't want food. I want answers. When did you find Adam?"

Tomas bit his lip and swallowed. "Four days ago."

"Four days?" White-hot anger sliced through me. I sprang to my feet. "Why didn't you call me?"

Tomas backed away. "I wanted to—"

Cruz caught me by the shoulders.

"—but the last time we talked you told me your phone would

probably be tracked. I couldn't risk it."

My heart pounded as I glared around Cruz. Never in my life would I have expected this from Tomas. I thought of the knives at my back. I had to wiggle my fingers to keep from reaching for them.

"You need to hear him out," Cruz said, his voice a measure of calm in my ear. Gently, he pressed on my shoulders.

Acid filled my stomach, but I sat.

Cruz stared at my hands.

I fisted them in my lap.

Nodding, he turned and motioned once again for Tomas to sit in the armchair. Tomas did. Cruz pulled the desk chair over and sat, blocking everyone's path to the door. Smart.

Tomas wagged his head and looked at Cruz. "You as peacekeeper. That'll take some getting used to."

"I'll be whatever she needs," Cruz said.

A sad smile crossed Tomas's face. "I know."

"Right now, I'd suggest you talk. She was reaching for her knives a second ago."

Tomas's eyes widened.

I tipped my head, not denying it. *I* wasn't the one hiding things. "Does our son know who you are?"

Pride filled a smile he couldn't hide. "Yes."

I wanted to rip the smile off his face. *I* wanted to wear that smile.

"Tell us everything," Cruz said.

"Hand me a sandwich first," Tomas said. "I'm starving."

Cruz opened the bag and passed sandwiches and water bottles around.

Tomas unwrapped his sandwich.

The savory scent of the pastrami reminded me I hadn't eaten in twelve hours, and my stomach growled.

"You remember that vision I told you about before you went to Albuquerque? The one where Adam was looking at me?" Tomas took a bite.

I nodded.

"In the vision, there was a puzzle on the floor. After you left, I kept thinking about that. It showed the eye in Orlando. Same as my puzzle."

"Eye?" I imagined the eye from the *Lord of the Rings* movies and knew that couldn't be right.

"The huge Ferris wheel thing," he said.

Realization hit. "It's an eye and not a Ferris wheel?" No wonder I hadn't been able to find it on the internet.

Tomas took another bite. "I dreamt about it that night. The next day I had a vision of people outside Gatorland."

"Gatorland?" Cruz unwrapped his sandwich.

"Theme park in Orlando," Tomas said. "I got to thinking. I had the eye puzzle and now another vision from Orlando. So I decided it was time for a vacation, and Gizmo and I took off."

My stomach growled again. "You went to Florida?"

"Yep. Stayed about a week. Didn't learn anything though." He looked at Cruz who'd swallowed his first bite of sandwich. "Good, isn't it?"

Cruz licked his upper lip. "Very."

Unable to deny my hunger, I unwrapped the paper on my own sandwich and bit into the perfect blend of spicy meat, dill pickle, and tangy mustard.

Tomas smiled when I moaned. Had to give it to him. The man knew how to make my taste buds happy.

"Anyhow," he said, "even though I didn't get anything useful in Orlando, the thing about the puzzles kept bugging me. We were already on the road headed home, so I kept driving west until we reached San Diego."

"Hell of a drive," Cruz said.

Wide eyed, Tomas nodded. "Four very long days. Some beautiful scenery though."

"What happened in San Diego?" I took another bite.

"At first? Nothing. I went to the places I had puzzles of and came up short. I was about to give up and head home when it occurred to me the places might not be the point."

"Because they're only places Adam's been," I said around my food. "Things he's seen. Not where he is."

Tomas froze. "How'd you know?"

I told him about Portland and Cruz's realization regarding the puzzles and tourist attractions.

"You got my puzzles?" Tomas asked.

"Hideo got them. And the postcard," I said. "He told us what they were. *He sees us.* That's about Adam, isn't it?"

Tomas's cheek dimpled. "Yes. I'll come back to that." He finished off the first half of his sandwich and unwrapped the second. "I spent a week checking out stores that stock puzzles. Eventually, I came across a little girl in a bookstore outside the city. She brushed past me, and I saw a vision of her and Adam sitting in the store doing a puzzle. So I asked her if she liked puzzles, and she told me about her friend, Jeremy."

Jeremy had been another name on my list of possible baby names.

"She said Jeremy's favorite puzzle showed a tent in front of a big, snowy mountain because it reminded him of his mom...who loved camping."

Electricity shot through me and my breath caught.

Tomas smiled. "That's how I reacted. When I got past the shock, I asked if she'd met his mom. She said no; he lived with his grandma, but she'd been to his house. Then she told me about this rocking chair his grandma gave him for his birthday and the way he kept tracing the symbol carved into it with his finger. I asked her to draw the symbol for me. It's one of my chairs, Luna."

A puff of air escaped me. "Oh my god." Tomas built beautiful wooden furniture, but his rocking chairs were what paid his bills. Our son did see us.

"Is that what you meant by *more* in your text?" Cruz said.

"Sort of."

"What else did the girl tell you?" I asked.

Tomas's smile faded. "Not a lot. She said Jeremy had moved

about a year before but she didn't know where."

I glanced at the clock on the nightstand. Two more hours before I could meet my son. My insides ached. How would it feel to hold him? To wrap my arms around my child and breathe in his scent?

Paper crinkled, and I looked over as Cruz carried his sandwich to the bed and sat beside me. He rubbed my back. "Soon."

I nodded, but in my head I thought, *not soon enough.*

Tomas watched us, a fleeting smile on his face.

"What did you do next?" Cruz asked.

Tomas gave his head a shake and his expression turned neutral. "I packed up. Based on the puzzles, my choices were Portland or this area. Money was getting tight, and I only had two puzzles from Portland but three from here, so this is where we came. Gizmo and I hiked in Arches and Canyonlands and saw Moab Man. At night we stayed here. Then one morning, I saw a woman in a bakery and nearly dropped my coffee. She looked exactly like you, Luna, but twenty-five years older."

Coldness filled my lungs. "Raina."

He nodded. "Your mom."

A flash of anger surfaced followed by the sadness I'd felt when I'd read her journals. I didn't know how I felt about Raina anymore. No longer the stranger or enemy she had been, and yet, still, a little of both.

"Why did she take our son?" I asked. "What did she say?"

Tomas leaned back in his chair. "I can tell you what she told me, but you should hear it from her."

Anger seethed inside me. "I don't want to hear it from her." I'd waited long enough.

Tomas tapped the arms of his chair. "Okay. She was at the hospital when you were in your coma. She says your tribe has these people who've been looking for you your whole life—"

"Trackers," I said.

"You know about them?"

I thought of our early morning escape in Vancouver and the

way the woman with the blonde streak had stared straight at us. A shiver slithered through me. "Yeah."

"Okay." Tomas nodded. "That helps. She said because of your lineage in the tribe, if the trackers found you and Adam in Gallup, they would have taken him and come back later for you. She doesn't really trust the tribe." He scratched his head. "I haven't been able to get her to explain why. I keep trying, but something always happens and I get sidetracked."

He looked genuinely confused by that, but I had a good idea what might be sidetracking him.

"Anyhow," he continued, "she said she wanted what happened with Adam to be your choice, not the tribe's, so she helped Adam's foster mom leave her husband and took her and Adam somewhere safe. Once they were set, Raina came back for you."

"But Luna had already woken up," Cruz said repeating what Jay had told us.

Tomas nodded. "And left the hospital. Raina searched for you for two weeks, but had to get back to Adam. She says they've been searching for you ever since."

Déjà vu had me shaking my head. Except for the hotel room, we could have been in Mojave having the same discussion with Jay. "And yet, as of four days ago when you entered her life, she could have reached me by phone and didn't." Instead, she'd had me wandering around on a damned treasure hunt, tearing my hair out and endangering my child.

"I'm telling you," Tomas said, "your phone's being monitored. Those tracker people are monitoring all calls coming and going. She's been trying to reach you another way. She's been trying for over a month."

"And yet you called me last night on a number I never gave you."

"Yeah," Tomas scratched his ear. "You wouldn't believe what we went through to get that."

Cruz and I stared silently at him.

Tomas got the point. "I called your house sitter and begged

and pleaded. He put me through an interrogation worthy of the FBI."

I smiled.

"I don't know if I passed or failed," Tomas said. "After about thirty minutes, your mom asked me to hand her the phone. She called him H, said it was her and told him you were in trouble. She also told him you had a son. Five minutes later, she hung up and told me he would get the number. Three hours later, he had it."

"And that's when you called?" Cruz said.

Tomas nodded. "That's when I called."

I sat stunned. My mother had told Hideo I had a son? It wasn't that I didn't trust Hideo. I did. But even I hadn't told him. I hadn't decided I wanted anyone from the tribe to know, but people kept finding out.

Cruz caught my hand. "You said Raina's been trying to contact Luna?"

"Yeah," Tomas said.

"How?"

"Through Kurt." Tomas balled his napkin and paper wrappers together. "She's been trying to schedule a tour with Luna for over a month."

My mouth opened as something clicked inside my head. All those messages from Kurt. "The woman and child."

Tomas nodded.

What were the odds? I'd been trying to find Adam for ten years, and the moment I'd gotten a break—the beginnings of a clue as to where to find him—Raina had tried to reach me.

I faced Cruz. "Kurt kept telling me about some woman desperate to schedule a tour with me. I've been putting him off."

Cruz nodded slowly.

I frowned. "Why then? Why'd she suddenly start trying to reach me when I took the job with Maria?"

A smile spread across Tomas's face. "Our son."

"Huh?"

"Adam." Tomas grinned. "He sees you when you're having strong emotional reactions, Luna. He saw you packing to go to Albuquerque and caught sight of one of your shirts." He glanced at Cruz. "Saw you too."

I remembered the night I'd packed. I'd just come back from leaving Gizmo with Tomas and had stood in my bedroom folding clothes and putting them in my bag. Cruz stood with me telling me about Maria and the job.

"It was one of your work shirts," Tomas said.

I had several work shirts in various colors and styles all printed with the Enchanted Wilderness logo. That was it? All it had taken? Me to be excited and anxious while I folded clothes? If I'd known that, I would have spent the last ten years starting arguments every time I'd done laundry.

I thought of the finger painting and the macaroni necklace and puzzle piece. "How much does he know about me?"

Tomas's smile held the warmth of a favorite sweater. "More than you'd believe." He leaned back in the chair. "You'll understand when you meet him."

I glanced at the clock. One o'clock. Still almost two hours to wait.

"Where will she meet him?" Cruz asked.

Tomas leaned back. "At the house. I'll pick him up from school and bring him there. We'll meet you at three."

"Three?" I whined. "That adds twenty minutes!"

Tomas's smile fell. "Believe me. You don't want to do this at his school with all the other parents looking on."

Cruz squeezed my hand. "He's right. Remember what happened in Portland?"

I thought of the after-school worker and the trackers' game on the website. It was why we'd agreed to travel at night. If twenty extra minutes would keep my child safe, I would give it time and again. "Okay."

⌗

I didn't know how to kill the minutes after Tomas left, but

297

Cruz suggested we visit a laundromat. When done, we each put on clean clothes then followed the directions Tomas had given us to the house where my son lived.

Located south of town, in an area called Spanish Valley, the modest ranch house was painted beige with brown trim. Flowers and small shrubs grew in the half-moon front yard and a hackberry tree stood in the corner. A long stone walkway led to the porch running the length of the house.

No cars sat in the driveway, and when I rang the bell, no one answered.

"We're early," Cruz said.

Disappointment gnawed. "How early?"

He checked his watch. "Ten minutes."

I clenched my fists and let out a breath.

To the left of the door sat two rocking chairs and a table. I checked the backs of both for evidence of Tomas's work. The smaller chair bore his initials and a carving of a wolf inside a dream catcher decorated with feathers.

Cruz smiled and ran his fingers over the carving. "He keeps getting better."

Tomas had once told me he'd tried to teach Cruz to carve fetishes when they were young. Cruz had attempted a bear and accidentally cut off the front legs and nose. At that point, he'd given up on carving and taken up throwing knives.

I sat in the smaller rocking chair while Cruz stood at the edge of the porch. Bear busied himself with sniffing and marking the yard. I doubted that would go over well with Gizmo.

I tugged at the hem of my jean shorts and smoothed the front of my peasant blouse then forced myself to fold my hands to keep them still. I ended up cracking my knuckles.

"They'll be here," Cruz said.

I frowned at my clothes and cowboy boots. "I should have packed a dress."

"Why?" Cruz glanced back.

"For today. Show respect. Look pretty. I want him to be proud

298

of me."

Cruz chuckled. "You don't need a dress for that. You're his mom. He'll think you're perfect."

I swallowed. "You think so?"

"I know so."

I wanted it to be true. But... "I don't think Raina's perfect."

"That's different." He whistled for Bear then stepped off the porch and turned back. "Just be yourself. He's going to love you."

Shorts and boots definitely fit the part about being me. But what if I wasn't good enough? What if I made a terrible mom?

A car sounded, and I jumped up.

Cruz shook his head. "Not them."

A full-sized Dodge Ram rolled by, carrying hay in the back.

My stomach churned. "What time is it?"

From the other direction, a light-blue panel van approached. I recognized the rust on the fender and stepped forward.

Cruz smiled.

My legs shook and my knees threatened to give out. I gripped the post in front of me.

Cruz offered his hand.

I made it down the two steps and Cruz wrapped his arm around my waist. The van drew nearer, and I spied two heads inside the cabin.

My mouth turned dry and my heart raced.

"Okay?" Cruz asked.

Unable to form words, I nodded.

The truck turned into the driveway and I watched the dark-haired passenger lean forward, hands on the dash.

My chin quivered.

I heard a bark, and a familiar black lab thrust its head through the open passenger-side window. The minute the van stopped and the door opened, Gizmo shot out.

"Shit." Cruz caught Bear's collar as the Rottweiler jumped forward to defend his people. "Heal!"

Oblivious to the threat, Gizmo sprinted toward me, ears

flapping while Bear barked.

"Gizmo!" I cried.

Skidding to a stop, the lab jumped and plopped his front paws on my chest. Unsteady on my legs, I stumbled back a step before Cruz caught me with his free arm. I removed Gizmo's paws and dropped them to the ground then knelt to hug my dog. He licked my face until I didn't know whether the wetness on my cheeks was tears or him.

"He loves you," a little voice said.

Twenty-two

S till crouched, I looked up at the boy with black disheveled hair and my heart swooped and swelled. His walnut-colored eyes searched my face, and his shoulders bunched beneath his blue T-shirt. A rip in his jeans revealed a Band-Aid on his knee.

"Adam?" I shot a glance at Tomas.

Tomas nodded. "He goes by Ben."

"Ben?" I looked at my son and thought of the list of baby names as I climbed to my feet. "Short for Benjamin?"

He nodded. "You can call me Adam though. We decided it's my middle name."

I nodded, my head moving separate from my brain. "Okay."

"I've seen you in my visions. Are you my mom?"

"Yes." Desperately I wanted to throw my arms around him, and tell him how I loved him. But to him, I was a stranger. I swallowed. "Can I hug you?"

He nodded and took a tentative step forward before wrapping his arms around my waist.

I wrapped mine around his back and gently held him.

"He won't break," Tomas said.

Looking over my son's shoulder I saw Tomas chuckling and Cruz nodding his head. So I closed my eyes, and pulled my child in close and really hugged him. Hugged him like I had longed to since I'd woken from my coma. Like he was mine and I would always be his.

His arms tightened around my neck, and I felt his love too. But far too soon, he loosened his hold. Some part of me knew I should let go too, but I couldn't. I never wanted to let go.

"You've got to let him breathe, Luna," Tomas said.

"Oh shit!" I pulled my arms back as if I'd touched an ember. Then, realizing I'd just sworn in front of my ten-year-old son, I covered my mouth. "I'm sorry." My gaze flew to Tomas who appeared to be biting back a laugh. I turned to my child and lost my breath. A thousand starlit skies would never be as beautiful. "Did I hurt you?"

He smiled and shook his head. "No. I'm real strong. Meemaw always says so."

"Meemaw," I said, "that's…your grandma?"

"Uh-huh." A bit of unruly black hair fell over Adam's eye, and he shoved it back. "She's almost as excited to see you as me." He looked around and frowned. "Where is she?"

Tomas ruffled our child's hair. "She wanted to give you and your mom some time alone. She'll be here for dinner."

Gizmo's cold nose butted my forearm, and Bear growled.

"Heal," Cruz said, his voice deep and low.

Teeth bared as he stood next to Cruz, Bear looked ready to spring into action the moment Cruz gave the command.

I patted Gizmo's head and took hold of his collar. Unable to separate myself, I kept my other hand on Adam's shoulder. "I should introduce you to Bear."

Adam held his hand out and let Bear sniff him while Cruz said friend. We tried the same thing with Gizmo, but Gizmo didn't understand formalities. Gizmo was a Welcome Wagon. He believed in sniffing butts, touching noses, and starting to play. Bear nipped at him.

"They'll figure it out," Cruz said.

"Who's he?" Adam's eyes narrowed as he studied Cruz.

"This is Cruz," Tomas said before I could answer. "He's a very special friend of both your mom's and mine."

302

"Hello." Cruz held out his hand. "It's nice to meet you."

Lips pursed, Adam glared up at Cruz.

"Shake his hand," Tomas said.

Adam did as told, but barely touched Cruz's hand before he dropped it and rudely turned his back.

I jerked my gaze to Cruz.

The right side of his mouth quirked upward. Amused.

Tomas mouthed *sorry*, but Cruz waved it off.

"Why don't you show your mom around?" Tomas said to Adam.

Adam took my hand and tugged me forward. I glanced back at Cruz. He wore the gentlest smile I had ever seen.

For the next hour I followed my son. He showed me every room in the house as well as the garage and backyard. He showed me how well he could climb his favorite tree and cheered for me when I climbed up behind him. I saw his bike and met his six-toed cat. I saw the LEGO models he'd built and the ribbons and certificates he'd earned at school. He told me about his soccer team and the game he had coming up that weekend. And through it all, I stared in wonder at this perfect, amazing little boy.

For ten years, I'd worried about my child. Considered every horrible possibility that might exist. Yet here he was. Safe. Thriving. Happy.

He questioned me about Gizmo and our home in New Mexico and if I had a room for him. He asked how far I lived from Tomas and if we would all live together and if Meemaw would live with us too. He asked about my job and my favorite places to camp and hike. He asked if I'd ever seen a bear or a snake and what other animals I'd come across and if I'd been scared.

He asked so many questions I ran out of words. And when that happened, I put my head down and wept and thanked God for this moment—this miracle I'd feared would never happen.

"I think your mom needs some time," Tomas said.

I jerked my gaze up. Tomas and Cruz stood in the doorway of Adam's room. I didn't know how long they'd been there, but I sensed it had been a while.

"How about you and I put together a snack and some drinks?" Tomas said.

Adam nodded and walked over to where I sat on the floor. He patted my shoulder. "I'll get you some of Meemaw's cookies. They always make me feel better." Then he wrapped his arm around me and gave the top of my head a kiss. "It'll be okay, Mom."

My breath caught and warmth exploded through my chest. *Mom.* I caught my son's hand and pressed it to my lips.

Tomas stepped into the room and put a hand on Adam's shoulder. "We'll be in the kitchen. Come join us when you're ready."

The look in his eye told me I needed to pull myself together, and he was probably right. But I couldn't. Every emotion I owned seemed to have raced to the surface. I didn't know how to handle them.

I let go of my son, feeling an ache the moment the heat of his body no longer touched my skin and then again when he stepped out of the room.

Cruz waited a moment, leaning against the doorframe before he walked over and crouched beside me.

He pulled me into his arms and whispered into my hair, "Let it out. Let it all out."

The tears poured out. Sobs of pent-up anguish and despair wracked my body. So many years I had worried. So many nights without sleep. So many days filled with fears. I cried until the tears ran out and the sobs drained away. And then I sat in silence still clinging to Cruz.

"He's okay," Cruz finally said.

I nodded as I released my hold and simply sat beside him. "He's perfect."

Cruz touched my knee where I'd scraped it while climbing the tree. "Good thing you chose shorts."

I smiled. "He called me Mom."

"I heard."

"It made my heart burst."

Cruz chuckled. "I think you can count on a lot of moments like that."

I hoped so.

"He's not very fond of me," Cruz said.

I winced. "I'm sorry. I don't know what that's about."

Cruz chuckled. "It's okay. I get it. I'm not his dad."

"I'm sure he'll love you." Tomas's nieces and nephews did. They couldn't get enough of Cruz.

He smiled. "You gonna be okay?"

I considered a moment. "I think so. I'm just...."

"Overwhelmed?"

That was exactly what I was. "Yes."

"Understandable."

"Really?"

He nodded. "Yeah. You've been through a lot. But right now, you've got cookies and a son waiting for you. Probably shouldn't keep them waiting."

We stood, and I hugged him. "Thank you."

"You're welcome." He brushed a kiss across my lips then gave my butt a gentle smack. "Mom."

In the kitchen, Adam and Tomas sat at the breakfast bar. A plate of cookies and four glasses of milk sat in front of them. A stack of photo albums sat at the end of the bar.

"Sorry about that," I said as I stepped into the kitchen.

Tomas stood and offered me his stool. "Come. Sit."

I did, unable to keep from grinning at the milk mustache my child wore.

Cruz stepped over and he and Tomas flanked Adam and me.

"What kind of cookies are they?" I asked.

Adam pushed the plate toward me. "Oatmeal raisin. My favorite."

"Mine too," Cruz said.

Adam shot Cruz a begrudging look and nudged the plate

toward him after I'd taken a cookie.

"Adam has something he wants to show you," Tomas said when the cookies had been eaten and the glasses were empty.

"What?" I asked.

Adam grinned and pointed at the photo albums to my left.

My heart leapt. "Are they pictures of you?" Was I finally going to see a baby picture of my son?

"No. Not these. These are cool. You and Meemaw can look at pictures of me later if you want. Those are boring."

Disappointment sat like a weight on my chest, but I tried not to show it as I pulled the top album off the stack and placed it between us.

Tomas put a hand on the cover and turned a serious gaze on our son. "You should know your mom will probably cry again. That's not bad."

Adam took a deep breath and nodded. "I understand. She's a girl."

"Hey," I complained. "Boys cry too."

Adam nodded again. "Sometimes. But not as often. Right, Dad?"

Tomas fought against a grin and lost. He looked at Cruz. Together, they nodded. "True."

We opened the photo album, and a well-worn and somewhat crinkled picture of a two-year-old Anna holding me as a baby stared up at me.

"That's you and Aunt Anna," Adam said.

A lump formed in my throat. "Yes, it is."

He flipped the page and proceeded to walk me through photo after photo of my childhood. Some I'd seen before. Some I had not. Clearly, these were the photos Gloria had sent Raina. Near the front of the album, were pictures of Raina and Gloria together, but after a couple pages there were only photos of me and occasionally one of Gloria and me.

Adam pointed at a picture of Gloria sitting on a horse with me. "Meemaw says Gloria was her best friend."

I nodded.

"That's who you lived with when you were little, right?" Adam said. "Like I live with Meemaw?"

Again, I nodded. It wasn't the same in my mind, but in his, I could see how it might be.

"Did you love her?"

"Very much. I wish she were here to meet you."

"She is."

I jerked my gaze to Adam. "What?"

He ducked his head and kicked his heels against the legs of his stool. His mouth clamped shut.

I looked to Tomas for help.

"He's worried what you'll think," Tomas said.

I blinked in surprise. How could I ever think my child anything but perfect?

"Is this about seeing people who've crossed over?" Cruz asked.

Adam's head shot up and he glared instant death at Cruz.

I took my son's hand. "Are you worried I'll think that's weird?"

He gazed down, refusing to meet my eyes. "Do you?"

I shook my head. "No. I think it's wonderful. Mr. Price, in Portland, told us what you told him about his mother and daughter. That was a gift you gave him. Telling me that Gloria is here is a gift too. I've missed her more than I know how to say. I wish I could see her like you can."

He squinted as if debating the truthfulness of my answer. Then he frowned and looked over my shoulder. "She keeps saying trust. Something about trusting yourself."

"Trust myself?" I asked.

He shook his head and his gaze returned to mine. "I don't know. She says you'll know when the time comes."

I stared, wondering what he was talking about.

"Grandpa's here too," Adam said.

"My father?"

Adam nodded. "He started coming to me this summer. That's how Meemaw knew he died. She cried a lot."

The thought of my father's death cast fresh tears in my eyes. I had hardly known the man, but his love had been pure. Until that moment, I hadn't fully understood why a man who'd only spent an hour with me would step in front of a bullet to protect me. But as I sat there watching my son, I understood perfectly.

"He was very special," I said.

Adam nodded. "He says you're special." He reached up and tapped his breastbone. "He keeps touching, here. Do you have something of his?"

I touched my chest and felt the locket Raina had left for me—the one Gilberto had given her. Reaching beneath the neckline of my shirt, I pulled it out. "This?"

Adam shook his head. "No. That." He pointed at the Leader's Ring also dangling from the chain. "He says that's where it should be."

I lifted up the ring. "On the chain with the locket?"

"No. He's pointing at you. I think he means with you."

I sucked in a breath and glanced at Cruz. He grimaced. I didn't want the job. He knew it. The entire tribe knew it. No doubt my father's spirit did too.

"He didn't want it either," Adam said, "but he's saying it goes where it needs to."

Great.

Tomas shot a questioning glance from me to Cruz.

Cruz responded with a miniscule headshake and mouthed, *later*.

I dropped the locket and ring beneath my shirt, and we returned to the photo albums, flipping through page after page of my life. The last shot showed me with a pregnant belly. The words *six months* were written at the bottom.

"That's me!" Adam pointed at my swollen belly. "Right?"

I nodded.

Cruz and Tomas stood behind us looking over our shoulders.

I smiled at them. For years I had wanted to show them images from my life—a picture of me pregnant most of all. Sharing it now—all four of us together—felt like the most natural thing I'd ever done. This was my family—a family that had started with the pregnant belly on display in the photo.

"That's his favorite picture," a female voice said behind us.

Twenty-three

I swiveled around and gaped at the woman standing in the doorway.

On the night I met my sister, I felt like I'd stepped into a Star Trek episode. Staring at the woman with shoulder-length black hair shot through with gray and eyes that matched mine felt even more like that. Fine lines creased the skin around her mouth and eyes and her neck had begun to sag. Seeing her was like looking at an age progression photo of myself.

I shivered.

Tomas sprang forward and caught the two pizza boxes tipping precariously from the woman's hands. He set them on the table as Cruz nudged me to stand.

My legs quaked.

"Pizza!" Adam cried, going straight to the boxes. "What kind did you get?"

Raina remained silent as she stared at me, eyes filled with water. "Luna?"

I swallowed and nodded as she drew closer.

I knew the look she wore. I'd seen it on my father the day I'd met him. And I imagined I'd worn the same expression hours before when I'd stared at my child for the first time.

The dam holding back the water broke, and tears streamed down her cheeks as she rushed to me and threw her arms around me.

I've never been a particularly affectionate person when it comes to displays. I'm not much of a hugger. But I'd hugged my child for all I was worth earlier that day, and Raina clearly wanted to hug me like that too. Placing my hands on her back, I squeezed.

My grandmother had hugged me once. It had felt stiff and cold. My father had hugged me too. It felt much like this. Warm on his end. Awkward on mine. But he had loved me. I understood that now. In spite of the things I had thought my whole life— could it be my mother loved me too?

We pulled apart and her hands flew to my face, touching my cheeks and forehead like a blind person.

"You're scaring her, Meemaw," Adam said.

Had I scared him when I'd behaved this way?

Raina pulled her hands back as if stung.

I shook my head. "It's okay."

"I can't believe I'm finally touching you," she whispered.

I couldn't believe I'd finally held my son. "I understand."

She shook her head and looked down. "I'm so sorry you do. I never wanted you to know this pain." Her voice broke and her shoulders shook as she continued to stare at the floor. "I'm sorry. I'm so, so sorry. Tomas told me you thought I'd kept your child from you on purpose. Never. I would never."

God help me. I believed her. "It's—" My words trailed off. I didn't know what to say. It wasn't okay, but I needed to say something. "We'll talk about it. We have a lot to talk about."

Chin quivering, she nodded. Glancing around the kitchen, her gaze stopped on Cruz.

"This is Cruz Whitehorse," I said, "my—"

"Your young man." She offered her hand. "It's nice to meet you."

Relief washed over me that I hadn't been forced to choose a term. I'd been going to say *boyfriend*, but the word didn't do justice for what Cruz had become. I couldn't think of a term that did.

He shook her hand. "Mrs. Bluefeather."

She stiffened before letting out a breath. "I haven't been called that in many years. I'm Raina Trujillo here. Please, call me Raina."

Cruz nodded. "Raina."

She let go of his hand and looked from him to Tomas to me. A crease formed between her brows.

"You change names every time you move?" I asked. "Both of you?"

She nodded.

Gloria and I had never changed names. But the world had changed so much—everyone so much more interconnected with the internet. Who knew? Maybe the fact that Gloria and I hadn't changed names was why we'd often come so close to being found.

"How do you get the records and documents you need?" Cruz asked.

Raina cast a pointed glance Adam's way, and I got the message. She didn't want to discuss it in front of him. "We'll talk tonight," she said in a light tone. "Right now, why don't we eat? Someone looks hungry."

Adam snatched his hand out from beneath the pizza lid. Judging from the grease on his fingers, he'd already filched a few toppings.

After dinner, I followed my son like a lost puppy until Raina said it was bedtime. He brushed his teeth and changed into pajamas then asked me to tell him a story. He lay beneath the covers while I sat on his bed and told him the only story I knew—the First Girls. By the time I finished, Adam's eyes were closed and his breathing even. I kissed his forehead and ran my hand through his hair. Tomas pulled me out of the room.

"He won't sleep if you keep touching him," he whispered in the hallway. "He's a light sleeper for the first hour or so."

"How do you know?" I asked.

He grimaced. "I made the same mistake my first night here. I refused to leave his room. He hardly slept because I kept checking him to make sure he was breathing."

I swallowed. Checking Adam's breathing was exactly what I wanted to do. I didn't want to let him out of my sight.

"It's okay." Tomas nudged me toward the living room. "He'll be all right."

I didn't want to leave, but I did want him to sleep, and I needed to speak with Raina. There were things we needed to discuss that Adam didn't need to hear.

Cruz stood in the living room when Tomas and I stepped out of the hallway.

He walked over and brushed his hand against mine. "Everything okay?"

Leaning into him, I wrapped my arm around his waist. "Yes."

His eyes narrowed in question as he looked down at me.

I tucked my head against his chest as his arms circled me.

In truth, with Tomas standing there, the moment was awkward. But that had been the point. Tomas and I were friends and we were partners in parenting. But I'd given my heart to Cruz, and I wanted both of them to know it.

Cruz kissed the top of my head, and I smiled up at him before stepping back. "Where's Raina?"

"In the kitchen."

"I need to talk to her."

Cruz nodded. "Go ahead. Tomas and I need to talk too."

Hopefully their discussion would include a make up in their friendship.

"Will you fill him in on everything regarding the Neme-i?" I asked.

Tomas frowned. "What's a Neme-i?"

"Her people." Cruz said.

I stepped into the kitchen. Steam rose from the kettle on the stove.

Raina pulled a box of mint tea from a cupboard and waved it at me. "Always helps calm my nerves. Would you like some?"

313

Under normal circumstances I might have asked for one of the beers I'd been offered before dinner, but I wanted a clear head. "I'll try it."

She prepared the tea and carried two mugs to the table where we sat across from each other.

"I don't know where to start," she said.

I didn't either. "I read your journals and the letters between you and Gloria. Thank you for leaving them." Unclasping the chain around my neck, I held out the locket and Leader's Ring. "I believe these are yours."

She took the necklace and ran her fingers over the locket. Then she turned it over and gingerly ran a finger over the inscription. "Your father was such a good man. I can't imagine how much I must have hurt him. He must have hated me."

"I don't think so." I told her about my one conversation with him. "When he told me about you, he spoke with love. Did he know your prophecy?"

She nodded as a tear spilled from one eye. "I told him a week before I left. He said I worried too much. I disagreed. I still worry what will happen when they learn it."

"Did you know the council voted to publicize the prophecies?"

She bit her lip. "I heard."

"As far as I know, they've only decoded some of the prophecies in Jay's possession. But they took him, so it's probably a matter of time for the rest. I was told he holds yours."

"They have him?" Pain lined her face. "You're sure?"

"Yeah."

She looked down.

"Do you know what they'll do to him?" He hadn't been willing to tell me, but I needed to know. What was the cost of all this?

"Yes." The word came out as a whisper.

"Tell me. Please."

She swallowed. Hesitated. "There are houses—well, shacks really—in the forest on Mount Lemon. I saw one once, when I was a girl. It had a staircase that led down into a cave with deeper

314

pits inside. They'll keep him in one of those and limit his food and water. Beyond that, I don't know the specifics. My father would never tell me. I know none of it is good though."

"For how long?" I asked.

"Until he breaks."

"So until he gives them his codes?"

She winced. "Maybe."

The hair on the back of my neck prickled. "What do you mean *maybe*?"

She twisted her mug in a circle. "Are you sure his codes are what they're after?"

I frowned as I recalled our conversation with Mo. "The council says he's missing some prophecies, but his daughter says they're lying."

"Are you sure? He never wanted them publicized. Maybe he held some back."

"No. I asked him to hold back Adam's. He wouldn't. He wouldn't hold back any."

She sat up straighter. "Adam's prophecy? You know it?"

"Yes." I slouched lower in my chair.

Her brow crinkled as she studied me and I could see the desire to ask playing through her eyes. Something else sparkled too—something fighting with the desire.

"You want to know it?" I'd seen Raina's love for Adam all night. She wouldn't hurt him. I knew that. She would protect him, same as I would.

She shook her head slowly. "No." Then she looked at her hands and scoffed. "All these years. You'd think I'd know better. Still, here I sit, as excited at the mention of a prophecy, as I would be about a baby on the way. I guess it's ingrained in me."

"I assume you know mine and Anna's?" I said.

"I do." Her gaze strayed toward the living room. "Do you want to know yours?"

I considered. On the one hand, of course I wanted to know. But knowing Adam's and Raina's brought worry enough. Did I want to risk adding to that? "Will you tell me one thing? Does mine say I'm evil or will do evil things?"

"What?" She stared at me as if the idea were preposterous. "Of course not."

I breathed out and felt the fear abate. "Thank you."

"That's all? You don't want to know more?"

"No." I smiled. "I don't."

She seemed perplexed by my answer but didn't press. Turning her attention to the locket and ring she still held, she removed the ring from the chain and pushed it toward me. "This is yours now. It hasn't been mine in many years."

I shook my head. "It's not mine either. Anna's the leader. I guess it's hers."

Raina pulled her tea closer. "It may become hers. But for now, it's yours. I gave it to you. That means something."

I had my doubts about that. Raina had effectively resigned her position as leader. She'd walked out on the Neme-i. I doubted they would care what she had to say anymore.

Picking up my mug, I swirled the contents and took a sip. The mint tingled my tastebuds.

"You must have questions," she said.

I had tons. But I kept it simple. "Tell me about Adam."

She told me everything. When he'd taken his first step. What his first word had been. That he was mildly allergic to insect stings, but not dangerously so. He was kind and giving and well-liked by his peers, a favorite of some of his teachers. He enjoyed school and got good grades (a fact that surprised and delighted me considering how I'd done), and he loved animals.

"He's loved having Gizmo here," she said. "Having Bear around will make him doubly happy."

"How does he handle the moving?" I asked.

"How did you?"

I shrugged. My sense was that Gloria had told Raina everything. She knew.

She sighed. "He's more outgoing than I think you were, so he makes friends easily. But...."

"There's more for him to lose with every move that way." I remembered the few times I'd left behind friends. Those moves had been the worst.

She slumped back in her chair. "The first few weeks are rough. But after a couple days at his new school, he finds a new friend and life goes on."

"What about you?" I asked. "How do you handle the moves?"

She shrugged and attempted a smile. "They used to be horrible. Now, they're just life. There are people I miss. Sometimes I get to see them again. Sometimes not. But there are also a few who've become constants. People I trust and who help us. We're lucky." She reached for her mug. "I understand you count yourself lucky not to move anymore."

"I do. I have friends I can count on, a home with a garden and a yard, and a job I love."

"The wilderness tours." She smiled. "Your boss seems quite fond of you."

I thought of Kurt with his dirty-looking socks and teddy bear personality. "I'm fond of him too."

"I take it he's one of your friends?"

I nodded. "I don't have a lot, but the ones I have are special. I like having roots." I lifted my mug then set it back down. "It's something I'm hoping to give Adam."

She took a sip of tea. "But...?"

"I'm scared."

"Of what?"

Was she serious? "Of the Neme-i and what they'll do when they learn about him."

She tapped a finger against her mug. "That's a wise thing to fear."

I waited, hoping she would offer more.

She sipped her tea.

Finally I asked, "What are you afraid of? Why are you still running from them?"

Raina tapped her fingernail on the mug, the sound growing louder with each passing second. About the time it became unbearable, she pushed her chair back and stood.

"I'm going to make another cup." She motioned at my mug. "Would you like some?"

I shook my head.

She returned the kettle to the burner. "Before I answer your question, I think we should join your friends. The answer will affect them too."

As soon as Raina's tea water boiled, we joined Tomas and Cruz in the living room. Cruz had explained to Tomas who the Neme-i were, but Raina and I had to describe what we could do. We explained the trackers and their pursuit of Cruz and me which led us to the prophecies and Jay and somehow that led us to the topic of my abductions which took us to my father's death, and that left Raina needing a minute and another cup of tea.

By the time we returned to the topic that had brought us to the living room, Gizmo lay sprawled on the floor snoring while Bear lay at the head of the hall. I'd long since given up on tea and joined Tomas in a beer. Cruz had turned to the sugar infused, caffeinated wonders of soda and Raina had produced two bags of microwaved popcorn along with her tea.

"So what are you afraid of?" Tomas asked her. "Why have you been running for thirty years?"

Seated in a brown, leather recliner with her legs curled beneath her, Raina balanced her mug on her knee. "At first I was afraid of what the tribe would do to Anna and Luna if they learned my prophecy."

"And that's why you left?" I said.

Raina nodded. "After you and I got away, I realized how much danger I put others in who helped us, so I cut all ties with the tribe. For a short while, that was good, but then I realized if the trackers found us and moved fast enough, they could kill us both and simply say we'd never been found. So that's when I left you with Gloria. I knew you'd be safe with her, and I knew the trackers would never think to look for you with anyone but me."

"Except they did." Gloria and I moved as often as we did because we'd been found. "Why?"

Raina regarded her tea. "Because a tracker found me and intercepted some of my mail. I got away—barely—but he got hold of a letter from Gloria that contained a picture of the two of you."

I wiped my hand on a napkin. "So that's how they sent the nightmares? But I thought you couldn't send a message based on a picture. Jay said it would end up going to the picture."

Raina sighed. "It's iffy, but it *can* work if the sender is strong enough."

The ice in Cruz's glass tinkled. "Who was the tracker?"

"Joey Two Paws."

I remembered the female tracker with the blonde streak in her hair. "His daughter's a tracker now, isn't she?"

"Yes." Raina seemed surprised. "How did you know?"

I started to say we'd come across her, but Cruz cut me off.

"Website," he said. "We saw her picture."

Tomas reached for the nearest bag of popcorn and pulled out a handful. "Is that who chases you now?"

"No." Raina sipped her tea. "For the most part, no one chases me anymore."

"Then why keep moving?" Cruz set his glass on the coffee table.

Curled against him on the couch, I rubbed my knuckles against his hip.

"Because I worry about Ben."

I was finding it hard to connect Adam with the name Ben, but I would get there. "What do you think they'll do if they find him?"

"Now that you are found"—she met my gaze—"I don't know. Before, when you were missing, I worried if they found us, they would take him and raise him however they wanted. I knew if they had him, they'd stop looking for you. They wouldn't need another leader-elect. They could tell your father they were still searching, but at best they'd be lying, and at worst, if they did find you, I worried they'd kill to keep you from entering the picture and complicating things."

"Who is *they*?" Tomas leaned forward. "Do you mean the trackers?"

Raina winced. "Maybe some of them."

"Some?"

"Yes, some. Some of them, some of the Revisionists, some of the council, some of—"

"The Sáanii Suntehai?" Cruz spoke quietly, but the silence that followed made his words boom.

Raina bit her lip and nodded.

Tomas gazed back and forth between us. "Who are they?"

I opened my mouth to answer but stopped and turned toward Raina. She undoubtedly knew more about the group than Cruz or I.

On the floor, Gizmo's legs twitched—probably dreaming about chasing a butterfly.

"The blessed women," Raina said. She let out a bitter chuckle and regarded me. "Did you know your grandmother's one?"

I nodded. "We've heard Anna might be too."

Raina jerked and seemed to deflate. "Of course."

"What?" I asked.

"Maria." Raina stared at her lap. "She invited me to join the group shortly after Gilberto and I married. But Father always said that group was dangerous. He didn't trust them. When I declined, Maria acted as if I'd insulted her and the group." Raina paused and wrapped both hands around her mug. "If Anna is a member, they've finally gotten what I believe they wanted back then."

"Access to the leader?" Cruz said.

Raina nodded.

"Hold on." Tomas made a face. "It's been what?—thirty years since you said no to the group? You really think they're nursing the same agenda today?"

Raina cast him a pitying glance. "They've nursed that agenda far longer than that."

"How long?" I asked.

"Since the First Girls."

Lovely. While the First Girls made for a nice, redacted bedtime story, their actual history left me wondering if they would have considered Adolf Hitler a creative pioneer.

Cruz drummed his fingers on the arm of the couch. "Jay said they were power hungry."

Raina sighed. "That's an understatement."

"You think they'll manipulate Anna?" I asked.

"I'm certain they'll try."

"Time out." Tomas held his hands up. "We're getting off topic. Tribal stuff's important, but we're talking about Adam." He turned to Raina. "I get why you ran and why you were worried, but Luna and I are here now. No one's cutting us out of his life ever again."

Raina grimaced.

"I don't mean you." Tomas waved a reassuring hand.

Raina nodded, but the grimace remained.

"I'm talking about this *them* you've been talking about. Are they still a threat now that Luna and I are present?"

Raina lifted her chin and pointed her gaze at me. "What do you think?"

This was the question that had plagued my mind. I'd batted it round and round the past couple days. But now that I'd found my child, things had changed. "I don't think it's *them* we need to worry about anymore. I think it's Anna."

"Your sister?" Tomas's eyes bulged. "Why?"

I frowned. "She's not like your sisters." Tomas and his sisters actually loved and cared about each other. "Anna and I are related by blood, but that's all. To her, I'm competition for the one thing she grew up believing she had an absolute right to have."

"Leadership." Cruz reached for the popcorn.

"Okay." Tomas said. "What's that got to do with Adam?"

"The tribe gives priority to a male leader over a female," Raina said. "He is the only male heir. There are many in the tribe who would name Luna leader just to be certain they'd have a male leader when your son comes of age."

"But Luna doesn't want to lead." Tomas looked at me. "Right?"

"Right." I took a drink of beer.

"And that works to Anna's benefit," Raina said. "But the situation remains the same. The moment Luna's son comes of age, the tribe could force Anna out of the position."

"Unless *she* has a son." I set my bottle down and grabbed a handful of popcorn.

"Is she pregnant?" Hope tinged Tomas's voice.

"No," I said. "Not pregnant, married, or engaged. Hell, not even bonded."

"Not bonded?" Raina put her feet down and leaned forward. "She doesn't have a boyfriend?"

"There are rumors she's messing around with Hideo's replacement," I mumbled.

"But they're not bonded?" Raina pressed.

"Not as of a week ago." I glanced at Cruz to be sure I remembered correctly.

He nodded. "They seemed friendly enough, but Jay said they weren't bonded and that there had been whispering about that."

Raina's mouth hung open. "I would think so."

"Okay," Tomas said, "back up." He stared at Raina. "You've mentioned bonds before when you talked about Adam being connected to Luna and me. What exactly are we talking about?"

Raina cocked her head and turned to me.

I didn't know how to explain it either.

"Connections," Cruz said. "For the Neme-i they're not just something felt between two people. Their men sense the bonds somehow—see them, taste them, feel them—I don't know. But they know when people are connected. Even small connections."

Tomas turned to Raina. "So you're saying Adam can…?"

Raina smiled. "You saw his face the moment he saw you. He

didn't need me to introduce you."

Tomas frowned. "I thought that was because of his visions."

"His visions are related to his bonds," Raina said, "but he didn't need the visions to know you."

"Related to his bonds how?" I asked.

Raina set her mug on the table. "He isn't clairvoyant. He's what is known as a remote viewer. He sees things happening in real time."

"That's unusual," Tomas said.

Raina nodded. "He doesn't see everyone. He sees people he's bonded to. Usually when our emotions are high."

"What do you mean?" I shifted on the couch.

"The two of you were in the desert recently." She nodded at Cruz and me. "On Mount Winnemucca, right?"

The hairs on the back of my neck prickled. "How did you know?"

"He saw you. And then he woke me. Sometimes, by touching me, he's able to send calming thoughts to you."

"You mean *you* send me a message?"

She shook her head. "No. I haven't known how to visualize you, so I haven't been able to send you a message. I mean he borrows from me. The messages are his own."

"Borrows from you how?" I said. "You mean like mukutekka?"

Raina snapped her gaze to me. "You know what that is?"

I nodded. "I learned about it in Winnemucca. Apparently I have it."

Raina's face seemed to glow. "Me too. And yes, you're right. That's what he borrows. It's usually enough for him to somehow let you know things will be all right or wake you up if you're having a bad dream."

"Or convince her to turn around on a highway?" Cruz raised an eyebrow as he looked at me.

"Yes," Raina said. "Exactly."

"That's amazing," I said.

323

She nodded. "It is, and I actually think he's been doing it since he was a baby. But it doesn't always work. When you were in Winnemucca it didn't. He said the trackers were about to find you."

"They were close." I motioned at Cruz. "We were crouched below a road, and they were above us. But something happened, and they left. Did he do that?"

"No," she said. "I did."

"You? How?" She'd just said she didn't send messages to me.

"Ben tried to describe the trackers as best he could, but he couldn't see them properly in the dark. All he knew was they were very close. So I sent a message to all trackers."

"A blanket message?" Cruz asked.

Raina nodded. "I sent an image of me."

I gasped. "An image of you doing what? Holding Ben?"

"No." She drew the word out as if I were crazy for even asking. "Just an image from an old photo. It shows me standing outside the zoo in Portland."

I looked at Cruz and saw the spark behind his eyes. He got it. That's what had been bigger to the trackers than sensing me. And that was why they'd been in Portland when we were. They hadn't followed us. They'd gotten there before us.

"Amazing," I said as I thought of what my son could do. But then my elation crashed. "The Revisionists. If they learn what Adam can do…."

Raina nodded. "They'll want him all the more."

"Fuck."

"Who are the Revisionists?" Tomas asked.

⚑

We kept Adam home from school the next day, and I spent the morning tramping outside behind him. We climbed his second favorite tree, kicked a soccer ball, bathed Bear and Gizmo and saved a colony of ants by building a miniature dam to protect their home. By eleven-thirty, I was exhausted and needed a break, so Tomas and Cruz took over.

Inside, I helped Raina make sandwiches for lunch. We called the others to join us and sat around the kitchen table. As he'd done at breakfast, Adam sat between Tomas and me where he helped himself to a mound of chips.

At the sound of the doorbell, Cruz stiffened. His sandwich returned to his plate. "Are you expecting someone?"

Raina stood and pushed her chair in. "Probably just a delivery."

Oblivious to the wide-eyed looks Cruz and I exchanged, Adam pressed forward in his questions for his father. "What do you call the special ceremonies in Taos again?"

"Bear," Cruz said quietly, "guard."

The Rottweiler sprang to attention and stood between us and the doorway.

In the entryway, Gizmo's toenails clicked against the tile in the familiar rhythm of his welcome dance. I glanced at Bear, wondering what he thought of such antics.

The door opened and I heard happiness in Raina's greeting. A female voice replied and grew louder telling me she'd been invited in. She called Gizmo by name, so I knew she'd been here before.

I let out a breath. *Friend,* I mouthed at Cruz. He nodded.

On the other side of Adam, Tomas raised an eyebrow but kept his attention on our son who'd begun conducting a poll on everyone's favorite type of chip.

Tomas's and Cruz's picks earned looks of approval. Mine earned derision.

"Barbeque potato chips?" Adam cried. "Mom! That's boring."

I shrugged. "I guess I'm boring."

Seated across from me, Cruz chuckled and shook his head as if I were anything but.

"We have a problem," Raina said as she stepped into the kitchen.

But it wasn't Raina I saw. It was the young woman trailing behind her. A young woman whose short, dark hair had a blonde streak in front.

Twenty-four

My heart raced. "Shit!" I jumped up, sending my chair crashing into the wall as I yanked Adam from his chair. "Ow!" he cried, trying to pull free.

I forced him behind me.

In front of us, Bear growled. Cruz stood, gun pointed at the tracker.

"No!" Raina jumped in front of the woman.

Tightening my grip on Adam, I reached for my knives. Nothing. *Shit*. I'd taken them off before going outside to play with him.

Rebecca Two Paws held her hands in the air. "I'm a friend."

"Prove it," I yelled.

"I didn't out you at the motel in Vancouver."

"You saw us?" I'd been so certain she would, but her act—if it had been an act—had fooled me.

"Of course I saw you," she said. "That floodlight was like a spotlight."

"Let me go!" Adam continued to struggle.

I held tight.

"You trust her?" Cruz asked Raina.

"Yes." Raina's eyes shot venom at him.

Cruz and I exchanged a glance. Tipping the gun toward the floor, he engaged the safety.

"You hurt me!" Adam cried, wriggling free of my grasp.

"Bear," Cruz said. "Check."

I turned to face my son.

Backed into Tomas, Adam glared like I'd become the enemy. My heart shattered.

Hands on Adam's shoulders, Tomas gazed wide-eyed around the room.

"It's not your mom's fault," Rebecca Two Paws said to Adam as Bear sniffed her. "She thought I wanted to hurt you."

Adam made a face as he rubbed his arm. "You'd never do that."

The tracker shrugged. "You and I know that, but your mom and Cruz didn't. The dog either."

"Friend," Cruz said.

"It's okay." Tomas nudged Adam toward me. "Your mom loves you."

Red splotches, the size of my fingers, blossomed on his skin. My first morning as a mother and I'd likely bruised my child.

I sank to my knees. "I'm so sorry."

"Becky wouldn't hurt me." He released his arm. "She helps take care of Meemaw and me."

"That's what your mom and Cruz were trying to do too," Tomas said.

I shot him a thankful look.

Adam eased away from his father and turned to regard Cruz. Slowly, he shook his head. "Meemaw doesn't like guns."

Gaze locked with Raina's, Cruz nodded. "I'm getting that."

"Mijo," Raina said, "I need you go to your room."

"Now?" Adam whined.

"Now," Raina snapped.

"Wait," I said. Still crouching, I closed my eyes. Would my son ever forgive me? "I will never purposefully hurt you. I promise. I'm so sorry I did this time. Can you forgive me?"

He patted my shoulder. "It's okay. You're still learning."

I nodded.

"Meemaw says everyone makes mistakes when they're

learning."

"That's true," I agreed.

"Will you do better next time?"

I nodded as I prayed there would never be a next time. "Can I hug you?"

He stepped into me and we embraced, quick and simple, but he squeezed enough that I knew he meant it.

"Ben," Raina said, warning in her tone.

"I'm going." He heaved a sigh and set off down the hall.

Raina watched him go then turned to Rebecca. "Tell them what you told me."

"Ethan's at my dad's house. Dad managed to text me just before his doorbell rang this morning."

"Where does your dad live?" I asked.

"Other side of town."

My stomach slid toward my knees. I turned to my mother. "You live in the same town as the man who tracks you?"

"Tracked," she said. "Past tense. He's a friend now. It's a long story."

Which we clearly didn't have time for.

"Do you know why Ethan's here?" Cruz asked.

"No. And I've tried calling. No one's answering. That's not good." Rebecca pulled her phone from her pocket. Frowning at the screen, she pushed a button. "Shit." She showed her phone to Raina.

Raina paled. "We need to leave."

"What is it?" I asked.

Rebecca moved to the table and turned her phone around for the rest of us to see. On the screen, a video feed showed a dark-haired man with a brown hat standing on someone's stoop.

"This is my video doorbell," she said, "and that's Ikal. He's Ethan's second among trackers."

My stomach slid further toward the floor. "They're looking for you too?"

She sighed. "Looks that way. We need to go."

"Grab your things and get to the car," Raina said. "We'll leave in ten minutes."

"Is she serious?" Tomas whispered.

Shades of Gloria shone in Raina's eyes.

"Yes," I said.

Raina hurried into the kitchen and opened the bottom cupboard next to the refrigerator. Crouching down, she reached up and in.

Fear shone in Tomas's gaze. "Where will we go?"

I heard the sound of tape peeling away from a surface.

"We'll figure that out when we're safely away." Raina stood holding an envelope with blue painter's tape overlapping its edges.

Déjà vu and nausea hit. It could have been Gloria standing in Raina's place. I'd promised myself I would never live this way again—picking up and running at the drop of a hat. The only thing I had ever gotten from that was a dead mother figure and a missing child. Yet, here I stood, an old familiar rush of adrenaline urging my feet to hurry, telling me to snatch my stuff and go.

"Ben," Raina called as she moved toward the table, "grab your go bag!"

Thoughts raced at me from all directions. Snippets and scraps of things I'd learned over the last month and a half. Raina's description of what could be happening to Jay. Anna's and Maria's offer to hide my child's prophecy. Ethan's self-congratulatory grin on Mount Lemmon.

"Luna?" Cruz said.

I remembered the sound of my father falling against the door after being shot. Noni's cheeks streaked with tears and the marks I'd left on Adam's arm.

Was this what running got you?

I glanced at Raina—lines etched her face as she hurried past the table. She'd been running for nearly thirty years. Would it never end?

"Stop," I said.

Cruz and Tomas looked at me, but Raina kept moving. I said it louder, "Stop!"

She halted abruptly. Turning, she took in the sight of Cruz, Tomas, and me still standing at the table. Her eyes widened with disbelief. "We need to *hurry*."

"We're not running," I said.

"What?" she jerked as if slapped. "We have no time for this." Once again she turned toward the hall.

"We're not leaving." My words stopped her.

Slowly, she blinked, as if trying to clear some confusion. "We can't stay. They'll be here. *Soon*."

"I understand."

Her face paled. "No, you don't."

"Yes, I do." For weeks, the questions had plagued me, rolling through me in sickening waves of fear and self-doubt. I'd played every scenario over and over in my mind. I'd prepared my chess board. And yesterday, my ten-year-old son had told me he could see Gloria's spirit telling me to trust myself. "Adam?" I called. "Come here."

Feet pattered down the hallway.

"You don't know what they'll do to him," Raina pleaded.

"I have an idea."

Adam appeared in the doorway. Raina reached for him, but he ducked past her and came to me. "Yes?"

I rested my hand on his shoulder. "Do you trust me?"

Perhaps it was a stupid question after the marks I'd left on his arm, but he nodded with the blind faith of a child.

Stunned and awed by that gift, I caressed his cheek. "Are Gloria and your grandpa here?"

He looked past me and nodded.

"Good." I smiled and returned my attention to the adults. "It's time to let the Neme-i know about Adam."

"What?" Raina staggered back into Rebecca.

"Luna." Tension sounded in Tomas's voice. "Are you sure about this?"

"Yes." I glanced at Cruz.

His face remained neutral—clear as a cloudless sky. "Mo's suggestion?"

I nodded. "At this point, most of the Neme-i who know I have a son are the ones who might...." I grimaced as I studied my child.

"Want to hurt me?" he suggested.

I blinked. Eventually I would have to consider how I felt about my ten-year-old child knowing such a thing. For now, it made things easier.

"Yes, that," I said. "And if no one else knows, it's very easy for those people to... do what they want without fear."

"But *we* know." Raina motioned impatiently at all of us. "And Jay."

"Yes," I agreed. "We do. A despised former leader, a tracker who may have betrayed her tribe, two outsiders—one of whom no one in the tribe has ever heard of—a dishonest teacher and seer, and me, a leader-elect raised by a crazy white woman whose paranoia probably rubbed off on her. How hard do you think it will be to discredit us?"

Raina and Rebecca exchanged an uncomfortable glance.

"Go on," Rebecca said.

"But there are others amongst the Neme-i—people I trust. Good people. If they knew about Adam, they wouldn't discredit us. They'd fight for us. For him. They'd demand he be protected." For me, only one road led forward.

Raina, Rebecca, and Tomas appeared to need more explanation.

Cruz cleared his throat. "If something happens to Adam, after the things that have happened to Luna, the Neme-i will be irate. They'll ask questions. It won't be good for Anna or the people tasked with protecting the tribe."

Rebecca's eyebrows arched.

"It's a gamble," Raina said. "You'd risk his life on a gamble?"

"No," I said. "No more than you would by running with him.

332

That's a gamble too. I want to ask Gloria and Gilberto. They know more than any of us. They see more." I gazed down at Adam. "Will you ask for us?"

He frowned. "You just did. They heard you."

He stared at a space past Cruz where I saw nothing but tile and the end of the breakfast bar but Adam clearly saw more.

Then he nodded and turned back to me. "They say trust yourself."

I sent the first message before I had time to question or doubt myself further. I sent it to Jay. I wanted him to know he didn't need to hold out and risk being tortured any longer—not for us.

Adam's eyes grew to the size of quarters. He'd clearly felt my message. But he didn't say anything.

"What about Raina?" Rebecca asked. "How do we keep her safe?"

Tomas frowned "From who?"

"The tribe," Cruz replied. "She abandoned them."

"They're still angry?" Tomas asked.

"They're hurt." I thought of Maria and Anna. "And yes, some are angry." I remembered the way Maria had erased Raina from the family photos and the venom in Anna's tone when she spoke of our mother. "Some very much so."

"So what do we do?"

Cruz blew out a breath. "Appease them."

"How?" Rebecca asked.

Cruz rested a hand on the back of his chair. "Give them something they want."

"Like what?" Raina snorted. "My head?"

A cool sensation splashed over me. "Leadership."

"They're not going to follow me," Raina said. "I left them."

"Not you." I glanced at Cruz to make sure we were on the same track. "Anna."

"What?" Raina looked like she'd gulped cough syrup.

"Technically, you're still leader of the tribe," I said. "They've only had temporary leaders since you. Until they name another full leader, you're still it."

A crease formed between Rebecca's brows. She turned to Raina. "She's right."

"Even if that's true"—Raina stepped toward the table—"*no one* is going to listen to me."

"Not if you try to lead them," I said and righted my chair. "But they will if you help them name another leader." Sitting, I patted Adam's seat beside me.

"What are you talking about?" Raina motioned for Rebecca to grab the empty chair from the corner and everyone sat with me.

"Leaders have the ability to name their successors, right?" I said.

"Recommend," Raina countered. "Leaders can *recommend* their successors."

"Fine," I said. "*Recommend* Anna. It's what she wants. It's what I want. It's what many Neme-i want. Take them out of the in-between time they've been stuck in since you left."

Raina looked at Rebecca. The tracker's mouth hung open as she inclined her head. "It would make a lot of people happy."

"But I don't *know* her."

"You don't have to," I said. "She's getting the job anyhow. You'd simply be speeding it along."

Gizmo let out a small *woof* and Bear followed suit as both dogs sprang to attention. Gizmo moved toward the front of the house.

"Guard," Cruz growled. "We need to hurry."

Gizmo barked again. Tires crunched in the gravel driveway.

Rebecca leaned back to see through the doorway and front windows. "Damn. Ethan and Ikal."

"Mom," I said, "this is the only way." Perhaps it was dirty, forcing Raina into the decision by sending a message that called the trackers to us. And yes, calling her Mom qualified as manipulative. But it was the right choice. I felt it in my bones.

"All right," Raina said. "What do you want to do?"

We all joined hands. I asked Rebecca and Raina to think of everyone they could within the Neme-i and I sent the message.

First an image of Adam and me hugging and then another of us with Raina.

The doorbell rang. I squeezed the hands I held tighter, warning no one to let go.

Heat built in my chest as a rainbow of colors steeped in shades of green streamed through my mind. I imagined the council members as well as Anna and Maria and saw the rainbow flowing to them. I added George and Noni, Catherine Rivers and Lalo, Hideo, Juanita, Mo, Jay, everyone I could remember from the leader's dinner. Then I placed my images of Adam, Raina, and me on the rainbow and let them float away.

Tingles filled my body, soft and pleasant as bubbles in a bath. As they dissipated, I became aware of pounding on the door and Gizmo's near deafening barks accompanied on occasion by Bear. Next to me, Adam sat rigid, face pale.

I wrapped an arm around his shoulders and kissed the back of his neck. "It's okay. We'll be all right."

"Did anyone send the message to the trackers?" Cruz asked, raising his voice to be heard over the cacophony of barks and pounds.

Rebecca and Raina both said they had.

Cruz looked at me. "So we know they're not calling the shots."

I nodded, understanding. If Ethan were the one making decisions, the pounding would have stopped.

Cruz moved to the kitchen doorway, keeping his body shielded by the wall.

"What do we do?" Raina grimaced as the pounding continued.

"Wait," Cruz said. "If the person they're answering to is within the tribe, they should be getting a message any minute now."

Bear growled and the hair on the back of his neck stood up.

The pounding ceased. Echoes of it filled the air until quiet seeped in, spreading through every corner of the house.

Still, we waited.

"Did they leave?" Adam asked.

Cruz peeked around the doorway. "Cars are still in the

driveway."

"So they're still at the door?" Tomas asked.

"Or sneaking around the house." Raina stood and quickly pulled the drapes across the sliding glass door. "We need to hide Rebecca."

Rebecca shook her head. "It's too late. They've already sensed my energy and seen my car."

Guilt filled me at the realization we'd probably just cost the tracker her job.

"I'm sorry," I said.

She waved it off.

"Now what?" Tomas asked.

Cruz looked at me. "You're sure about this?"

I glanced at the spot where Adam had said Gloria and my father both stood. "Yes."

"Then we answer the door."

Raina sat up straight. "Mijo?" Her voice sounded calm, but there was a tightness to her tone. "You and Rebecca go to your room. Wait there till we call you."

Adam slid off his chair and drug his heels as he followed Rebecca down the hall.

"I'm going to recommend one last message," Raina said, "in case things go very wrong."

"What?"

"An image of the trackers standing at the door the moment it's opened."

I glanced toward the entryway. What would happen if things went wrong? Would the trackers try to kill us or just take us with them? At least Raina's suggestion would ensure someone knew who had last seen us if things went bad. "Who should I send it to?"

"You'll only have a moment," she said, "so it will need to be one message. Send it to all the Neme-i you know."

"All?" My brain stumbled at the thought. "I don't think I can send to that many."

"Yes you can." She leaned across the table and offered me her hands. "It's easy."

I glanced at Cruz and Tomas. Both watched expectantly as I took Raina's hands.

"Close your eyes."

I followed her direction.

"Imagine all the people you know standing together in a crowd."

"No trackers," Cruz said.

I cracked one eye open and noted the annoyed expression on Raina's face.

Cruz stared at me. "We need to see what they'll do when they think no one knows."

Raina sighed. "Okay. Imagine everyone you know except trackers. See their faces in your mind." She paused a moment. "Do you have that?"

"Yes," I said.

"Now draw a band around that crowd or a ring—something that keeps them inside, separate from what lies outside."

I saw the crowd and mentally put a gold band around them— endless and unbreakable, like a wedding ring. "Okay."

"Now memorize it. See it clearly. When you send, that crowd is who you'll send to. Because they are one group in your mind, it will go to them all."

"Are you sure?" I asked.

She gave a wan smile. "Yes. This is one thing I know."

"Who will you be sending to?" I asked.

She shook her head. "I won't be. I'll be answering the door."

"No," Cruz said. "Not safe. I'll do it."

Warmth filled my heart. My mother had been snippy toward Cruz since he'd pulled his gun, but he would still risk his life to protect her.

Raina shook her head. "You can't." And before Tomas could speak, she added, "Neither can you. In case they send you messages the moment the door opens, you both need to be touching Luna. You are bonded to her. If either of you is made to do something dangerous, she'll be able to stop you."

Tomas frowned. "I won't—"

Cruz shot him a glance. "You won't have a say. Trust me."

Gravel crunched and Gizmo and Bear began barking as two more cars pulled into the driveway.

"Who's that?" I asked.

Cruz glanced around the doorway again. "More trackers, I'm guessing."

The sandwich I'd eaten felt like a brick inside my stomach. "Great."

"We need to go before they have the whole house surrounded," Raina said.

We all stood, but the moment we'd stepped into the front room, I whispered "Wait" and ran down the hall. Retrieving my knives from the dresser, I strapped them to my waistband and returned to the group.

The knocking had started again, but friendly this time—more like the knock of a neighbor than the threatening pounding of before.

"Guard," Cruz told Bear.

Standing at the door, Raina placed a hand on the handle and glanced at me. "Ready?"

I nodded.

She held up her fingers, counting 1-2-3 then opened the door, stepping back with it.

Ethan and his partner stood on the stoop. Next to them stood Ikal in his brown hat and a young gum-chewing woman who wore her ponytail high and tight. Past them, in the driveway stood four other people—two men and two women.

I saw the image of them like a snapshot and sent it to my group.

Ikal and Ethan exchanged a glance. Undoubtedly, they'd felt the surge in my energy.

Raina, who had stepped back with the door to offer me a clear view, raised her eyebrows. I nodded. The message was sent.

Taking a deep breath, she stretched herself to her full height and stepped around the door.

Everyone on the stoop froze.

"Kwichania," Raina said. "Hello."

Twenty-five

G izmo jumped and planted his front paws on Ethan's chest. "Gizmo!" I called. "Down!"

For once, my dog actually listened, removing his paws from Ethan without being forced.

"Sit!" I said.

Gizmo whined and took a seat beside Raina in the doorway.

Ikal tipped his hat back. Words seemed to escape him.

Eyes blazing, Ethan stared at Raina. He returned her greeting, but didn't offer to take her hand or bow his head in the formal greeting due a leader. Not surprising, really. I doubted he considered her his leader. But he also didn't reach out and seize hold of her like a criminal. I took that as a good sign.

Ethan glanced back at his partner. She pulled out her phone and quickly typed on the screen. Probably reporting that the message we'd sent of being with Raina was not a lie. But why send a text when she could have sent a message?

"How can we help you?" Raina asked.

I had to give it to her. Back straight, chin high, Raina looked like a leader.

"I think you know," Ethan replied.

"I may," she said cooly, "but it remains your responsibility to tell me."

Next to me, Cruz kept a hand on his gun, practically straining against the barrier created by Raina, Gizmo, and Bear. It probably killed him to stand this far back.

Looking over Raina's shoulder, Ethan caught sight of Cruz and me. "Luna. Cruz."

I nodded. "Ethan."

"Are you all right?" he asked.

"Yes," I said.

"You're not being kept against your will?" He gazed pointedly at Tomas.

I chuckled. Tomas would never be a threat to anyone. Building the dam to protect the ants that morning had been his idea. "No. I am exactly where I want to be."

Ethan nodded, switching modes. "The council sent me to find you. They've been worried since they couldn't reach you and you weren't with John."

Cruz stepped forward. "That was my choice. I was concerned we were being followed."

Raina eased to the side, offering Cruz and Ethan a clear view of each other.

"Without letting the council know?" Ethan raised an eyebrow. *Smug bastard.*

Cruz tipped his head. "Since only the council knew our plans and we were still followed, I insisted we not tell them."

Ethan shifted his weight and glanced at Ikal. "It may have been us following you."

Cruz nodded. "That occurred to me."

"Are you satisfied now that you are not being followed?" Ethan asked.

"Considering you just showed up here? No," Cruz said. "I'm certain we are being followed."

Sighing, Ethan shifted his gaze to me. "May I inquire what you're doing here?"

Cruz looked back at me. This was my question to field.

"I received a clue I'd been searching for. Cruz and I followed it."

"A clue?" Ethan tipped his head toward Raina. "About your

341

mother?"

"No," I stepped forward to stand beside Cruz. Tomas came with me. "My son."

"Our son," Tomas said.

Ethan's head jerked, his gaze taking in Tomas for the first time since he'd dismissed him as a threat. "Your son?" He motioned between us.

"Yes." I turned toward the hallway and called out, "Adam, will you come out here please?"

"Would this be the child you gave birth to in Gallup?" Ethan put one foot on the doorstep. After a glance at Raina, he removed it. "The one who disappeared with his foster mother and later went to school in Portland?"

He'd done his homework. I'd give him that. How he'd put it all together, I had no clue.

Something flashed in my peripheral vision, and I turned as Adam stepped into the hallway. He paused in front of his door.

"It's okay." I held my hand out to him and prayed I was right.

When he reached the head of the hall, Adam took my hand. I pulled him close and he settled between Tomas and me.

"I present Adam," I said.

"Kwichania." Adam spoke slowly and softly, careful to pronounce each syllable correctly.

Ethan fell back a step while the remaining trackers strained forward for a better view.

"Kwichania," the four on the stoop replied, each bowing slightly.

I smiled at my beautiful son and ruffled his hair.

"Why didn't you tell the council about him?" Ikal's partner, the gum chewer, asked.

The question earned her a glare from Ethan, but she rolled her eyes in response. I liked her.

I edged forward in case I needed to shield my child. He tried to move with me, but Tomas held him back. "I told Anna and Maria, but I asked them not to tell anyone else. I've been searching for my child for ten years. Until I knew I could find him and keep him safe from everyone, I wanted no one to know."

The gum chewer met my gaze. Emotion clouded her eyes.

"You'll need to speak with the council," Ikal said.

"I know." I took a breath. "I'll call Ivan tonight."

"*We* will call them," Raina said.

Ethan nodded. "Ivan is unwell. May I suggest you try Joseph Peshlakai?"

My hackles rose. I would never voluntarily call that prick. "I'll call Crow and Trujillo."

Raina's eyebrows lifted. She seemed to enjoy my answer.

"They'll want to see you and meet the boy." Ethan rested a hand outside the door frame.

"I understand." I touched Cruz's elbow. "We'll do that when we're ready."

"We'd be happy to escort you," Ikal offered.

Cruz bristled, and I squeezed his arm before he could respond. "Thank you," I said. "We'll let you know if you are needed."

Cruz growled.

"It's not like they're going to leave us alone," I whispered.

Ethan turned his attention back to Raina. "The council will want to speak with you too. I'm sure your oldest daughter will have some things she'd like to say as well."

"Of course." Disdain dripped from Raina's voice. She shifted her weight, and Gizmo stepped back. "You may tell them I will accompany my daughter and grandson. Good day." She closed the door firmly and turned the bolt. For several seconds, she didn't move. When she did, she slumped against the door, hands shaking.

"Welcome back to the tribe," I offered.

A tear escaped her eye as she let out a puff of air that might have been a laugh.

⚎

I woke to the scent of bacon and the beautiful sound of my son's laughter. Opening my eyes, I looked at the mattress beside

343

me. Empty. I pulled on a pair of shorts and an over-sized T-shirt before padding down the hall.

Rounding the corner into the kitchen, I spied Raina sitting at the dining table sipping coffee while Cruz, Tomas, and Adam destroyed her kitchen. A plate overflowing with bacon sat in front of her.

"More eggs!" Tomas called from the counter where he stood whisking liquid in a bowl.

"More eggs," Adam echoed. He scurried to the refrigerator, pulled two eggs from the carton and delivered them to Tomas.

"Flipper!" Cruz called.

"Flipper," Adam echoed. He hurried to the stove, took the spatula from Cruz and carefully inserted it beneath a pancake.

"Ready?" Cruz asked.

"Ready." Using two hands, Adam lifted the pancake and turned it while Cruz slid the pan an inch to accommodate the novice flip.

"Good morning," I said to the group.

"Good morning, Mom! We're making a feast," Adam said. "It's man's work."

"Man's work?" I looked at Raina.

She shrugged. "It seems women only make regular breakfasts."

"Have a seat," Cruz said over his shoulder. "Coffee's on the way."

I slid into the seat across from Raina and helped myself to a slice of bacon.

Tomas poured coffee into a mug then turned to Cruz for directions on what to add for me. I sincerely doubted Tomas had forgotten how I liked my coffee, but he hadn't forgotten who now filled the role of my partner. Cream and sugar added, Tomas handed the mug to Cruz who took a sip and approved the taste before handing the mug to Adam.

Adam moved toward the table spilling a few drops on the way.

"We're going to have to clean your kitchen," I whispered to

344

Raina.

She closed her eyes and nodded. "We'll need to clean the whole house if we're to receive visitors."

I'd called Crow and Trujillo the night before as I'd said I would. Both had asked if they could represent the council and come to meet Adam. They explained that Ivan usually would have made the trip as leader of the Spirit clan, but his latest round of chemo would not allow for it. I had the right to choose any council member I wanted in Ivan's place. I chose them both. As for meeting the leader, that trip would apparently fall to us to undertake.

Stopping in front of me, Adam placed the mug on the table, a giant grin on his face. "Here's your coffee, Mom."

"Thank you." I pulled him close and kissed his forehead. "Good morning."

He giggled and gave me a quick squeeze before stepping back and watching me. "Aren't you going to taste it?"

I reached for the mug and took a quick sip then smiled as I stared into his walnut-colored eyes. "Perfect."

He grinned and turned. "Perfect coffee!" he called as he hurried back to the action.

"Perfect coffee!" Cruz and Tomas replied in unison.

I took another sip and turned to Raina. "How long has this been going on?"

"About half an hour," she said. "They were just starting when I got up."

I nodded at Adam and Cruz. "They seem to be getting along."

Raina nodded. "I believe Tomas and your son had a long talk this morning. Cruz joined in at the end. As far as I can gather, Cruz and Tomas are planning to help him make a pocketknife and you and Cruz are having a throwing contest this afternoon."

I felt my eyebrows arch. "Really?"

"He's ten," Tomas said as he handed a stack of plates to Adam. "It's time he had a knife."

Adam brought the plates to the table and set them all around.

"I'll start my training soon." He grinned with pride.

I smiled as he returned to the kitchen.

"He's never handled knives before," Raina whispered, her face drawn.

A tendril of fear squirmed inside me as I imagined my child severing a finger or nicking an artery, but as I glanced at Cruz and Tomas, I knew Adam would be safe. "They're great teachers. He'll be fine."

"They taught you?" she asked.

I nodded.

"And that knowledge saved your life?"

"Maybe." We still didn't know what Hernandez had intended to do with me. "It definitely helped me escape."

"So it's been a useful skill?"

Mostly it had been a hobby, but it had paid off tremendously when I needed it. "Yes. But they won't start with throwing knives. Right?" I raised my voice and directed the question to the kitchen.

"Right," Cruz replied. "We'll start with safety and respect." He shoveled a pancake on top of a tall stack.

In the corner, the toaster popped and Tomas called, "Toast up."

Adam scrambled to the corner and quickly exchanged the golden pieces of toast for two fresh pieces of bread and pushed the button. "Toast down."

I took a sip of coffee and returned my mug to the table. "There's something I want to talk to you about."

Raina took a piece of bacon.

"Cruz, Tomas, and I stayed up talking about this last night."

She took a bite and chewed slowly.

"If you're okay with it," I said, "we'd like to stay another week, but then we need to go home."

"Back to New Mexico," she said.

I nodded. "We all have work we need to return to."

She swallowed the bite she'd taken and put the remainder of the bacon strip on the plate in front of her. Head bowed, she said,

"And you want to take your son?"

It was more than want; we would take him. No question about that. But the conversation didn't need to be adversarial.

"Yes," I said.

Raina had gone to bed early the night before, saying our run-in with the trackers had worn her out. I'd gotten the feeling it was more than that. The prospect of being part of the tribe again—seeing the consequences of her actions and dealing with the aftermath—weighed on her. Although she'd gone to bed early, she looked like she'd hardly slept.

I reached across the table to offer my hand. She took it.

"We'd like you to come with us," I said.

Her gaze shot up. "You mean…take a vacation?"

I shook my head. "Move."

Raina's mouth opened as her eyebrows arched. "You want me to move with you? Why?"

I sighed and reached for another piece of bacon. In the kitchen, Cruz shoveled more pancakes onto the stack while Tomas helped Adam dump a pan of scrambled eggs onto a plate.

"When I was a kid, I understood home was supposed to be my safe space. Everybody talked about home like it was everything. All those moves? I handled them by telling myself I didn't need a house or a town or a school or group of friends. As long as I had Gloria, I was home."

Raina nodded.

"Tomas and I are hoping New Mexico will become home for Adam, and that he'll learn to see us that way. But for now he doesn't. For now, his home is with you. And if we take him to New Mexico without you, New Mexico will never be home for him."

Raina sipped her coffee while I took a chomp out of my bacon.

"So you want me to come with you for his sake?" she asked.

"Yes." I put the bacon on my plate and wiped my hands on the napkin beside it. "I don't know anything about being a mom. I'd appreciate it if you could help me learn."

Head bowed, she said nothing.

"Also," I continued, "I don't know anything about being your daughter. But I'd like to learn that too."

She looked up. Tears welled in her eyes and her chin quivered. "You would?"

I nodded wishing like hell I knew if her tears represented hope or sadness.

"Eggs," Adam said as he set a platter of steaming, scrambled goodness on the table.

Right behind him came Tomas and Cruz with the pancakes and toast.

Pulling out chairs, the three joined us at the table.

"Did you ask her yet?" Cruz said as he forked two pancakes onto his plate.

"Yes." I held the platter of eggs while Adam scooped a mound onto his plate.

"And?" Tomas asked as he took the platter from me.

"I don't know." I accepted the plate of pancakes from Cruz. "You interrupted before she could answer."

We all stopped passing and scooping and turned to Raina.

"What do you say?" I asked. "Will you come with us?"

Tears rolled down her cheeks and splashed on her plate dangerously close to her toast. "I'd love to."

"Happy tears?" Adam asked.

She smiled down at him. "Very."

He blew out a sigh of relief.

So did I.

THE END

Please consider leaving a review of this book. It will be appreciated more than you know!

Keep reading for a preview of *Blood Moon*, the third and final book in the Blue Moon series coming in 2025.

Acknowledgements

Thank you to the members of critique groups who generously read and gave their comments on this manuscript. From San Escondido, thank you to Veronica Baird, Penny Paugh, Glen V., and Lisa. From Kansas City and surrounding areas, thank you to Erin McCoy, Darlene Deluca, Kristie Gannon, G.A. Edwards, and Virginia Magers.

Thank you also to:

Nicole Pulliam, for another outstanding job of copy editing and finding my many mistakes and inconsistencies.

Arnau-Soler through Unsplash.com for a beautiful picture and to Ghanipixels at Fiverr.com for turning that picture into an amazing cover.

My mother and Cheryl Dewey for being my beta readers and pointing out the mistakes, confusing explanations, and annoying repetitions they found.

Cindy Munoz, for all the advice and encouragement over the years. I still tell the tale of how one of my very first critique partners, told me she hated my main character because I'd written nothing to like about her and that I should delete my first five chapters. (The story always ends with how right you were.) I couldn't and wouldn't have done any of this without you.

EJ, for putting up with me for many years and keeping your promise to remain my friend. You may not remember this, but you are the reason I learned to write every day.

MaryGrace. You were the kindest, strongest, and bravest person I have ever known. You always asked about my writing, and because of that, you were sometimes the reason I put my butt in the chair and wrote.

My parents, grandparents, and sister, for loving and encouraging me even when my head was so far in the clouds, I often didn't hear what I was being told. I love you all.

Emily, Chris, and Nick, for accepting me as a part of your family and for giving me a chance to learn a little about what it means to be a mom. I love you.

Finally, thank you to my late husband, Michael. I didn't believe in romance or love stories before I met you. You made me eat every nay-saying word I ever spoke on the subject. I've never been so happy to admit I was wrong. I miss our laughter and love and all the stories you told me (even the ones about cottonmouth moccasins). Your belief in me and your support while I wrote this book was amazing. I miss you so much.

About the Author

Carper Smith grew up in Northern California where she began writing stories at age nine. She also raised pigs, played softball, and danced with a junior ballet company. She attended Dominican University of San Rafael and graduated Cum Laude with a degree in creative writing.

She has been a fast-food ice cream cone maker, waitress, retailer, grocery store clerk, secretary, ballet teacher, English teacher, P.E. teacher, and once for three days, she was a vacuum cleaner salesperson (she was terrible at it).

She has lived in Northern and Southern California, New Mexico, Oregon, Missouri and Florida in a series of homes and apartments that seem to regularly find their way into her stories. She now resides in the Sacramento Delta area of Northern California with her cat, Gracie (the wonder muse).

If you would like to connect with Carper or get information about upcoming releases, go to: **carpersmith.com**

Preview Draft of Blood Moon

T he cemetery in Oracle, Arizona was filled with dirt. Brown, dry dirt. Here and there a tuft of wild grass or a cactus provided a splash of pale green against the white headstones, but the overall impression was...dirt. It reminded me of something out of an old Western movie. Yet, somehow, as I stood amongst the crowd gathered for the burial of my clan leader, I couldn't help but think how lovely it was. Flowers left in front of headstones stood out even brighter amidst all that brown, as if the love they signified was stronger. Everything was simple. Honest. Pure. It seemed a perfect final resting place for Ivan Yellowhair.

The sky was blue, the crowd was somber, and the temperature felt like the kind of summer day you dream about. Unfortunately, I wasn't from Arizona. I was from the high desert of New Mexico where, a week before Halloween, we expected our first snowfall any day. In the two-hour window I'd been given to plan and pack for this emergency trip, I had packed for New Mexico weather, not this. As a result, I now stood facing an open grave dressed in a black sweater dress and tights trying not to squirm while beads of sweat pooled inside my bra. Much longer, and I suspected heat exhaustion might become an issue.

Shuffling my feet, I eyed the shade of a nearby oak. In the afternoon the tree would cast welcome relief over Ivan's grave. At ten in the morning, the line of shade went the other way. If I stood in it, I might not be able to hear my sister, Anna, leader of the Neme-i, speaking at the head of the grave, but I didn't care. I had a niggling feeling she had considered killing me just before she shot Paul Hernandez, and I hadn't gotten over it.

The gun pointing had happened four months before, after she and I had been abducted from the council meeting in Albuquerque—the same meeting where I met Ivan Yellowhair, leader of the Spirit clan. Seated near my father at the council table, long white hair hanging in a braid, Ivan had called me "Daughter" and welcomed me home to the tribe I'd been born into but only recently learned existed.

Nudging my boyfriend, Cruz, I nodded at the shade, and we moved a couple steps backward. My grandmother, Maria, who stood a conspicuous distance from where Anna had stood with her boyfriend, Leonard, glanced over and scowled. I shrugged. She'd disapprove more if I fainted. Cruz and I moved twice more before my sightline no longer included Maria or the gaping hole with the casket above it, but instead focused on a small, raised headstone with the beautiful shape of a flying bird chiseled into the marble next to the name Isaiah Yellowhair.

"Ivan's and Inez's son," a familiar voice whispered behind me.

I turned to find Jacy Crow, leader of the Fire clan and my new favorite council member since Ivan had passed. Dressed in dark jeans and boots, he wore his purple dress shirt open at the neck revealing a large turquoise pendant. In the still air, his long black hair hung like a drape down his back.

"How old was he?"

"Nine. Hit by a car on his way home from school."

My stomach clenched as I glanced at Cruz. "And you wonder why I don't want Adam walking to school."

"Did they catch the driver?" Cruz asked.

Jacy grimaced. "The man was having a heart attack when he went off the road. He died too."

Heaviness settled like cement inside me.

"Where's your son?" Jacy asked, glancing around.

354

"Home." I stared at the grave while I doled out the lie Cruz and I had planned. "He and his dad had plans this weekend. We didn't want to mess them up."

Jacy nodded.

In truth, Tomas's and Adam's plans had nothing to do with the decision to leave Adam home. It was Adam's abilities that had caused us concern. Like every Neme-i male, Adam could sense energy. But in addition to that, he was also a remote viewer and a medium. He could see things happening to the people he loved in real time—no matter how far away—and he could see and hear the spirits of those who had crossed over. Given the fact we were trying to keep his extra abilities under wraps, at least until Cruz and I figured out who amongst the Neme-i we could trust, surrounding him with a crowd of people in a graveyard hadn't seemed wise.

At the head of the grave, Anna finished speaking and stepped aside. A young girl began to sing—a haunting melody of words I didn't understand from the language of the Neme-i.

Ivan's widow, Inez, stepped forward and placed a bundle of lavender on top of the coffin. A three-year-old boy named Johnson held her hand. His short black hair brushed his collar while the fingers of his second hand sat securely in his mouth. Inez bent down and spoke to him and Johnson nodded. Pulling his fingers from his mouth, he trailed saliva as he put his hand on the coffin and said a few words. Inez squeezed the hand she held and the two of them stepped back as an older, barrel-chested man I'd never seen before wandered around the coffin sprinkling sage. Something about him seemed familiar.

"Who's that?"

"Ivan's brother, Victor," another familiar voice said.

I glanced left and found Willy Trujillo, leader of the Air clan, standing beside Cruz. He wore his usual silver cuff bracelets, but in the charcoal dress slacks and suit jacket he'd donned for the occasion, he looked nearly as hot as I felt.

"You two going to the church after this?" Willy whispered.

Cruz nodded.

"Good." Willy kept his gaze on the ceremony. "We need to talk."

The song came to an end, and Willy and Jacy stepped away. As they moved toward the grave, the other three council members joined them. Each man carried a feather. The five men surrounded the coffin and lifted their feathers to the sky then placed them on top of the polished lid—one in each corner and the fifth feather, placed by Willy, in the center. The men stepped away from the grave and formed a half circle around Inez and Victor—creating a wall of protection. A small whirring sounded, and Inez's shoulders shook as the coffin descended into the grave.

The hairs on the back of my neck prickled, and I looked up to find my sister staring at me. A satisfied smile tugged at the edges of her mouth and caused her eyes to crinkle. Behind her, her boyfriend, Leonard, said something and when she turned to look at him, the smile promptly faded. An icy shiver slid through my middle. Whatever that smile had been about didn't feel good.

A final prayer was said, and then Victor led Inez toward the parking lot. Anna and the council members followed, signaling the end of the ceremony. As they moved past, Anna slid a glance my way, the smile forming on her mouth once again. I allowed a similar expression to form on my face and continued to stare at her until she looked away.

To the casual observer, it probably looked like a warm, sisterly greeting. But it wasn't. The only thing warm in our relationship was the blood in our veins that made us sisters.

"You doing okay?" Cruz asked. Wearing a bone choker, brown dress shirt, and dark jeans he had earned unabashed stares from most of the women we'd seen that morning. Usually women tried to hide their interest when they saw he was with me, but when he dressed up and put on cologne, it was lambs to the slaughter. No one hid anything.

"I'm burning up," I said in response to his question. No need to point out the obvious about Anna. Cruz knew the score, and he'd seen the smile as clearly as I had.

"There's water in the car."

I sighed. Short of pouring the water over my head, I doubted anything would make a difference until I got out of my sweater-dress. At least inside the car, I'd be able to crank the air and wrestle my way out of my tights. That would offer some relief.

The crowd began to disperse, and I turned to follow, but Cruz caught my hand and held me back.

"Fence line," he said.

I scanned the periphery of the cemetery until I saw what Cruz had seen. Two men stood against the fence nearly two hundred feet away. The younger one tall and lean with short dark hair. The older one—nearly a head shorter than the first—wore his salt and pepper hair shoulder-length. His frame had thinned since I'd last seen him.

"Jay." I let out the breath I'd been holding since I hadn't found him in the crowd. "Why's he back there?"

Cruz shrugged. "Been there a while."

Leaving the crowd behind, we moved in the direction of the two men. The younger man, who I now recognized as George Tsossi, a highly gifted member of the Spirit clan, remained by the fence, but Jay stepped forward and met us halfway.

"Luna, Cruz." He held his hand out for a shake.

Bypassing his hand, I wrapped my arms around him in a hug.

He stiffened for a second then relaxed and gave me a gentle squeeze. The man was my uncle, my teacher, and the only adult I had known as a child who remained alive. On top of all that, he had sacrificed his freedom and comfort to help protect me and Adam. If he thought a handshake was ever going to be enough to satisfy me again, he had another think coming.

"You're burning up," he said as he disengaged himself.

"It's this stupid dress." I tugged at the front of it. "I wasn't expecting it to be so hot."

"Usually isn't in October. Weather's about a month behind." He nodded at my dress. "Probably wouldn't have been cold enough for *that* but…." He let the sentence trail off then added, "I'm glad you made it."

"Me too."

"Are you two staying in town tonight?"

Cruz nodded. "At the Chalet Village."

"Good. If you're okay with it, George and I would like to swing by later on. We need to talk."

"About what?" I asked.

Jay looked toward the parking lot before returning his attention to me. "You're going to be approached about filling Ivan's seat on the council today."

I jerked. "What?"

"Before you give your answer, we'd appreciate you hearing us out."

Made in United States
Orlando, FL
11 July 2024

48854490R00219